They were approaching the restaurant, which had half a dozen umbrella-covered tables set outside. She stopped and looked about, caught in full sunshine. Her hair was an incredible color, he thought, not red, but a dark auburn and shot through with rich fiery highlights. Thick and lustrous, it fell to her shoulders, wanting to curl in Houston's humid air—going its own untamed way. He preferred her looking natural and feminine, as she did now in jeans and soft T-shirt. As for those green eyes... A man could learn to love the look of a woman like Liz.

"Liz—" He stopped her as she started inside. She turned, giving him a questioning look. "After this is over, would you have dinner with me? Could we get to know each other better without all the complications of Austin...and everything else?"

"I...don't know." She frowned.

"Are you seeing somebody?"

"No. It's just—" Shaking her head, she looked sort of frantically at the traffic. "I'm really not interested in...that."

He smiled, a half tilt of his mouth, knowing the risk he took teasing her. "Don't tell me Austin's tacky accusations were right after all?"

"Austin's—" She looked confused a second or two before she understood. "Oh, that Gina and I—" She stopped, giving a soft laugh. "No, his accusations were probably a fantasy in his own mind. He's just that sick." She glanced at the door. "Are we having lunch or not?"

She hadn't promised to go out with him, but he hadn't been completely shot down, either, he thought. He felt hopeful. "Want to sit outside?"

Also available from MIRA Books and
KAREN YOUNG

FULL CIRCLE
GOOD GIRLS

Watch for Karen Young's next novel

IN CONFIDENCE

Coming February 2004

KAREN YOUNG

PRIVATE LIVES

MIRA

ISBN 1-55166-679-0

PRIVATE LIVES

Visit us at www.mirabooks.com

Printed in U.S.A.

ACKNOWLEDGMENTS

I'm grateful to several people for advice, information and moral support in the writing of this book. To Metsy Hingle for the idea and a long list of other favors. To Emilie Richards for being a sensitive and insightful sounding board when I needed it most. To my daughter, Alison Simmons, who is tireless and patient with me in avenues of my career that do not include sitting at my computer and writing. To Jon Salem for his canny grasp of the workings of the publishing world, and the world at large, and his willingness to share it with me. To my nephew, Mike Farris, for the boat stuff. And finally, to my editor, Valerie Gray, with thanks for her astute suggestions and attention to detail.

One

"Lizzie. What's wrong? You're pale as a ghost."

"I don't believe this, Louie." Elizabeth Walker's attention was riveted on an article in the Sunday newspaper. Her picture was front and center in the article, but it was the content of the piece that dismayed her. "You remember that reporter from the *Houston Chronicle* who interviewed me a couple of weeks ago?"

"After a bit of pressure from your publisher?" Louie Christian broke a piece off his bagel and tossed it from the gazebo to his dog, Archie, who caught it with a quick snap of his teeth. "Is the article in the paper today?"

"It's the front page feature in the 'Lifestyle' section."

Louie leaned over to see for himself. "Nice photo. You look very professional sitting at your computer."

Elizabeth's response was a disgruntled snort. "I knew I shouldn't have agreed. Listen to this." She moved her coffee cup aside and spread the paper flat on the low table across from Louie. Grimacing, she read aloud, "'Houston author Elizabeth Walker, winner of the prestigious Newbery Award for children's books, leads an almost reclusive life. Repeated attempts to interview her were unsuccessful. It was only after her publisher intervened that Walker, an auburn-haired beauty who looks more like a runway model than an author of sensitive stories for children, reluctantly agreed to the interview at her home in the ex-

clusive Memorial area. Consequently, her reluctance had
this reporter's nose aquiver. Deeper research revealed a
very interesting history quite apart from her life as a
writer. Walker, it seems, is the daughter of Matthew Scur-
lock Walker, a judge who was once a powerful political
figure in Houston legal circles. After his death in a mysterious house fire twenty-five years ago, Walker left behind three daughters. Elizabeth, the eldest, was five years
old at the time. Having no other relatives, her two younger
siblings were adopted, but Elizabeth landed in the care of
the state of Texas, then spent the remainder of her childhood in and out of various foster homes.'''

Elizabeth stood up abruptly and began to pace. "What
possible relevance does any of this have on my career,
Louie?"

"None, specifically, but you'll have to admit it adds
spice to the reporter's article."

Bending, she swept up the article. "I suppose this part
is also titillating," she said, snapping out the page smartly.
"'According to sources, Walker has had no relationship
with her siblings since their adoption. She has not seen
them since the night of the fire.' How does he know that,
Louie?"

"Deeper research, I suppose."

She muttered something unintelligible and tossed the
paper aside. Moving to the steps of the gazebo, she looked
out, tears blurring her vision. "What's missing from the
reporter's story is that my sisters' adoptive parents never
made the slightest effort to contact me."

Behind her, Louie picked up the paper and scanned the
article. "You can't let something like this upset you,
Lizzie. Your success makes you an interesting person to
the public at large. The reporter struck it lucky when he

researched a little deeper and discovered your past to be a bit extraordinary.''

''I feel violated, Louie. It's almost like…rape.'' She closed her eyes and took a deep, unsteady breath.

Louie sighed, knowing her well enough to leave it alone for now.

But Elizabeth wasn't ready to leave it. ''It's no wonder the media is suffering from a reputation only slightly better than used car salesmen,'' she said bitterly, turning to face him. ''I'm amazed at my own naiveté, Louie. The questions he asked were so benign, such as, 'How do you get your ideas?' and 'How difficult was it to get published?' and 'What made you choose to write books for children rather than adult fiction?' And I actually thought that was what the article would be about.''

''He appears to cover that, too,'' Louie said, still reading.

She turned and looked at him, then after a beat, she managed a short laugh. ''I'm overreacting, right?''

Louie put the paper down. ''I wouldn't say that, since he's opened your life to the world, but your editor and your agent would probably remind you that any publicity, favorable or otherwise, is good.''

She made a disgusted sound and picked up her cup. She could always trust Louie to spin even the most awful experience in a positive light. She knew that he understood her reaction to the reporter's insensitive exposé of her history, knew that to her it was like pouring salt in a wound that had never quite healed. Still knowing all that, he wouldn't let her wallow in self-pity. She studied him over the rim of her cup with affection. At seventy-one, his white beard gave him a distinguished air even though she'd noticed he'd begun to stoop a bit. She wondered if she could persuade him to have a full physical.

Louie had been her neighbor for about five years, but they hadn't become friends right away. Her fault, not his. Those years in foster care had shaped her well. She'd learned early the hazards of trusting too soon. But Louie had patiently persevered. Elderly and lonely himself, he'd finally breached her shy defenses with a variety of neighborly gestures: offering tomatoes and cucumbers from his garden, bringing her newspaper to the door on rainy days, returning her trash can to the garage after the garbage was picked up. And, best of all, assuming a vital role in Jesse's life.

A sharp shriek from across the lawn brought her to her feet. But it was joy, not distress making Jesse squeal. The little girl and her best friend, Cody, were in wild pursuit of Archie who now had not a bagel, but something dark blue and crushable in his teeth. There was no likelihood that the big golden retriever would be overtaken, but both kids were giving the race their personal best.

"Is that something valuable in his mouth?" Louie asked, moving up behind her.

"Cody's cherished Texans ball cap? Priceless." Elizabeth smiled, watching Jesse try to outsmart the dog by circling behind while Cody stood out in front and yelled as a distraction. Squealing, Jesse leaped on the playful retriever from behind and Cody dived gleefully into the tangle of little girl and big dog. Amazingly, Cody emerged from the fray with his cap. Archie got up, too, shaking himself vigorously, tongue dangling in a doggie grin.

"Maybe we'd better go check for broken limbs," Louie said dryly as the two five-year-olds sprawled on the lawn, winded and giggling.

"Whose, Archie's or the kids?"

"Good point."

Smiling, they watched as the children tore off in another

direction, Archie between them, barking joyously. Elizabeth felt a rush of love. Jesse was a delightful mix of tomboy and sprightly femininity. And a constant delight, despite the fact that lately her welfare was a constant concern.

And on that thought, Elizabeth's smile faded. Gina D'Angelo, Jesse's mother, was living with Elizabeth now after her longtime lover, Austin Leggett, had finally broken off their relationship. Elizabeth was holding her breath praying the affair was truly over this time. It wouldn't be the first time she'd opened her home to Gina and Jesse after one of Austin's tirades, but in the past he would soon apologize, Gina would forgive all, and the whole dysfunctional cycle would begin again. It was frustrating and painful to Elizabeth to see that Jesse was forced to live in an atmosphere of fear and violence. Gina was an adult and free to make her own choices, but Jesse, the child of their stormy relationship, was without options. Maybe this time the split would be permanent, as Gina had confessed that she suspected Austin was having an affair. She had no wish to see Gina hurt, but she knew the relationship would end only when Austin decided to end it. For Jesse's sake, she hoped the time had come. The fact that Gina had hired an attorney and a law suit was filed regarding Jesse's custody gave Elizabeth hope. On the other hand, she worried about Jesse's fate if the breakup turned ugly. As the little girl's father, Austin Leggett would have considerable standing in the eyes of the court.

"Is Gina sleeping in this morning?" Louie asked, his eyes still on the kids.

"She has a lot on her mind lately." Elizabeth knew what he was thinking. It should be Gina out here watching her daughter, not Liz. But Gina hadn't come home last night until after eleven. In spite of the fact that she was forced to move on with her life, she was devastated by Austin's rejection and stressed out over the upcoming custody hearing. Seeing that she felt cooped up after weeks in the house, Elizabeth had suggested she take in a movie. But hours after the movie was over, when she still had not come home, Jesse had been worried. Elizabeth was sympathetic over Gina's situation, but she didn't—couldn't—condone Gina's occasional lapses in parental responsibility.

Finally, Gina had called, apologetic and contrite over waiting so late to check in. She'd taken in a movie and then decided to browse in the Galleria, she told Elizabeth. Next, she'd bumped into a friend who was a paralegal in the law firm where Gina no longer worked, thanks to Austin, and simply lost track of the time. Was Jesse okay, she'd asked. What if she weren't, Elizabeth had thought with some irritation, but she'd reassured her and agreed to give the little girl her bath and put her to bed.

"One more book, Aunt Lizzie, pul-eeezze," Jesse had begged later when Elizabeth was trying to coax her into settling down for the night. Sleepy-eyed, her tattered Barney clutched tight to her chest, she was doggedly determined to wait for her missing mommy. Elizabeth closed *Miss Spider's Wedding* and tucked an equally tattered blanket snugly around her.

"Three's the limit, Jesse-girl," she said, letting her touch linger on the child's cheek. "It's way, way past your bedtime. You know how hard it is to wake up in the mornings when you go to bed too late." Elizabeth rose from the side of the bed, but Jesse caught her hand, stopping her.

"Will you stay beside me until I go to sleep, Aunt Lizzie?"

It had been weeks since Gina had arrived in the middle

of the night with Jesse, pale and frightened and clinging to her mother's jeans, but the ordeal was far from forgotten by the child. Jesse played hard during the day and even seemed okay at kindergarten, but at bedtime her anxieties surfaced.

Elizabeth was sympathetic to Gina's plight, but her first thought had been for Jesse that night when she'd opened the door and the little girl had flung herself into her Aunt Lizzie's arms. There was no telling what the child had witnessed in that final scene between Gina and Austin, as Gina had never quite revealed all the ugly details. But tension—and worse—between the child's parents had taken a toll whether Gina allowed herself to see it or not.

"I think I will just have a seat in this old rocking chair," Elizabeth had said in a reassuring tone as she pulled the antique close to Jesse's bed. "I'll rock awhile and you can count sheep."

"Don't turn off the light, Aunt Lizzie."

"I won't."

"And don't close the door."

"No way. G'night, sweetheart."

Jesse's eyes darted to the window. "Does my daddy have a key to this house, Aunt Lizzie?"

"No, darling. Only your mommy and I have a key."

"She might give it to Daddy."

"She won't. She promised. It's just for her."

"Good." Jesse paused a beat or two. "Could he get in the window, do you think?"

"No, sweetheart. I have a security system, remember? When a door is opened or a window is raised, it goes off and the police hurry over here."

"Police are good. They help people." Reassured somewhat, Jesse yawned widely, eyes heavy at last, wanting to close. "We learned that in school."

"Yes, police help people." Elizabeth had reached over and rubbed the child's back, her own throat tight with emotion. It wasn't fair for a child to have these fears! "Don't worry, Jesse. You're safe here with me. Always."

"Is my mommy safe?"

"I'm sure she is, but she's probably stuck in traffic, sweetheart. She'll be home soon."

"I'm glad you're not stuck somewhere, Aunt Lizzie. I need you to be here…with…me." Words had slurred into silence then. And with a last flutter of lashes, Jesse had finally surrendered to sleep.

Elizabeth had actually felt the tension easing from the child's body. Recalling it now, Elizabeth wrestled with conflicting feelings of loyalty to Gina and her love for Jesse. With a sigh, she rested her hands on the railing of the gazebo and felt frustration and not a little fear. Jesse was safe now, and yet Elizabeth knew how tenuous that security was. She was unable to control the other forces threatening this child of her heart. How many lectures had she given Gina about her responsibility to Jesse? And how little did anything she said matter when Gina's obsession with Austin was so much stronger? It mystified Elizabeth how Gina could choose the brutal, unsafe existence she had with her lover over other options. And to subject Jesse to it defied understanding.

The truth was, no matter how Elizabeth wished it otherwise, Gina was basically flawed as a parent. She was a less-than-perfect mother. Of course, Elizabeth would never tell her that, or anyone else. She, above all others, understood Gina, knew where she came from. Her personality had been set in their early years as they'd been shuffled from one foster home after another, both longing for permanency and parents of their own. Knowing first-hand the damage that was done when children were denied the stability of a good home, why didn't Gina do the right thing? It was this failure on Gina's part to protect Jesse from the damage they'd suffered that confounded Elizabeth most.

Watching Jesse now, Elizabeth knew the bittersweet pain of loving someone else's child. If Jesse were hers, she'd never be subjected to the terror of feuding adults. If Jesse were hers, she'd treasure the child as a gift from God. If Jesse were hers, it would be a second chance for her and she'd be a good mother the second time around. And this time, she'd never let go.

Two

Elizabeth received an e-mail the day after the article appeared in the newspaper, and her first reaction was total surprise. The address on the screen was unfamiliar, but the subject grabbed her instantly, which was exactly what the writer intended, she decided later. Usually, she went through her messages and deleted anything she didn't recognize, as well as annoying advertisements and worse. How she'd managed to get on some of those lists, she hadn't a clue. But the highlighted e-mail wasn't an advertisement or a pitch to draw her into a porn site.

"Daughters of Judge Matthew S. Walker," she read. The sender was somebody named Blackstone at a local television station. The name meant nothing to Elizabeth. She decided it was probably something to do with the article in the newspaper yesterday. Unlike Elizabeth, her editor had been pleased over the publicity. She'd probably dance a jig at the possibility of a live TV spot in a market as large as Houston. Still…

"Daughters of Judge Matthew S. Walker," she read again, her hand hovering on the mouse. Being only human, curiosity got the best of her and she opened the e-mail.

Hi, Elizabeth.

You don't know me yet, but it's my hope that you will want to. I'm Lindsay Blackstone. You may have seen my show on WBYH-TV, "Lindsay's Hour," which is now canceled, I'm sorry to say. Anyway, I read the article about you in the Sunday Chronicle *and, guess what? My sister Megan and I are your sisters! After Judge Walker's death twenty-five years ago, we were adopted by Joseph and Emily Blackstone and now we would like, more than anything, to meet you.*

Elizabeth's heart was beating wildly in her chest now. Her sisters' good fortune had been hard for the five-year-old Elizabeth to accept. While they'd been basking in the attention and care of two loving parents, she'd been surviving the trauma of numerous foster homes. Everything about that time was so painful that she never—absolutely never—allowed it to surface in her mind.

Megan is doing her residency at Hermann Hospital and hardly has a life at all, but she'll make time to meet you. She's as eager to know you as I am. Also, I was telling my producer here at Channel 6 about you being my sister. He saw the article, too, but as he has small children, he already knew about you and that you'd won the Newbery. Oh, by the way, congratulations on that! He said he hoped I had inherited some of that talent. He's always trying to one-up me, but this time I have to agree. However, I hardly think my gift of gab is in a class with your awesome talent as a writer. Which brings me to this: When can we get together, Elizabeth? Just name the time and place. It'll be wonderful to reconnect, don't you think? Please call.

Elizabeth stared at a string of numbers, three for Lindsay, her office phone, her cell phone and her home, as well as numbers for Megan. There was even a number for the Blackstones at home. She'd signed the e-mail, "Love, Lindsay."

She sat looking at that salutation for a long time. Rejecting it. Disbelieving it. Drumming up some kind of relationship with her biological sisters was the last thing she wanted or needed now.

Her throat was tight and her hands, resting on the keyboard, were unsteady. First, the article exposing facts from the past that she'd worked so hard to forget, and now this. She had known when she won the Newbery Medal that some of her cherished privacy would be compromised, but she hadn't expected her whole life to become an open book. Hand on the mouse, Elizabeth deleted the e-mail.

She clicked the icon to bring up her word processing program and opened a new document to begin work, but thoughts of her sisters were not as easily zapped as an e-mail. Her peace of mind was destroyed. Her thoughts were in chaos. Lindsay's interest was too late. Not wanted or welcomed now. After twenty-five years, they expected just to knock on her door and she'd open her heart and life to them? Even if she was somewhat curious about them, it wouldn't happen. Couldn't happen. She had all she needed in her life now and it didn't include them. She had her career, she had Gina and Jesse, and yes, even Louie, although he'd probably react to that with an ironic twitch of his mustache considering how difficult it had been to become her friend. Another thought struck her. Lindsay's sudden desire to "reconnect" now was probably a ruse to get an interview, not a genuine need to get to know a long-lost sister. More intrusive publicity. Nothing could be less appealing to Elizabeth. She had enough on her plate without reuniting with two people who were virtual strangers to her. And in Gina, she had a sister in the truest sense of the word. Together, they'd shared the hell of growing up as wards of the state and that was a bond far stronger than some distant blood connection with no memories attached.

She clicked on her file list and opened the document

she'd been working on yesterday, determined to get back to work. The tension in her began to ease eventually as she immersed herself in a world that she controlled, a world of discovery and wonder, a child's world. Something that Jesse had said last night had given Elizabeth an idea for a scene. Jesse, to her delight, proved a rich resource for her books. Focused again on her work, she had the scene almost completed when Gina rushed in.

"The hearing's Friday morning at ten," she said breathlessly. "Maude just called. She wants you to be a character witness. And Louie, too."

Elizabeth saved the document before turning to look at Gina. "Did Maude say she wanted to talk to me or Louie about our testimony?"

Gina wrapped both arms around herself, looking anxious. "No. I mean, I don't know. I didn't think to ask. I just freaked out once I heard the hearing was actually scheduled. He's going to steal her from me, Lizzie, wait and see!"

Elizabeth suspected the same thing herself and had been diligently trying to figure out how to counter whatever maneuver Austin had up his sleeve. Knowing if she revealed her fears, Gina would be even more panicked, Elizabeth rose from her chair and went over to a leather couch, patting a place beside her. "Try not to panic, Gee. Austin would have to produce very damaging evidence against you before a judge would rule in his favor."

"He wouldn't have to look very hard to find stuff," Gina said, sitting gingerly. "I'm unemployed, I can't afford an apartment for us on my own, I've got a mountain of debt on three maxed-out credit cards, I—"

"Those debts were incurred by both of you," Elizabeth said, thinking there were worse things than debt and homelessness that would be unflattering to Gina as a mother if Austin's lawyer chose to use them. "Besides, you wouldn't be in such desperate circumstances if Austin hadn't forced you out of the firm. This is probably just harassment on his part and he doesn't want Jesse at all, Gee. Deep down, it's your claim to a financial settlement that's driving him."

"Maybe so, but I know he'll try to take Jesse."

"And Maude will argue that he's been a sorry excuse for a father."

"Nothing will stick," Gina said bitterly. "Trust me. Somehow his lawyer will make me out to be a…a slut or something. And probably unstable, too."

Although Elizabeth believed that was a very real possibility, she wouldn't say it. As it was, Gina was dangerously close to meltdown from the stress of the breakup. In spite of the fact that Austin was cruel, insensitive and violent, there was clearly something about him that drew Gina.

Eight years ago, Gina had been hired as a paralegal at the law firm where Austin's father was a senior partner. Why he had fallen for her was understandable. Gina was beautiful, a dark-haired, vivacious person with a sharp wit and ready smile. She was good at her job, too. In fact, Elizabeth had tried to persuade her to go to law school, but that would have meant time away from Austin. Still, it wasn't long before Austin's controlling ways and ungovernable temper took some of the bloom off the romance and dashed Gina's rosy expectations. He wouldn't marry her, but he wanted her. Their life together was stormy and unpredictable, up one day, down the next. Crazy. Why she'd stayed in such a relationship still mystified Elizabeth. But now, because he was Jesse's father, it made sense to tread carefully.

"Who is his lawyer?" Elizabeth asked.

"Wait'll you hear," Gina said gloomily. "It's Ryan Paxton."

"So? Who is he?"

"Just the best that Leggett, Jones and Brunson has when it comes to winning in court." Gina got up to pace, rubbing her forehead and frowning. "I told myself it couldn't be Ryan, at least I didn't think he'd take on something like this. He's not exactly a friend of Austin's. In fact, I always got the feeling that he disliked Austin, or at least that he found him kind of…well, he didn't have much respect for him. He knows Austin got into the firm through his father while everybody knows that Ryan is where he is because he's smart, he works like a dog and he brings in a ton of clients." She stopped and grabbed Elizabeth's phone. "I'm calling Maude back. I need to warn her just how formidable Ryan can be in the courtroom."

Elizabeth watched her dial, then listened as she spoke to Maude Kennedy. The conversation was brief and when she hung up, she knew by the look on Gina's face that Maude had failed to reassure her.

"I'm in big trouble, Lizzie. Maude says she knows Ryan's reputation and I'm right to be concerned. She wants me to think about what to say on the stand, but it's hopeless. Ryan will wipe the floor with me." Gina gave a choked cry. "The man's a barracuda! He never loses."

"Every lawyer loses once in a while."

"Then for Ryan, it's once in a very rare while. Frankly, I don't recall him losing even once since he's been with the firm."

Elizabeth stood up. "Actually I see an advantage here, Gee." She gave her a little push toward the door. It was time for lunch. Jesse had half a day at kindergarten and was now playing in the yard under Louie's watchful eye,

but she would be coming inside soon. She didn't intend
for the child to get wind of any stress, especially regarding
her contemptible father. "If Paxton has been in the firm
that long, then you're hardly a stranger to him. No matter
what gossip he hears, it's facts he must present in court."

Gina was still wringing her hands. "I can't count on
that. I was a paralegal, not a lawyer, and I worked exclusively for Austin. When it comes to taking the side of
some lowly ex-employee at LJ and B over someone whose
father is Curtiss Leggett himself, guess who'll come out
on top?"

"Austin forced your resignation from the firm, Gee.
When he realized you planned to demand child support
for Jesse, you had to go. Just as he forced you to move
out of the house where the two of you have lived together
for eight years. Maude will reveal all that in court. When
this is over, you should file a civil suit against the firm.
You have every right to bring your own case."

"Hah! That's all Austin is waiting for," Gina said bitterly. "I can't bear to think what he'll do if I don't just
shut up and let him have his way."

"Does that include handing Jesse over?" When Gina's
eyes filled with fresh tears, Elizabeth felt a pang of remorse. Gina knew what was at stake without being reminded. "I don't think you need to worry too much about
Paxton digging up dirt on you, Gee. He'll be aware that
you've been a conscientious employee. Knowing this,
he'll hardly go for your jugular."

"You don't know him." Gina looked defeated. "Wait
and see, he'll destroy me."

"I don't care how you do it, just destroy her."

Ryan Paxton placed his pen on the legal pad and leaned
back in his chair, watching his fellow colleague stalk

about the office, tight-lipped and furious. "That's a pretty harsh statement, Austin." Ryan glanced at the notes he'd taken. "Nothing you've said so far is going to give a judge sufficient cause to deny Gina compensation after a live-in arrangement that lasted eight years."

"That's why we have to destroy her."

Ryan sighed with frustration. Austin Leggett was his client only because Curtiss Leggett, senior partner at Leggett, Jones and Brunson and Austin's father, had approached Ryan and asked him to represent his son in "a delicate matter." Curtiss wanted a quick, quiet and final resolution to a sticky situation without a hint of any unpleasantness to the firm. Ryan studied his notes. Making that happen was going to be tricky. Gina D'Angelo had been a paralegal at LJ and B and Austin had been shacking up with her for eight years. They had a child, a little girl, five years old. Now Austin wanted out of the relationship and he didn't want any expensive consequences. Tuning out Austin's ranting, he briefly considered telling Curtiss he wanted no part of Austin's sleazy life. But as a partner in the firm, the reputation of LJ and B was as important to Ryan as it was to Curtiss. Too bad Austin didn't have the same concern.

"I guess you didn't consider the firm's policy of non-fraternization when the two of you became lovers," Ryan said to him now.

Austin shrugged. With his hands stuffed deep in his pockets, he looked like a petulant teenager being forced to discuss a misdemeanor. "We had some good times. In the beginning."

"I hope it was worth a couple of thousand a month in palimony, buddy. Because that's what I'd expect from you if I were her lawyer, plus child support."

Austin was shaking his head, dismissing the possibility.

"Not a problem. The attorney she's hired is some bleeding-heart female who specializes in family matters. You can run rings around her without half trying. Name's Maude Kennedy."

"I know Maude Kennedy. I've seen her in court where the only bleeding is from wounds inflicted by Maude herself. No, Austin, you've got to have something more than hostility and wishful thinking to get out of this one with your assets intact." Ryan rested farther back in his chair, crossing his arms behind his head. "Frankly, it's the kid that complicates everything."

"What do you mean?"

"Well, if you didn't have the little girl..." He moved forward, paged back in his notes, found a name. "Jesse, is it? If you didn't have Jesse, Gina's case would be a lot weaker. Come on, Austin, she's your flesh and blood. You want to do the decent thing for your daughter, don't you? It's Gina you've fallen out of love with, not Jesse, right?"

Scowling, Austin resumed pacing in the cramped office. Ryan had a tendency to stack material on any empty surface, including the floor. Case files littered the thick carpet along with reference books, computer printouts and—Ryan winced—the empty pizza box from last night's take-out when he had been burning the midnight oil on a real case, and not some irritating domestic dispute between two former lovers who now hated each other. But if the clutter hampered Leggett, or if he even noticed, he gave no indication. He was too intent on coming up with a strategy to stiff Gina, even if it meant his own daughter's quality of life suffered.

"What if I sued for custody of Jesse?"

Ryan felt a pang of sympathy for the little girl. "You'd have to prove Gina unfit, since she'll probably put up a fight. Mothers are funny that way,'' he added dryly, but Austin was busy thinking and missed the irony in his tone.

''She had a rough upbringing.''

''Gina?''

''Yeah, she was raised in foster care. Lived with a dozen families, the way she tells it. Then struck out on her own when she was about sixteen. She's been around the block more than once.''

''No crime there.''

''It shouldn't be difficult to prove she isn't the best role model for a five-year-old girl.''

''Starting with…?''

''Hell, I don't know.'' He rubbed both hands over his face. ''There's gotta be something. Nobody's perfect.''

''You'd be the best judge of that after observing her as a mother for five years. I'll need specifics and so far, I haven't heard any. I don't know Gina personally. Except for an occasional encounter in the halls, I don't think we've ever talked. But she seems pretty solid to me. She's a damn good paralegal, according to my assistant, Jean Johnson.''

''Yeah, well, give me a day or two and I'll compile a list that'll guarantee she's unfit to mother a stray cat, let alone my daughter.''

''It has to have the ring of truth, Austin. You go at it from the angle of proving her unfit with bogus charges and Maude Kennedy will hang us both out to dry.''

''Well, shit!'' Austin flung himself into a chair.

''For starters, Maude will produce a couple of character witnesses. I don't need to remind you that they say nice things.''

Austin looked up. ''But we'll diss the witnesses, right?''

Ryan shrugged. ''Depends. You'll need to cast doubt

on their veracity. But...I'm warning you, you screw that up, it could do your case big-time harm.''

Austin grunted with irritation, rubbing the fingers of one hand along his jaw, thinking. "I bet I know who she'll call.''

Ryan clicked his pen, ready to write.

"She'll probably persuade that tight-assed bitch she's moved in with to lie about her on the stand. Those two are disgusting when they get together. And they're together permanently now, just the way Elizabeth has always wanted it. I've always known she had the hots for Gina. Talk about feminism gone rampant.''

"She's living with a lesbian?'' Ryan jotted a note on the pad and added a question mark. It paid to take Austin's statements with some skepticism.

"Wait'll you meet her...and that old goat they've practically adopted next door. He'll be witness number two. I tell you, it's like a sixties compound over there when they all get together. Elizabeth writes, if you consider books for kids real writing, and the old man doesn't do much of anything, far as I can tell. Mostly acts the doting grandfather. Wait and see, between the two, they'll pressure him into swearing they're all saints.''

Ryan put his pen down. "Have you considered the fact that her friends might actually be decent people? And that Jesse might be better off with surrogates who really love her?''

"You think I don't?''

"I think you're so obsessed with putting an end to your relationship with Gina that you're in danger of losing sight of what's best for Jesse. You can bet the judge won't. That'll be uppermost in his mind. And in his ruling.''

"All I'm obsessed with is blocking Gina's plan to take me to the cleaners. Jesse'll be fine with me. I—''

Ryan lifted a hand to halt him as the phone rang. A glance at caller ID showed his daughter's cell phone number. Jennifer had strict instructions not to disturb him short of an emergency, but lately she'd been stretching the definition of *emergency*. He reached for the phone. Almost everything was an emergency to a fifteen-year-old girl, he thought with a sigh.

"What's up, Jen?"

"Dad, did you call Mom like I asked you to?" Without waiting for a reply, Jennifer rushed on in a whiney voice. "She's so impossible, Dad. She's treating me like I'm ten years old or something." Her voice climbed several notes in distress. "I don't know how much longer I can take this!"

Ryan spun his chair to face the skyline. "Take what, Jen? And make it quick as I'm with a client and you know—"

"Excuse me, but I hope I'm equal to a client," she said frostily. "I'm your daughter. Do I have to make an appointment to talk to you on the phone?" She drew an impatient breath and regressed to teenager mode again. "And you didn't answer me. Did you talk to Mom or didn't you?"

"I haven't made the call yet, Jen, and I'm not sure what you thought it would accomplish anyway. Your mother has rules that seem reasonable to me."

"You promised, Dad!" she cried shrilly.

Ryan shifted the phone a bit from his ear. "And I will, Jen. I just haven't managed to get a—"

"Oooh, this is so...so...not okay! If you had to live with her every day you'd see what I'm talking about."

"What exactly is the problem, Jen? How is she treating you like a baby? Be specific."

"That sounds so like a lawyer," Jennifer said with disgust.

"I am a lawyer," Ryan said dryly.

"Well, here's the problem." He heard the bounce as she flopped on her bed. He pictured her settling back, taking her time—and his client's—to spin her side of the latest battle between her and his ex. "Jeff Landon invited me to this party and I saw these really neat boots, but Mom just acted so...so...as if we were on food stamps or something. She said no. Just a flat no, I couldn't have them, they were too expensive. That I—"

"Maybe you didn't need them, baby."

"I did! They were too cool. Via Spigas. Perfect with my new outfit." She took a breath, dropping her tone. "It's not just the boots, Dad. It's that she doesn't have time for me anymore. She's got this new guy friend. He's gross. He's bald, Dad."

"Jennifer, is this about new boots or about your mom's new friend? And remember, I'm working. If you were a client, I'd be billing you big bucks."

"Oh, funny, Dad. In other words, you don't have time for me either, right? Mom doesn't have time, you don't have time. I don't have any friends anymore. Jeff will probably dump me if I have to wear something *old!* If it weren't for Mocha, I'd be totally alone in the world. My whole life sucks!"

Mocha was Jennifer's chocolate lab. The aging dog had been faithfully devoted to her since she was five years old. Ryan swung back around, removed his reading glasses and tossed them on the desk. "So far I haven't heard anything from you that sounds so awful," he said, rubbing a spot between his eyes. "And don't swear. You know the rule. And it goes for me as well as Diane, damn it."

"Do as I say, not as I do, right?" Jennifer said sarcastically. "That just figures."

"Tell Diane that I'll be calling," he ordered, his patience exhausted. "Tonight, provided she's staying in."

"I won't hold my breath for either one of you," Jennifer muttered.

He clamped his teeth, struggling to hold his temper. "I said I'll call her, Jennifer. And be there yourself. You hear me?"

He winced as the phone crashed in his ear. She'd hung up on him.

"Problems?" Austin asked with a cynical twist of his lips.

"Be careful what you wish for," Ryan said. "Jesse will be a teenager one day."

"I can handle it." Austin moved to the window. "I was thinking as you talked. What about this?" He turned to look at Ryan. "My mother's been making noises about Jesse visiting with her now that Gina and I are finished. This guy she's married to now is okay with it, she says. As far as TLC is concerned, there's plenty of it waiting for her with them."

Ryan frowned, trying to shove the dilemma of his own daughter in the back of his mind. If Jennifer kept this up, she was going to wind up in trouble. What the hell was the problem with her and Diane? His ex had demanded primary custody after the divorce, then after about six months, she'd remarried and moved to Dallas. Incredibly, less than two years later, she was divorced again. He didn't claim to be a perfect father, but at least he was more stable than Diane. Still, it was hard trying to do the right thing by Jen long-distance. If he wasn't fielding complaints from her about her mother, he was trying to soothe Diane as she whined about Jen. He rubbed a hand over his eyes and put his glasses back on and brought his thoughts back to Austin's domestic problems. "Where does your mother live? Nearby, I hope."

"Actually, it's Arizona. But so what?"

"That's a long way from Houston. Judges try to keep kids within reasonable traveling distance of both parents. You heard what just transpired between me and my daughter. It's difficult when parents can't share the ups and downs of raising a kid. If you remove Jesse from Gina's immediate orbit, you'll have to shoulder most of the responsibility. It can get sticky, take it from me."

"I can handle that, too."

Ryan took in a long breath and tucked the yellow pad with his notes into the file. "I don't know, Austin. Unless you can come up with specifics to taint Gina's character or cast aspersions on her as a mother, this won't be a cakewalk."

"Don't give me that bullshit, Ryan. You could build a case against Mother Teresa in a courtroom. As for Gina's faults, she's got a million. It's your job to sniff them out."

He had two options, Ryan decided, squinting beyond Leggett to the stunning view of Houston's skyline visible in the floor-to-ceiling windows. He could tell this insensitive prick to get someone else to do his dirty work, or he could show up in court, take a fresh, personal look at Gina and decide in his own mind whether Jesse was better off with her and her unconventional live-in, or with Austin's mom. In spite of the fact that he'd seen Gina in the office for several years, he knew very little about her. The judge might be someone who frowned on unmarried couples cohabiting, much less having children. But whether the judge would consider that a strike against her remained to be seen. Poor little kid. It was a foregone conclusion that Jesse wasn't going to have a future with her daddy regardless of the ruling by the court. The sheets were barely cool in the bedroom he'd shared with Gina and Ryan suspected he was already on the scent of a new lover.

"I'll put something together about Gina and the witnesses," Austin said, rising to go. "You can take it from there."

Ryan stood up. "Make it good."

Ryan handled three more appointments that day before finding time to open the folder containing the material Austin had furnished about Gina. He spent an hour reading Austin's descriptions of the woman's behavior over the years. Finishing, he groaned and rubbed both hands over his face. He preferred to avoid cases like this because of the courtroom carnage that resulted when couples decided to part. And once their lawyers got into the act, people who once viewed themselves as fairly well-matched were suddenly accusing each other of being evil incarnate. It had happened to him and Diane when they divorced, and Jennifer had been the victim. In spite of his efforts to provide some stability for his daughter, it had been traumatic for her. She'd been nine at the time. As for Diane, he'd been beyond caring about her then. Discovering her infidelity had killed his love for her outright.

He fingered the notes he'd taken earlier. Skewed, of course, to Austin's point of view. He was primed to play hardball and if the allegations he'd made to Ryan were true, there should be little difficulty painting Gina as unstable and unfit. On the other hand, was Austin telling the truth?

Ryan paged over to the character witnesses. Louis Christian. The folder contained only a single sheet. Retired business consultant, the facts of his career going back fifteen or so years. Property records showed Christian's house had been purchased three years ago, but Austin hadn't been successful in ferreting out more details, not even a former address. Also missing was anything potentially damaging that might taint his testimony. A note from Maude Kennedy was clipped to the page. Christian respectfully asked to be deposed rather than to appear in court. Health reasons. With a shrug, Ryan scribbled a note to his secretary to call Maude and agree. If, after reading the deposition he noted anything that sent up a red flag, he'd force the witness to appear in person.

Ryan set that folder aside and opened the next one with Elizabeth Walker's name printed on it. He paused for a moment, trying to capture a fleeting memory, but whatever it was danced just out of reach. The top page was a photocopied author bio, courtesy of her publisher, Ryan noted. So she wasn't just some hack writer playing at writing kids' books as Austin said. She was multipublished and award-winning. He quickly scanned the basics: born in Houston, graduate of city public schools, a master's degree from the University of Texas. Brainy and successful, he realized, noting the string of honors mentioned in the bio. Attached to the bio was a photo. Her face was a perfect oval with high, model-quality cheekbones and a mouth that was wide and softly appealing. Kissable. But it was her eyes that caught and held the viewer's gaze. In the black-and-white photo, they appeared crystallike in clarity, wide apart, the brows naturally arched. The color would have to remain a mystery, but he found himself wondering…blue, gray, hazel? No mention of a husband, siblings, hobbies or other interests in her life. In fact, there was so little personal information that he was suddenly curious.

Settling back he studied the face of Elizabeth Walker.

A woman with a face like that could use it to her advantage. He wondered if she was that kind of woman.

Turning the photo facedown, he picked up the next item, a newspaper clipping, again photocopied. And recent, too, he noticed, with a glance at the date. A feature article in the Sunday edition of the *Chronicle*. He didn't recall reading it himself, but he often played golf on Sunday and sometimes only glanced at the features section of the paper. As he began reading, the vague familiarity he'd been unable to grasp earlier suddenly came into hard focus. He swore softly, reading more intently, his eyes now flying over the words. The publisher's bio had skipped the juicy stuff, but the *Chronicle* reporter hadn't. Ryan shuffled through the pages and came across another photo, one that had been used in the feature. She was pictured in her office sitting at her computer. Live plants with cascading greenery enhanced her work area. She was surrounded by bookcases, all volumes neatly shelved. Small art objects and mementos were tastefully placed around the room. He peered closely at her. This time, she smiled. Too fixed to be natural, he thought. Clearly it had been produced on demand by a photographer.

He closed the folder and sat back, his frown as dark as the twilight swiftly falling over the skyline. Old pain stirred in his chest. Old rage. According to the article, Elizabeth Walker was the daughter of Judge Matthew Walker, a high-profile figure in Houston politics who'd died in a house fire in the late seventies. But it wasn't that that interested Ryan. What he recalled about Judge Walker was more personal—Matthew Walker was the man responsible for his father's death more than twenty-five years ago.

Three

"Let's see if I understand you, Ms. D'Angelo." Ryan Paxton gave the judge a small smile, two men sharing a male moment. "You claim you were physically abused by my client, not once, but several times during your... relationship?"

"Yes, that's right," Gina said, her tone almost inaudible. Both hands were knotted together in her lap. Elizabeth, watching from the front row in the courtroom, felt Gina's distress. She looked pale and frightened. If only there was a way she could go to her, put a hand on her shoulder, encourage her with a warm hug. Gina had been right. Ryan Paxton was a barracuda.

A very attractive, confident, skillful barracuda. Gina's words, but they were an inadequate description. Elizabeth simply hadn't been prepared for the force of Ryan Paxton in person. He was younger than the mental image she'd conjured up. Not yet forty, she decided, closer to mid-thirties. Very impressive for the level of his success. He was Texas born and bred, of course, she knew it just from the look of him and the lazy drawl in his voice, although there was nothing lazy about his rapier sharp mind. His legs were long, his body well toned. His suit probably cost a couple of thousand dollars. When he moved around the courtroom—which he did a lot—it was with the rangy ease of a man who might have been born in a saddle.

Likely a total misinterpretation, she thought with a quiet little snort. He was probably a lot more at home in Houston's trendy Sierra Grille than either hunting, fishing or riding in Texas's hill country.

"Speak up, please," the judge ordered sternly.

The judge was worrisome, too. It was Gina's bad luck that Lawrence Hetherington was presiding. He was known in legal circles as Lock 'em up Larry, notorious for his hard-nosed rulings. Gina had fared well during Maude Kennedy's questioning, but she was literally trembling with fear now and Paxton was taking skillful advantage of it.

"Ms. D'Angelo?" the judge prodded.

Gina cleared her throat before replying. "Yes. Austin was abusive. Frequently."

"But not so frequently that you quit shacking up with him, right?" Ryan quizzed.

"Objection, Your Honor!" Maude Kennedy was on her feet.

"Sustained," the judge intoned. "Mr. Paxton, watch yourself."

Ryan strode to a table, flipped open a folder and took out a sheet of paper. "This is a list of every hospital and emergency room within a fifty-mile radius of the dwelling you shared with my client, Ms. D'Angelo. Nowhere is there a record of you ever being treated…for anything. How do you explain that?"

"I never went to a hospital," Gina said, her tone faltering again.

"But you were badly injured?" Paxton was clearly skeptical. "More than once?"

"Yes."

"Describe these injuries that you claimed in your testimony were crippling."

"Well, there were bruises on my arms and legs and b-backside, you know, when he'd shove me and I'd fall against the furniture. Sometimes I'd be limping for days. Or…or he'd twist my hair in his fist, pulling it out by the roots. He's struck me in my face, too. One time—"

"And your co-workers never noticed these bruises? Never inquired about a black eye? Never commented when you appeared on crutches at the firm?"

"I never needed crutches."

"Oh…" Ryan nodded slowly, unconvinced. "And the bruises?"

"Well…" Gina licked her lips and glanced at Judge Hetherington. "He was always careful, Your Honor. Usually we'd be away from Houston, like at a weekend getaway or on vacation somewhere. So by the time we returned, the bruises had faded or I could cover them with makeup."

"Direct your answers to Mr. Paxton, Ms. D'Angelo," the judge instructed.

Nodding, Gina obediently turned to face Ryan.

"You took vacations together during the eight years of your relationship," he said, looking at a sheet he'd pulled from the folder.

"Yes."

"Often, according to my client. And this list." Ryan waved the paper in the direction of the judge. "From it, I see you were in Saint Croix, then Hawaii—two times—Europe, Canada, Boston, San Francisco, Washington D.C., New York…hmmm, four, five, six. Six times you visited New York with my client. Like New York, do you?"

"Austin liked New York."

"Were these trips business related?"

"We attended legal conferences, yes."

"How often?"

Gina shrugged. "Three, four times. I'm not sure."

"I'm counting over twenty very posh vacation spots. And, by the way, how often was Jesse allowed on these trips?"

"As often as I could persuade him to let her go," Gina said, darting a quick glance at Austin, who was sprawled behind the defendant table looking bored. She had avoided meeting his eyes during her testimony.

"How many times, Ms. D'Angelo?" Ryan pressed.

Gina was shaking her head. "Three times," she replied hesitantly.

"But being such a caring mother, you cheerfully waved goodbye to your little girl…let's see, about seventeen times, it appears. Leaving her with…who?"

"Her godmother." Gina met Elizabeth's gaze across the courtroom. "Elizabeth Walker."

"Your close friend."

"My best friend," Gina said.

Ryan turned abruptly to the judge. "I don't see a pattern of abuse here by my client, Your Honor. On the contrary, my client took Ms. D'Angelo with him when he vacationed, he opened his home to her, she lived well beyond the means she would have been able to provide for herself while keeping company with my client. Furthermore, I believe Austin Leggett is well qualified to have full custody of the child, Jesse. He acknowledges paternity, he loves his daughter, he wants only the best for her."

"Is this your summation, counselor?" the judge asked.

Ryan gave a short, charmingly sheepish grin. "Not yet, Your Honor. Sorry about that." He turned again to Gina. "How do you propose to support Jesse, Ms. D'Angelo?"

"I'm a qualified paralegal. I should be able to get a job at one of the major law firms in the city."

"But do you have a job now?"

"No."

"Why is that?"

"I was only...I left Leggett, Jones and Brunson only a month ago. They paid me three-month's severance and—"

"If you're so good at your job, why were you terminated?"

Gina glanced warily at Austin. "I wasn't terminated. I resigned."

"Why, Ms. D'Angelo?"

"Austin...suggested it." She turned again to the judge. "I know it makes me sound sort of irresponsible, Your Honor, but Austin made it intolerable for me. He—"

"Direct your answers to counsel, Ms. D'Angelo," the judge repeated with some exasperation. "Don't make me repeat myself again."

Gina's shoulders fell as she turned back, gazing not at Ryan, but at her hands. "He was going to accuse me of irregularities in the handling of some of his clients' matters. He specializes in estate law. He handles millions of dollars in other peoples' assets. It would be easy to manipulate funds here and there."

"What exactly are you accusing my client of?"

"Nothing, no. Only the threat of doing it. If I didn't leave peacefully." Gina pressed trembling fingers to her mouth. "In his position, it's easy to move money around from one client's portfolio to another without actually—"

"Come on, Ms. D'Angelo. What you're accusing my client of is a serious charge. In fact, some might call it slander."

"It isn't slander if it's true." Gina's tone rose with her agitation. "Do you think I'd walk out of a job where I'd worked for almost nine years if I didn't have a compelling reason? Knowing Austin wanted to dump me and I'd be without a place to live? Knowing there'd be no way I could support Jesse? I don't think so, Mr. Paxton," she added bitterly.

"But you do have a place to live," Paxton argued. "Your best friend and Jesse's godmother, Elizabeth Walker, has been only too eager to take you in. No, I think you orchestrated this whole scam, the abrupt resignation at LJ and B, the allegations of abuse and irregularities with the firm's most valued clients, the threat of legal action against my client...all toward one end. You want a hefty financial settlement. You want a lot of money in return for walking out of his life."

"No, I—"

"No more questions, Your Honor." Ryan turned on his heel and strode to the table. Dropping into a chair, he didn't look at Gina again, nor did he glance at his client. Instead, he flipped the folder shut, leaned back with his hand spread flat on the folder as if to guard the contents and gazed moodily out a window. If his goal had been to destroy Gina, Elizabeth thought, studying the set look of his features, he'd succeeded. But he didn't look like a man who was pleased with his success.

"You may step down, Ms. D'Angelo," the judge said. And as Gina rose unsteadily, Maude Kennedy stood up.

"I have one more question, if Your Honor would allow it?" She raised pencil-thin eyebrows in question. The judge nodded and motioned Gina back into the chair.

"How much money are you requesting from Austin Leggett, Gina?"

"Two thousand dollars a month," Gina replied. "And for child support only, nothing more. Jesse will stay in the school where she's presently enrolled in kindergarten. One thousand will pay her tuition and the other will be placed in trust for her to go to college."

Maude Kennedy looked at the judge. "That's all, Your Honor. Thank you."

"Step down, Ms. D'Angelo," the judge ordered. As Gina rose and left the witness box, he studied a paper in an open folder in front of him. "You want to call your first character witness, Ms. Kennedy?"

Still standing, Maude said, "There is only one witness, Your Honor. We have a deposition in lieu of testimony from the second witness, Louis Christian. He is presently at Elizabeth Walker's residence taking care of Jesse. As you'll see once you've read the deposition, Mr. Christian is not a blood relation to Jesse, but he could very well be her grandfather. He sees her daily. They're very close."

"Then call the witness who has shown up, counselor," the judge replied. He removed his glasses and rubbed both eyes with thumb and forefinger as if his patience was at an end. Her face carefully blank, Maude nodded to the bailiff.

"Elizabeth Walker," the bailiff intoned.

Elizabeth was already on her feet. She approached the gate in the bar separating spectators in the courtroom from the players and slipped through it, made her way past the two lawyers' tables to the witness box and turned to take an oath to tell the truth. She was nervous. None of her experience in courtrooms had been pleasant, but this wasn't about her, she told herself, taking her seat gingerly. It was about Jesse. Gina. Their future.

Maude seemed to sense her apprehension and gave her a reassuring smile as she asked her address and occupation. Then, "How long have you known Gina D'Angelo?"

"Since we were both five years old."

"You're not related?" Maude asked, knowing the answer.

Elizabeth smiled faintly. "Not by blood, no. But we sometimes feel as if we're related. Sisters almost." She took a small breath. "We were both wards of the state when we were orphaned at age five. As luck would have it, we were in the same foster homes off and on during our teenage years."

"That explains your willingness to share your home with Gina now."

"In a way, I guess. Actually, we're no different from biological sisters who see a lot of each other," Elizabeth said, feeling more at ease. Maybe this would be more positive than she had thought. "We live in the same city, we share holidays, lunch, we shop together, we share gossip and clothes. I was at Gina's bedside when Jesse was born. In fact, I was her birthing coach. So now that she's in difficulty, it's very natural to have her move in with me until she's on her feet again."

"Why wasn't Mr. Leggett Gina's birthing coach?"

"He said he didn't have time."

"Where was he when Jesse was born?"

"In Europe. On one of the many excursions he took without Gina," she added dryly.

"How would you characterize Gina? In a few words."

"She's loving, smart, honest, impulsive, funny. Jesse adores her. She's everything a sister and best friend should be. My life would not be nearly as rich without Gina."

"Thank you, Elizabeth."

The moment she feared was upon her. She tried to blank the apprehension from her mind. And the utterly irrelevant thoughts she'd had about Ryan Paxton as he'd questioned Gina. It was her turn now and Jesse's life was in the balance.

Ryan was speaking as he got up from his chair.

"You've been very supportive to Gina for many years, haven't you, Ms. Walker?"

"What do you mean?"

"You've bailed her out of trouble countless times."

"She's never been in serious trouble."

"Did you co-sign for her to get a credit card when she couldn't get one on her own?"

"Yes, but that was years ago."

"Did you pay her tuition when she trained to become a paralegal?"

"Yes."

"Were you her tutor in high school when she almost didn't qualify to graduate?"

"She…she had some unpleasant experiences while we were in foster care."

"Did you have some unpleasant experiences, too?"

"Foster care isn't an ideal situation for anybody," Elizabeth answered dryly.

"And yet you didn't require a tutor?"

"Well…"

"And you weren't in trouble with school authorities?"

"I—"

"Yes or no, please, Ms. Walker," Ryan said.

"No."

"Tell us more about yourself today, Ms. Walker. You're an author?"

"Yes. I write books for children."

"And very successfully, too, according to the recent article in the *Chronicle*."

"I've been lucky."

"I actually read one of your books last night, the award-winning book. I wouldn't say it was luck that won you the Newbery, Ms. Walker. That book was very clever, whimsical and fun while delivering a very solid message.''

''A moral message. I try to do that in each of my books.''

''It was about a little girl's difficulties with her school friends—what was her name?''

''Jasmine.''

''Jasmine. Because her mother had chosen an…ah, alternate lifestyle. The other kids found that odd and weren't shy about saying so.''

''Children can be hurtful.''

''The main character—Sophia, was it?—befriended Jasmine. Came to her defense at school. Sort of fixed everything for Jasmine, but got in some hot water herself for doing it.''

''I tried to show how courageous behavior can be rewarding, but you may have to pay a price.''

''What price will you have to pay for your courage in defending your friend Gina today?''

''Price?'' Elizabeth frowned. ''I don't understand.''

''The article about you in the *Chronicle* made clear your aversion to publicity, Ms. Walker. You're almost a recluse. A hearing such as this is bound to stir up more unwelcome interest in you.''

''With all due respect, Mr. Paxton, I don't think the media can have much interest in me.''

''I did a bit of research into your background after reading that article.''

Elizabeth felt her heart bump into a faster rhythm. Maude rose. ''Objection, Your Honor. Ms. Walker isn't on trial here today. If Mr. Paxton has a question, let him ask it.''

With eyes locked on Elizabeth's, Ryan said, ''No one's on trial here today, Your Honor. I'm within safe legal grounds to question the credibility of Gina D'Angelo's character witnesses.''

"Overruled," the judge said. "But ask a question, counselor."

"Are you comfortable knowing the media is in the courtroom, Ms. D'Angelo?"

Elizabeth glanced beyond him to the sparse gathering of people seated in the spectator area. Several onlookers met her eyes, three women and half a dozen men were scattered here and there. A group of twentysomethings looked on with interest, possibly law school students. "I have no interest in the media," Elizabeth said quietly.

"Not even if someone were to question your lifestyle?"

"Question my lifestyle?" She frowned. "In what way?"

"You and Gina are very close. You said as much and so did Gina. Exactly how close are you, Ms. Walker? Would you describe your relationship as intimate?"

"Objection, Your Honor!" Maude said fiercely, surging to her feet.

"Sustained. Move on, Mr. Paxton," the judge said, looking mildly irritated.

"How do you come up with ideas for your books, Ms. Walker?"

"As most authors," Elizabeth began, struggling to control the angry tremor in her voice, "I'm an observer of human nature. I read newspapers. I watch television. I read."

"The kid in your book is named Jasmine. That's very close to Jesse. Was there some connection there?"

Again Maude Kennedy jumped to her feet. "Your honor, I object! Mr. Paxton's insinuations are scurrilous and have no foundation in fact."

"Withdrawn, Your Honor," Ryan said, unfazed. Going

to the defendant's table, he picked up his notes. "December 24, 2000. Does that date mean anything to you?"

"Christmas Eve?" Elizabeth guessed, but, again, her heart was beating fast.

"A couple of years ago," Ryan acknowledged, nodding. "Tell us what happened that night."

"What happens to anyone on Christmas Eve," Elizabeth replied. "It depends on your family traditions. My Christmases are usually very quiet."

"But not that year, right? Didn't the cops ring your doorbell sometime after midnight? You'd gone to bed, I believe."

"Your honor," Maude Kennedy said, "if Mr. Paxton has anything of substance to add to this hearing, would he please get on with it?"

Ryan faced the judge. "This is a hearing about Gina D'Angelo's suitability to gain custody of a five-year-old child. The facts I'm about to elicit from this witness will cast grave doubt on Ms. D'Angelo's character."

"Again," the judge intoned, "I want you to get on with it, Mr. Paxton. There's no place in my courtroom for grandstanding."

"Understood." Ryan turned back to Elizabeth. "Where were we, Ms. Walker? Oh, yes. Midnight. Your front door. Cops ringing the doorbell. What was that all about?"

"Gina had been in an accident. She was—"

"Drunk?"

"It's not the way you make it sound." Elizabeth's tone was soft, pained. "Gina and Austin had been at a party. They had a quarrel in front of the other guests. They'd both been drinking. Everybody at the party was drinking, but—"

"But nobody else stormed out into the night—by the

way, it was raining. A downpour. To be more specific, one of our torrential Houston storms. But that didn't deter Gina as she spun out into the street in Austin's eighty-five thousand dollar Porsche, did it?''

"She knew if she got into the car with him he'd become violent," Elizabeth said fiercely. "He'd done it before."

"Well, we have only your speculation about that, don't we?" Ryan said, giving the judge a droll look. "What we know happened was that she ran onto a neighbor's curb, knocked down a mailbox, bogged down in a planting of sago palms and incurred substantial damage to the Porsche."

"She had to swerve onto the curb to avoid hitting a cat that darted in front of the car!" Elizabeth cried.

"A cat. In the rain. In a neighborhood with stringent leash restrictions on all animals. Even cats."

"Maybe it was a possum," Elizabeth said, knowing she was being baited. Still, she was doggedly determined to defend Gina. "Maybe it was a raccoon. There's a stream running behind those houses. Animals are common."

"Critters, huh?"

"Was that a question, Your Honor?" Maude inquired with disgust.

Striding away, Ryan tossed the notes onto his table and sat down. "I'm finished with this witness, Judge."

Elizabeth turned in her chair to look at the judge. "Austin would have hurt her that night, Your Honor. That's why she took the car. And he would have hurt her even worse if she'd asked a guest at the party to help her. That would have revealed the trouble in their relationship. It would have made public Austin's cruelty."

"Your honor—" Ryan was on his feet.

"That's enough, Ms. Walker. Step down, please." The judge drew in a deep breath. "Let's recess for lunch, folks.

We'll resume at two o'clock.'' Banging his gavel, he rose impatiently, striding out of the courtroom in the billowing folds of his robe, slamming the door behind him.

It was a subdued trio who were seated for lunch in a restaurant near the courthouse half an hour later. "I'm sorry, Gina. I made a mess of that." Elizabeth rubbed at her temples, eyes closed, but unable to banish Ryan Paxton's smug expression from her mind. If only she'd been more clever, faster on the uptake on the stand. Instead, she'd been pathetically inept in Paxton's skillful hands. "You were right about Paxton. He's tough."

"Worse yet, I think the judge is on Austin's side," Gina said, gazing morosely into a glass of iced tea. "His body language during the entire morning says it all."

"Not all. The game isn't over, ladies." With reading glasses resting at half-mast on her aristocratic nose, Maude Kennedy studied the menu. "It's never possible to predict a judge's ruling. Has anyone tried the trout amandine?"

"How can you have an appetite, Maude?" Gina exclaimed. "I'm never going to eat again."

"Of course, you are." Maude looked at them both. "How about a cup of crab bisque and that old standby, a Caesar salad?"

"I'll just have the bisque," Elizabeth said, laying down her menu.

"Did you see the way he slammed the door of his chambers when he left?" Gina asked, clearly still focused on the judge.

"I repeat, judges are unpredictable." Maude paused and motioned a waiter over. "And whether he may have seemed so or not, Judge Hetherington has a reputation for fairness. He's tough, even a bit chauvinistic, but when it comes to the welfare of a child, he'll be very careful."

She removed her glasses and looked at Elizabeth. "By the way, Elizabeth, you didn't *mess up* on the stand. Your reputation and demeanor go far in adding credibility to your testimony. Judge Hetherington won't dismiss lightly the fact that you've actually seen Gina bruised and hurting."

"Even though he thinks we're two lesbians?" Elizabeth said bitterly.

"That was below the belt," Maude conceded. "I was surprised at Paxton."

"A barracuda," Gina repeated. "Didn't I say it?"

"I have to think the lie originated with his client," Maude said.

"Austin knows that's pure garbage!" Gina said. "I knew he'd play dirty, but I didn't expect him to go that far." She crushed a roll in her fingers. "But the worst thing was dredging up that old drunk driving charge."

"I believe Judge Hetherington heard Elizabeth's explanation even though he had to silence her," Maude said, taking a sip of water. "Let's order, ladies. I'm famished."

"I hope the worst is over." Elizabeth leaned her head back against the leather padding in the restaurant booth and closed her eyes. They were due to return after lunch at two o'clock, but after being subjected to Ryan Paxton's ruthlessness, she wanted nothing more than to go home, close up in her office and turn on her computer where she could enter a safe and idealistic world, a world he'd described as whimsical, somehow making the word sound weird.

"Remember, Ryan Paxton is used to winning," Maude Kennedy said, "but there is enough substance in both your testimonies that I have hope the judge will not rule in Austin's favor."

After taking their orders, the waiter collected the menus

and hurried away. "What was that about media?" Elizabeth asked, frowning. "Was the reporter who did that feature on me lurking around?"

"He wasn't in the courtroom," Gina said. "I looked."

Maude broke open a roll and buttered it lavishly. "There are always reporters assigned to the courthouse beat, but they seldom have an interest in custody hearings unless the people involved are in the public eye. As much as Austin might fancy being in the public eye, he isn't. No, I think Ryan was just trying to rattle your cage, Elizabeth. Trust me, you did very well up there. Your sincerity shone through." She smiled at them both. "I, for one, find the friendship between you heartwarming."

"Excuse me…" A woman, smiling slightly, stopped at the booth.

"Yes?" Maude said, her thinly penciled brows going up. But it wasn't Maude the woman's gazed fixed on. It was Elizabeth.

"I know this is so…well, pushy, but I told myself if I don't grab the opportunity, I might not get another." Her pretty face lit up in a wide, warm smile. "Hi, Elizabeth. I'm Lindsay."

Elizabeth could think of absolutely nothing to say. After the fiasco of both her and Gina's testimony, she'd thought the day couldn't get any worse. She'd been mistaken.

"Lindsay," she repeated.

Gina gave a little gasp, then covered her lips with her fingers. She glanced quickly at Elizabeth. "Is this—"

"Lindsay Blackstone." Lindsay's smile went even brighter, if possible. "And I've just sat in on your hearing so I know who you are." She gave Elizabeth an imploring look. "Please don't be offended, but I just wanted to introduce myself." She stuck out her hand and her smile flashed again. "I don't think you'd welcome a hug, would you?"

"Hello." Elizabeth took her hand, gave it a brief squeeze. What else could she do? "This is my friend, Gina D'Angelo, and her lawyer, Maude Kennedy. Gina, Maude, this is Lindsay..." She paused, unable to bring herself to say the *S* word.

"I'm Elizabeth's sister," Lindsay said with a wide smile.

There was a moment of stunned silence at the table. "We've had some e-mail correspondence lately," Elizabeth explained in the lull.

"I was aware that you had a sister," Maude said, studying them both with frank interest. "And now that I've seen you together, the physical resemblance is definitely there."

"I never made a connection with *the* Lindsay Blackstone on TV," Gina said on a note of wonder. She gave Elizabeth a wide-eyed look. "This is the Lindsay you mentioned who sent you the e-mail? Your sister?"

"It seems so," Elizabeth said dryly.

"You mean you didn't go around bragging about me?" Lindsay teased with an amusing laugh. "I'm hurt."

"Sorry." Elizabeth was vaguely familiar with the canceled show—"Lindsay's Hour"—but she hadn't made a habit of watching it. Mornings were her peak writing time, so she didn't watch much television at all during the day. She recalled seeing it, though, but had never guessed at any connection between herself and the woman who was the show's star. The woman whose life seemed charmed.

Lindsay's charm was now fully unleashed. "Well, as they say, pride goes before a fall. I guess that'll show me."

"I was a big fan," Gina said.

"Thank you."

"The similarities between you two are quite amazing," Maude said, gazing from one to the other. "But you're certainly different types as far as hair and eyes go." Elizabeth's dark auburn hair and clear green eyes were startlingly different from perky, blue-eyed and blond Lindsay.

"I've only figured it out recently," Lindsay said, still smiling. "According to my adoptive parents, we were separated by some stupid mix-up in the courts. This happened when Megan, our other sister, and I were still infants. We never knew that Elizabeth existed, can you believe that? It all came out when she won the Newbery. I guess you could call our reaction a mix of delight and amazement and...well, we were furious and sad, too. You should have been there when we confronted our parents. They had a lot of explaining to do, I can tell you."

Elizabeth drew a long breath. "Lindsay, I don't think this is the time to discuss our personal circumstances." But inside she was trying to take in the fact that her sisters hadn't known about her until the newspaper article. Had Lindsay mentioned that in her e-mail? She'd zapped it after that first, fast read-through. Had she missed it?

Eyes wide, Lindsay put a hand against her cheek and looked somewhat apologetic. "You're so right. Like I said, I'm pushy sometimes. Megan's always telling me I talk first and think later. But how could I pass up this opportunity when it's been so difficult trying to reach you?" She gave Elizabeth a cajoling smile. "Can we get together...please? It would mean so much to Megan and me."

Their orders arrived just then and Elizabeth escaped having to reply. Not to be deterred, Lindsay shifted to one side, waiting while their plates were placed in front of them. Then she laid her card at Elizabeth's place. "I'll go now and let you enjoy your lunch, but please use my private number to call me…anytime. Or Megan. I've jotted hers down, too. She's doing her residency. Presently it's an ER rotation. I think that lasts six weeks, then it's—'' She stopped, smiled again in charming apology. ''Okay, okay, I'm done. Call one of us, Elizabeth. Please? Now that we know you exist, we'll have all the time in the world to get to know each other. After all, we're family. What could be more natural?'' Still smiling, she backed away.

''So that's what a TV personality looks like in person,'' Gina breathed as they watched Lindsay make her way through the lunch crowd, waving to first one then another of the seated diners. One man rose hastily, beckoning her over to an already full table. With a bright smile of recognition, she went over and stood talking.

''I wonder how it feels to have a face that everybody recognizes?'' Gina mused.

''Not everybody,'' Maude said, giving Elizabeth a smiling look. ''I never saw her before. I take it she's a local celebrity?''

Gina, not Elizabeth, answered. ''Yeah, at least she is in Houston, I guess. She had her own talk show produced at WBYH, but it was canceled after—'' She looked at Elizabeth. ''It ran about a year, didn't it, Liz?''

''I really don't know.''

''Are you like me, Elizabeth, not much time for television?'' Maude might not be a fan; nevertheless, she was intrigued. Her gaze was on Lindsay, still chatting across the room. ''Why was the show canceled?''

Gina shrugged. ''Ratings, I suppose. Isn't that always the reason a show is axed?''

Maude smiled faintly. ''Again, I plead ignorance.''

''But now that I've actually seen her,'' Gina said, noting the buzz among the lunch crowd as they began to recognize the celebrity among them, "I'm surprised she didn't make a go of it. She's very charismatic, isn't she? And talk about *cogones,* she's got 'em! It took balls to approach Liz after she ignored the e-mail. I've seen Liz squash lesser individuals who tried to intrude on her privacy." She gave Elizabeth a thoughtful look. "Are you telling me you never knew the Lindsay who sent that e-mail was one and the same as Lindsay Blackstone of television fame?" There was obvious admiration on Gina's face.

"I guess I'm just not the starstruck type," Elizabeth said with a shrug, knowing it was difficult to resist someone with Lindsay's infectious personality. But she was honest enough to admit her reaction seemed less noble now that she'd learned her sisters never knew she existed. They hadn't chosen to shut her out of their lives. They hadn't known about her. She studied her soup without enthusiasm. Maybe sometime in the future she'd make an effort to get to know Lindsay and Megan, but for now, the time just wasn't right.

Even though her appetite was gone, Elizabeth picked up her spoon. "Can we eat our lunch now?"

Four

"Hot damn, I think you did it, Ryan!" Slapping his hand on the tabletop, Austin grinned with glee as he watched Ryan collect papers and notes, a couple of pens and a scattering of paper clips, then toss them into his briefcase. "I knew you'd cream Gina on the stand, but it was really inspiring the way you rattled that bitch she's living with now." He rubbed his hands together. "Hell, you made it look easy. We've got 'em, haven't we?"

Ryan closed the lid of his briefcase and snapped the locks shut. He preferred spending the lunch recess alone. He stayed focused that way, but Austin was like a pesky pup, dogging his tracks and peppering him with questions. He'd done his best to prepare him for his testimony this afternoon, but he didn't have a good feeling about it. "It's a mistake to count your chickens before they hatch, Austin."

Something about the grim set of his features finally signaled to Austin that his lawyer's behavior was something less than joyful. His glee morphed into impatience.

"It's not chickens we're dealing with here," he snapped. "It's a couple of dykes with an agenda. Which is to take me to the cleaners. So I repeat, do you think we've destroyed their case? Am I going to come out of this without writing a check that'll make me very unhappy or not?"

Ryan was silent. He'd been pretty brutal to Gina and her friend and he wasn't feeling particularly proud of himself. Elizabeth's testimony had been especially powerful and he'd had to use strong tactics to make his point. Hell, it was natural she'd want to stick up for Gina. That's what character witnesses did. Their mission was to paint a glowing picture of the person they'd mounted the stand to defend. Elizabeth had done that all right, big time. As a result, he'd crossed a line professionally grilling them both the way he did. He knew in his gut the women weren't lesbians. And Elizabeth's explanation about the New Year's Eve party had the ring of truth. Whether both were telling the truth about Austin's abuse was more difficult to judge, and that was troublesome. There were no hospital records, Gina had never called the police, she'd made no formal complaints anytime, anywhere. With no paper trail, it was Gina's word—and her friend Elizabeth Walker's—against a man Ryan himself had known for several years. On the other hand, his acquaintance with Austin was not personal, but almost exclusively professional. And very casual. Still, word of that kind of behavior got around, didn't it? And although he had never heard a word about it, the gossip mill at LJ and B was alive and well. On the other hand, anyone gossiping about Curtiss Leggett's son would be severely chastised at the firm. That, in itself, would keep a lid on gossip. So, the question remained, were the allegations of the two women manufactured to put the squeeze on his client, as Austin claimed? If so, that kind of mean-spirited, grasping behavior deserved the full brunt of his expertise to rebut it.

He paused with a sheaf of papers in his hand. All this soul-searching and second-guessing of himself was a useless exercise. His treatment of Elizabeth Walker on the stand had nothing to do with her connection to the man who'd driven his father to suicide, and everything to do with his client. That would have been over the line, and he didn't consider himself petty.

"Hello? Counselor...anybody home?"

"Hmm? Oh, sorry, Austin. I was just practicing my closing statement," Ryan lied. He picked up his briefcase from the table and fell into step with his client, both headed for the doors. "Why don't you go grab yourself some lunch and I'll meet you here when we reconvene?" He shot back a cuff to look at his watch. "In about an hour and a half."

"You didn't answer my question," Austin said, ignoring the dismissal.

"I didn't hear a question."

"Is she going to be awarded big money?" he repeated in exasperation. "Jesus, Ryan, what else would I be asking about?"

"What about custody? Isn't that what you're most interested in?"

"Custody and the settlement amount go hand in hand," Austin said, getting more agitated by the minute. On the steps of the courthouse now, he suddenly faced Ryan. "What's going on here? Are you having doubts about the case? Are you starting to believe those two? Because if you are, I need to know about it. I can get another lawyer—"

Ryan stopped, fed up with the whole nasty situation. "Listen, Austin, if you don't like the way I'm handling your case, there are thirty-five or forty other lawyers at LB and J who would jump to take my place. I didn't ask for this job, I was put in a position by your father where it was flat-out suicide to refuse it. And now that I'm up to my ass in your life, I realize that Curtiss Leggett wasn't particularly looking out for your welfare in ordering me to wrap the whole thing up neatly. What your father wants besides that is to shield the firm from any hint of scandal. Now, the question remains, Austin…why would he think there was a chance that the firm would be embarrassed?"

"I don't know what he thinks." Austin sounded like a surly teen.

"Maybe there's some substance to those allegations Gina and Elizabeth Walker were making? Maybe your old man has picked up something from the office grapevine? Or maybe he has a more reliable source."

"Meaning what?" Austin's face was turned away, closed.

"Meaning he's family, Austin. Your family. Families have secrets."

"He doesn't know my secrets," Austin said sourly, his gaze on the lunch hour traffic. "There's nothing for him to know. Gina's lying. Liz is lying."

"Everybody's lying," Ryan said evenly. "But not you."

Austin turned and looked him squarely in the eye then. "No, not me."

After a moment, Ryan began to walk again. "Then if you stick with that attitude on the stand this afternoon, you'll be in good shape, depending on what you really want. If it's to avoid writing a big check, maybe. Gina claims she doesn't want much. But if it's custody of your little girl, that's more iffy."

"You worry too much," Austin said, his good humor restored by the prospect that he might not have to part with real money.

"Yeah, well, that's my job," Ryan said. Approaching his car, he opened the door and tossed his briefcase inside. What was really sticking in his craw was the custody issue. When it came to the little girl, Ryan had a bad feeling about handing her over to Austin. He'd felt these vague negative stirrings before in other cases…and it was always when he'd gone to the wire for a client who, when it was all over, turned out to be a liar.

Pity that little girl.

"Jesse, we're home!" Gina tossed her purse on a chair, kicked off her shoes. "God, I feel like an ex-con getting out of prison. How do you stand being cooped up all day in front of that monitor, Liz? I'd go crazy. Louie! Jesse!" She pulled the comb from her hair and freed her thick, dark mane. Balancing on one leg, she reached for one of the staid, black pumps borrowed from Elizabeth for the hearing and took it off. She glanced into the den while massaging her cramped toes. "Where are they?"

Elizabeth tucked her purse into a drawer. "I'll check my office." Jesse had quickly learned to play simple computer games and she sometimes broke the rule not to open the machine when Elizabeth wasn't there to supervise. "Not in here," she told Gina. "They're probably outside."

"Probably." Gina headed across the den to the patio doors. "If Louie would let her, Jesse would spend the whole day outside. She's such a tomboy." Gina sighed, savoring the cool wood floor on her bare feet. "My feet feel as if they're out of prison, too," she muttered, opening the French doors to a burst of enthusiastic barking in the area beyond the patio. "Louie! Jesse! Where are you?"

"Over here." Louie's voice came from the gazebo. He began to rise from an old-fashioned glider. There was no sign of Jesse. "How'd it go?"

"We'll know tomorrow," Elizabeth said. "The judge will give us his decision then."

"Oh, shoot, I'll ruin these panty hose if I go out there." Stepping back, Gina lifted the hem of her skirt—also borrowed from Elizabeth—and wiggled out of the panty hose. Then, sighing with relief, she stepped barefoot onto the flagstone surface. "Where's my honey?" she called, raising her voice in the singsong way that Jesse loved.

Jesse squealed, emerging from a pile of raked leaves that hadn't been there when they'd left this morning. "Here I am, Mommy!" Laughing, she ran flat-out for her mother, arms open wide. The golden retriever raced by her side. Both outdistanced a tow-headed boy, who was just a fraction of an inch taller than Jesse. Gina laughed as thirty-five pounds of small female energy crashed into her legs and two short arms closed tight around her thighs. The dog leaped around them, grinning and barking ecstatically.

"Missed me, didn't you, punkin?" Gina framed Jesse's small face between her hands and gave her a kiss on the nose.

"You were gone a long time, Mommy."

"It sure seemed like it to me, too, baby." Gina plucked a few dead leaves from her daughter's tangled mop. "But I came home as soon as I could. Hi, Cody," she said to the little boy, who smiled shyly while hanging on to the dog's collar.

"Was she a good girl, Louie?"

The aging man was dusting leaves and debris from his pants. "She's always a good girl," Louie Christian said, giving Jesse a wink.

"What is it with that wink?" Gina asked, pretending to frown.

"Don't go in Papa Louie's kitchen, Mommy," Jesse warned. Beside her, Cody buried his face in the dog's ruff.

"Why, what would I find in Papa Louie's kitchen?" Gina asked.

"They wanted to make play dough," Louie explained. "From scratch."

"No, from flour and salt, Papa Louie," Jesse said.

Louie gave Gina another wink. "My mistake."

Gina's hands went to her hips. "So you said absolutely not because a kitchen is no place for two five-year-olds, except for eating. And besides, fooling around with flour and salt and who-knows-what-all to make play dough is a project to be supervised by moms. That is what you said, isn't it, Louie?"

Louie scratched his bearded cheek. "Well…"

Jesse was jumping up and down and Cody was grinning. "He let us do it because we knew how, Mommy! We learned at school, didn't we, Cody?"

"Uh-huh." Blond head bobbing.

"I'm afraid I didn't realize exactly what was required to make play dough," Louie said apologetically. "And then there seemed to be flour everywhere and Archie was going to track it back into the den, so I turned my back for a moment to put her outside, then Cody said he knew how much water it took, but apparently he overestimated a bit and then—" He was shaking his head. "Actually, it was the mixer that did most of the damage, I'm afraid."

Gina reached up and flicked something white and sticky from Louie's beard.

"Oops." Jesse covered her mouth and her smile. "I thought we cleaned you all up, Papa Louie."

"But did you clean up Papa Louie's kitchen, young lady?" she asked sternly.

"Papa Louie said we'd better go outside while the gittin' was good," Jesse said. "So we did."

"It was too overwhelming for them to clean up," Louie

said, looking pained. "And I couldn't leave them outside without supervision. You wouldn't want that, would you?"

"Oh, no, I wouldn't want that." Gina rolled her eyes. "Look, Louie, you're going to have to be more forceful with them, Jesse especially. She can talk the tail off a tiger if you let her. Now, next time—"

"Next time I won't let them in the kitchen," Louie said, looking relieved to get only a lecture.

"No, next time you won't let them talk you into beginning a project that even an experienced childcare worker would hesitate over." After a moment, she gave a resigned sigh. "Okay, the damage is done, but we have to go over to Papa Louie's house now and clean up." She took Jesse's hand and motioned for Cody to follow. When Louie made to join them, she shook her head. "Uh-uh, Louie. They did the mess, they'll clean it up. You go back to the glider and let Elizabeth tell you about the hearing."

"Good idea." Elizabeth, smiling faintly over the situation, nudged Louie toward the gazebo.

"Is it good news?" Louie asked, not ready to sit.

"Tell him, Liz." And with that, she picked up her pace, tugging Jesse along with Cody, and headed toward Louie's house just visible through a thick hedge of oleander.

"Want some more iced tea?" Elizabeth asked, noticing the glass on the table beside the glider.

"No, no, I'm nearly floating now." Instead of relaxing, Louie sat up straight on the edge of a cushion as Elizabeth took a seat in a white wicker chair. "I'm surprised the hearing's over. I thought it would go into a second day. Did Austin do the decent thing and withdraw his motion?"

"Austin and decency is an oxymoron," Elizabeth said

with a grimace. "Gina and I testified this morning, then he took the stand after lunch. Judge Hetherington—"

"Old Lock-'em-up Larry," Louie muttered as he tossed what was left of his drink into the grass.

"You know him?" Elizabeth asked.

"I've watched him preside in a couple of high-profile cases," Louie said, "but that was years ago. I hope he's mellowed in his old age."

It always amazed her how informed Louie was for a man who seldom left his house except to stroll over to hers. He had an opinion about politics, about social problems, about current faces in the news. It shouldn't surprise her that he recognized the names of locals in the legal community. Judge Hetherington had been on the bench in Houston for over thirty years. Where Louie Christian had been for most of that time was a mystery. He was vague about his past, which was fine with her. She wasn't one to pry into anyone's past. It was the present that mattered where Louie was concerned. For one thing, he was the nearest thing to a grandparent that Jesse had, since Austin's father was a cold fish and his mother lived with her second husband in Phoenix, Arizona, and had never expressed any interest in spending time with the little girl. Louie had an endless supply of anecdotes about his boyhood that enchanted Jesse. Elizabeth herself was charmed by his tales, so much so that she'd used a couple to illustrate themes in her books.

"Let's pray that he has mellowed," Elizabeth said now, plucking a spent bloom from a camellia. She'd have to think about getting her yard man to put in some petunias soon. And possibly some daylilies. The lantana would return on its own, flourishing in Houston's heat. One of the perks of the climate was that her yard was alive with color year-round.

"Exactly what happened today, Liz?"

"Ryan Paxton was brutal to both of us on the stand. Then Austin lied outrageously when it was his turn. There's no one to refute what goes on between two people in the privacy of their home, Louie, so he painted a picture of Gina that could have made even me wonder if she was an unfit mother. Maude did a good job trying to show that Austin was motivated by a self-serving need to give Gina nothing in the way of decent financial support, but what concerns me most is Austin's claim that she is unstable." She stared beyond the trees to the older man's house, frowning. "She'll be lucky to come out of this with equally shared custody, Louie. Even worse, it'll be a miracle if she gets a pittance in the way of child support, too."

"Hetherington will have to award her reasonable child support."

"But what if he believes she's unstable and primary custody goes to Austin?" she asked anxiously.

"Isn't that what you think?"

She looked at him with surprise. "What?"

Louie was shaking his head. "You haven't admitted it to yourself, have you? You've been Gina's guardian angel since the two of you were prepubescent, Liz. You've watched her make crazy choices even as you begged her to be reasonable, you've stepped in to grease the way back when she's been irresponsible, you've lectured and cajoled, you've sympathized and nagged. When are you going to insist that she grow up?"

Elizabeth was on her feet now, hugging her middle as if to arm herself against what he said. "That's a little harsh, isn't it? And somewhat judgmental."

He muttered something she didn't quite catch, then said, "But is it wrong?"

"Some people find it harder to overcome the hardships of childhood than others."

"Yes, and she can thank the good Lord that you aren't one of them. Pity poor Jesse-girl if both of you were as damaged as Gina. As it is, the child's got you as a second mother figure and a stabilizing influence." Louie gazed through the trees to the patio of his own house where the two children romped and squealed and Archie barked in joyful accompaniment. "The real fear here is that Austin might change his mind and renew their affair. She won't be able to hold out if he does."

The same thought was making Elizabeth's nights long and sleepless. But it made her feel guilty and disloyal to discuss it. To be honest, it was Jesse's welfare that concerned her more than Gina's. After all, Gina was an adult, a fact she'd often reminded Elizabeth of when they got on the subject of her relationship with Austin.

Louie was looking at her keenly. "I don't hear a denial, Lizzie."

She rubbed her forehead with one hand. "Not this time, Louie. I think the possibility of getting back with Austin is hopeless. He's tired of her at last and that's the only way this whole miserable situation is ever going to end."

"And now, all we have to worry about is what happens to Jesse."

"Yes, that's all."

Seeing the enormity of her fear, Louie rubbed his chin and looked wise. "I wouldn't be too worried about that, Liz. Frankly, I can't see a man like Austin wanting the responsibility of a young child. That takes an emotional toll, not to mention time and energy. He'll avoid all three like a bull avoiding a rattlesnake."

"I know he's not concerned about Jesse's welfare. He never has been. If there had been any doubt about that,

he proved otherwise when he tried to force Gina to put
Jesse on the stand. He had no thought of how devastating
that might be for a five-year-old child. He's shameless!''

''And selfish.''

''Well, to Gina's credit, she refused,'' Elizabeth said.
''What I worry about now is that he's so vindictive that
he'd separate Jesse from Gina and never even consider the
heartbreak that would cause both of them.''

''And you.'' Louie was looking at her with sympathy.
''You have too much invested in this, Liz, and no control
over the outcome. You need a husband and children yourself. You'd be a terrific mother, but you've invested so
much emotionally in these two that you aren't even open
to the possibility of a family of your own.''

She had been once, she thought, watching a dragonfly
settle on the back of a chair. And she'd believed herself
so close to realizing that dream. Once. ''I'm not past the
age of possibilities yet, Louie,'' she said dryly. ''I'm
thirty, not fifty. There's still time for me to marry. In the
meantime, I'm concentrating on doing everything I can to
help find a happy ending for Jesse. And Gina, of course.''

''Hmm. Meanwhile, let's be grateful that we're finally
seeing the end of that sorry relationship,'' Louie said, adding in a wry tone, ''if we're lucky. And even though it's
Austin doing the walking. Hell, it's years overdue, but
now's not the time to look a gift horse in the mouth.''

''It's so frustrating.'' Elizabeth watched the dragonfly
lift off and fly away. ''But the more I know about people
in abusive relationships, the more I can see Gina conform-
ing to type. I remember the first time I saw purple marks
he left on both her arms. I insisted that she pack up, leave
him and file an official report with the police. She didn't
have Jesse then. It would have been so much easier than
now. You know what she said?'' Louie still sat silent.

Unable to stand still, Elizabeth began pacing. "She said she'd provoked him, that it was as much her fault as his. I couldn't believe it. She was battered and bruised and I think he'd made a mark on her cheek that she'd tried to cover up with makeup, which meant he'd struck her in the face, for heaven sake." Her arms were again tight around herself and her eyes had a suspicious brightness. "That was the beginning and it only got worse. Gina's reaction was right out of a textbook. Sadly, you're right that she'd go back today if Austin smiled and crooked his finger."

"Well, we can hope that won't happen," Louie said, rising with a painful grunt. He'd hurt his back a few weeks ago while preparing his vegetable garden. Of course, he'd refused any help from Gina and Elizabeth even though he would share its bounty. Next season, he would use a motorized tiller if she had to purchase it herself. "And even if he does manage to get primary custody, he'll soon be bored and more than willing to hand Jesse back to Gina."

Elizabeth smiled thinly. "Yes, but until he gets bored, there will be nothing and no one to protect his victims."

They were seated in the courtroom a few minutes before ten the next day. Judge Hetherington arrived precisely on time, seated himself with an air of importance, then peered over his reading glasses to locate Gina and Austin. With a curt nod of his head, he addressed them both.

"This was a very difficult case. When the facts are as murky and uncertain as I've found them to be herein, I can only adjudicate with what's given to me in testimony or in deposition. Ms. D'Angelo, I believe you love your daughter and genuinely seek what's best for her. I also believe—" he turned his gaze on Austin "—that you, Mr. Leggett, have demonstrated a fatherly concern for Jesse, although your time and attention as a parent differs from your…ah, ex-partner's parenting behavior, as well it should.'' He studied notes in front of him silently for a few moments. ''The difficulty in deciding this case lies in the accusations made by each of you about the other. In essence, the court has only the word of each of you that you are being truthful. I believe Ms. Walker is sincere in defending your character, Ms. D'Angelo. But she was not present when you and Mr. Leggett were alone behind closed doors. Therefore, her testimony must be considered hearsay. I find the same to be true of the deposition of one…ah—'' he turned over several pages of a yellow pad ''—Louis Christian.'' Looking up, he gazed sternly at Ryan. ''It would have been helpful to have a character witness for your client, Mr. Paxton. I have read the deposition of one…Marilyn Leggett Bingham, but—''

''That would be my mother, Your Honor,'' Austin said, ''Jesse's grandmother.'' He had begun to rise from his chair, but was halted when Ryan jerked hard on his coattail.

The judge's gaze became a glare. ''You had your chance to respond when court was in session yesterday, Mr. Leggett.''

''Sorry,'' Austin mumbled, subsiding.

The judge reviewed his notes again. ''Mrs. Bingham's deposition was very favorable, as one might expect from a mother, but I am forced to point out that she is not in residence nearby and hasn't seen the child in more than a year. Her testimony was not helpful in that context. I repeat, I find myself in a difficult situation.''

Listening, Elizabeth held her breath. In front of her, Gina sat fidgeting and looking scared. And no wonder, Elizabeth thought. Judge Hetherington clearly wasn't convinced that they'd told the truth about Austin. Was the man going to get away scot-free?

"I'm favorably impressed by Ms. D'Angelo's modest financial demands," the judge continued, "as well as her intention to set aside some of it for the child's education later. I'm granting that amount. I'm also increasing it by two thousand dollars each month to apply to rent and day-care since Ms. D'Angelo has stated she needs to seek employment and it's unreasonable to assume that she can enjoy her friend's hospitality indefinitely. If she does indeed find suitable employment, I'll take another look at her financial situation."

Gina made a soft, incoherent sound, but was sternly quashed by one look from the judge. Focusing again on his yellow pad, he studied his notes in silence, then continued. "I'm also favorably impressed by Mr. Leggett's generosity in providing for Ms. D'Angelo and the child for the entire duration of their relationship. Without hospital records or police statements to back up the allegations of abuse, I'm powerless by law to consider that an issue here today. Consequently…" He paused, finished with his notes, and began tidying up. When the pad and all documents were neatly stacked in front of him, he reached for his gavel. "I'm granting joint and equal custody of the minor child, Jesse Elizabeth Leggett, to you both, Gina D'Angelo and Austin Leggett, and directing that you work out an amicable arrangement for sharing the responsibilities of parenting her. There's no such thing as equal custody, of course, but you both live in the same town and that is an advantage. Since Jesse attends kindergarten, I'm directing that she live with her mother during the week and that you have visitation rights as often as you wish, Mr. Leggett. I leave it to you both to work out weekend visitation, but I'm again directing that it be each and every weekend if you so desire, Mr. Leggett. Also, you are to take turns with holidays, Christmas, Thanksgiving, Labor Day, whatever. If you are unable to come to an agreement, then the court will appoint someone to do it for you.'' Stern-faced, he leaned forward and pointed the gavel at them. ''I strongly urge you both to work this out between yourselves. I'll expect a document from your attorneys within thirty days as to the terms and conditions. I don't need to point out the difficulties in dividing a child's life into two equal parts, but if you care about Jesse as much as you've testified to me, then I'm confident you'll both do the right thing. Now, this hearing is adjourned.''

Crack! His gavel banged and it was over.

Five

"Can we talk, Ms. Walker?"

Ryan Paxton spoke from behind Elizabeth as she stood in line at Starbucks waiting for the cappuccino she'd ordered. She turned, startled, and found herself looking into his eyes. They were a clear, almost silver, gray. He'd unbuttoned his shirt and pulled the knot of his tie loose. But it had done nothing to detract from the classy elegance of his suit, as expensive as yesterday's. Would anything? Dangling from one hand was his briefcase. The other was anchored by a thumb in a pocket. She wasn't fooled by his casual air. There had been nothing casual about the way he'd gone after her and Gina on the stand yesterday. And this close, he seemed taller and more intimidating than he'd been in the courtroom.

She resisted an urge to ease back and held her ground. "I don't know what we could possibly have to say to each other, Mr. Paxton."

"You heard the warning Judge Hetherington gave Austin and Gina. I thought you and I might help ward off the Third World War."

"The way I heard it, the judge assigned that task to you and Maude Kennedy." Elizabeth glanced toward the attendant who was brewing the cappuccino. With a hiss of the machine, he completed the creation and handed it over. She took it and began walking away. Ryan followed.

"I'd still like a minute to talk about it." With a light touch on her arm, he steered her toward an empty table. Wishing she hadn't indulged her craving for coffee, Elizabeth allowed him to pull out a chair for her. After the session in the courtroom, she'd left Gina and Maude to begin hammering out some kind of workable agreement with Austin and Ryan, telling Gina to meet her at the coffee bar in an hour. It surprised her that Ryan had left his client unprotected with Maude Kennedy. She hoped Maude was taking advantage of his lapse in judgment.

When she was seated, he took the chair opposite. "You must be feeling pretty good about the judge's ruling," he said.

"What makes you say that?"

"It's obvious, isn't it? Gina gets the kid, the money...two thousand bucks more than she asked for. Plus, you're off the hook. She can get an apartment and you get your privacy back."

"Do you practice being obnoxious, Mr. Paxton? Or were you simply born that way?"

"You mean you wouldn't mind if Gina stayed with you indefinitely?"

"I mean exactly that. Gina and Jesse are family. I love them both. They're welcome in my home as long as they want to be there."

He slapped his briefcase into the empty chair at the table and dropped his head back, looking at the ceiling for a moment before straightening up. "I'm screwing this all up."

"Screwing what up?"

"My peace mission. Trying to get your help on this whole stupid situation before it turns into something we'd all rather avoid."

"Like what? Like Gina might get attacked again by that

sadistic jerk? Or, worse yet, he might turn on Jesse? How would you like that, Mr. Paxton? How would you feel if he lost his temper when Jesse spills her milk or…or leaves a toy on the stairs or breaks something that he prizes? Children do that, you know. How would you like it if she landed in the ER with a broken arm? Or a concussion? Or worse!"

He was shaking his head. "Come on. You're exaggerating. Nobody produced a scrap of evidence proving Gina was roughed up by Austin. And you're not going to make me believe he'd hit that little girl."

"I'm not going to be able to make you believe anything except what you want to believe," Elizabeth said bitterly. "You've convinced yourself that Austin's okay. Odd, since you probably don't even particularly like him. At least, I didn't see much evidence of strong male bonding between the two of you during the two days I've had to observe. Your attitude is so typical. You won't let yourself think that a fellow lawyer, a well-educated contemporary from a privileged background could be a cruel, vindictive, violent creep, will you?"

"Not without something more than the word of two—"

"Lesbians?"

Again, he was shaking his head. "Ah, I don't believe that."

"Then why did you insinuate it to Judge Hetherington?"

"I'm a lawyer. I use whatever tactics I can to benefit my client."

She stood up, nearly tipping the coffee over. "I never could understand why anybody would want to be a lawyer and you've reassured me about my instincts."

Ryan touched her hand. "Wait, wait a minute, Ms. Walker." The look she gave him was so furious that he fell back. "Look, I'm sorry. I didn't approach you to stir things up worse than they are between Austin and Gina. Believe it or not, I'm trying to do some good here."

"How, in God's name, are you trying to do good?" she asked, genuinely baffled.

"I need your help in trying to get Gina and Austin to work something out for the sake of the kid…for Jesse's sake. And I don't think it's going to happen if it's left to them."

"I can promise that Gina is more than willing to do whatever it takes to work out something for Jesse's sake. She loves her child more than life itself."

"And Austin doesn't, is that what you're saying?"

"If the shoe fits." She wadded up her soaked napkin and tossed it and her unfinished cappuccino into the trash. "And now, if you'll excuse me…"

He caught up with her just as she stepped outside into bright sunshine. "Don't you even want to try?"

She put a hand up to shade her eyes and stared at him. "Excuse me, but it's difficult for me to believe that you're thinking of Jesse and Gina, Mr. Paxton. The only way this could have been worse is if Austin had been given full custody of Jesse. Then she really would have been lost to us. This way, Austin will still be in her life and in Gina's, I'm sorry to say."

"Ryan."

She blinked. "What?"

"I'm Ryan, not Mr. Paxton."

"Look," she said, drawing a weary breath and digging for her car keys, "the only two people who are relevant in this…this agreement that the judge has decreed are Gina and Austin. And nothing you or I can do is going to affect that. I don't quite understand why you felt comfortable leaving your client with Gina and Maude, but without you they may be able to work something out. Maude is smart and coolheaded and even Austin must respect her.''

''Yeah, and it would be nice if Maude was in there with them. Unfortunately, when they booted me out, they booted her out, too.''

Keys forgotten, Elizabeth stared at him. ''What do you mean they booted her out?''

''Just what I said. She—'' He stopped abruptly as a sporty BMW stopped at curbside, brakes squealing. The driver was a woman. ''Damn it all,'' Ryan muttered as she got out of the car and looked over the top of the car at him.

''Where the hell have you been?'' she growled, snatching sunglasses from her face. ''Why do you have that damn cell phone if you aren't going to bother answering it?'' She was halfway around the front of the car now. ''I've been trying to reach you for hours, Ryan. Damn it! You're impossible. You're—you're—''

''Excuse me a moment,'' Ryan said to Elizabeth in a grim tone, adding, ''Don't go away. I still want to talk to you.'' He intercepted the furious woman, catching her by the arm just as she stepped up on the sidewalk. But even though he turned to shield their conversation, the woman was oblivious to an audience.

''You're taking her, Ryan. This time, I've simply had it. She can come live with you. I'm tired of fighting it. We'll see how you cope if she's with you 24/7.''

''Calm down, for God's sake, Diane. The whole world can hear you!''

''It's too damn bad *you* can't hear me, Ryan.'' She shoved her sunglasses back on her face and turned away, lips trembling. ''Oh, hell, I know I'm wasting my time.''

She drew in a shaky breath. "I've been trying to reach you since early this morning."

"I've been in court. Which is why my cell phone was off. What's going on?"

"It's Jennifer, of course."

Ryan looked at the ground as though taking a moment to count to ten. "What now, Diane?"

"She's really done it this time, Ryan. She stole a car. Can you believe that?"

"What!"

"It gets worse. She had an accident."

Ryan's attitude went instantly from shock to concern. "Is she hurt?" He looked at the car as if expecting to see Jennifer. "Where is she?"

"She's not hurt. She's at your house. I dropped her there and told her I was going to find you." She pressed a hand to her lips. "She's in serious trouble, Ryan."

"Are the police involved?"

"I haven't called anybody yet." She pushed her hair back and looked directly at him again. "She left the scene. She hit somebody who was biking in Hermann Park. There was no other car involved. And then she—she just drove off, Ryan." Diane spread her hands in a gesture of pure bafflement.

"Jesus Christ." He leaned against the car, then turned to see Elizabeth watching. Straightening, he caught Diane's arm and moved out of earshot. "Go back to my house and wait for me there. I'll clear up what I've got going here and be there within an hour. Don't talk to anybody else about this. I'll do that when I get home."

"I called the hospitals to try to get some information about the—the victim," Diane said hesitantly. Her face was tight with strain. "No luck. I—I didn't call the police to see if he was—"

"I'll handle it." Ryan reached out and squeezed her shoulder. "Try not to worry, Di." His jaw went rigid. "And tell Jennifer—" He stopped, waited a moment or two as if reconsidering. "Tell her to sit tight and we'll talk when I get there."

Diane's face was bleak as she met his eyes. "I can't believe she did this, Ryan."

"Yeah, she's out of control. We've both seen it coming." He shook his head. "I don't know what to tell you."

"You're going to have to take her. She needs a stronger hand, Ryan." She pushed a hand through her hair wearily. "I'm just at the end of my rope."

"It's okay," he said, nodding. "We'll work something out. Go back now and stay with her. She shouldn't be left alone too long under the circumstances."

She nodded wordlessly, then as she stepped off the curb to go around her car, she glanced about and saw Elizabeth. "I'm sorry," she murmured. "I guess your friend heard everything. Or is she a client?"

"Neither. Drive carefully now."

He stood watching as she walked back to the BMW, got in and started it. He lifted a palm and waved her off, his face troubled. Finally, he turned where Elizabeth was waiting. "Sorry about that."

She gave a small shrug and smiled sympathetically. "Looks like you'll have your hands full for a while."

"I'd like to keep this private, Elizabeth. My daughter seems to be going through a bad patch."

"Certainly. Consider it forgotten."

"Thanks."

"You were saying that Gina dismissed Maude when you left. I can't believe that."

"See for yourself." He looked beyond her as Austin's Porsche pulled into a parking slot across the street from the coffee shop. Gina got out and even from this distance, Elizabeth could tell she was flushed and animated. At a signal from Austin, she waited for him to come around the car. He bent and said something in her ear. She nodded, not quite smiling, but she looked far less fragile than she'd been in the courtroom less than two hours ago. Tucking his hand beneath her elbow, they started across the street. There was no sign of Maude Kennedy.

"Hello," Ryan murmured, watching them. "Looks as if they're all made up."

"Thanks to you," Elizabeth said bitterly. "Once Austin got her alone, he would have wasted no time convincing her that they didn't need anybody to help them work this out. So now he's got a free hand to persuade her to anything he wants. Trust me, it won't be to Gina's advantage."

Ryan looked down at her. "You really despise him, don't you?"

"He's a despicable human being."

Both were silent as the couple approached. Gina's smile, when she spotted them, was a little too bright. "Lizzie, I'm glad I caught you. Hi, Ryan. Are you two getting acquainted?"

"Mr. Paxton was just leaving," Elizabeth said, then added coolly, "Hello, Austin."

"Liz." Austin's pale eyes sliced over her.

"Austin and I are going to lunch, Liz. We're going to talk this over ourselves, try to put something together without the…the lawyers." She gave a quick, embarrassed half laugh. "No offense, Ryan. So, Liz, you needn't wait around to give me a lift home as we'd planned."

"What are you doing, Gina? You know why the judge directed you to work out an agreement with the help of your lawyers. These things are handled best with people who aren't emotionally involved." She gave Austin a quick glance, unmoved by the venom in his glare. She expected Austin to try an end run around the judge's order, but why would Gina give him the opportunity after the abominable way he'd treated her? "If you go with Austin now, you give up any advantage you might have in negotiations. You know how he is, Gina."

"Oh, Lizzie—"

"Yeah, Lizzie," Austin said, with sarcasm, "however Gina decides to work this out is none of your business. And even if she wants advice from her lawyer, that's Maude Kennedy, not you. So butt out. Now."

Ignoring him, Elizabeth focused on Gina, but it was a struggle to keep the edge from her voice. "Does Maude know you're going to handle this without her and does she approve, Gina?"

"She—she was a little reluctant, but—"

"C'mon, Gina. I'm ready for some fresh air." With his arm around Gina's waist, Austin's razor-sharp smile included Ryan as well as Elizabeth. "That judge was so full of shit that it'll take me and Gina a while to shovel through it and come up with a reasonable plan, but we can do it, can't we, honey? And without the help of lawyers."

He took a step or two, but stopped as another thought struck him. There was no smile on his face when he addressed Ryan. "Hey, Ryan, you'll want to stick to criminal defense if your performance today is an example of what you can do in a civil suit. Luckily, Gina's going to be reasonable about this and we'll let you and that ballbuster who represented her know how it comes out." Lifting his hand, he pushed Gina ahead a little more forcefully than she expected, but she quickly regained her balance and picked up her pace to match his as they headed toward the car.

"Seems in a hurry," Ryan observed, watching as Gina was hustled into the Porsche.

"It's necessary…before she changes her mind."

Ryan shifted his briefcase to his left hand and urged Elizabeth into a walk. "I think I've just been dissed bigtime," he said dryly.

"I wouldn't expect a bouquet of flowers tomorrow from your client if I were you," Elizabeth said, still frowning at the Porsche that was peeling out into heavy traffic. But concern and disappointment were a thick knot in her throat. He'd done it again. He'd smiled and mouthed a few smarmy words and Gina had caved, just as she and Louie had feared.

"All I need now," she said mostly to herself, "is to get back home and find a message that she's decided to go back and live with him again." She was barely aware that it was Austin's lawyer beside her.

"I don't think that'll happen."

"Oh, it could. She's done it many times."

"It might be difficult this time. Three's a crowd and I'm not counting Jesse."

She gave him a quick glance. "He has another woman already?"

He shrugged. "He hasn't admitted it. I'm just repeating gossip."

"Isn't that a breach of ethics? The man's your client."

"As I said, it's only gossip. Besides, Austin's parting salvo makes me think he'll be looking for fresh representation soon."

She would have laughed, but she was simply too disheartened. "It won't matter. He's in damage control mode and we'll only know how much damage he's controlled when Gina gets home tonight.''

"I thought they were just having lunch," Ryan said.

"Oh, they'll have lunch all right…and then he'll persuade her to spend the afternoon with him to give him more opportunity to get her to rethink her attitude. Then he'll treat her to dinner in a great restaurant. It'll be expensive and romantic, a place to remind her of all the perks that come from sleeping with the enemy.''

As they neared her car, Elizabeth fished her keys out of her purse and chirped the remote to unlock it. But before she climbed inside, Ryan stopped her.

"May I ask you a personal question?"

"Ask anything you want, but I certainly don't promise to answer.''

"It's about your friendship with Gina. Anyone can see that the two of you are nothing alike. From what I learned about her after I took on the case, Gina's made some really bad choices. Granted, Austin's not a very reliable source, but on the stand yesterday you said the two of you have been together as foster kids since you were five years old. Tell me, why is her personal life a wreck and yours almost the exact opposite?"

"Almost?"

"Well, nobody's perfect. So, unless you're going to tell me something bad, my comment stands. And my question.''

"I'm not going to tell you anything, Mr. Paxton. My personal life is just that, personal. And private.'' She got into the car, but he caught the door before she could close it. "What?'' she demanded. Both hands on the wheel, she looked straight ahead.

"You have a reputation for avoiding publicity, for reclusiveness. Don't you know that the more mysterious you seem, the more intriguing you are to your fans? Avoiding them just adds to your mystery. Throw a few scraps out there and they'll back off. And it's Ryan, not Mr. Paxton.''

"Reporters don't want scraps, they're hunting red meat. I have a right to avoid anyone prying into my life. Thanks for the advice, but no thanks.'' She put the keys into the ignition and started the car. Getting on a first name basis with Ryan Paxton was another thing she wanted to avoid. "And my fans won't care—because they're children.''

"How do you communicate with them, other than your books, of course? By e-mail on the Internet? Letters? What?''

"Letters mostly.'' She could just drive off, but he'd unknowingly touched on something she was not reluctant to share. "And I answer them all, each and every one.'' Her fan mail came from children, innocents who wrote from the heart. Elizabeth understood that need to communicate. She knew how it felt to write a letter when you still believed there was someone out there who would listen. And she knew how it felt to wait expectantly for a reply that never came.

"Kids send you letters,'' he said, considering that with a half smile. "You must get some real cute stuff.''

She thought of the eight-year-old whose letter lay even now waiting for a reply in her in basket. The child's younger sister needed a heart transplant. Would Elizabeth please tell the child's parents that she would like to give her sister "half of her heart?'' "Sometimes they aren't very cute.''

He still blocked her leaving, standing with his weight on one hip, his left hand resting on the door frame of her car. She didn't wait to hear what else he had to say about her career or her personality drawbacks. Instead, she reached for the handle of the door, forcing him to move back, and closed it smartly. "Goodbye, Mr. Paxton," she muttered to his receding outline in her rearview mirror.

Ryan stood for a minute watching Elizabeth drive away. Okay, he'd satisfied his curiosity. He'd had a conversation with her out of the courtroom. Away from her pal and soul mate, Gina. He hadn't made up the reason for seeking her out, not exactly. He knew, if left to his own devious devices, Austin would chew Gina up and spit her out, sans any financial settlement, no matter what the court decreed. And just to ease his conscience, he was going to give Curtiss Leggett an earful about his prick of a son. He might not be as black as the two women had painted him, but he wasn't a boy scout either. So, Ryan's motive in talking to Liz was honorable. Sort of. He also wanted to talk, one on one, with the daughter of the man who was responsible for John Paxton's death.

He'd watched her for a few minutes at the coffee bar before approaching her. She was easy on the eyes, as gorgeous in person as her press photo. In fact, he'd had a hard time keeping his thoughts in line when he had her on the stand in the courtroom. He admired her loyalty, too. She was as fierce as a mama tiger defending Gina. Or possibly, it was the little girl, Jesse, who stirred the fires in her breast. Beautiful breasts. He'd had no trouble imagining the feel of them in his hands as he stood talking to her, even in that severe suit with the starched blouse underneath. But he didn't intend to get caught up in any sexual fantasies about Elizabeth Walker. He had other, more compelling reasons for getting to know her better.

Her old man was dead, killed in a house fire just a day or two after his dad's suicide. That much was public knowledge. But information beyond that about Judge Matthew Walker was extremely hard to come by. Maybe Elizabeth was a possible source. She'd been only five when he died, but she probably had his papers, his files, a record of the cases he'd been involved in at the time of his death. If she hadn't destroyed them. Being a foster kid, her possessions might have been lost as she'd been palmed off to one anonymous family after another.

He felt a pang of sympathy, but for only a moment before shutting it off. Unlike Elizabeth, he'd had both parents until he was fifteen, two-thirds longer than she'd had anybody. Tough luck, but she'd managed. Pretty damned good, too. He admired her accomplishments. No, he wouldn't waste sympathy on somebody who clearly didn't need it.

Six

"Have you got a minute, Curtiss?"

Curtiss Leggett looked up from a seemingly vacant perusal of Houston's skyline and motioned Ryan into his office. He swiveled in his chair so that he faced forward as Ryan quietly pulled the door closed behind them, ensuring privacy. "How'd it go?"

"Hetherington awarded joint custody to Austin and Gina. They're to share holidays and vacations. They're to work out an amicable plan together."

Leggett grunted. "What about child support, palimony?"

"Her request was modest. Hetherington doubled it. Austin's hit for about four thousand a month unless the two of them can come to an agreement for less." Ryan frowned. "I thought he would have called you by now."

Leggett's laugh was brief and without humor. "He knows better than to bring up the subject of that woman with me. He should never have moved in with her. I know it's the thing to live together now, but wouldn't you think he'd choose someone of his own class? She's trailer trash, that's an apt description. I've been after him for years to send her packing." He drew a disgusted breath. "I never could understand what he saw in her."

"What about Jesse?"

Leggett turned his face, avoiding Ryan's gaze. "Another mistake. Why the hell he didn't make her abort is another mystery to me.'' Shaking his head with more disgust, he said, ''The whole thing has been distasteful to me from the beginning. I'm just glad to see the end of it. Of course, I'll talk to Hetherington about reducing the money. Four thousand's ridiculous. What does she expect, to be kept in the style of a real ex-wife? You've got to have a marriage for that. Steering clear of matrimony was Austin's only smart decision.''

Ryan felt himself doing a slow burn. He'd felt no particular affection for Gina D'Angelo while representing her ex-lover, but she seemed a decent person. She'd made some bad choices in her life, but, hell, didn't everybody once in a while? But she wasn't trailer trash and she didn't deserve the treatment Leggett father and son would no doubt cook up for her.

''Something else emerged during the hearing,'' he said, wishing hard that he was on the golf course. He found he couldn't sit down. He was too close to telling this bigoted old fart where to get off. ''I know you were concerned about the firm's reputation and any scandal that might grow out of the hearing...or out of Austin's involvement with Gina.'' He paused, giving Leggett a chance to be reminded that it wasn't only Gina who was to blame for the situation. ''There is some exposure, I think.''

Leggett was in the act of reaching for an elaborate humidor where he kept his stash of Cuban cigars. He stopped now, giving Ryan a keen look. ''In what way?''

''Gina and her character witness, Elizabeth Walker, made some serious accusations about Austin. Do you have any knowledge of abuse in their relationship?''

''Abuse? Not sexual? Nothing about the little girl, eh?'' He barked the questions out, like bullets.

''No.'' Jesus, why would he even think that? Ryan

watched him lift the lid of the humidor and select a cigar, taking his time. Did he know what was coming next? "They claimed Austin was often physically abusive, that he made a habit of beating up on her. That he had an ungovernable temper and when it went out of control, Gina was the victim."

"Preposterous." Leggett busied himself preparing his cigar. Looking at it, not Ryan, he meticulously clipped the end, moistened it by rolling it round and round in his mouth, then he picked up a sterling silver lighter. Now, holding the cigar in his teeth, he put the flame to it and puffed energetically until the immediate area around his head and shoulders was thick with smoke. Only then did he look up at Ryan, his eyes squinting against the acrid cloud. "What kind of evidence did they have for that?"

What kind of question was that? Ryan wanted to shoot the words back at him. It was as if Leggett accepted it for the truth, but lawyerlike was seeking a way out. "They didn't produce any evidence," Ryan told him. "That was the reason the judge went with the joint custody thing. If they'd had a hospital report or a police report, or if they managed to come up with an actual eye witness when Austin did what they claimed, it would have been much worse for him. As it is, only Elizabeth Walker, Gina's friend and godmother to Jesse, claims to have seen bruises. She was a sort of way station when Gina would go into seclusion."

"Bullshit."

"Maybe." Ryan was beginning to have grave doubts about the character of his client. "But if Austin's smart— and there is some grain of truth to what both women claim—he'll need to be very careful around Gina and his daughter in the future. It wasn't a closed hearing, Curtiss. There were some students there, law school types from

Rice, I think. And the usual courtroom junkies that hang around just to watch the legal system in play. But hear this. The person who really concerns me is Lindsay Blackstone, a television personality at WBYH-TV. She heard everything. My paralegal tells me that there was a series on her show last year about the escalating violence against women from husbands and lovers. I just hope she wasn't there doing more research for a follow-up. I don't think so, as there was no camera, but you never can tell.''

"Goddamn it!" Leggett rose abruptly from his chair, his frown thunderous. "Why didn't you see to it the hearing was closed, Paxton? That's why I chose you to handle this...mess.''

"If I'd suspected what Austin was going to be accused of, I would have,'' Ryan said in an even tone. Did he have to remind the old coot that he'd walked into this case blind? And whose fault was that? The first rule in defense was to come clean with your lawyer.

Leggett grunted and puffed furiously on his cigar while he thought. He then gave Ryan a sharp look. "You think anything'll come of it?''

"Only if Austin gets stupid and hits her again.''

Ryan was out of Leggett's office and on his way to his car when he realized what he'd revealed in his parting remark to Austin's old man. Leggett clearly was unsurprised to hear that his son was accused of beating up on a woman. That was disgusting enough, but what was just as disgusting was the absence of any shock and sympathy on Leggett's part for the victim. The whole thing left a bad taste in Ryan's mouth. He wished he'd never gotten involved.

Seven

Austin lifted his wineglass and smiled into Gina's eyes. "To peace and harmony," he said, his voice low and sexy. "To a better understanding, and especially to a history that can't be wiped out by asshole lawyers."

"Present company excluded, I assume," Gina said dryly.

He touched her glass to his and grinned wickedly. "Damn right."

Gina tasted the pinot grigio and found it fragrant and light. At one time she would have enjoyed it, as well as the hushed, intimate atmosphere of the restaurant. Anthony's was pricey and the place to see and be seen in Houston, but considering that they'd spent the past two days in a bitter court fight, Austin's motive in bringing her here was pretty obvious. She should have asked him to take her home after lunch, but he'd suggested they take in the new exhibit at the museum and then they'd stopped at happy hour at a bar he liked. And now...

When the menus were placed before them, he set his glass down and rubbed his hands together. "So, let's see what's wonderful tonight. I've heard the tomato tower is great. Let's try it. What do you say?"

She ordered without much enthusiasm and sat back to wait for the meal while Austin chatted with ease about everything except the one subject that they should discuss. "So how's your job search coming?" he asked as soon as their salads were served.

"I've had a couple of interviews." She toyed with the garden greens. "I think I would have been hired by a small firm last week, but the personnel manager was spooked by the circumstances of my leaving LJ and B."

"Not a problem." He poured more wine for both of them. "Have them call me. I'll give you a recommendation that won't quit." He lifted his glass. "Cheers, babe."

"It's too late, Austin. I needed the recommendation before they notified me that someone else had been selected." Since that had been before the hearing, she didn't need to be a rocket scientist to understand why there'd been blank silence from Austin.

"It's their loss, sweetheart." He reached over and touched her cheek. "Next time."

In spite of her suspicions, she felt a quick, familiar warmth as his hand lingered, cradling her face. Austin in this mood was dangerously seductive. And the emotion he kindled wasn't from the wine. No, it stemmed from some deep need in herself that Austin had always been skillful in tapping. Struggling to resist it, she glanced at her watch. "I really need to get back, Austin. Liz will be wondering what happened to me."

The easy charm disappeared at the mention of Liz's name. He dropped his hand and his voice went flat. "Liz knows you're with me. Forget her." He lifted his wine-glass, but found it empty and set it down with a hard thump. Refilling his glass almost emptied the bottle. Looking about with irritation, he located the waiter and with a curt gesture ordered another.

"Austin, I'm serious." Gina covered her glass with one

hand. More wine would undermine her ability to resist him. "It's not just Liz I'm concerned about, it's Jesse."

"She's asleep, for Christ sake! Or she damn well should be at this hour."

"She is, because Liz is so conscientious about everything to do with Jesse. But I'm responsible for her even so. I hadn't planned on having dinner with you this evening. What if Liz had plans of her own?"

"She never has plans. She's a goddamned recluse!"

"You make her sound weird or…or antisocial, or something. She isn't any of that. She's the best kind of friend a person could have, especially to Jesse and me. I honestly don't know what I'd do without her."

"We probably wouldn't be in this mess without her," he said in a biting tone, then added, "And don't forget good ol' Louie."

She looked again at her watch as the waiter approached with a fresh bottle of wine. "I really have to go, Austin. Stay and enjoy your meal. I'll get a taxi."

He stood up with a short obscenity and pulled out his wallet. Sensing trouble, the waiter backed away and stood at a discreet distance as Austin peeled off several bills and tossed them on the table. The waiter wasn't the only one who sensed trouble. Gina recognized the signs all too well. She quickly stood, grabbing her purse. On the ride home, Austin's irritation would grow with every mile. He'd be tense and silent, seething with rage. But tonight, thank God, she wouldn't be going home with him.

She stole a quick look at him and felt an odd regret. For several hours today when he was so utterly focused on her, when he'd turned on the full force of his appeal, she'd come dangerously close to forgetting who he was. What he was really like. Just a moment ago, in the heat of his gaze and his touch, she'd allowed her defenses to slip. Then she'd mentioned Liz's name. That, coupled with her reluctance to stay until he decided it was time to go, was all it took. His good humor was gone in a flash. A dash of cold water couldn't have brought her back to earth quicker.

With a weary sigh, Gina stood quietly beside Austin while the valet brought the Porsche around. The trip would be a harrowing experience. Austin drove like a maniac when he was ticked off. She'd lost count of the many instances in their long relationship that had ended this way. She'd say something, or do something that set him off and the fat would be in the fire. Tonight, knowing she was not going to be his victim, she could almost view his behavior with humor.

They were barely seated in the Porsche when he pulled away in a wild screech of tires. He was like a teenager, she thought, hiding a smile. In fact, a kid would probably have more self-control. Jesse certainly did. Apparently she hadn't inherited her father's black temper, another point for which to thank God tonight.

"What?" he growled.

"Nothing." She cleared her throat and looked straight ahead. He was pretty mad at her right now, but if he guessed she was laughing at him, his temper would really explode. "Just thinking of something funny that Jesse said," she lied.

"Liar, liar, pants on fire."

She gave him a startled look and saw that he was smiling slightly. Austin…laughing at himself?

"Okay, I was an idiot back there. I apologize."

She made some incoherent sound.

"Yeah, I apologize. You're right. You can't impose on

somebody who's furnishing free room and board, plus baby-sitting.''

"It's okay," she said faintly. Wow, a touch of gratitude. This was a new twist.

"I was just disappointed that we couldn't stay and enjoy the atmosphere. And the company." He winked and gave her a wicked smile. "Anthony's is a place where you bring somebody you feel special about."

"Don't push it, Austin. You don't feel special about me anymore."

"I'll always feel special about you, babe. We've got history, good history."

"And some not-so-good history," she said dryly.

"Yeah, but I can see the error of my ways. I hate for it to end this way, both of us with regrets and wishing it could have been different. I think we can still salvage something good out of all this."

"We'll definitely salvage something good. That's Jesse."

"Yeah, which is exactly what we need to focus on, babe. We need to think about Jesse. How all this is going to affect her. I mean, if Liz and Louie are always bad-mouthing me behind my back and you're hounding me about palimony, how's that going to look to Jesse? She needs to feel that we still care about each other."

"I wasn't hounding you, Austin. I asked for a reasonable amount of child support, a thousand dollars of which is going into trust for Jesse's education. You can set it up at LJ and B if you want. It was the judge who increased the amount, not me. And Liz and Louie don't ever mention you to Jesse. They wouldn't do that. They know how that can confuse and hurt a child."

"Now you're saying they never mention me. Hell, that's almost as bad."

She gave an exasperated sigh. "Austin, listen to yourself! Just exactly what in all this would make you happy?"

"That's easy." He signaled to exit the Interstate. "Just you and me handling our business without anybody else interfering."

Now they'd reached the neighborhood where Liz lived. Memorial was dense with tall trees, good landscaping and upscale residences. Much of Houston proper was hot and arid with an excess of stark, towering skyscrapers and roads frequently in a state of ongoing "improvement," but the Memorial area was quiet and understated. Even as successful as Liz was, she couldn't have afforded living here if it weren't for the trust fund left for her by her father.

Suddenly, instead of driving the final mile to Liz's house, Austin pulled into the parking area of a posh condominium complex. At this late hour, no one was stirring and Austin stopped the car near a thick hedge of oleanders. He killed the engine and lowered both her window and his own with a button, then turned so that he faced her.

"Nice night, huh? Quiet and peaceful in this neighborhood, too. Hell, if I didn't need my health club and the convenience of living five minutes from the office, I might live in Memorial myself."

For a bittersweet moment, Gina recalled the dreams she'd had during the years of their relationship. When she discovered she was pregnant with Jesse, she had fantasized about being married to Austin, buying a house in Memorial or the University area, having the kind of life she and Liz had planned as foster children. They'd both have super careers, meet and marry two great guys, have two and a half kids each and live in the same neighborhood. Turning away, she gazed from her window at the lush bank of oleanders. How many years had passed now and only a fraction of that dream had materialized, little of it for her. Liz, of course, had a great career and her house truly surpassed their girlish expectations. Gina idly fingered the strap of her purse. She, meanwhile, was still waiting and hoping and dreaming…

In daylight, the oleanders would be bright pink. She thought how much nicer a barrier the flowers made than a conventional fence, wood or stone. Somewhere nearby there must be night-blooming jasmine as its sweet, unique scent hung heavy on the air.

"We need to talk, sweetheart." Her heart fluttered when he touched her shoulder. Then his fingers slipped beneath her hair and began gently rubbing the taut neck muscles. "I meant what I said a minute ago. We don't need lawyers to work out whatever's best for Jesse." Deep, low, husky, his voice alone was almost a caress, more intimate than a kiss. His fingers moved in a soothing, hypnotic rhythm. "We don't need people who call themselves friends to tell us what we should do. We're the ones with the history. And we have the power to make our own decisions."

Power. She knew what power was all about and it was hardly a two-way street with Austin. She knew how he wielded it, how he'd manipulated her almost from the first day they'd met so that she'd been happy to give him anything he wanted. Everything, if that was the price to be paid to realize her dreams. He leaned closer, finding a spot he knew well. Heat stirred in her belly. Her breath caught in her throat. Her eyes were closing. Thank God it was dark and he couldn't see her. But he knew what she was feeling. He knew.

"Maude is going to tell you that we need our lives to be spelled out in a document." Still low and husky, his voice was like the stroke of his hands, compelling and hypnotic. "You'll call her tomorrow, won't you? Tell her you don't need her anymore."

"Hmmm."

His laugh was low and sexy, feathering over her ear, her hair. She'd always been susceptible to that laugh. "Is that a yes, babe?" His hand was still tangled in the hair at her nape, working magic on the muscles of her neck, the curve of her shoulder, finding the shell of her ear. His lips at her ear, he whispered, "I need to hear a promise, sweetheart."

"Promise…"

"Ahh, that's my girl." He rewarded her with an erotic sweep of his tongue in her ear. In spite of herself, she moaned with the sweet rush of pleasure. It had been so long. So long. Her breasts ached to feel his mouth. Between her legs, she was wet and wanting. If he touched her anywhere, she would—

Oh, God. His hand slid along her inner thigh and found the ready softness. Ah, he knew so well what to do. What to touch. And how. She made a small sound, then bit down hard on her lip to silence herself. To keep him from knowing. But he did know. He did.

"Do you like that, Gee-gee? Is my sweetheart feeling good?" He was crooning in her ear now, his breath hot and exciting, his fingers busy, skillful, all-knowing. "Aren't we something, sweetheart? This is so right, isn't it, love? C'mon, now, come for me, c'mon, c'mon, babe…" Then his thumb found just the right spot. She felt the rush of heat consuming her. And need, so strong, so impossible to resist. And with a soft cry, part joy, part anguish, she gave in, shuddering with the force of her orgasm.

She was weak and still senseless with pleasure when he suddenly pushed away, got out and in half a dozen urgent strides was at her side of the car. He jerked the door open and hauled her up and out. Dazed and still in the grip of her orgasm, she didn't resist as he stripped her of her skirt. Her knees were like rubber, lacking the strength to hold her up. But he had her buttocks clamped in both hands, guiding himself to the softness between her legs. She caught a glimpse of his face, dark and brutal. No love there, she thought in anguish as the glow of her orgasm faded. His hands were hard, cruelly so as they positioned her. Then, growling deep in his throat, he buried himself to the hilt in one hard thrust.

As always when aroused, he was rough. Caught now in the throes of his own need, he set a savage, mindless rhythm. It was not just sexual gratification he was seeking, she realized. He was punishing her for her transgressions. For having to restrain himself in the restaurant when she'd defied him. For her temerity in forcing their battle into the legal arena. For daring to reveal his violent attacks. For her audacity in taking the initiative in the welfare of their child. She pushed at him with a broken cry of self-loathing. But it was like pushing against a stone wall. Too late, too late, too late, she wailed inwardly, bearing the brutal assault in misery until finally, with a loud shout, he came.

A few minutes later, after he'd tossed her skirt to her, zipped up his pants and was again behind the wheel of the Porsche, he turned to her and said, "You won't forget your promise, will you?"

Her gaze was fixed on the dark landscape at the side window. She was so bruised and miserable and angry that she couldn't manage a reply at first. It was reckless to defy him in this mood, she knew. "What promise, Austin?" She was suddenly past caring.

There was black silence for the space of a heartbeat. Then, in burst of rage, he lunged at her, forcing her face up to his in a killing grip. "What the hell was this all about then?"

She could barely breathe and her heart raced, but fright and despair combined in a reckless cocktail. She was tired of him thinking all it took was a quick orgasm and she'd readily do his bidding. She caught at his hand and tried to free herself. "What's this all about?" she repeated, her mouth twisting in disgust. "It is so totally obvious what *this,* as you call it, is about, Austin. It's just more of your disgusting way of manipulating me with sex. You really must think I'm a complete idiot."

He shoved away, releasing her, but still breathing hard with the force of his rage. "I didn't notice any disgust when you were coming so hard I practically had to hold you down or the whole goddamned neighborhood would have heard you screaming."

"I didn't scream."

He snorted something obscene. With shoulders hunched over the wheel, he looked straight ahead. "Next you'll be saying you didn't come."

"No, I came. Thanks for that, I guess. I'm just disgusted with myself for getting in this situation. I knew what you were doing when I agreed to leave with you today and I did it anyway. I knew what you were doing when you came on to me just now and I did it anyway. It was weak of me. Sick, even. But having sex didn't turn my brain to complete mush. Here's the deal, Austin. I'm not agreeing to defy the judge, if that was your aim. I would be an idiot to do that. I'm going to call Maude and arrange another meeting with your lawyer.''

''If you mean Ryan, I fired his sorry ass!'' he snarled.

''Then I imagine the judge will appoint someone to negotiate.''

He turned then to look at her. The power of that look was so explosive that it was nearly palpable in the car. ''You're not going to get away with this, Gina.'' His voice was soft and deadly, so threatening that she felt a cold chill. He waited a few moments—for her, harrowing moments—then when she remained stonily silent, he started the Porsche and pulled out of the parking lot. She braced for a wild and reckless ride, but he drove the scant mile to Liz's house at a moderate pace. It was so out of character that she was more unnerved than she would have been had he reverted to habit. Still, she sat with her arms wrapped around herself and her teeth clamped to keep them from chattering. Then, finally, Liz's street. And escape. She was out of the car and hurrying away almost before he stopped. Once safely at Liz's front door, she stole a wary glance back and saw that he was out and watching her from over the top of the Porsche. Just…watching.

If looks could kill.

Shivering, she slipped inside and quickly closed the door behind her.

Curtiss Leggett sat in the library of his splendid home in River Oaks waiting for Austin. He'd left messages on his son's cell phone, his home phone and the pager he carried. No matter what the hour, he told Austin, he would expect to see him.

Women, the disgruntled lawyer thought, swirling the best brandy money could buy in a Baccarat snifter. How his life would have been eased without the complication of women, his ex-wife, his many mistresses, his daughter, now married to some itinerant artist out in some godforsaken corner of California. Even his mother, and he didn't give a damn whether her soul rested peacefully or not. What a domineering tyrant she'd been. An occasional display of masculinity from his father would have shown her who was boss, but his father had buried himself in his professorial work and never noticed or cared about anything else. Including Curtiss.

That was not the way Curtiss Leggett had run his life.

At the sound of a key in the lock, he stirred in the deep leather chair, but didn't get to his feet. He wouldn't bother. As spineless as Austin was, the lecture and subsequent threat could be delivered as effectively in the comfort of his chair as otherwise. Thirty-six years old and Curtiss still had to wipe his ass for him. His son was a great disappointment to him. His daughter, Julia, should have been his heir. She was full of defiance, possibly as bright as Curtiss himself. Focused. An independent thinker. As God was his witness, he couldn't see any strength in Austin.

Not the kind of strength evident in Ryan Paxton. Now, there was a real man, Texas born and bred, tough as nails, smart as a whip. Steel in his backbone, too. Leggett sighed, bringing the snifter up to his mouth. And look at his old man. Killed himself. No steel there. A weakling. Genes were odd things.

He heard the door open. Then close. "In here, boy!" he called, finishing off the brandy.

"How are you, Dad?" Austin entered the library, his smile wary, eyes cautious. He scanned the room, saw that his father was alone. "Sorry I couldn't make it over until now, but I had an appointment that couldn't be rescheduled." He watched Curtiss set the snifter on the table at his elbow and then walked over to the sideboard to pour himself a brandy.

"Hold up there. You can drink after I've had my say."

Austin put the glass back and slowly turned to face his father. "Is something wrong?"

"Wrong? Is something wrong, you ask?" Curtiss had planned to stay in his chair, but found he had to get up or, swear to God, he'd blow a gasket. "I don't want to think you're as stupid as it appears, Austin, but what I learned today makes me wonder." He shot a beetle-browed look at his first born. "You finally had the balls to dump the trailer trash slut you've been shacked up with for more years than I want to think about, but now instead of a clean break, you get yourself called before Judge Hetherington and he hears that you've been knocking her around. Have I got it right, Austin?"

"She's lying."

"Ryan Paxton doesn't think so."

"You've seen Ryan? He's talked to you about this?" Austin slammed a hand down on the sideboard. "Goddamn it! That's a breach of client-attorney privilege. Did he come around whining to you about the judgment?"

"He came to bring me a report of the hearing because I asked for it."

Austin made a dismissive sound. "Well, he sure isn't

the legal eagle you think he is, Dad. I could have represented myself and come out of this looking better.''

Curtiss Leggett simply stood looking at his son for a
beat or two before turning in disgust. He stared at the dead
ashes in his fireplace for another long moment before turning to face Austin. ''I want the truth and I want it plain
and simple. Don't lie to me, I warn you. Have you been
knocking that bitch around?''

''What kind of question is—''

''Did you hear me?'' It was a roar and it stopped Austin
in his tracks and killed whatever defense he might have
attempted. Another moment passed while Curtiss calmed
himself. ''Have you been slapping her around?'' he repeated, speaking each word precisely.

Austin cleared his throat, looked anywhere but into the
knowing eyes of his father. ''We have disagreements like
most couples.''

''And you express yourself with your fists?''

''Do I hear outrage, Dad?'' Austin's tone was suddenly
less subservient. When Curtiss didn't reply, Austin was
emboldened. ''I didn't think so.''

''Watch yourself, Austin.''

''Yeah, it's me we're talking about now, not you, eh,
Dad?'' Austin reached for a glass in defiance of his old
man and recklessly poured brandy in it. Then eyeball to
eyeball with Curtiss, he tossed most of it back in one gulp.
''I don't know why you'd be shocked,'' he said, wiping
his mouth with the back of his hand. ''It couldn't come
as a shock to you, a man handling a troublesome woman
with a little show of force. I sure didn't act shocked when
you did it. I guess I thought everybody's mom wore sunglasses in the house as a regular thing, night or day. Until
I wised up.''

"I'm not shocked that you did it, Austin," Curtiss said in disgust, not bothering to deny what was fact. Hell, it was years ago and Marilyn was long gone. Good riddance, too. "I'm pissed because you've brought it out like so much dirty family linen. You're a reckless fool and I just hope to God Paxton can pluck your sorry ass out of the fire."

"Speaking of asses, I fired his today." He looked defiantly at Curtiss.

"You what?"

"I'm out four thousand bucks a month because of his incompetence," Austin said, letting his fury loose. "So I fired him. I'll work out something less with Gina, just the two of us, no lawyers. You'll see."

For a full minute, Curtiss just stared at him. "Austin, I'm only going to tell you this one time. And you better hear me good. Call Ryan Paxton ASAP, or better yet, go see him in person. Now. Tonight. Do whatever it takes to get him back on board in this miserable mess you've created. But don't let the sun rise tomorrow without being able to tell me that he is still representing you. Now—" his tone went lower, more menacing "—do you read me?"

For a long moment, Austin seemed tempted to defy the order. But the moment passed. "Yes, sir," he said, the response weak, but the look in his eyes was anything but. He finished off the brandy, set the snifter down with a thump and walked out.

As soon as she heard the car door, Elizabeth set her book aside and rose from the chair in the den. She'd been on edge the whole evening, reading with one ear cocked to listen for Austin's Porsche. The hours had dragged by.

It was crazy for Gina to be alone with him, especially tonight when his temper would be on a hair-trigger. Did she forget how dangerous Austin could be when thwarted? He was clearly enraged that she'd dared to air the facts of their relationship in a court of law. He'd made no secret of that from the moment he was served with the papers. And he would be furious with the judge's ruling today, more so because, in his arrogance, he'd believed that he would prevail. Parting the blinds, she saw the Porsche pull away from the curb and felt deeply relieved that Gina was now home safe.

That idea died with her first glimpse of Gina's face in the dimly lit foyer. She stood with her eyes closed, back against the door. By the look of her, breathing heavy with arms clamped around herself, she must have run from the car. Alarmed, Elizabeth reached for the light switch. "What happened?"

Gina turned her head slowly and looked at her without speaking. Overhead light caught the glint of unshed tears in her eyes. Elizabeth's gaze narrowed at the sight of Gina's face. With a shocked sound, she moved closer and touched Gina's face, turning it gently to get a better look. Brutal marks on either side of her jaw clearly showed the imprint of fingers. They'd be purple bruises by morning. "My God, Gina, did he do this?"

Gina, still shaky and pale, glanced at herself in the mirror above the table. She lifted her hand and touched her face. "Don't freak, Liz. He didn't hit me. He just—I just refused to go along with what he wanted and he—"

"He retaliated by manhandling you, reminding you who was boss, right?" Angrily, Elizabeth tilted Gina's face this way and that, examining the marks thoroughly. "He may not have actually punched you, but he left fingerprints. Wait'll you see yourself tomorrow.'' She turned away, shaking her head. ''He's an animal, Gee. It takes brute force to mark someone like that.''

''I shouldn't have argued with him. It was really dumb of me, but I just got fed up.''

''Why not get fed up before you agreed to spend the day with him? Why did you do it, Gee? What were you thinking?''

''Actually, it wasn't so bad…at least not at first,'' she added under her breath. ''He was trying to—to make a point. I honestly don't think he realizes his own strength.''

''Gina, Gina, Gina…do you realize how screwed up that sounds? He knows his own strength, you can count on that. He uses it often enough. But no matter what his intent, you shouldn't wind up bruised and hurting.''

''I know how to handle him, Liz. If I'd pretended to go along with him, he would have let it go. He lost it when I told him I was going to do what the judge instructed.''

She pushed her hair back from her face wearily. ''Can we talk about this tomorrow, Liz? I'm beat.''

Liz's gaze narrowed. She moved closer and saw another mark on Gina's neck, one that didn't look like a bruise. ''What's this?''

Gina put her hand up quickly, covering the mark. ''It's…nothing.''

Liz then stepped back. In her concern about Gina's face, she hadn't really taken in the disheveled look of her. Now she saw that the tail of her blouse was untucked in places. Two of the buttons were undone. Her skirt wasn't quite straight and her hair was a mess. ''No, Gina.'' Disbelief flickered across Liz's face. ''Tell me you didn't have sex with him.''

Turning away, Gina waved a mute hand and headed for the stairs.

"Gina…aaa…ah…" Liz played out the name with disapproval.

Gina stopped. "I don't need a lecture, Liz. I know I've been a bad girl. Worse, I've been an idiot. In fact, I probably deserved what just happened," she said bitterly. Then, with a foot on the first tread, she turned slowly to face Liz. "I know you don't understand. Even if you were in dire straits, you would somehow find the strength to do the right thing. The smart thing. It's like you always control your emotions while my emotions control me. I'm weak when it comes to Austin, Liz. It's like a sickness. Honest to God, that's the only way I can describe what happens when he…when we…are—" she spread her hands helplessly "—together."

It hurt for Liz to hear herself portrayed as being bloodless. It was so completely wrong that she wanted to grab Gina and scream that she had loved with a passion so consuming that everything else in her life paled to nothingness. Had Gina forgotten that dark year of her life? Liz wished to God that she could bury the memory.

"I'm human, Gee, believe me. And I've been in love, or at least I thought it was love. But it's not love that drives your relationship with Austin. I don't know what to call it, but it isn't love."

"Oh, hell, that came out wrong, Liz. Of course, you're human. But you're good at keeping emotion at a distance. I'm not like that. Tonight, when Austin touched me, I knew what he was doing. I certainly know he doesn't love me anymore…if he ever did. But it was just so…delicious and it had been such a long time, you know? Never mind that I was going to regret it. I wasn't thinking about that.

I wasn't thinking anything except how good it felt. Then, somehow, I just let myself go with the feeling. Instead of doing what you would have done and run away from it, I gobbled it up. I wanted it so much that I was willing to take whatever consequences came from it.''

"Even if the consequences are another child?''

She turned her face away. "That won't happen.''

"Are you sure? Did you remember to use protection?''

"You know how bad my endometriosis is. Having Jesse was a miracle. The doctor said I'll never have another pregnancy. Besides, it's a safe time in my cycle.''

"I certainly hope you're right.'' Still shaking her head, Liz dragged fingers through her hair. "It's none of my business if you and Austin are intimate, Gee. I just hate to see—''

"I know, I know. You're concerned that he'll take advantage of me, which of course he will if I'm dumb enough to allow it.'' Gina suddenly walked over and put her arms around Liz, hugging her and somehow managing a smile. "You don't have to tell me what a fool I am. He's a selfish bastard and I would have to be an idiot not to see what he was doing by taking me out today, being so attentive, wining and dining me. We had lunch, we went to the museum, then onto Anthony's, would you believe? But I left before the entree arrived. Now I guess I'll never know what the tomato tower is or whether I liked it.'' She gave a short laugh. "But the pinot grigio was very nice.''

Liz was shaking her head. "I can call Ryan Paxton right now and ask him to come over. One look at your bruised face and he'll believe everything we said about Austin. Will you let me call him? Let him see firsthand what kind of temper his client has?'' But even as she suggested it, she knew the chances were slim that Ryan would respond. He would be up to his neck in his own problems tonight.

"God, no! I still need a reference from the firm."

"You can get a job without a reference from those people, Gina!" Exasperated, Liz threw her hands wide. "Even if it takes six months, what does it matter? You can stay here until it happens."

"No, I don't need to impose on you any longer."

"It's not an imposition. We're family, Gina. Jesse's my godchild. How can you even think I wouldn't want to help you now?"

Gina had started back up the stairs, but at the mention of Jesse, she stopped again. "How did it go tonight with Jesse? Was she okay? Did she settle down at a reasonable hour? I know how she snookers you into delaying bedtime."

"She seemed fine. We played with Legos. She loves building things. I explained that you were delayed with last-minute business."

"Good. She understands that. God knows, I've had to disappoint her many times when Austin needed me to work late." She hesitated, then asked, "Did she mention Austin?"

"No. Not a word."

Gina frowned. "He has visitation rights, Liz. I'm worried that she might not want to go with him when the time comes."

"I think you're right to be concerned." Elizabeth felt Jesse showed good sense in being wary of Austin's unpredictable temper. More sense than her mommy.

"Louie doesn't believe he's going to bother with a five-year-old." There was hope in Gina's face. "What do you think?"

"It doesn't matter what any of us think. It's what Austin thinks and does. If Jesse is frightened, she must not be forced to see him alone, Gina."

Gina's arms were wrapped around her waist in distress. "But what can I do about it, Liz?"

"I don't know." Elizabeth ran her fingers through her hair. "Maybe his lawyer could do something. He's a father. Maybe he could persuade Austin to give it some time."

"Yeah, that's good. That's something to try." Looking hopeful, she turned and began climbing again. "I mean, the fact that she doesn't want to talk about him isn't normal, I know that. If she doesn't even want to talk about him, she certainly isn't going to want to spend any time alone with him." At the top of the stairs, she stopped and looked down at Elizabeth. "Thanks for baby-sitting, Lizzie. I honestly don't know what we would do without you."

"How many times do I have to say it? You're welcome. Good night, Gee."

"Night."

Elizabeth watched with a troubled frown as Gina turned at the top of the stairs and headed for the room where Jesse slept. After she'd slipped quietly inside, Elizabeth walked back to the den, picked up the book she'd been reading, then switched off the lamp. At the foyer, she checked that the door was securely locked and, although she didn't always do so, fixed the chain in place. Gina seemed to dismiss the likelihood that Austin's rage might extend beyond herself, but Elizabeth knew him to be unpredictable and she vowed to be extra vigilant until this whole sorry affair was resolved.

Upstairs a few minutes later, she settled herself in bed,

opened the book and tried to pick up where she'd left off reading earlier. But instead of losing herself in the story, she found herself thinking of Gina's remark that Elizabeth couldn't understand how a person could love with such abandon. Had Gina's own problems blurred her memory of that summer when Elizabeth's whole world had collapsed? Giving up the thought of reading, she closed the book and dropped it to the floor.

His name was Evan Reynolds. Now, looking back on the affair, it was all so obvious how it happened. Why it happened. Elizabeth was a senior when they met at the University of Texas and utterly focused on her plan to enter law school after graduation. At the death of the judge, a trust fund had been established for Elizabeth and her sisters, so the cost of her education had not been an issue. But the years in foster care had turned her natural shyness into near reclusiveness. She'd not adjusted well to the social demands of college life. Instead, she'd thrown herself into achieving her goal.

She didn't remember a time when she didn't visualize attending law school and then passing the bar and finally earning the credentials that would put her in the same exalted profession as her father. She'd been five years old when she lost him and ever since she'd been locked into a lifelong dream to follow in his footsteps. Once that was accomplished, she'd fantasized, it would make her father proud, had he lived.

That kind of ambition and her dreams didn't leave much time for a social life, had she been so inclined. Maintaining a grade-point average at the level necessary to get into law school with no connections prevented many of the dates and social events she might otherwise have enjoyed. So, when she met Evan on a holiday weekend with a friend and her family, she was ripe for his smooth line and quickly dazzled by his slick sophistication. He was seventeen years older than Elizabeth. He was handsome and sexy. He was a judge.

He was also married. His wife was currently on a sabbatical at Oxford University in England, but Elizabeth didn't know that until she'd fallen deeply in love and plunged into a sizzling, dizzying affair. She lavished on Evan Reynolds all the passion that had had no outlet when she was shuffled back and forth between foster homes growing up. She loved his intelligence, his confidence, his profession. She loved *him*. Then, when she found herself pregnant, he told her she'd have to get rid of the baby and why.

She spent an agonizing summer trying to decide what to do. Somehow, the thought of an abortion was abhorrent. On the other hand, she knew firsthand how it felt to be a child without a father. Marriage to someone else was out of the question, even if she'd been so inclined to trust another man. Ever. Once burned, twice shy. Finally, she decided to have the baby and put it up for adoption. It was the single most difficult decision she'd ever made, before or since. Even today—after ten years—she was unable to see dark-haired, dark-eyed little boys without feeling a pain so deep and wrenching that it took her breath away.

She never told anyone about her pregnancy except Iris Graham and Gina, who was having a difficult time herself then. Iris, case worker for both Elizabeth and Gina, had been one of the few constants in their lives. Sometimes she seemed more mother or caring aunt than employee of the state of Texas. Looking back, Elizabeth thought that Iris must have wished herself retired and living anywhere else except Houston that summer. Both her "girls" were in trouble.

Gina had not yet met Austin Leggett, but she was establishing a pattern then that permanently characterized her relationships with men. She invariably chose flashy, selfish, insensitive types who put their own interests far above Gina's needs.

Elizabeth's pregnancy changed all her plans—and thus, her life. Evan's rejection was hurtful, but the humiliation of having been duped and lied to was equally damaging. She'd been a shy and introverted adolescent, overly sensitive about everything from her red hair and startling green eyes to her circumstances as a ward of the state. Clearly, Evan Reynolds had seen her striking looks as sexy and appealing, but those painful adolescent memories had rushed back in the wake of her disastrous pregnancy.

She gave up plans for law school and went back to Houston where she got a job working at an independent bookstore in the Village during her pregnancy. She had the baby and after an all too brief hour with her tiny dark-haired baby boy, gave him up to a childless couple she'd personally chosen with Iris Graham's help. The adoptive parents lived in Denver, Colorado.

While working at the library during her pregnancy, she'd been assigned to the section featuring children's books. She loved the contact with kids. She loved reading to them. Soon, she was thinking about ideas for books that she might write. And then she began writing them. Maybe it was the influence of early memories when her mother read to her that motivated her. She'd been only four when her mother died in childbirth and the memories were vague, but they were there. And real. Or maybe it was recalling the refuge to be found in books as she'd moved from one foster home to another. Or maybe she turned to writing for children to assuage the loss of her own child. Whatever the motivation, to her amazement, she was successful beyond her dreams. And it was success that ended her comfortable, safe, reclusive lifestyle.

She removed her glasses and reached over to turn off the lamp. Success in the form of winning the Newbery Medal had brought her to the attention of her sisters when Elizabeth would have been satisfied to keep that chapter of her life closed. And now that Lindsay had actually introduced herself, it probably wouldn't be long before she heard from Megan. Both would show up again on some pretext or another.

So would Ryan Paxton. Elizabeth thumped her pillow and tried to get comfortable. Ryan had been distracted from his mission to enlist her help with Gina and Austin by his daughter's mishap, but he wasn't the type to walk away from a client even if Austin was looking to blame Ryan for the judge's ruling today. Austin would cool down and then Ryan would be back looking for a way to take advantage of Gina. If only there was a way that he could be made aware of what happened tonight when Austin was alone with Gina. Should she call and tell him? Shifting onto her back, she stared at the ceiling. At least it would be on the record if anything happened. And something would happen. She knew it.

Eight

Austin Leggett and his troubles were not on Ryan's mind when he got home. His own problems were front and center tonight. Diane's car was parked at the curb out front. She must have taken him at his word, which was a good thing. They needed to present a united front to deal with Jennifer's latest scrape.

Unlocking the door, he let himself inside, stooping to pick up the mail which had been deposited through a brass slot in the door. Ordinarily, he would have poured himself a Scotch and sipped it while glancing through his mail, but that was a treat he'd have to forgo tonight. Often he cooked something. He'd found he liked the rhythm of preparation, chopping, slicing, mixing, as well as the creating. And the end result was, more often than not, pretty good. Funny thing was, he'd never been in the kitchen before his divorce except to put out the garbage.

He wasn't in the mood for cooking tonight.

"We're in here." It was Diane's voice. He wouldn't have had any difficulty finding her, as the smell of her cigarette was enough. He tossed his jacket on a bench in the foyer and headed for the family room. A misnomer for sure. The house wasn't the one he and Diane had owned together during their marriage. He'd bought the town house after the divorce. It was in a spiffy location off San Felipe, but that wasn't his motivation for buying it. It was a good investment and only twenty minutes from his office. Diane, on the other hand, had insisted on pulling up stakes and moving with her new husband to Dallas. And taking Jennifer with her.

Looking impatient and annoyed, she now paced the rug that a decorator had chosen to complement the leather sofa and club chair. Jennifer was curled up in the corner of the sofa clutching a pillow to her tummy. She looked pale and scared.

"Hi, Daddy." Her eyes were wary and watchful. What, did she think he was going to beat her or something? He smothered a sigh and thought with longing of his night-time Scotch.

"How's it goin', Jen?"

"Not too cool, I guess."

He pulled at his tie as he crossed the room and loosened the collar button on his shirt. She looked up at him, eyes filling as he ruffled her hair. "Seems like you've messed up big-time, baby."

"I guess," she said again, now studying the pattern on the pillow.

"You want to try to explain?"

"Yes, that would be helpful," Diane said, exhaling smoke. "Try to explain stealing a car and running down a biker, then fleeing the scene, *baby.*"

"I've asked you not to smoke in here, Diane." Ryan went to the French doors and pushed them open. Wide. Then turned back to Jennifer. "You have anything to say, Jen?"

Mouth trembling, she picked at a ragged cuticle. "I didn't see him. We were sort of acting rowdy, you know? A CD was blasting, I guess."

Diane sighed. "I've told them so many times to lower the volume, Ryan. They couldn't hear a train, let alone other traffic."

"Who's we?" Ryan said, after shooting a glare at Diane.

"Jody Reinhart and Melissa Maness."

"The car belonged to Melissa's parents." He knew that much. He'd spent the past three hours doing damage control. James Maness could have gone ballistic, but he'd been damned decent. He and his wife were going through a pretty rough patch with Melissa, and Maness suspected the "theft" of the car had been a group decision. Of course, fleeing the scene of the accident had been Jennifer's decision since she was driving. As for the Reinharts, there had been no answer when he called.

"Melissa said they wouldn't even notice it was gone," Jennifer murmured.

Ryan's eyebrows went up. "And your point is—"

"Huh?" She gave him a blank look.

"What relevance is it to the situation that the Manesses wouldn't notice their car was missing? Did you have permission from them to take it? And how did you know they wouldn't need it later? Come on, Jen. Since when do you help yourself to someone else's property? And how the hell did you come up with the notion of driving all the way to Houston!"

She teared up again. "I know it was wrong, Daddy."

"It was wrong to hit some guy on a bike and run away, too. You must know that, as well."

"He wasn't hurt bad. We could see that." Her voice was almost inaudible.

"Oh? And you based that opinion on what? Your extensive medical training? Your ability to judge a person's injuries through the rearview mirror? The judgment of your two passengers?"

"He got right up afterward," she whispered, hands twisting in her lap. "I mean, he didn't stand up, but he

sat up on the ground. He was looking at us. I mean, he
wasn't unconscious or anything. And before you ask, yes,
I saw all this through the rearview mirror.''

He gave her a stern look before turning away, muttering
something vile. "I don't think I've ever been as disappointed over anything as I am about this, Jennifer. I'm
shocked that my daughter would take a friend's vehicle
without permission—and you with no license, mind you—
drive that vehicle from Dallas to Houston, joyride around
Hermann Park, strike a man on a bike and then simply
haul ass.'' He turned back, pinning her with another hard
look. "Did you once think about helping him? Did you
even slow down? Did you *care,* for God's sake!''

"It happened real fast,'' she whispered.

"Too fast for you to call 911 on your cell phone?''

"We were afraid they'd trace the call.'' Head bent, she
stared miserably at her hands.

Diane was suddenly fed up. "Listen to yourself, Jennifer! Your father and I want to hear you take responsibility for what you've done, not simply mouth a few weak
excuses. I'll just be frank here. I'm at a loss as to what to
do about this. Grounding you for starters, I suppose. Although that seems too lenient a punishment for nearly killing someone.'' She reached for her cigarettes on the table
and started to click her lighter.

"Don't, Diane.'' Ryan pressed a hand to the back of
his neck. "Go out on the patio to smoke.''

"Gladly,'' she huffed and stalked across the room,
flicking the lighter as she went.

"She hates me,'' Jennifer said woefully, watching as
her mother paced angrily on the patio.

"She doesn't hate you.'' Ryan was shaking his head,
wondering at the friends he had who were raising several
kids. How the hell did they keep from going crazy? He

had just one and she was out of control. "Your mother's disappointed. Both of us are baffled over the number of bad choices you made in just one evening." He stopped in front of her. "Look, you can be honest with me, Jen. I've been around the block a time or two and I know how it is when you're with your buddies. Things get out of hand. Somebody wants to show off, prove how grown-up he is. He might have a little beer. Some pot. Everybody tries it eventually. Is that what happened?"

"No!" Jennifer looked truly shocked. "No, Daddy. I wasn't drinking and I've never even thought of using drugs. Why would you even think something like that?"

He studied her face. "I'm searching for something to explain what you did, Jen. If you'd had some beer or smoked a joint, that would impair your judgment. It would tell me how it happened that my little girl behaved so callously. And when you say you didn't, it makes your actions even more incomprehensible. And flat-out wrong."

"Now you hate me, too!" She jumped up from the couch with both arms wrapped around her waist. Turning away, she began crying. "Nobody underst-stands! I didn't m-mean to do any of this. I didn't m-mean to steal the car. But once we were in it, I wanted to come to Houston and see you. Mom and I had had a big fight. She's always on my case, Dad. And then—and then—we were in Hermann Park and this guy sort of swung out of the bike lane and I sort of sideswiped him. It was an *accident!*"

He watched her dissolve again into noisy sobs and resisted an impulse to reassure her. He'd done a few dumb things as a teenager himself. He could tell her that one mistake—albeit a doozy—didn't mean her life was over. She could make amends to the kid she'd hit. Looking at her, his features softened. Baby-fine hair curled sweetly at the nape of her neck. He remembered looking at her the day she was born, marveling at the perfection of her tiny body. He had a fatherly urge to hug her, to tell her that he and Diane both loved her. But instinctively, he knew she needed to suffer more severe consequences for what she'd done.

He waited for her tears to subside somewhat. "Fortunately for you, Rick sees it that way, too."

She turned to look at him, her face wet and bewildered, big blue eyes watery and red. "Who?"

"Rick, the kid you nearly creamed on the bike."

"You've talked to him?" She blinked, wiped her cheeks with both hands.

"Yeah, I've talked to him." Ryan went to the French doors and motioned for Diane to come inside. She took a long drag from a half-smoked cigarette and crammed it deep into the soil of a potted sago palm, then crossed the patio.

"You need to hear this, too, Diane." Dipping his fingers into his shirt pocket, he removed a business card he'd used to scribble on earlier. It had taken some sleuthing, but Ryan had finally located a couple of students who'd been jogging in the vicinity when it happened. They knew the biker and had come to his aid when Jennifer drove off. They'd been glad to identify him to Ryan, who'd driven straight to the kid's house. Rick Sanchez, sixteen years old, had not been seriously hurt, but he was banged up and bruised. He had been traveling in the biking lane and admitted to Ryan that he had swerved to avoid a pothole in the asphalt just as Jennifer sped by in the Manesses' SUV. None of which excused Jennifer's fleeing the scene.

"He was damned decent about it," Ryan ended. "You

owe him an apology and you're paying for his bike out of your own money. It's totaled.''

"Okay," she said meekly, chewing on her inner lip.

Diane sat on the edge of the couch, shapely legs crossed, fingers clasped around one knee. "Mr. Maness came by a couple of hours ago to pick up his car," she said.

"Yeah, we talked earlier. He could have complicated things.''

"By pressing charges?''

"Exactly.''

"Melissa and Jody went home with him," Jennifer told Ryan. Color had returned to her cheeks now. She no longer looked as scared, but she kept darting little glances between her parents. Clearly, she was waiting for the other shoe to fall.

"Now…" Ryan went to the bar on the other side of the room and took down a tumbler from the glass-front cabinet. The Scotch was a rich, warm brown. He took a satisfying swallow, then wiped his mouth with his hand. "Here's the deal. You're moving in with me, Jen." He frowned when her face brightened. "And before you begin celebrating, I want you to know that it won't be a walk in the park living with me instead of your mother. I've been in Family Court often enough to know that kids tend to think the grass is greener at the house of the parent they don't live with. I'm taking on this responsibility not because I think your mother has failed, but because you've behaved badly. I'll be running a tight ship, I just want to warn you, Jen.''

"What about school?" She was trying, but not quite succeeding in putting on a sober face when Ryan guessed that inside she was jubilant.

"I would expect you to buckle down and prove to me that you've turned over a new leaf."

"My grades were okay in Dallas," she said, her mouth turned down in protest.

"Okay won't be good enough here," he told her.

She glanced at Diane. "When does this start?"

"I think this is the best thing," Diane said, scooping up her purse as if Ryan might change his mind if she delayed. "I'll have her things shipped tomorrow," she told him. "And good luck."

He watched color flare in Jennifer's cheeks. Although she'd been begging to come live with him for a year or so, it must hurt to see Diane so eager to get rid of her. He wondered if their inability to get along meant they were too much alike. He'd never believed that, but what did he know about mothers and daughters? For that matter, what did he know about fathers and daughters? Since divorcing Diane, he'd been a very spotty parent to Jen. She'd been only nine years old at the time. More than once today, he'd wondered what he was getting himself into by taking on the full-time parenting of a fifteen-year-old girl.

"Do you need a bed for tonight?" he asked Diane. He had only one extra bedroom, which would now be occupied by Jennifer, but she could share with her mother this once.

"No, I'm heading back."

"She has a new boyfriend," Jennifer said with spite, getting in a hurtful jab of her own. Diane rolled her eyes and said nothing.

"Get your jacket, Jen," Ryan ordered, thinking to separate them before he had to referee a catfight. If they acted like this often when they were together, it was no wonder Jen was desperate to get away.

"Why do I need my jacket?" Jennifer paused in the act of dabbing at her eyes with a tissue. With her mascara smudged from tears, she looked like a little raccoon.

"It's turned chilly outside," he said, picking up his own jacket. "We've got a date with Rick Sanchez. Or rather, you have."

"Daddy!" she wailed, looking as if he planned a walk over red-hot coals for her.

"It's called taking responsibility for what you've done, baby." He went to the front door, giving her a stern look. "Get your jacket and that's the last time I'm asking nicely."

"It's so *late!*" She shoved her arms in the denim sleeves.

"It's never too late to do the right thing," he said, thinking he sounded pretty pompous, but hell, he was doing his fatherly best. "Besides, Rick's expecting us."

Outside, Diane was pulling away from the house in her car. He hadn't put his own car in the garage, so they headed to the drive where he'd parked. Jennifer's pace lagged a little, but Ryan urged her forward, unlocked the SUV with a chirp of his remote and opened the passenger door for her to get inside. As he stepped back, a car arrived, skidding to a stop behind them.

It was late and no part of Houston was entirely safe, especially after dark, including this neighborhood even though it was gated and a guard challenged most unfamiliar vehicles. Ryan quickly closed and locked Jennifer inside the SUV before turning to face the driver. As he stood there, Austin Leggett got out of the car and headed around it toward Ryan. "Hey, man, glad to see you're still up," Austin said, giving a jaunty wave to Jennifer. Sidling up to Ryan, he caught him by the sleeve and tugged him off to the side, out of earshot of the teenager.

"What are you doing here, Austin?" Ryan demanded, freeing himself. "I was just leaving with—"

"Yeah and I'm sorry to put you out, but this couldn't wait and it won't take long." He glanced up and down the street as if checking to see no one was listening. "It's about Gina."

Ryan instantly thought of Elizabeth's concern for Gina, which he'd dismissed as exaggerated bias. "What about her?"

Austin shifted his weight from one hip to the other, scratched his head and looked as if he bore the weight of the world on his shoulders. "She's not gonna cooperate, man. I thought if I could spend a little time with her today, or rather tonight, she'd roll over on this deal, see reason. You know we need to talk her out of dragging that she-devil lawyer and her buddy Liz into the negotiations, but—"

"Whoa, whoa…" Ryan put up a hand. "I'm out of this, Austin. You fired me today, remember? You're strictly on your own with Gina and her lawyer now, buddy."

"Aw, hell, Ryan, you know I didn't mean what I said then. I was hot because the goddamn judge went off the deep end like that. Who'd ever think he'd double the freakin' child support? But it's water under the bridge now, my man. We've got to put together a plan, otherwise she's going to hurt me. Four thousand a month, shit! Add that up over a year and pretty soon we're talkin' real money here." He was walking in tight little circles now, throwing his hands out, gesturing wildly to the streetlight, the moon, the night. He stopped suddenly with a look of desperation at Ryan. "I'm gonna need your help."

"Look, Austin—"

"I know, I know, you don't generally do this type of case, but—"

"It's not that. I just don't think I want to get involved

again. The case is going to get sticky. It didn't look good for you in the courtroom today. You saw for yourself that Maude presented a solid case for Gina. And Elizabeth sounded honest and sincere. The judge believed her, I think.''

"Even though there was no evidence that I'd ever—'' he looked away briefly "—been…you know…physical?''

"The word is *violent*, Austin. Both those women painted a vivid picture of an abusive relationship between you and Gina. I'm not surprised that Liz managed to talk her out of going along with any pitch you made after separating her from Maude.''

"It wasn't Liz," he said petulantly. "She turned on me at the restaurant. You believe that? I thought I'd talked her into us handling this stuff on our own, but she got a wild hair midway through the meal. Then on the way home—'' He was shaking his head. "I've never known her to…well, just say this, she's got a bug up her rear. She's gonna go with the judge's ruling unless we can talk her out of it.''

"Like I said, Austin, that'll be your job. I'm out of the picture.''

"Hey, I apologize for shooting off my mouth today, okay? I need you to fix this. Tell you what, Ryan. I didn't mention it before, but I'm pretty strapped for disposable income right now. I lost a lot of my net worth in the market and I just don't have four K to toss to the winds. Every month! Ad infinitum! I'm serious, man.''

"You can present that argument to the judge through any attorney,'' Ryan said, jangling his keys in his hand. "You don't need me.''

"Look—'' Austin hung his head, shuffled from one foot to the other, then drew a fortifying breath before looking directly at Ryan. "I don't want this to get back to the old man. He'll be royally pissed that I've got myself involved in something with the potential to bring unsavory attention to the firm. I'm not asking much, just this. Gina thinks anything that Liz says is chiseled in marble and right up there with Moses on the mount. It looked to me like the two of you were hitting it off pretty good today, you and Liz. How about you just taking one more shot for me, huh? See if you can persuade Liz to talk Gina into something less…less solid, you know what I mean? They—Gina and Maude—get this agreement in writing, man, I'm in it for life, you see?" He glanced at the car where Jennifer sat staring at them. "You understand how it is, Ryan. You've got a kid. And an ex-wife. They're expensive, right?"

"I don't think of Jennifer as an expense, Austin. Anything I provide for her, I do because I'm her father. I love her. In fact, just tonight I was thinking—" He stopped. What was he doing speaking of his concern over Jennifer to this cretin? It was Jesse, not Jennifer, whose future was at stake here. On the other hand, with Liz in the picture and having some influence, maybe it was possible to keep the situation from deteriorating into just another bitter custody battle where the kid was the ultimate victim. Maybe he should do it for Jesse's sake.

"What d'you say, Ryan?"

He nodded, but with reluctance. "I'll talk to Liz."

"What was that all about, Daddy?" Jennifer turned in her seat and watched as Austin screeched away in his Porsche, the powerful engine roaring as he exited the gates of the complex. "He looked sorta crazy, the way he was pacing and waving his arms and all. Who is he?"

"A client," Ryan muttered, adding, "a soon to be ex-client."

"Whatever he was excited about, it must have been something else."

"It was his daughter."

"Huh?" Startled, she turned to look at him.

"Not your concern, baby," he said, patting her skinny little knee. "We've got our own problems, you and me. And we're taking the first step to getting things all straightened out right now. The Sanchezes live about ten minutes from here, nice neighborhood, nice young man. Let's see how nice you can be when expressing your extreme regret for leaving him lying in a ditch after knocking him off his bike."

"Daddy!" Another wailing protest. "It wasn't like that. And there was no ditch."

"Whatever," Ryan muttered. "Let's see if we can fix it."

The ride to Rick Sanchez's house seemed all too brief to Jennifer. She thought it was going a little too far for her dad to make her go over and apologize in person. She could just as well have done it on the phone. It was probably going to be a bad scene. She knew how she'd feel if someone ran her over and then just drove off, leaving her for dead. What if he was really mean or something? But he couldn't be that bad if he wasn't going to tell the cops. That would have gotten her in big trouble. Not that she wasn't in big trouble anyway. It was the last straw for her mom, and her dad was only letting her come live with him because there was nowhere else for her to go. If she had grandparents or anything, she'd be dumped on them, she bet. Nobody wanted her. Nobody really cared about her, and that was the truth. Her mom and her dad had their lives and there wasn't room in it for her. She turned her face and looked at the houses, obscured by lush landscaping and the wan light of a sliver-thin moon. Why did people have kids and then divorce and leave them just hung out to dry? It was like getting a puppy and then finding him too much trouble, so you took him to the pound and everybody knew what happened to pets then. Which is exactly what would happen to throw-away kids if there wasn't a law against it.

She stirred as her dad slowed to make a turn. "I think it's here," he murmured. "Broken Bough's the street."

The neighborhood was nice. So were the houses. They were sort of dated, like they were built a while ago, but they had a look of...well, like they were there for all time. Permanent. And meant for families where kids grew up in the same room and didn't leave until they went to college. As they cruised and her dad searched for the address, she saw bikes and sports stuff in the garages. Some teenage boys were shooting baskets in the driveways. No little kids, 'cause it was night. But if it was daylight, she thought somewhat wistfully, there would be little kids playing outside. She had never lived in a neighborhood like this.

"Here we are." Before shutting off the engine, Ryan looked at her. "Have you been rehearsing what you'll say?"

She shrugged. "What's to say besides I'm sorry?"

"You might inquire about his injuries."

"Well, sure. I guess."

"You might mention that you plan to pay for his bike."

She shrugged again. "Whatever."

"And you might lose the attitude. In fact, I'm ordering you to lose the attitude. You owe this boy, Jennifer. And if you screw up this opportunity to make amends, you're going to wish you'd stayed with Diane."

She crossed her arms in a huff. "I don't know why

you're acting like this, Dad. I didn't have to tell anybody anything, you know. I could have just driven back to Dallas with Jody and Melissa and nobody would ever have known anything.''

"Except for the fact that you'd swiped the Manesses' car.''

"So they'd ground us for a week or something.''

He sat looking at her in silence, making her feel like a worm. Inside she was miserable. Why was she arguing with her dad like this? She was in the wrong and she knew it, but why did everybody just want to rub her nose in it more and more? She was going to do the right thing. He'd dragged her here, hadn't he? She didn't have any choice.

"Get out of the car," he ordered with a look of disgust and pushed his door open. "Go up there, ring the doorbell and make it good, Jennifer.''

Her insides were shaking and so were her hands when she rang the doorbell. This was worse than getting stopped at Blockbuster when Deanna Rivers tried to swipe a movie. Even worse than the time last month when she had come home at two o'clock in the morning, three hours late on her curfew after having a few beers at Jody's house. The Reinharts were never home and it had seemed like a good idea at the time. Just as taking the car last night had seemed cool. At the time.

The door was answered instantly by a guy she assumed to be Rick Sanchez. He was really tall, she saw now, but she hadn't had time to notice that when he was down on his butt on the street. And he had coal-black hair and gorgeous gray eyes. Even with that horrible bruise on his cheek, he was really hot. Wow, wait'll she told Jody and Melissa!

"I thought you might have decided not to come, Mr. Paxton.''

Okay, he was looking right through her, speaking to her dad and ignoring her existence. Fine, she thought. Just because he was hot didn't mean she wanted him to...well, *see* her.

"Hello again, Rick." Ryan extended his hand and they exchanged a handshake. "This is my daughter, Jennifer."

"Hi," Jennifer squeaked, sounding to herself like a sick mouse.

"Hi," Rick said. "Come in. My parents are in the den. They'll join us if you want, Mr. Paxton."

"Up to you, Rick."

"Okay, it's just us."

"And please, call me Ryan."

"Yes, sir."

"And drop the sir."

"Right."

Jennifer watched Rick grin, a beautiful transformation of his features that made him even more fabulous-looking. Maybe this wasn't going to be as bad as she thought. Even if she remained invisible. She followed him as he turned to lead them into an area that they probably called the living room. That was when she noticed he was limping. Also, he had an Ace bandage around his wrist and two fingers were wrapped. Oh, Lord, had she broken his fingers?

The room was actually a living-dining area combined, a pretty sort of formal room. She was glad to tear her gaze from Rick's injuries to the china cabinet. His mom's pattern had lots of roses on it. Delicate and feminine, nothing like her own mom's sterile black-and-silver geometric choice. His mom must collect cranberry glass as there was a lot of that, too. She recognized it because Melissa's mother had a sizable collection.

They sat down on a couch, which had a coffee table in

front of it loaded with pictures of their family, she guessed. The frames were really cool, all mixed up designs, some funny, some traditional. Many of the photos were of Rick and somebody that looked a lot like him, only she was a girl. His sister, for sure. A boy and a girl, a mom and a dad. Nice house. Perfect family. Rick sat in a chair opposite her and her dad and propped one leg on an ottoman.

"My daughter has something to say." Ryan prompted Jennifer with a stern look.

Her tummy gave a flip. She put her hands together, laced her fingers tight. She met Rick's eyes, felt her face get hot. "I'm sorry for hitting you with the car last night," she said, her voice low. "I didn't know I was that close to you until it—it happened. I didn't mean to hit you."

"I realize it was an accident," Rick said.

"I— Were—" She licked her lips. "I mean, I can see you're hurt. I didn't think so then, because you were just sitting there on the ground looking at us. I mean, you weren't lying down. Or—or bleeding or anything. It was wrong for me to drive off. I should have stopped."

"I was sitting there because I was dazed." He frowned. "What did you say your name was?"

"Jennifer."

"Jennifer. I knew nothing was broken, but it was no fun getting blindsided by an SUV…a big one at that." He chuckled, shaking his head.

She glanced at his fingers, wincing. "Are your fingers broken? I'm really sorry."

"No," he said, lifting his hand and showing the wrapped wrist and fingers. "Just sprained. They'll be okay." He shifted on the chair, reached for a cushion and tucked it behind him. "So, where do you go to school?"

"Not here. I live in Dallas." She glanced at Ryan. "Or I did. But I guess I'll be enrolling somewhere around here. I'm going to be living with my dad."

Rick looked at Ryan. "Will you try to get her in Kincaid?" His attitude suggested that he knew Ryan would want the best for Jennifer.

"Kincaid's not possible as they're entering the second semester. There's a long waiting list. I tried Saint Andrews, too. Neither has to cater to parents who spring a new student on them at the last minute." His smile took any sting out of his words. "Are you at Kincaid?"

"Whoa, not me." Rick was shaking his head with a rueful smile. "The tuition's way too steep for my folks. I'm at Memorial. It's public, but the best, in my opinion."

"You've been checking?" Jennifer asked, looking at her dad in surprise. "Why? For how long?" Did that mean her mom had just been waiting for her to screw up so she could dump her?

Ryan didn't answer that, but kept talking to Rick. "Looks like she'll be going into Memorial, too. My town house puts her in that district."

Rick looked at Jennifer. "Maybe I'll see you there, Jennifer."

This time, her heart really did flop right over. "Even though I almost k-killed you?"

His grin widened. "Hey, accidents happen."

"That's pretty generous, Rick." Ryan looked at Jennifer. "Isn't it, Jen?"

She managed a nod. She was blushing like mad. She could feel the heat in her face as if she was on the beach in August! "Thank you," she croaked.

"I believe there's something else Jen wants to say," Ryan prompted.

"Huh?" She gave her dad a blank look, but her brain was mush.

"Rick's bike. Don't you have something to say about it?"

"Oh. Oh! Yeah, your bike." She lifted her shoulders, her smile weak and embarrassed. "I'm…ah, I would like to pay for it. Dad said it was a total loss, so…how much did it cost?"

"Twelve hundred dollars."

She stared at him. Did bikes really cost that much? She didn't have much experience with biking, but that sure had to be unusual. "No kidding?"

"It's not your average Kmart special," he said, smiling at her reaction. "I'm training for a cross-country this summer. It's custom-built for the terrain we'll encounter."

"Oh, where's that?" she asked weakly.

"Colorado."

She cleared her throat, looked to her dad for help. She'd never be able to come up with twelve hundred dollars. Not even if she sacrificed for a year! No more CDs or makeup or even if she gave up her cell phone. "Um, could you accept a payment plan?"

"Possibly." Rick's expression was sober, but his gray eyes were bright. He was laughing at her! "What terms do you think you can manage?"

"Well—"

Ryan stood up. "You can leave that to Jen and me, Rick. She's going to have a lot of time on her hands here in Houston until she can make new friends. Until then, there might be something she can do to earn a few bucks."

"Twelve hundred dollars is more than a few bucks, Dad!" she cried. She was convinced they were putting her on now.

"Yeah, so the sooner you get started, the sooner Rick will be able to resume training. Right, Rick?"

"That's right." He shifted forward in the chair and got to his feet, wincing a little. "I'll take it easy until my ankle is better and by that time, the wrist should be good as new, too." He looked at Jennifer. "What do you say to…three weeks?"

She looked in absolute desperation at Ryan. "Dad?"

"You'll have a check in three weeks, Rick. And thanks for being a good sport about this."

"Forget it."

"Jen?" Ryan looked at her.

"Oh, okay. I mean, yes, thank you." Feeling her cheeks begin to heat up again, she fled the room and was out the door before Rick, hobbling beside Ryan, could say anything else to make her feel worse.

She was nearly in tears as Ryan started the SUV and backed out of the Sanchez's driveway. Rick's outline, as he stood in the doorway backlit from the light in the foyer, was a blur. "Dad, I don't know how I'm going to get twelve hundred dollars even if Rick would be willing to wait a year! Mom only gives me fifty dollars a week for my allowance and I have to buy my lunch every day with that. What'll I do?"

Ryan disciplined the grin that wanted to escape. "I'll think of something."

Nine

"She doesn't want to talk to us, Megan." Lindsay sat on the floor in what served as her sister's dining area, her legs tucked in a lotus position, eyes closed, shoulders relaxed. "No, that's not it. She doesn't even want to know us."

Megan stood at the stove tossing shrimp and Chinese vegetables in a wok. "You're not supposed to talk while doing yoga."

Lindsay opened one eye. "Don't you care? She's our sister. Aren't you just the least bit curious about her?" She uncurled her body and flopped back on a huge black floor cushion. "She's beautiful, Meggie. And so...so... cool. I mean, not cool as in hip, but like an iceberg. In fact, *iceberg* is a pretty good description. Most of her real self is hidden beneath the surface, if you ask me."

"She's probably far from cool to the people in her life." Megan rummaged in her fridge looking for a lemon.

"She was certainly fierce in her defense of Gina D'Angelo."

"Well, they have a history."

"And how. You should have heard the testimony of that slug, Austin Leggett. He said some really vile things about Gina. What I want to know is why he stayed in a relationship with her if she was so screwed up. How come he had a child with her? Why get involved with her in the first place?''

Megan reached for a spatula. ''Did you believe her when she said he was abusive?''

''I thought she seemed credible.'' Lindsay took a baby carrot from a bowl sitting beside her on the floor. ''But even if she was iffy, Elizabeth was anything but. She defended Gina with a sincerity that was very believable.''

''She would, considering the bond they share.'' Megan stirred the ingredients in the wok. ''Was the little girl there?''

''No, just Elizabeth, Gina and Maude Kennedy, her attorney. And wow, they were a solid team, those three. Even with the sexy Ryan Paxton doing his thing, the day belonged to those gals.'' Pausing with a carrot in her fingers, Lindsay looked thoughtful. ''She didn't have a clue who I was when I approached her at lunch, Meggie.''

''Must have bruised your ego a bit.''

''Not really.'' She made a wry face. ''Well…maybe I did feel a pang when only Gina had seen my show. What is it with Elizabeth? I've tried e-mail, I've called her, but I get her answer machine, of course. She just doesn't want to know us.''

''Not me, you. I'm not the one pestering her.'' Megan cut the lemon in half. ''As I said—and from what you've described of the court appearance—she has a life with her foster sister. And the little girl, of course.''

''But why not make room for us, too?'' Lindsay reached for bottled water and unscrewed the cap. ''We're nice. We're not going to bug her like—like rabid fans, or anything. Besides, her readership could hardly turn vicious. I mean, kids don't usually even communicate with authors, do they? And besides, we're *related*. What's the matter with her!''

"We may be related, but we're strangers."

"We're sisters, Meg."

"Only biologically. And since the year we were all separated, we're strangers who have nothing else in common with her. That's obviously the way she sees it." Megan took the lid off a saucepan to check that the rice was ready. "As I told you the last time we talked about this, I think you should leave Elizabeth alone. If and when she ever decides she wants to meet us, she'll know where to find us. You, more so than I."

Lindsay suddenly looked glum. "If you mean I'm visible on TV, I'm not so sure. I'm hanging on by the skin of my teeth. Filling in for various anchors isn't my idea of success. For one thing, it's not enough exposure. And working behind the scenes is definitely not me." She saw the knowing lift of Megan's eyebrow. "I know, I know, I'm vain and shallow, wanting to be a star, but actually, I'm more comfortable when I'm on camera. It just feels right." She sighed and made a little moue of dissatisfaction. "I simply need to find the right venue to be able to persuade Jack Bigelow to give me another shot. He's receptive, but when I approach him, I want to have something he simply can't refuse."

Megan lifted the steaming wok and dumped the contents into a wide serving bowl. "But getting back to Elizabeth, I don't quite understand your obsession there."

"It's not an obsession, Meggie. It's a natural thing, I think, wanting to include her in our lives." Lindsay stood gracefully, her sleek body long and willowy-looking in black leotards. Now on her feet, she drank from the water bottle, then set it aside before pulling an elastic scrunch from her hair, which fell to her shoulders, a thick mass of streaky blond curls. To keep the current straight look, she spent much time taming it before appearing in public.

Passing the large mirror mounted above an artistically dec-orated chest, she checked her reflection. Classic features were enhanced with unique almond-shaped eyes and a lush mouth that loved the camera, assets that hadn't been overlooked by producers at WBYH-TV when they had cast her in her own show.

She mounted a tall stool at the bar as Megan dished up the food. "You know what we need to do," she said, accepting a plate. "If we had something she wanted, she'd come around."

"Give it a rest, Lin." Megan tasted the shrimp-and-veggie concoction and closed her eyes in ecstasy. "Hmm, this is so good. I haven't had real food in a week."

Lindsay frowned. "You're going to pay for neglecting yourself, I'm telling you, Meggie. If not now, then some-day." Lindsay was ruthless in adhering to her own health and exercise regimen. She worked out at the gym daily, ate healthy, obsessed over food additives and the problem of obesity in America. "What's your cholesterol count?"

"It's 176."

"Oh. Well—" Undaunted, she pointed her fork. "You're lucky it's in the safe range, but one of these days—"

"I'll collapse from overwork, not a heart attack. Only six more months of residency and I can ease up. Quit nagging."

"You're the doctor," Lindsay said popping a shrimp into her mouth. "It should be you nagging me about keep-ing fit, not the other way around."

"You were saying about Elizabeth—"

"Oh, yeah," Lindsay said. "I was thinking."

"Really?"

"I was thinking," Lindsay repeated doggedly, "about things we have in common that might interest her. Not our careers. You're in medicine, I'm in television, she writes books for children. Not much in common there. You and I were raised as sisters, but even though we're equally related to her, she chooses not to acknowledge it. What she can't ignore is that we have the same father. And that's the ticket, Meggie.'' Lindsay pushed her plate aside. ''What do we really know about Judge Matthew Walker?''

''I thought we knew a lot.''

''We don't know anything except what we were told by the parents when they finally outed the fact that we had another sister. Okay, Matthew Walker was a judge and our mother died in childbirth having me. They got married while students at the University of Texas. Their parents are long deceased, which is the reason no one came forward when we were orphaned. We know the judge died in the house fire that could have killed us, too, except that we were rescued.''

''Actually, that sounds like a lot to me.''

''Facts. Dry facts. Or maybe not.'' Forgetting her plate altogether, Lindsay hunched forward to make her point. ''Have you ever wondered if it really was an accident? The fire, I mean. What if—''

''Oh, for Pete's sake, Lindsay!'' Megan took her plate to the dishwasher, put it inside and closed the door with a thump. ''And they say Elizabeth's the one with the active imagination.'' She grabbed a dishcloth and began briskly wiping the counters. ''Where do you come up with these off-the-wall theories? He was a smoker. He fell asleep with a smoldering cigar in his hand and a fire started. It happens.''

''How do we know it was that simple? Have you read an autopsy report?''

''No, but I assume if there was anything even remotely

suspicious about that, it would have come out at the time. And I believe Mom and Dad would have mentioned that when they finally did get around to telling us that we were adopted. They were pretty up-front about the circumstances when they did come clean, if you recall.''

''I don't necessarily think they would have been told those details.'' Lindsay brought her plate around and stowed it in the dishwasher. ''I mean, what purpose would it serve to tell prospective parents that?''

''Tell them what, Lindsay? That the judge might have been murdered? That is what you're saying, isn't it?''

Lindsay caught her hair up in her hand, lifting it off her neck. ''Not necessarily. It might have happened just as they say it did. He was relaxing at the end of a long day, lit up a cigar. Maybe he had a couple of stiff drinks. He nodded off, the smoldering ashes dropped on the carpet....'' She stopped, frowning. ''I wonder if it was the carpet or something else, like a trash basket with paper in it. That'd go up pretty fast. But it would also wake somebody up, too. I mean, if a waste basket flamed up beside me at my desk, I don't think I'd just continue snoozing. Oh, wait. There were no alcohol or drugs found in his body at the autopsy, so that wouldn't—''

''Wait.'' With a shake of her head, Megan held up a hand. ''Wait a minute here. Are you saying you've looked at the accident report? You've read the autopsy?''

''No, but I nosed around until I located one of the detectives on the case who's now retired. He remembers it well. He told me there was a lot of speculation about that fire. He said he remembers the investigation because it was so brief, too brief in his opinion.''

''How old is this detective, Lindsay? All this happened twenty-five freakin' years ago.''

Lindsay shrugged. ''He's old. But he had no difficulty

remembering it. Judge Walker was well-known in Houston. His death was a big deal.'' She waited a beat before adding, ''And as for the autopsy and accident reports, you're right about that. I should take a look at them. I met a guy the other night who might be a good contact. Name's Jake Farrell. He's in the DA's office.''

Megan dropped her head down, braced herself with both hands on the countertop. Waited a long moment before looking up. ''Okay, I'll accept that you have some interest in exploring the death of our biological parent. But what does all this have to do with Elizabeth? About forging some kind of relationship with her?'' Now Megan's tone turned rich with irony. ''I can just imagine how overjoyed she'll be when you approach her with your theory that the man she remembers—and we don't, mind you—didn't die an accidental death. Possibly. He was murdered. Maybe. For a really sinister reason, about which you don't have a clue. And, by the way, you can't prove anything just yet, but hey, it could happen.''

''You just said it.'' Lindsay pounced on the remark she considered relevant. ''The man she remembers is the key, Megan. I need to have a conversation with her about Judge Walker. She might remember something vital. She might—''

''She was only five years old, Lindsay.''

''So? Kids that young have memories. I can remember my first day at kindergarten and I was only five at the time. Mom held my hand as we looked for the right room. I even remember what color the door was when we found it. It was orange and had a clown poster taped on it.''

Megan rolled her eyes. ''You're grasping at straws here, Lin. The best way to build a relationship with Elizabeth is to come at it naturally. She's a very private person, but maybe she wouldn't be offended by a note on her birthday, or maybe you could go to one of her signings when her next book comes out. Or you might bump into her at the grocery store where she shops, try approaching her there...just to say hello, nothing more. Sooner or later—''

"That could take years!"

Megan looked at her, then spoke quietly. "She has a right to acknowledge you as her sister or not, Lindsay. Accept it and move on."

"I'd really like to have a conversation with her about Judge Walker." Lindsay was off the stool now and pacing. "She might be able to shed some light on the case, point me in a direction that was overlooked by the police. But if she—"

"Wait just a minute." Megan abruptly shut off the water at the sink. "I'm beginning to get it now. This isn't about Elizabeth at all, is it? It's about digging up info on the judge, right?"

"Not totally." Lindsay shrugged. "And what's the harm if there's nothing there as you suspect?"

"And the reason you want to find something irregular about the judge's death is because it may possibly interest Jack Bigelow, who will then—possibly—let you do a feature on 'Evening Magazine.'" Megan was shaking her head. "It took a while, but I'm finally getting it. You're right. I should eat more sensibly. My brain was really slow on the uptake on this one."

"Oh, c'mon." Lindsay flopped back down on the huge floor cushion. "It's not that reprehensible. You make me sound like a sleazy opportunist."

Megan gave her a knowing look and said nothing.

"Well, just acknowledge this and I'll shut up...for now." Resuming a new yoga position, Lindsay stuck her leg straight up in the air with ease and rotated her foot at the ankle. "Judge Matthew Walker's death was surely advantageous to a few people who had cases on the docket at the time. What if one of those cases turns out to have some really suspicious elements? What if there's a deep mystery just waiting to be solved? What if he really was murdered?''

Megan tossed a wet sponge into the sink and turned off the kitchen light. ''Yeah, and what if pigs could fly?''

Ten

Elizabeth muttered something vile as the telephone rang. Resigned to quitting for the day, she saved the text in the current document and closed down. The ringer for the phone on her desk was turned off, but she could hear the sound when other extensions rang. More irritating, she could hear the messages as callers spoke. Like now.

"Hi, Elizabeth. It's me again. Lindsay. Just reminding you to check your e-mail today. I'd love to firm up a lunch date. There's something important I want to talk to you about. I've uncovered some really interesting facts about the fire the night that Judge Walker died. Let's see…" Brief pause. "I'll be at this number until five. Will you call me? Thanks. Talk to you soon."

Elizabeth stood staring at the phone. Ignoring Lindsay clearly wasn't working. She was going to have to send her a stern e-mail to end the harassment, that is, if she wanted to maintain some distance between herself and her sisters. But since learning they never even knew about her, she was struggling with whether or not to open up a dialogue, at least. Maybe they could have lunch, possibly include Megan. Elizabeth admitted to a curiosity about her sisters. When she was still young and feeling the crushing pain of losing them, she'd fantasized meeting them in a grocery store. Or at the mall. Or in the library. Her imagination had taken her only so far. She couldn't remember how she'd planned to react if they had chanced upon one another. And now that the door was cracked when it had been firmly closed against the possibility of a relationship with her sisters, she was finding it difficult to ignore what might be behind it. Rubbing her forehead, she pressed a button to hear other calls.

"Gina. Austin." The tone was abrupt, harsh with irritation. "We need to talk, so pick up." Long pause. "Goddamn it, Gina! This is the third time I've tried to reach you. What's the problem? Is Liz monitoring your calls?" He paused again, then muttered an obscenity. "I thought this whole thing was about you taking control of your life, but if Liz is advising you, that's hardly a declaration of independence." He waited again, two, three, four seconds. "You're gonna have to talk to me sooner or later, Gina. I'll be in my office the rest of the day. Call." He slammed the phone down.

Elizabeth stood, debating whether or not to delete the message. But shielding Gina from Austin's bullying would be validating his accusations, wouldn't it?

"Go ahead, zap it. I've already heard it."

Gina appeared from the vicinity of the kitchen, drying her hands on a dish towel. Lately, she'd been taking over the chore of cooking and cleaning, insisting on doing something to pay for room and board for herself and Jesse. "I should have deleted it myself. I don't want to talk to him, but you know how he is. He'll keep on pestering me until I simply give in."

Elizabeth punched the delete button. "You don't have to give in, Gina, and you don't have to tolerate any harassment. Have Maude call him and lay down the law. That's what lawyers are for."

"I guess I should do that."

"Are you comfortable with the judge's ruling?"

"Of course. I never expected to get what I petitioned for, let alone that it would be doubled. I'd be crazy to change anything. It's just that…" She went to the window where Jesse and Cody played while Louie looked on from his favorite spot in the gazebo. The kids were trying to teach Archie, the dog, to retrieve a Frisbee. New at the game, Archie simply ran from one child to the other, barking and wagging his tail wildly, while basically ignoring the Frisbee. There was a lot of squealing and laughing.

"So Jesse's the reason you're hesitating."

"I don't like the idea of her being alone with Austin, Liz. I know what he's like. He doesn't want Jesse. He just wants out from under any financial burden. So, if I sign the agreement, I'm financially secure, but what about Jesse? Will she be safe in his care?"

Since those were basically the same concerns Elizabeth had, she could think of nothing reassuring to say. She knew Gina's fear was based on the reality of living with Austin. But what were the options? Nobody but Maude and Elizabeth believed Austin posed a threat. In hindsight, she realized it had been a mistake not to call Ryan Paxton after Austin manhandled Gina the day of the hearing. Paxton was the type of man who went with the evidence of his eyes. He wouldn't have been able to defend Austin if he'd seen those bruises on Gina's face. Too late now. The bruises had faded in the two weeks since it happened.

The phone still blinked, signaling one more message. With a sigh, Elizabeth pushed the button to hear it.

"Elizabeth, Ryan Paxton here. I've been trying to reach you for a couple of weeks now. Didn't want to leave a message. I'd rather talk to you personally than to rely on voice mail. Remember our discussion at the coffee shop? We need to get together to try to work something out between Gina and Austin. I know you've got some concerns about the whole thing, but I think for Jesse's sake we could work something out.''

Somehow she'd missed hearing that one. Elizabeth quickly deleted it, resisting the instant leap of her pulse at hearing his voice. "What he'd like to work out," she said, fiddling with the notepad beside the phone, "is a way to get Austin off the hook financially."

She opened a drawer and dropped the notepad inside. "But sooner or later this has to be settled, Gina. Austin's going to appear and demand his visitation rights with Jesse. And you won't have a leg to stand on."

Jesse burst through the door just then with Archie galloping beside her, his tongue lolling in an ecstatic smile. She was grimy from head to toe after only an hour outside. One pink sneaker was untied, shoestrings trailing, limp and dirty. How she avoided tripping over them was a mystery to Elizabeth.

"Aunt Lizzie, somebody's coming and they're almost to the front door right now." With both her arms wrapped around the dog's neck, Jesse strained to avoid being licked in the face. "It's a man and he has somebody with him who looks like Britney Spears!"

Elizabeth gave Jesse's nose a playful tweak as the doorbell rang. "Well, it's not Britney Spears, you can take my word for that, sweetie."

Jesse's smile faded as she was struck by a new thought. "It's not somebody wanting us to leave, is it? So they can live with you and not us."

"Of course not, Jesse." Elizabeth ruffled her hair as they headed to the door. It always gave her a pang when Jesse voiced her fear of more upheaval. Surely, if Austin realized how anxious his daughter had become, he'd know how vital it was to quickly resolve the issues between himself and Gina and hopefully give Jesse some peace of mind. "You'll be staying here with me as long as you want to, Jesse."

With the little girl beside her, she checked the peephole to see who was at the door. Her heart bumped against her ribs as she recognized Ryan Paxton. Pausing a moment, she took a breath and reached for the handle.

"Hi, Elizabeth," Ryan Paxton said, flashing a grin. When she didn't reply, he gave a boyish shrug, "Hey, we were in the neighborhood." Elizabeth's gaze moved to the teenager beside him. "My daughter, Jennifer," he said, still exuding good humor. "As I said, we were in the neighborhood and I hoped I might catch you at home." His gaze dropped to the small face tucked close to Elizabeth's legs. "Hi there, I bet you're Jesse."

"Uh-huh." Jesse ventured out a little farther to get a better look at Jennifer. "Do you know Britney Spears?" she asked, wide-eyed.

Jennifer rolled her eyes and made a huffy sound. "No."

"Jennifer," Ryan said with a note of warning in his tone, "say hello to Jesse."

"Hello."

"O—ka-a-y…" Ryan's smile now had a slight edge. "If you could spare a minute, Elizabeth, maybe we could have a conversation about the…ah, situation." His glance went briefly to Jesse.

"Mr. Paxton—"

"Ryan."

Elizabeth sighed. "Ryan. I don't think—"

"Hello, Ryan," Gina said, materializing at Elizabeth's shoulder.

Another flashy grin. "Gina. How you doin'?"

"Okay. Thanks."

"I was just saying to Elizabeth that, being in the neighborhood, I thought I'd pop by and see if I might bum a cup of coffee." He glanced down at Jesse. "Or something."

Gina smiled. "Guess what? You're in luck. I was just thinking of making a fresh pot." She took Jesse's hand. "And I've still got some of those chocolate chip cookies left from yesterday." She smiled at the teenager. "Jennifer, if you don't know Britney Spears, I bet you know a lot about her and Jesse would be your slave forever if you'd be willing to share a few tidbits."

Jennifer hesitated, not thrilled about munching cookies and talking with a five-year-old.

"Jen loves chocolate chip cookies and Britney Spears," her father said in a tone that left no room for argument. "Fifteen minutes, hon."

"Whatever," Jennifer said with a toss of her head, but she stepped around Ryan, giving him a last dark look before following Gina and Jesse down the hall toward the kitchen.

Still standing outside the door, Ryan's grin now had a rueful tilt as he watched her go. "I'm in for it when we get back in the car," he said to Elizabeth. "She's been mad at me ever since the accident."

"How serious were the biker's injuries?"

"Not too bad, fortunately. He's young and healthy. He'll be good as new in a couple of weeks." He stared for a moment at his feet, then looked up at her. "Look, I know this was pushy and you've done everything except rent an airplane with a sign saying you don't want to talk to me, but I really believe it's in the best interest of that little girl to try to work something out before it's left to us lawyers to screw things up."

She stepped back and motioned him into the house. "We can talk in here." Heading for her office, she waited until he stepped inside and then closed the door. He looked around with interest, noted the classics side by side with popular fiction in her crammed bookcase, walked closer to examine a wall with framed citations, various photographs, her college diploma and the Newbery. "Very impressive," he said, motioning to the crowded wall. "Only one thing surprises me, or maybe I should say, only one thing puzzles me."

She moved past him to get behind her desk. Somehow she felt safer with something substantial separating them. "And that is?"

"Why you keep such a low profile." He looked about, choosing a chair. "May I?"

"Of course."

"But we've already talked about that, even though I'm still trying to figure it out."

Elizabeth eased gingerly onto the edge of her chair, all too aware of the size of him in her clearly feminine lair. He was so…male. "You wanted to talk about Gina, not me," she reminded him. "How do you think we can do anything? And before you start, I want to tell you what happened that day after the hearing when Gina left with Austin in his car. They were gone for hours. I know, I know, it was her choice," she said, stopping him with an upheld hand. "She came home very late, looking upset. She'd found the courage to refuse when he wanted her to disregard what the judge recommended and allow him to deal with the issue of child support as he saw fit. He wants no formal agreement of any kind. You and I know that would leave her up a creek and him in a much more advantageous position regarding child support or anything else. Anyway, when he realized she was actually going to defy him, he attacked her. Her arms were black and blue from his grip and there was a mark on her neck. That was what I saw for myself. I don't know if there was anything else.''

"You're saying he tried to choke her?"

"No." She hesitated, frowning. "Actually, I don't know. Gina wasn't willing to tell me very much. I wanted to call you then, to show you that we weren't lying about Austin.''

"Why didn't you?"

"Gina worried that the firm wouldn't give her a recommendation to get another job if she made waves. And I didn't push it because I knew you'd just learned about your daughter's hit and run and you'd be preoccupied with that. Besides, I thought he'd fired you.'' She looked at him. "What happened? Did he change his mind?"

"Yeah." Ryan stood up, clamped a hand on the back of his neck and took a few restless paces around the room. "This is a helluva mess."

"Then you believe me?"

He looked at the wall, at a bulletin board with several childishly written letters pinned to it, at snapshots of her fans. "Let's just say I don't disbelieve you."

She was surprised at the satisfaction that gave her. It wasn't just that Ryan's opinion boosted Gina's chances to be dealt with fairly. It was more personal. She actually wanted him to believe her. Exactly why that should be, she wasn't quite sure. "Then what can we do?" she asked him. "Austin isn't going to just give up and write monthly checks to Gina, regardless of the fact that if he doesn't, his own child will do without."

"With all due respect, he knows that won't happen," Ryan said. "He knows you'll take care of her."

She opened her mouth to dispute that, but it was true. She would never let Gina or Jesse get into dire straits.

He went to an antique library table crowded with

framed photos. Bending close, he picked up one of Jesse and Louie. "Who is this?"

"It's Jesse."

"I know that. Who's the elderly gent? He looks familiar."

"Louie Christian." She watched him studying the photo. "You have his deposition as one of Gina's character witnesses."

Ryan snapped his fingers. "Oh, yeah. I remember now. I gather he's a close friend."

"He lives next door. He's the only grandfather figure in Jesse's life. Austin's parents just can't be bothered."

Ryan gave a short laugh. "Curtiss Leggett isn't exactly the grandfatherly type, is he?"

"I've never met him."

He replaced the photo, then turned to look at her. "I guess you don't remember much about your parents."

"No."

"What were you, four, five years old when they died?"

"Five. Actually, my mother died in childbirth. It was a year later that my father died." She laced her fingers together tightly and rested them on top of the desk, wondering why she was telling him this when she always avoided any reminders of that time. First the reporter from the newspaper, then Lindsay, now Ryan Paxton, all probing painful memories. She'd gone for more than two decades when no one cared enough to mention that time, even casually. Why now? Why all the curiosity when a little publicity years ago might have been helpful in changing the circumstances of her childhood? And why this man, of all others?

"We were talking about Gina," she said to end the questions.

"I know, but I lost my own parents at an early age and

it's pretty unusual, meeting someone who's been there and done that." Leaning close, he studied a certificate from the mayor with her father's name on it. Without turning, he said, "Actually, we have more in common than the fact that we're orphans. My dad was a judge, too."

"Here in Houston?"

"Yeah. Right here."

"What happened, I mean, that you lost both parents? Was it an accident?"

"Actually, my father committed suicide."

"Oh, I'm sorry."

"Yeah. And would you believe, it happened right about the time of Judge Walker's death."

She frowned at the strange coincidence. "Twenty-five years ago," she murmured in sympathy for the trauma he must have suffered.

"Yeah, two judges in the same jurisdiction."

She was puzzled by something in his attitude. "They must have known each other."

"Must have."

She watched him reach up and straighten the framed certificate. Just a tiny nudge to align it with the other pictures on the wall. His touch was delicate, respectful. But there was something in the set of his shoulders, in the bleak silence. "And your mother?" she asked, still trying to pin down the reason for this odd underlying tension.

"Pancreatic cancer six months after my dad."

"Oh," she murmured with more real sympathy.

"Yeah, it was pretty hard to accept."

She had a brief vision of a grief-stricken boy. She didn't want to feel sympathy for Ryan Paxton, but how could she not? "Some of the most touching letters that I receive are from children who have lost a parent," she told him, thinking to turn their conversation into less personal territory. "It's utterly bewildering to them. Of course, most of the time their loss is as a result of an accident or incurable illness, as in the case of your mother. Sometimes it's inner city violence, but the result is often the same no matter what the reason. They're angry and resentful, blaming the dead parent for being so cruel as to leave them."

Ryan turned from the wall of memorabilia. He smiled, but it had a grim edge. "I didn't blame my father so much as the man who drove him to it."

Elizabeth now felt certain she'd missed something significant, but still couldn't imagine what. Of course, the loss of parents in childhood was traumatic. Nobody knew that better than she. But it had been a long time ago. Could be he felt the same reluctance to stir up old memories as much as she did. Still, he'd been the one to bring up the subject. And to reveal painful details.

He had moved to her bookcases and was examining the titles. "Do you remember much about your father?" he asked.

"My father?" Changing the direction of her thoughts, she frowned. "Not very much, just vague…impressions more than memory."

"How much is much?"

The nightmares. Fire and chaos. The flash of red lights and sirens. Sympathetic adults. Caseworkers. One after another until Iris. And the letters with never a reply, because for years as a child she couldn't believe her father was gone. Wouldn't believe it. What made her plight worse was that there had been very little left of the household contents after the fire, and nothing worthwhile had gone with her into the system. She remembered having no clothes and going with someone to a department store— probably a caseworker, not Iris, not then. She was bought new things, but nothing for her sisters. She'd worried about that. They hadn't told her until later that she wouldn't be seeing her sisters again. Then, a few years ago, she'd been notified by her father's aging secretary, Millie Wainwright, that there were some things from the judge's chambers that rightly belonged to Matthew Walker's family. The certificate was one of them, as well as the judge's law school documentation, his college diploma, and several snapshots of him taken with various political figures in the seventies. She'd been so pathetically glad to get anything. Anything.

"Can we get back to the subject of Gina?" Determined now to change the subject, she watched him pull out a tattered edition of *The Secret Garden*. "I've been over and over the possibilities and it seems to me that there's no better option than putting it back in the hands of Austin's lawyer, whoever he is, and Maude Kennedy."

"There is one possibility," Ryan said, carefully replacing the book. "It wouldn't be in Austin's best interest for the senior staff at the firm to learn what's going on. Of course, his relationship with Gina is no secret, but the details of their split aren't generally known. Right now, it's assumed that Austin is in the process of breaking up with Gina and they're experiencing the usual contentious issues of any divorcing couple. If it got out that Austin is accused of roughing up Gina, there would be uncomfortable repercussions for him."

Now Elizabeth was on her feet. "Are you saying you'd be willing to use such a tactic to force him into real negotiations?"

"Eventually, if it came to that." Ryan faced her, his hands tucked into the back pockets of his jeans. "Actually, I don't think it'll come to that because Austin will back down just at the possibility."

"Are you sure?"

He gave a humorless laugh. "Trust me."

Jesse scooted her tiny rear end onto the cushioned glider while holding cookies in a plastic bag high enough to avoid Archie's eager nosiness. Beside her, Jennifer sat with arms crossed in the corner of the glider, wearing attitude and a sulky look. Jesse took one of the cookies from the bag and offered it to the teen, who had a blunt refusal ready, but her rude retort died after one look into the kid's big eyes. She took the cookie reluctantly and got a delighted smile in return. Jesse, oblivious to the teen's attitude, turned to share with the dog. "My mommy makes really good cookies, doesn't she?"

"Yeah, sure."

"Can your mommy make cookies?"

"She doesn't cook anything." Jennifer craned her neck toward the house, but her dad was nowhere to be seen and she was stuck out here with this kid until he decided they could leave. She didn't know why he had insisted on coming over here in the first place. From the way the writer person had looked when she opened the door, Jennifer had expected the door to be slammed in their faces.

"But if she doesn't cook," Jesse said with a frown wrinkling her forehead, "what do you eat?"

"We eat out."

"Oh." Jesse's small head bobbed in understanding. "McDonald's. I love to get a Happy Meal, but Mom and Aunt Lizzie say I can only have it for a treat."

"Good. You'll stay healthy that way."

More bobbing of the head. "I'm healthy. I'm very healthy, everyone says so. I had a bad cold a long time ago and it got okay really fast."

Jennifer moved restlessly on the glider. "So, do you live here with your mom and your Aunt Lizzie?" She glanced at her watch and felt like going inside and yanking her dad out of there. Melissa was going to call her right after school and if she didn't get back to the condo soon, she'd miss the call. Not that her dad would care. He had taken the cell phone as punishment for the hit and run and he was simply deaf to all her arguments that she needed it to keep in touch with her friends in Dallas. She didn't know anybody at Memorial. Well, nobody except Rick. She felt a little leap of something inside just thinking about Rick Sanchez. He said hi to her in the hall today and almost stopped to talk to her, but one of his friends pulled him away. Rick was the only thing that was good about being here. It was so different living with her dad than she'd imagined. Plus, he had discontinued the maid service and now it was her responsibility to do the job, all in payment for Rick's stupid bike. He even made her do the bathrooms! Yuck. It would probably be ten years before she got out of debt.

"I'm going to live here forever," Jesse said, carefully picking out a chocolate chip and offering it to Archie.

"You mean here with your mom and Aunt...ah, Lizzie?"

"Uh-huh."

"What about your dad?"

Jesse's small fingers went still. Her pink sneakers had been beating a monotonous rhythm against the glider as they sat. Now all movement stopped as Jesse thought hard. "I don't think there's room for us with him anymore."

"Why, did they get a divorce and he got the house?"

"What's a divorce?"

"Uh, never mind." Jeez, she didn't want to say something to upset the kid. Maybe it was a divorce, maybe something else. Whatever, it was none of her business. "You get to visit your dad anyway, don't you?"

"No, I don't want to."

"You don't want to visit with your daddy?"

"Uh-uh. He yells and throws things. I have to get under the bed when he does it. Then my mommy cries."

"No joke?"

"Did you think that was funny?" Face upturned, Jesse looked puzzled.

"Funny? Oh. Oh! A joke." Jennifer managed a smile. "No, that was just an expression."

"What's a 'spression?"

"An expression is a ummm…a brief way of saying something."

Not quite getting it, Jesse moved on with another thought. "I think I need a new daddy now," she said decisively.

"Really," Jennifer muttered in total agreement. "But you can't just get a new dad the way you go to Toys "R" Us and pick out a new bike."

"Why?"

"Because…well, just because. Dads are people, not things."

"Well, maybe I could share your daddy. Would that work?"

Hardly, Jennifer thought. She herself wouldn't be living with him right now if she hadn't screwed up royally with the hit and run and everything. But she felt momentary sympathy for the kid. It was awful when your mom and dad split and it was even more painful when your dad had no room in his life for you. What she didn't know about was living in a house where you had to scramble under the bed because your father was on a violent rampage.

"Tell you what," Jennifer said, reaching over to tie the kid's dirty sneaker, "you can visit me and my dad sometimes if it's okay with your mom."

"Really?"

Jennifer shrugged. "Sure. Why not?"

Jesse's smile was almost too big for her little face. "You want another cookie?"

Jennifer buckled herself in beside Ryan a few minutes later and struggled to keep quiet until he backed out of Elizabeth's driveway. Both her parents treated her like a baby and she knew she'd get nothing out of her dad if she just burst out with what the kid said. She would have to be real cool going about it. "Ah, Elizabeth Walker writes children's books. I guess you know that."

"Yeah. I didn't know until lately, but I've seen her current release and I was impressed. She won a prestigious award, did you know that?"

He'd seen Elizabeth's latest book? It dawned on Jennifer that her dad might have the hots for the woman. "Jesse told me the story."

"Cute kid, huh?"

"Uh-huh." Maybe he was interested in the divorced mom.

He glanced at her, smiling. "How were those cookies?"

"Good. Her mom made them."

"Gina."

She gave Ryan a quick, shrewd look. "Is she a client?"

"Gina? No."

"Well, it can't be Elizabeth because I don't think we'd have been invited inside if she were. It was only after Jesse's mom said okay that we got in the door, Dad."

Ryan gave a playful tug to her hair. "You noticed."

She ducked away. "So neither one is a client."

"Neither is a client."

"Then why were we there?"

Finally he realized she was going somewhere with the

questions. He turned onto Westheimer before looking at her. "Is there some reason for all this curiosity? I recall I had to drag you kicking and screaming when I wanted to stop there. Were the cookies that good?" He was smiling.

"Are you interested in one of them...as, you know, dating and stuff?"

"No, honey, it was a business call."

She turned her gaze straight ahead, frowning. "Then I don't get it. You don't represent either one of them, but—" She gave a little gasp and bumped her forehead with the heel of her hand. "Oh, I get it now! It's a divorce thing and you represent Jesse."

He stopped for a traffic light. "Wrong again. What is this, Jen, twenty questions?"

She stared momentarily at her hands. "Dad, would you just please answer the question? If it's business that made you stop there, then you maybe should hear what Jesse said."

He studied her face in silence, then said, "Jesse's dad, Austin, is my client. You saw him the other night when we were leaving to go see Rick."

Her mouth fell open and she quickly covered it. "Now I remember. And he was acting really hyper. I even said to you that he seemed out of control, didn't I?"

"You did." He pulled into the parking lot at Le Peep and killed the engine before turning to face her. "Now, what did Jesse say that's got you upset?"

"You're not going to like it."

"Try me."

"She said she and her mom had to move out of the house, that there was no room for them there. She also said he has a mean temper, that he yells and throws things. She hides under the bed when that happens and he makes her mother cry."

"Ah, hell." Ryan released a sigh and rubbed a hand over his face wearily.

"Why would you represent someone like that, Dad?"

"He's a partner in my law firm, honey. It's customary to use representation in a firm for a colleague who's in need of it."

She wrinkled her nose. "That sounds like a bunch of baloney to me."

"You may have a point."

Eleven

"I wish you'd reconsider, Gina." Elizabeth sat on the edge of the bed watching Gina wiggle into a pair of skin-tight jeans. "You know what happened the last time he talked you into meeting with him alone. And if he finally gets the message that you're really not going to be talked out of this, only the devil knows how he'll react."

"I'll be all right, Lizzie. I'm not getting in the car alone with him. I told you, I'm driving my own car. We're meeting here and going to a safe place, a restaurant or a coffee shop. Since Jesse'll be with us, it might even be McDonald's. Just someplace where there will be other people around."

"That worries me, too. Do you have to take Jesse?"

"He does have visitation rights, even if we haven't formally agreed as the judge requires. Refusing would just get his back up." She sucked in a breath and finally managed to zip the jeans.

"His back is already up. He's desperate, Gina. Desperate people do crazy things."

"Tell me about it," she muttered.

"What?"

"Nothing." Gina looked around in distraction. "What did I do with that sweater? I had it in my hands a minute ago."

"You were steaming the wrinkles out in the bathroom when I came in here."

"Oh, yeah." She disappeared into the bathroom for a moment. It worried Elizabeth that she was taking such pains to look her best if this was simply an opportunity for Austin to spend some quality time with Jesse, as he claimed. She wouldn't expect Gina to wear something unflattering, but the outfit she'd chosen was special, chic and sexy. What would Austin assume when he saw her? What was Gina's intention?

Lately, other things had been troubling Elizabeth. Gina had been oddly distracted for several days. What was that all about? And it was unusual for Gina to be so unforthcoming as Elizabeth gently probed for information. Usually, to Elizabeth, she was open and candid to the point of embarrassing frankness. They'd shared secrets for years. Maybe she was simply nervous over another one-on-one date with Austin, considering how the last encounter ended. Yet, the plan had just come up today when he'd reminded her of his legal right to see Jesse, or so Gina said. Elizabeth hoped she wouldn't have agreed to see him at all otherwise.

"I'm having to brush off doggy hair, would you believe," Gina complained, emerging from the bathroom with the sweater in one hand, brush in another. Hands, Elizabeth noted with concern, that were shaky as she fumbled trying to rid it of Archie's hair.

"Jesse and Cody like to play hide-and-seek in that closet," Elizabeth said. "And, of course, they can't do anything without including Archie."

"Tell me about it." The brushing done, Gina pulled the sweater on, then stood at the mirror and adjusted it over her hips. "Will you fix this collar for me?"

Elizabeth stood up and adjusted the cowl collar of the

sweater, tucking the label, which had reversed, out of sight. Then, with her hands resting on Gina's shoulders, she met her eyes in the mirror. "You're trembling, Gina. What's wrong? If you're not worried about going with Austin, then why the case of nerves?"

Gina's laugh was brief, forced. "You know me, if I didn't have something to be nervous over, I'd invent something." She leaned forward to outline her lips with a peachy gloss, fluffed her hair one more time, then stood back to survey the result. "How do I look?"

"You look good, as always."

She wrinkled her nose. "Just good?"

"You look chic, smart, spiffy."

Now Gina's laugh was genuine. "Okay, okay."

"I recognize those jeans. Neiman's, right?"

Smiling wryly, Gina smoothed her hands down both thighs. "Austin bought them for me. The sweater, too. For my birthday last year."

"Belated, as I recall. Didn't he lock you out of the house that night, then refused to let you in the garage to get your car?"

"And you had to come pick me up." Her smile faded. "Me and Jesse."

"The outfit was an expensive peace offering."

Another brief shrug. "It was over a baby-sitting screwup. I got real busy at work and waited until the last minute to try to find someone to stay with Jesse. When I finally did, the restaurant had canceled our dinner reservations. You know how they are at some restaurants in Houston if you're a few minutes late. Austin freaked."

"What a guy."

Another shrug. "He lost his temper, Lizzie. It happens."

Elizabeth simply looked at her. They stood before the

mirror in complete understanding for a long moment. Elizabeth felt a dark foreboding down deep. Gina's continued resistance was bound to aggravate Austin's dicey temper. If she planned to hold out against him, it was downright dangerous to be alone with him.

"Don't go, Gina," she said again.

Gina smiled…sadly? "I have to, Lizzie."

"Then are you absolutely sure you want to take Jesse?" Gina was an adult. Subjecting a child to Austin's uncertain temper was another thing. Elizabeth felt temper stirring in her own breast. It was frustrating to watch Gina make mistakes that might harm her, but to expose Jesse was— She searched for a word and the only thing that came to mind was *immoral*. To put your own child in harm's way was immoral.

Gina seemed to focus on the flame of an aromatic candle that burned on the vanity. "Do I have a choice?" Dropping her gaze, Gina began sorting through a maze of glitter in her jewelry box.

"I'll say it again, Gina. Please reconsider. For Jesse's sake."

Gina slipped a diamond-studded watch on her wrist and brightened her smile. "We'll be in a public place. What could happen?" Then, as if shaking off her qualms, she grabbed a cashmere shawl draped over the back of the vanity chair, scooped up a tiny, but pricey shoulder bag— another peace offering from Austin after another brutal incident—and blew out the candle. "Okay, I'm ready."

"Don't forget your cell phone. And keep it on."

"Got it." She patted the small bag. "Where's Jesse?"

"Hopefully waiting on the patio. I helped her get dressed and made her promise not to get too grimy while you finished dressing."

"I hope it wasn't over ten minutes ago," Gina said dryly.

"Barely." Elizabeth followed her out of the bedroom. "I didn't tell her anything about your plans tonight." Hoping against hope they wouldn't pan out. But that was a futile wish.

"Great." Gina breathed in a deep sigh.

"If you won't reconsider, just let me call Ryan and find out if he's had a chance to talk with Austin yet."

"Give it a rest, Liz."

"You're flirting with disaster, Gina! I think I have a right to—to—"

"To nag me?" Gina laughed shortly, humorlessly. "Yeah, I guess if anybody deserves to lecture me, you do. Haven't you always done the right thing? Always resisted the devil's whispers in your ear?"

Elizabeth threw her hands out in exasperation. "What are you talking about? This isn't about me. You have a chance to start a new life and flirting with Austin is the best way to screw that up. That's what I'm trying to make you see. If Ryan has spoken with him, maybe—"

Suddenly Gina was angry. "Didn't you hear me, Liz? I'm going. I've already set it up. Even if Ryan has talked to him, Austin will just think of something else another day. The best thing I can do is try to play him the way he's playing me. Obstructing him is sure to piss him off. Tonight, of all nights, I don't want him pissed off." Tired of talking, she jerked open the French doors to the patio. "Jesse! Where are you?"

"Here, Mommy." Jesse appeared with Archie, both breathing hard. Miraculously, Jesse's shoes had remained tied. Her shirt was reasonably neat, but her jeans were smudged at the knees. Otherwise, she was still fairly presentable.

"Ready to go, muffin?" Gina picked a bit of leaf from her daughter's bangs.

"Where are we going, Mommy?"

"It's a surprise, sweetie. Daddy's coming and we're going to follow in our car. Won't that be fun?"

"No." Looking alarmed, Jesse ran to Elizabeth and locked her arms around one leg. "I'm staying with Aunt Lizzie."

"Don't you want to see your daddy?" Gina asked.

"No."

Elizabeth met Gina's eyes over the child's head. "I'd be happy to—"

"No, Liz." Taking a firm grip on Jesse's arm, Gina pulled her away from Elizabeth and hustled her into the house. "Daddy's due any minute now and we don't want to keep him waiting."

"I don't want to go anywhere with him, Mommy!" Jesse tugged at Gina's grip, trying to free herself. "You can't make me. I hate him!"

Elizabeth took a step to intervene just as a car wheeled into the drive with a loud blast of the horn. She'd always deplored Austin's rudeness in honking to announce his arrival rather than coming to the door. It was just one more indication of his lack of respect for Gina. For Jesse.

"He's here," Gina said, scooping Jesse up as the child struggled in earnest. Her arms flailed wildly while her legs churned, kicking and thrashing.

Distressed and helpless, Elizabeth followed them to the door. Jesse was now hysterical. She watched as Gina wrestled the red-faced, screaming child down the sidewalk to the street where Austin was parked. Apparently, the plan was for Jesse to ride with him, but it was going to be a trick to get her in the car and buckled up. Austin, of course, sat waiting for Gina to manage the feat on her own. But Jesse was having none of it. Gina couldn't even get the door open. Elizabeth now ventured forward, determined to try again to persuade Gina not to force the child to go.

But before Elizabeth reached them, Austin suddenly decided to intervene. He got out of his car, stopping Elizabeth in her tracks with a murderous glare. Then, looking fed up, he stalked around the back of the car and instead of forcing Jesse inside, he said a few quick, scathing words to the little girl that cowed her into abrupt silence. He then took her by her small arm, ignoring the fear on her face, and marched her to Gina's car that sat parked and waiting in Elizabeth's driveway. Jerking open the door, he buckled her in and closed the door with a force that rocked it on its wheels. Next, he gave Gina a wordless order with just a curt dip of his head before stalking around to climb back behind the wheel of his car. His face now a thundercloud, he watched while Gina meekly climbed into her car and started it. Elizabeth stood in the middle of her driveway transfixed. It was only when Austin turned to check traffic behind him that Gina gave a quick, furtive flutter of her fingers to Elizabeth. He roared away. Gina looked tearful and pale as she backed out to follow. Then they were both gone.

"Check."

Elizabeth pulled her gaze from the window and stared blankly at the chessboard. Louie's last move, she noted, had rendered her queen helpless. With a sigh, she shoved her chair back and stood up. She had no heart to finish. Chess was not a game to be played while distracted. Archie, sensing her distress, rose instantly and followed her over to the window. "I'm sorry, Louie. I just can't concentrate tonight."

"So it seems," he said and began carefully placing the chess pieces in a velvet-lined case. He prized the elaborate set and the game, and had been delighted when he discovered that Elizabeth liked to play.

"I thought I heard a car." For the umpteenth time in the past hour, she parted the plantation shutters at the window and peered, frowning, at the dark and empty street.

"Worried, are you?"

"They should have been back by now." She stroked Archie's silky head absently. "Something terrible has happened, Louie. I know it."

He paused with a knight in his hand. "You don't know any such thing, Lizzie. Don't let your imagination run away with you. It's fine for writing your books, but at a time like this, you want to keep it under wraps, hon."

"I had a feeling like this once before," she said, focusing on nothing special in the shadowy stillness outside.

"Oh?"

"It was the night of the fire."

Louie was silent a beat or two. "Fire?"

She turned then and gave him a tight smile. "The fire that burned the house down where I lived with my father and sisters."

He took a moment to reply. "We've never talked about that, Lizzie." There was an odd note in his voice, but she was focused on the past.

"No, because contrary to what all those counselors said during my childhood, I never could see the point in discussing what couldn't be changed. My life was changed from that night. I had to accept it and go on. Actually, I've been pretty good at stuffing it—that's another psychological term, you know—until that article in the *Chronicle* when I won the Newbery. I don't quite know how, but that reporter seems to have opened the door to my past." Her mouth twisted in a bitter smile. "An uninteresting past but mine alone, and I wish it had stayed that way."

Louie still held the knight. "I don't believe there was any intent on the reporter's part to expose facts about your life that would hurt you. You're an author, a famous one now. People are interested in who you are."

Again, a tight smile. "Well, I learned my lesson. No more interviews."

His beard sometimes hid Louie's smile. As now. "Until the next award."

"That article flushed my sisters out. I was really stupid not to guess what would happen when I agreed to talk to him."

"I think we've had this conversation," Louie said dryly, then added more soberly, "And it's troubling to hear you refer to your sisters as being 'flushed out.'"

She sighed. From the start, Louie had encouraged her to renew her relationship with Megan and Lindsay, insisting that family was important. He'd dismissed her argument that it was too late, that there was no relationship as she had no memories of them. Sisters were meant to be together, he'd argued, however late it was or whatever the past.

She watched him tuck the knight into its niche, then take off his glasses and begin polishing them. "Are you going to lecture me again about the importance of family?"

"Not tonight, Lizzie." He put the glasses on and brought her back into focus. "Besides, it's only Lindsay you've heard from, isn't that right?"

"She wants to pick my brain for details of the night my father died."

He halted in the act of reaching for the queen. "What makes you say that?"

"She claims she's been researching his death. I'm sure she wants to know what, if anything, I remember about that night. Or about anything out of the ordinary I might recall during the time leading up to that night. She's hinted at having uncovered some interesting facts—I'm quoting her—which she'll share with me. All I have to do is let her into my life and my head." With a bitter sound, she turned back and parted the blinds to check the street again. It was dark and still. "I don't know what it'll take to convince her that I know nothing. Or even if I did, I don't want to talk about it. I don't want to remember that time. It beats me that she doesn't understand why it's so much more painful to me than it is to her. Or Megan."

"Because they were adopted and you weren't?"

She released the blind and turned to face him. "Is that so odd?"

She didn't wait for his reply. Moving to a small table, she picked up a framed black-and-white photograph of her parents taken at their wedding. Badly damaged, it was dark from smoke and water stains, beyond restoring, although Elizabeth had given it to an expert to try to salvage it. "To tell the truth, Louie, I work at not thinking about that time in my life, but you can't always keep things buried. I've never quite believed in repressed memory. By that, I mean the kind of memory that a person claims they've never let out of the dark box inside them until an event or an experience or someone triggers it. Then suddenly, they recall a murder or a molestation or something so personally traumatic that it just must be exorcised. I simply don't accept that."

"Some people aren't strong enough to face harsh realities, Lizzie."

She shrugged and carefully set the photo back in its place. "If you say so."

"So you do have some memories of that night?"

She gave a short laugh and made a knot of both hands locked together. "Right here in my own personal dark box." But then with a sigh, she dropped back into her chair across the game table from him. "Unfortunately, my demons come swirling up out of that box at the most distressing times."

Louie's hand wasn't quite steady as he stored the chessmen back in their velvet niches. "And this is one of those times?"

"I can almost smell the smoke."

Louie reached for a rook. "You weren't even six years old, Lizzie. You're probably recalling what you were told and your imagination is doing the rest."

"Maybe, but the feeling's there all the same." Too restless to sit, she got up again and went to the window. Still no sign of Gina. "I remember my dad reading me a story that night. He didn't always do that. He was very busy and I think he spent a lot of time in a room that I now know was his study. I took the book down there to ask him to read to me. I missed my mother dreadfully. She had already taught me to read, but I wanted the time with him, you understand?" Frowning, she rubbed her forehead, thinking. "I remember that he was at his desk. Just sitting there. He took me up in his lap and he read the book to me. I don't remember what it was. I wish I did, but it must have been destroyed in the fire."

"It's a good thing you didn't stay in his office."

"Don't you think I've thought of that a million times?" she asked, turning from the window. "If I'd stayed, maybe he wouldn't have lit up that cigar. That's what they said caused the fire, you know. He was smoking at his desk and he must have fallen asleep and the ashes ignited the papers he was working on.''

Louie replaced the final chess piece. "You aren't thinking to take responsibility for your daddy's accident, are you, Lizzie?"

"No, of course not. But as a child, I often replayed the events of that night. If I'd curled up in one of the leather chairs in that room, would it have happened? Maybe I would have noticed him nodding off and rescued the burning cigar.''

"Counseling should have helped you with those feelings." Louie snapped the lock on the chess case. He bent down to stow the case beneath his chair. Archie, sensing tension in the room, whined and looked from one to the other.

"I guess they tried. Maybe I was just locked into my own private little hell. Maybe in the state's underfunded bureaucracy, nobody was particularly noticing a kid who didn't make much noise. Maybe all the counseling in the universe wouldn't have helped." She stroked Archie, soothing him. "Actually, Iris Graham, my caseworker, was more helpful than the overworked psychologists. She seemed to develop a personal interest in both my case and Gina's. It was Iris who suggested I write to my father."

"Why, if your father had died in the fire?" Louie had again removed his glasses and was rubbing his eyes.

"I don't know, really." She was looking thoughtful. "Maybe she knew how devastating it was to lose both my parents within a year of each other and was trying to ease the loss. Or maybe she thought it would be good therapy, who knows? Anyway, I did what she suggested. I wrote letters to my dad...." She paused in stroking Archie, remembering the care and thought she'd taken in telling the judge every little happening in her life. The laugh she gave was soft and bitter. "It wasn't good therapy. It kept me hoping and hoping, you know? That was cruel. I must have written a hundred of those letters and Iris would take each and every one with a promise to put it in the mail. Of course, I knew long before I stopped writing them that it was dumb to write letters to a dead man, but I still did it. I was ten or eleven—definitely old enough to know better—before I finally just quit doing it."

"I'm sure she meant well," Louie said.

"Probably." Archie licked her hand and she bent down to hug him. "But at thirteen, I was pretty angry. And not only with Iris, but with my father, if you can understand that. I would lie in bed at night and scream at him. You can imagine how that went over with some of my foster families. I felt a lot of anger. I hated my sisters. I hated my father for dying. I hated him for setting up a situation where my sisters were given new parents and I was a ward of the state. I hated him for abandoning me to that fate."

She looked up to find Louie watching her through a blur of tears. She managed a laugh, a brief, deprecating dismissal of the pain of that time. "Does that sound sick? I know it was unreasonable, but I really did hate him. Not my mother, because dying in childbirth seemed something beyond a person's control. But to die by carelessly falling asleep with a cigar in your mouth!" She made a disgusted sound. "I still find it hard to forgive him for something so stupid."

"He's probably in hell thinking the same thing."

Now her laugh was soft, more natural-sounding. "I hope not. I've learned to…well, put it in that dark box. But sometimes it just seems to burst open, like a jack-in-the-box. Like tonight."

Louie shoved his chair back. "I believe I need to visit the little boy's room, Lizzie."

"Oh, okay." She watched him rise, his movements stiff and careful. She'd upset him and hadn't meant to. "I shouldn't have gotten carried away like that, Louie."

"I'll just be a minute. Why don't you check your own cell phone? Maybe Gina left a message there, although I can't imagine why she'd do that instead of calling...." His voice trailed off as he disappeared down the hall. Elizabeth heard the sound of the door of the powder room closing. She sat down abruptly. She'd broken a rule, talking about her father and the fire, dredging up old ghosts. What had gotten into her? She never did that.

As Louie suggested, she picked up her cell phone and turned it on. Gina would have no reason to call it, knowing Elizabeth wouldn't be away from the house. Still...she watched it go through a series of electronic tricks before indicating its readiness. As she expected, no messages.

She looked up as Louie returned. His face was drawn with fatigue and his color was off. "You should go home, Louie. It's so late. I'll call you when Gina returns, if you like."

"I'm staying, Lizzie."

She knew that tone and didn't bother arguing. "I think I'll try her cell phone again."

"You're sure she has it with her?"

"I saw her put it in her bag." She replaced her cell phone and picked up the cordless which had stayed within reach on the game table while they played. Gina's number was programmed and she punched the button. Voice mail kicked in instantly. Disconnecting without bothering to add another message to the numerous ones she'd already left, she looked at Louie. "Do you think I should call Ryan Paxton?"

Louie stepped carefully over Archie, who lay sprawled

on the floor now, and settled back in his chair. "Why would you do that?"

"He would probably have Austin's cell phone number." But would he give it to her, even if he had it? She felt a rising sense of panic. Gina knew Elizabeth would be concerned by the lateness of the hour and she wouldn't have turned off her cell phone. Besides, it was a school night for Jesse, another point Gina wouldn't ignore. It was difficult for the little girl to get up if she didn't get to bed by nine at the latest. It was now long past that time.

"It's worth a try."

"What?" She looked blankly at Louie.

"Paxton." Louie leaned his head back against the ladder back of the chair and closed his eyes. Lately it seemed he was showing his age more and more. Elizabeth had been urging him to have a checkup. He hadn't refused outright, he'd just put her off. She made a mental note to get him in to a doctor soon, no matter what.

"Louie, please go home and get some rest."

"I'm not going anywhere 'til we hear from Gina," he said stubbornly. "As you say, Austin would have given his lawyer his cell number. What's interesting is that you'd want to call him."

She didn't *want* to, did she? Except that she was desperate. She'd thought about having a conversation with Ryan more than once since he'd dropped by out of the blue a few days ago. He'd seemed genuinely concerned about Jesse, although she didn't know if he was truly convinced yet that Austin was dangerous. And because he wasn't convinced, she'd resisted calling.

"We can't just sit here and do nothing, Louie." She looked at the clock again as Archie got up and shook himself vigorously. "Gina knows we worry, especially when she's with Austin."

"You've convinced me, Lizzie. Call him."

"It's pretty late," she said, picking up the phone with some hesitation. "What can he do except hang up on me?"

Louie got up, joints popping, and opened the French doors to let Archie outside. "You have his number?"

"He's been calling me lately claiming we can work this out more amicably without going through the courts." Unaware of Louie's surprise on hearing that, she began scrolling through Caller ID on her phone. Ryan had left several messages she'd ignored, but his number should still be in the phone's memory. Sure enough, it came up and with no more wavering, she punched it in, thinking it would serve her right if her call got the same treatment she'd given him. She put the phone to her ear and listened while it rang.

"I wonder why he'd do that?" Louie mused, scratching his beard thoughtfully.

Elizabeth still felt some skepticism, but tonight she was willing to forgo doubt as to Ryan's motives. "For Jesse's sake, or so he claims."

Ryan stirred, resisting the strident sound of the alarm. With a groan, he fumbled for the snooze bar on his clock and missed, knocking it off the bedside table onto the floor. It didn't kill the sound. Then he identified the noise as coming from the television. He'd fallen asleep watching the news. Swearing, he sat up, rubbed both hands over his face and realized it wasn't the television or the alarm ringing, but the telephone.

On the floor, the red numbers displayed the time. Eleven oh nine. Who the hell— Then he realized it must be somebody calling Jennifer. Didn't these kids ever sleep? Jesus. Growling like a bear routed out of hibernation, he reached for the phone and barked into it. "Paxton. And make it good."

"Ryan? It's Elizabeth Walker."

Elizabeth? Elizabeth Walker. Ryan came awake abruptly and sat up on the side of the bed.

"Hello? Ryan?"

"I'm here." It came out a croak. He cleared his throat, tried again. "Yeah, Elizabeth. What's up?"

"I'm sorry to disturb you so late, but—"

"Not a problem. I was…uh…" Forty fathoms deep in sleep. He blinked strongly a couple of times, trying to think. "Is something wrong?"

"Do you have Austin Leggett's cell phone number?"

"Austin's—" He stopped, frowned. "Why?"

"Because Gina left with him this evening and they should have been back hours ago. I'm worried. I've tried calling her cell, but I keep getting her voice mail. She wouldn't just ignore a call from me."

He took a deep breath. "She would if she didn't want to talk right now, Liz."

It was a moment before she caught his meaning. "I don't think anything like that is going on."

"Really?"

"Look, could you just give me his number. Please."

"You know I can't do that, Liz. It would be a violation of my client's rights." He stood up, ran a hand over his hair and clamped it to the back of his neck. "Hell, maybe they're working things out after all. In their own way. Take my advice, go back to bed and—"

"I haven't even been to bed yet! How can I go back, damn it!" She paused to bring herself under control. "Look, Ryan. Please. This is very disturbing. Gina wouldn't stay out so late without calling me. Or even if she forgot to call, she wouldn't ignore her phone if it rang. I've tried several times and—''

"Maybe she has it turned off, Liz. It happens."

"Not when she has Jesse with her."

Ryan had wandered to the bathroom and was now looking at himself in the mirror. "Jesse? They have Jesse with them?"

"Yes, yes. That's another reason I'm so concerned. I don't like the idea of Gina being alone with him, but nothing I said changed her mind." She drew a shaky breath. "But there's Jesse—" He heard the tiny catch in her voice, but she sounded in control when she spoke again. "They should have been back by now or at the very least called."

"Okay. Okay." He left the bathroom and made his way across the floor to the armoire. On top lay everything he'd emptied from his pockets: keys, his wallet thick with credit cards, loose change, somebody's loose business card, a tiny penknife, a money clip and his cell phone. He picked it up, turned it on and began scrolling.

"Ryan?"

"I'm here." Squinting—damn, he couldn't see shit— he selected a number and put the phone to his other ear. "Hold on while I try to reach Austin. I've got a couple of numbers here besides his office line." After five rings at home, Austin's voice mail kicked in. Ryan left a brief message to call back, no matter what time. Then he dialed Austin's cell where, again, he got a voice message. He left the same call-back message, disconnected and tossed the cell phone on the bed.

"I don't seem to be able to raise him, Liz." He sank down on the mattress. "Do you know what their plans were for tonight?"

"Dinner, but I don't know where."

"You're sure she would be aware that you're worried?"

"Yes!" Again she tried to subdue her tone. "Yes, especially since she has Jesse with her."

He stared at his bare feet, wincing at her distress. He found himself wishing he could think of a way to reassure her. Where the hell were they anyway? And what was Austin up to now? If the son of a bitch did anything more than buy Gina and Jesse dinner and pay for a movie, he'd live to regret it. Even more inexplicable was that Gina risked leaving with him after what they claimed he'd done the last time they were alone together. The woman was asking for trouble!

"I tried to talk her out of going," Elizabeth said, as if picking up on his thoughts, "but she insisted that refusing would only irritate him and he could be very nasty when irritated."

"What time did they leave?"

"Around seven-thirty."

A sound brought his gaze around to the door of his bedroom. Jennifer stood watching him. Listening. She was swallowed up in one of his double-X size T-shirts, looking sleepy-eyed and very young. "I don't know what to tell you, Liz. You'll just have to wait it out. They'll probably show up any minute."

There was a long moment of silence. "Yes, well…thanks anyway." With a soft click, she hung up.

"I heard the phone," Jennifer said. "I thought it might be Mom."

"No, it was…a friend." He stood up, pulling at the low-riding Joe Boxers he'd been forced to sleep in since Jennifer moved in.

"I thought she wasn't a friend." She blew at a strand of blond hair near her mouth.

"Who?"

She rolled her eyes. "Dad. I heard you call her Liz. That's Elizabeth Walker. I was with you when we popped by her house unannounced the other day, remember?"

He crossed the room toward her. "Okay, she's not exactly a friend, but she's not a client either. That call was half business."

"What does that mean?"

"She needed information, Jen. You don't need to know more."

"Because it's none of my business, right? Like I'm still a kid, no matter what the subject is. That's the way Mom treats me and now you, too! When will I be old enough, when I'm forty-five?"

"This is not about withholding information from you, Jennifer. The call doesn't concern you. Case closed."

"Ooo, the lawyer again." She shook the fingers of one hand, her mouth twisting with sarcasm. Then suddenly, there was a new look on her face, a dawning thought that widened her eyes. "I know! She's hot for you. That's why she called. Wow, am I a dork. I should have seen it when we were at her house a few days ago."

"Well, you see a helluva lot more than I see," he muttered, gritting his teeth at her impudence. He caught her arm, turned her and marched her down the hall. "Liz barely speaks to me."

"The oldest trick in the world."

Lord, how old was she? Fifteen going on thirty-five? He sighed, wondering if he was up to the challenge of coping with a teenager, even temporarily. They stopped at her bedroom door. "Get to bed, Jen. Tomorrow's a school day. It'll hurt when that alarm goes off."

She freed herself, but couldn't resist a parting shot as Ryan turned to leave. "I'm telling Mom."

* * *

The call came not long after Elizabeth spoke to Ryan. No matter how much she'd insisted, Louie had refused to leave until Gina and Jesse got back. And he had refused to lie down until she did so. So she'd stretched out on the sofa in the den, wrapped in an old afghan, not so much for its warmth, but for its soft familiarity while Louie lay on the sofa's matching twin. But lying still had proved impossible. It had been torture to wait until she heard Louie's breathing deepen into sleep, then she'd thrown the afghan aside with relief and escaped quietly to the kitchen where she made herself a cup of tea and then sat letting it grow cold…waiting.

Her heart had stopped, literally, when the phone rang. She grabbed for it, jostling the cup in its saucer and splashing tea on the table. Ignoring the mess, she stared at the number and name displayed. Hermann Hospital. With her heart pounding, she fumbled with the talk button. "Hello."

"Elizabeth Walker?"

"Yes." Standing now, Elizabeth pressed a hand to her middle.

"This is Megan Blackstone, Elizabeth. I'm a resident in the Trauma Center at Hermann Hospital."

In some distant corner of her mind, Elizabeth registered the name, but only in the most vague sense. "Gina," she said in panic. "Is it about Gina?"

"I'm afraid so," Megan said in a gentle tone. "There has been an accident."

"An accident." Elizabeth repeated the word while her mind shrieked denial.

"Yes. A car accident. Can you come to the hospital now? Do you have transportation?"

"Jesse." With her hand at her throat, she managed to ask, "What about Jesse?"

"Is that a little girl, dark hair and eyes? Five or six years old?"

"Five. Yes. That's Jesse. Gina's daughter."

"Jesse appears unhurt. Just some bumps and bruises." Megan took a deep breath. "Is there someone to drive you, Elizabeth?"

"I...yes. No." She licked her lips. "It doesn't matter. I'll get there. How—how bad is it?"

"We really aren't sure yet," Megan said, speaking softly, her tone rich with concern. "Just...if I were you, I'd hurry."

Twelve

The Trauma Center at Hermann Hospital was packed with people when Elizabeth arrived. She scanned the faces of medical personnel, seeking someone to tell her where Gina and Jesse were. Finding nobody else, she headed for a clerk who sat behind a desk in the admissions zone. "I'm Elizabeth Walker. I had a call from…ah, Megan Blackstone that my—my friend, Gina D'Angelo, is here. With Jesse, her little girl. They've been in an accident. I'd like to see them, please."

"Gina… What's the last name again?"

"D'Angelo. Gina D'Angelo. And Jesse. Jesse Leggett. I had a call—"

"Uh-huh." The clerk wore a blue name tag with Lashanda printed on it. Without looking up, she ran one of her long, bloodred acrylic nails down a list. While Elizabeth agonized, Lashanda finally found what she was looking for. "She's in Trauma Six. If you'll have a seat, someone—"

"Please. I was told it was urgent. If you could page Megan—"

"I'm sorry, but you'll have to wait for one of the staff."

"She is staff! She called me. She—"

"Elizabeth."

Elizabeth turned at the sound of her name. She knew instantly that it was Megan Blackstone. She was tall, dark-haired and serenely beautiful. Her eyes were a luminous gray and her face was so like pictures of their mother that for a moment, Elizabeth could only stare.

"I'm sorry that we have to meet this way." Megan put out her hand, her features soft with sympathy. "I'm Megan Blackstone."

"I'm here for Gina," Elizabeth said, trying to read more in Megan's expression as she took the extended hand. Lately, she had been curious about the second of her biological sisters, but in her anxiety over Gina and Jesse, Megan was now simply a medical person and a source of information.

"I'm doing a trauma rotation, and tonight, when they came in, I knew who they were, of course." Megan wore plum-colored hospital scrubs and paper booties on her shoes that meant she'd come straight from a treatment room.

"Yes. Is Gina okay?" Elizabeth wrapped her arms about her waist, prepared for she knew not what. Then, before Megan could tell her, someone came up behind her and a strong, male arm settled around her shoulders, squeezing reassuringly.

"Here you are." It was Ryan Paxton's deep voice. "Austin called me," he explained at her startled look.

Her reaction amazed her. She felt a crazy urge to simply lean into him. He was tall and warm and real. If she was about to hear horrible news, she would need— She would need help—maybe—but not from someone whose loyalty was to Austin!

Withdrawing so that his arm fell away, she drew herself up with a deep, deep breath and looked directly into Megan Blackstone's eyes. "Please, I'm not going to fall apart. Is Gina... Has she been...killed?"

"Gina is alive," Megan said.

Elizabeth's knees went weak, but only for a second. "And Jesse?"

"We can talk in here." Megan motioned them inside a small room. She waited as Ryan urged Elizabeth to sit on the sofa, then took a seat beside her. He didn't attempt to touch her again, but sat close, almost protectively.

Megan sat, too, in a chair opposite them.

"What about Jesse?" Elizabeth repeated.

"Jesse was banged up some. She's having a CAT scan as we speak. Just as a precaution," she added when Elizabeth looked alarmed. "She appears to be in good shape."

"But Gina isn't?"

Megan's face was grave as she sought for the right words. "We aren't quite sure the extent of Gina's injuries yet. There is extensive head trauma and her left arm is broken. There's internal bleeding, probably from a punctured lung. Of course, that's just a guess at this point. But we'll need to find the source. As for the brain trauma, that will require surgery."

"Then she's not conscious?"

"No. She was unconscious when the EMTs arrived on the scene and she remains unresponsive." Megan reached out and touched Elizabeth's knee. "It doesn't look good, Elizabeth. As it stands, she is in critical condition."

Elizabeth pressed fingers to her lips to keep from crying out. She felt Ryan's arm steal around her shoulders again. And again, she felt a weak, needy urge to take a time-out, just until she could absorb what Megan was telling her. But there was no time-out and no escaping the fact that Gina could be dying. She straightened and tried to speak around the knot of fear in her throat. "Will she survive, do you think?"

"Only God knows." Megan was shaking her head slowly. "It's so hard to say at this point considering the scope of her injuries. I've seen patients in worse shape survive, but to tell you the truth, only rarely. And the prognosis for the future is often pretty bleak.''

Elizabeth closed her eyes for a second. ''Brain damage,'' she murmured. When, after a long moment, there was no reply, she asked, ''Does anyone know what happened?''

Ryan spoke for the first time. ''Austin was there.''

Austin. Of course. ''He called you?''

''Yeah, not fifteen minutes after you hung up the phone. I tried to reach you, but apparently you'd already left for the hospital.''

''What did he say?''

''They were in separate cars after leaving the restaurant. Austin was following to see that they got home safely.''

Elizabeth couldn't prevent a twist of her lips at the thought of a chivalrous Austin Leggett, but she said nothing.

''It happened on Memorial Drive. You're familiar with Memorial, right?'' At her numb nod, he went on, ''It twists and turns and it's pretty narrow in places. According to Austin, Gina was going at a good clip. She lost control somehow, ran off the road and slammed into a tree. Austin was unable to free them from the car and had to leave briefly to get help. The road was pretty deserted at that hour.''

''And where is he now?'' Not with Gina or Jesse, she'd bet. He would be busy fabricating his version of the accident.

''He's with the police filling out a report of the accident.''

And probably rejoicing over the possibility of fate taking a problem off his hands if Gina died, Elizabeth thought bitterly. But it took too much energy to dwell on Austin just now. She dismissed him from her mind. It was Gina and Jesse who mattered. "When will we know something?" she asked, turning again to Megan.

"About Jesse...probably very soon—when she's done with the CAT scan. As for Gina, I wish I could give you an answer, but with injuries such as hers, it's almost impossible. There's going to be some swelling of the brain, which in itself is a serious danger. She needs to get into surgery as soon as possible. First and foremost, we need to try and stop the internal bleeding. We'll know more after that."

"I want to see her."

"And I understand that. I really do." Again, Megan looked sympathetic. "But there's no time just now. She's surrounded by a trauma team and everyone is focused on saving her life." She stood up. "I know you're anxious, but until she's out of surgery, we won't even know the extent of her injuries."

"And you're sure Jesse's all right?"

She sat down again with a smile. "Nothing's sure in this business, but I saw her myself and there were no obvious injuries other than a bruise or two. Is she very shy?"

"Shy? No, not really." Elizabeth glanced at Ryan. "Why? What does that have to do with anything?"

Megan's smile faded. "We tried several times to get her to tell us whether she felt any pain, but she wouldn't answer. Usually we can get a child's name and frequently their age, but Jesse refused to talk." Two lines appeared as her brows drew together in a frown. "It happens sometimes when a child is traumatized, which is certainly the case here. At any rate, as soon as she has that CAT scan, providing we find nothing wrong, I'll see that she's brought here to you. That should reassure her. She can probably go home.''

''Is there someone to leave her with at your house?'' Ryan asked.

Elizabeth looked at him blankly. She'd almost forgotten he was there. ''What?''

''Is there someone she can stay with? I'm assuming you'll want to be at the hospital tonight until Gina comes out of her surgery, right?''

''Oh. Yes, of course.'' Elizabeth put a hand to her forehead and tried to think. ''Louie. He came with me to the hospital. He dropped me at the entrance then went to find a place to park the car. He'll stay with her. Next to Gina or me, Jesse would choose Louie.''

''I'm here, Lizzie.''

Everyone turned as Louie came into the room. His face was creased with concern as Elizabeth stood up. One look at her and he opened his arms. ''Is it bad?'' he asked, taking her into a bear hug of an embrace. He seemed to take no notice of anyone else.

''I think he's killed her, Louie,'' Elizabeth said, her control breaking now. Here at last was someone she could safely lean on. Burying her face in his shoulder, she gave in to despairing sobs. ''I told her not to go! I knew he was dangerous, but she was afraid of what he'd do if she refused.''

''Gina's dead?'' Over her head, he looked piercingly at Megan, her scrubs identifying her as the only medical person in the room.

''No, but she's critical,'' Megan told him.

''And Jesse?'' Louie looked suddenly grave. The hand stroking Elizabeth's back went still.

''She's having a CAT scan,'' Elizabeth managed with

a swipe at her nose. On his feet now, Ryan took a box of tissues from a table and offered them.

"Here, sit down, Lizzie." Louie urged her back to the settee and sat down beside her while she dabbed at her face with the tissues. "Now, give me some details. What about Gina? Will she make it?"

"This is the person to ask," Elizabeth said, with a look at Megan. "Dr. Blackstone says it's impossible to tell right now."

Louie shot another glance at Megan's name tag, taking note of it. He looked keenly into her face. "Is that right, Dr. Blackstone?"

"Yes. Gina's critical, but Jesse—as far as I'm able to tell—seems fine. But to double check, we're giving her a CAT scan, as Elizabeth said. Now," she moved to the door, "I've given everyone as much information as I know. I need to get back to Gina."

"You do your best, Doctor," Louie said, as Elizabeth blew her nose. She'd probably shocked him and Megan with her outburst about Austin, but it was true. She knew he was responsible and knew, too, that he would go to his grave denying it. "Gina's special to us," Louie told Megan. "And her little girl needs her. So you keep that in mind as you do your job, you hear?"

"Yes. Yes, I will." Her tone quiet and confident, Megan gave them the briefest of smiles. But at the door, she paused and looked back at Elizabeth. "I meant it when I said I wish we'd met under happier circumstances, Elizabeth. I'm so sorry it had to be this way."

Elizabeth pressed damp tissues to her mouth. "Just don't let her die. Please."

It was a promise no doctor could make. Megan said instead, "There's a chapel on this floor. It never closes.

In case you need help from someone with far more power than a doctor.''

"Thank you." Elizabeth felt her throat go tight with the threat of more tears.

"Blackstone," Louie said, his gaze lingering on the doorway after Megan was gone. "So that's your sister, eh, Lizzie?"

Sitting back on the settee, Elizabeth rested her head against the wall. "It seems so," she said.

"Funny the way things work out," Louie said, stroking his beard. His expression was unreadable as he watched the door.

"Yeah, funny." She'd already upset him once tonight blabbing about her childhood. She wasn't getting into that again.

"Good to have Jesse and Gina in the hands of your own flesh and blood," Louie said now, giving her a keen look.

"Let it go, Louie," she said and turned her face to the wall.

Elizabeth hated hospitals. Her very earliest memory had been the day she'd waited in the hospital with her father while her mother gave birth. She remembered going to the newborn nursery and being lifted up to look in the wide window where the babies were displayed like so many wrapped peaches in specially formed trays. They all looked alike to her, except some were in pink blankets and some in blue blankets. If her father had pointed out their new baby, she didn't recall it, although he must have. Then, the next time she'd been in the hospital, it was to await the birth of another baby barely a year later. Only that time she had been robbed of her mother. She didn't recall leaving the hospital or being told that her mother had died. She just recalled being at home with a stranger who said Elizabeth could call her Nana. A year later, there was the fire and she was told that her father had died in a hospital.

She felt the same deep foreboding now as then.

Thirteen

"Jesse should be finished with her CAT scan by now, don't you think?" Elizabeth rose from the settee to take a worried look down the hall. Seeing nothing, she glanced at the clock on the wall. Another half hour had passed with no word about Gina or Jesse.

"You'd swear the clock stopped by the way time slows down in a hospital," Louie said, offering her a can of cola. "Here, a little sugar and caffeine'll buck you up some. Megan would let us know if anything was wrong, Lizzie. Try not to worry."

Ryan had been aware of the older man's solicitous attitude to Liz since the moment he'd entered the waiting room. Louie clearly had a soft spot for her and from his reaction when he'd heard about Gina and Jesse, he cared for them, as well. Why else would he be here in the hospital in the middle of the night? Even so, it seemed his efforts weren't making much difference. Elizabeth couldn't manage anything close to a smile to reassure him.

"It's impossible not to worry until Gina's out of the woods, Louie." Her voice had a smokey, sexy quality after that spate of crying. In her anxiety, she kept running her hands through her hair. It was now a tangle of rich, auburn curls framing her face. A beautiful face, he found himself thinking, even without makeup. He'd never seen her looking anything but buttoned up and unapproachable in a man-tailored suit or in a crisp shirt and trim pants. Caught off guard by the call from Megan, she'd thrown on well-worn jeans and a soft T-shirt. The effect was more to Ryan's taste.

Damn! He got up from the chair and walked to the door. He thought of Jennifer's suspicions that Liz had a thing for him and decided that his little girl had it backward. He was more attracted to Liz than she ever could be to him, in spite of what he knew of their connection through her father.

"You have to put a good face on it," Louie cautioned her now, "for Jesse's sake."

"Yeah," Ryan said, deciding to throw in his two cents. "Be careful making rash statements about Austin killing her as you did a few minutes ago. First of all, she's alive, not dead, and even if she doesn't survive, making accusations like that could land you in some very serious trouble."

"Austin may have a good story," she said with color flaring in her cheeks. "In fact, he's probably working on it right now, but you'll never convince me that the accident happened the way he'll tell it."

"Shouldn't you hear it before condemning him?" Ryan asked.

"I don't believe we've met," Louie said, standing now and looking at Ryan.

Ryan put out his hand. "Ryan Paxton."

"Austin's lawyer," Elizabeth explained as they shook.

"Well, he's got to have one," Louie said with his usual lack of rancor. "Everybody does, even abusive bastards."

Ryan shot a keen look at the old man. "You have proof of that?"

"Nothing that would hold up in a court of law," Louie said, sinking back onto the settee. "If I did, I'd've testified

to it to Judge Hetherington. As it is, I only have my ob-
servations of that girl for the past five years or so that I've
known her. Had the look of an abused woman, if you
know what I mean.''

"Not really," Ryan said, intrigued by something about
Louie Christian. "I don't have many acquaintances who
go around abusing their wives and children."

"Gina wasn't his wife," Elizabeth said, in a bitter tone.
"And he never had any intention of marrying her."

"Do you think she knew that?"

"I think she was in denial over everything about Austin."

"Even though you say he was frequently violent? What
was going on that she stayed in the relationship for so
long? Why didn't she walk away after the first time?"

"Good question." Louie stood at the door looking toward the elevators down the hall. "Why don't you ask
Austin himself? He just got out of the elevator and he's
heading this way."

A moment later, Austin appeared. His expression was
appropriately grave as he glanced briefly at the three people in the room. "I was told everyone was in here," he
said to Ryan, speaking in a somber tone. "Did you tell
them what happened?"

"Yeah, as much as I knew…which wasn't a lot." Ryan
let a moment of silence linger. "Do you have any news
or did you come straight from HPD?"

"About Gina? No. You know how hospitals are, especially the ER. They don't tell you squat." Austin raked
fingers through his hair, then rubbed both hands over his
face. "God, this is a nightmare."

"Gina's critical, Austin," Elizabeth said. "She might
not make it."

"Jesus." He sat down abruptly and dropped his head in his hands.

"Was she upset when you left the restaurant?"

"Upset?" He raised his head and looked directly at her. "No. What makes you think she was upset?"

"Ryan said she was driving too fast. She knows Memorial Drive well. She knows it twists and winds and that it's not always well lit at night. She wouldn't drive recklessly unless there was a good reason. What did you do to upset her?"

Austin looked suddenly at Ryan. "What the hell did you tell them? She got in the goddamned car and drove like a maniac because that's the way she acts after a few drinks. She hit a tree."

Elizabeth looked at him coldly. "You're saying she was drunk, Austin?"

"I'm saying she had a few drinks."

"She wouldn't get drunk while Jesse was with her. So something else must have been going on."

"Well, if something else was going on, I don't know about it. We had dinner, we talked a little in the parking lot, then we both got in our cars and left." He glanced at Ryan. "Hell, I even followed them to be sure they got home okay."

"But you didn't think she was too drunk to risk your daughter's safety then," Elizabeth questioned, openly sarcastic. "Is that what you're saying?"

"I'm saying I could have misjudged whether she was drunk or not."

"And speaking of Jesse," Elizabeth said deliberately, "you haven't asked about her. Or do you care?"

He looked quickly from Elizabeth to Louie to Ryan. "She's okay, isn't she? I mean, when we got her out of the car, she didn't seem to have any injuries. A scratch or two, kinda shaken up, but nothing else. She wasn't even crying.''

''Maybe she was in shock, Austin,'' Elizabeth said through set teeth.

''Where is she now?'' He looked around as if he might have missed her in the room.

''She's having a CAT scan,'' Ryan said, moving to the door. ''Why don't you and I step out into the hall and discuss the arrangements for Jesse. If—''

Elizabeth was suddenly on her feet. ''What do you mean, arrangements?''

''He means arrangements for taking Jesse home with me,'' Austin said with spite. ''Where she belongs.''

Ignoring Austin, Elizabeth appealed to Ryan. ''Don't let him do this, Ryan. If you'd seen her when they left tonight, you'd know that turning her over to Austin is the worst thing that could happen. She's traumatized already by the accident and by seeing Gina so badly hurt. She needs to be with Louie and me right now.''

''She needs to be with me!'' Austin said, and shook off the hand Ryan put on his shoulder.

''She screamed and begged Gina not to make her go with her father tonight, Ryan,'' Elizabeth said, still ignoring Austin. ''Please do the right thing.''

Austin's face went tight with fury. ''Hey, I don't have to hang around and take this kind of shit, Ryan. Do any of you realize that I've been through hell tonight, too? I'm taking my kid home with me...where she belongs, as I said before. Where she's always belonged.''

''Ryan—'' Elizabeth's eyes clung to his. Her hand was at her throat as if something threatened her ability to breathe. ''Please believe me. Jesse refused to get in his car just to ride to the restaurant. They finally forced her into Gina's. She didn't want to go! What does that tell you?''

Louie had been silent and watchful, but now he spoke up. "Lizzie's right, Ryan. I can vouch for that. For some reason, Jesse has been reluctant to see or talk about her daddy lately. It seems best for Austin to leave her in Lizzie's care just until the first fright of this night has eased somewhat. For the sake of the little girl.''

"C'mon, Ryan, we're wasting time here." Unmoved by anything said so far, Austin took a few steps, but Ryan put up a hand to delay him and spoke to Elizabeth.

"When I mentioned arrangements for Jesse, it was my intention to suggest she stay with you, Liz. I—"

"What the hell!" Austin exploded, looking ready to square off to Ryan. "Who're you representing here, for chrissake?"

Ryan's stare would have stopped a speeding train. His patience with his client was wearing thin and it showed on his face. Austin must have seen it. He swallowed whatever else he wanted to say and turned away in disgust. "Give me a few minutes with Austin, okay?" Ryan said to Elizabeth.

She finally nodded reluctantly, then watched as Ryan urged Austin ahead of him with a not-so-gentle nudge. Austin, sputtering and furious, shifted away irritably, then as if to demonstrate he wasn't going to be maneuvered, picked up his pace and stalked off down the hall. With a last apologetic backward glance, Ryan followed.

Neither Austin nor Ryan noticed as Lindsay stepped hurriedly from the elevator. She paused to get her bearings, breathing hard as if she'd been running. Spotting the waiting room, she rushed directly to it, startling Elizabeth and Louie. She dropped her shoulder bag on the floor and went to Elizabeth.

"Megan called me," Lindsay explained, putting a hand on her heart. "'Scuse me, I'm out of breath. I jogged all the way from the parking lot." Pushing aside an old issue of *Time* magazine, she sat down beside Elizabeth. "She told me about Gina's accident. I got here as soon as I could. How is she?" She reached for Elizabeth's limp hand and brought it to her cheek. Her blue eyes were soft with sympathy. "I'm so sorry. Have you heard anything?"

Had the accident to Gina happened a few weeks ago, Elizabeth would have been cool to Lindsay for just showing up and assuming she had a right to be here. But tonight, she was too bombarded with emotion. Sympathy and concern on the part of her sister was hard to resist. Later, when she had more energy, she would reestablish boundaries. "No, we're still waiting," she said.

"That's so tough, isn't it?" Lindsay was now stroking Elizabeth's arm.

"Yes." Elizabeth felt tears start to her eyes. She should move away, but somehow…

"Maybe Megan can give us an update," Lindsay suggested in the tone of someone used to demanding results. "Have you seen her?"

"Yes, but it's been…awhile. I think she's with Gina…in surgery." She touched a tissue to her nose and blew gently. "Right now, we're waiting for someone to tell us about Jesse."

Lindsay frowned. "Megan said Jesse was okay. Has something happened to change that?"

"Who knows?" Elizabeth said.

"I'm afraid we're out of the loop," Louie said.

Lindsay glanced at him as if seeing him for the first time. She smiled, but it was nothing like her usual celebrity-bright greeting. There was curiosity with a hint of puzzlement as she noted the ease that existed between the old man and Elizabeth. She leaned forward, putting out her hand. "Hello, I'm Lindsay Blackstone, Elizabeth's sister."

"Hello, yourself." Louie got to his feet, ignoring the polite sounds she made that it wasn't necessary and took her hand. He studied her face with the same intense look he'd given Megan. "Louie Christian, Elizabeth's neighbor."

"I'm glad there's someone here to be with her," Lindsay said, before turning back to Elizabeth. "A hospital waiting room is a lonely place, isn't it?"

"Very."

"Seems like we've been here days instead of hours," Louie said. "Time's moving about as fast as a gallstone."

Lindsay chuckled softly. "I don't think I've ever heard that one."

"Stick around," Elizabeth murmured, managing her first near-smile since she left her house. "He's got a million more where that came from."

"Watch out," Louie said, shaking a finger at her. "I'll copyright 'em and then you won't be able to steal 'em and put 'em in your books."

"Is he the source for those hokey sayings in *Sophia's Secret*? I got such a kick out of them."

"Been reading your sister's books, have you?" Louie looked pleased.

"Of course. I just finished *Sophia's Christmas Gift*," she said, turning to Elizabeth. "It was wonderful. Sensitive and funny."

"Thank you." It was a distracted response. Elizabeth's worried gaze strayed again to the door. Seeing it, Lindsay rose and checked for activity in the hall. "I think I'll try to get a progress report on Jesse." She gave them both a little wave. "Watch my bag, will you. Back in a jiff."

"I'm gonna feel foolish if she's successful," Louie said, watching her stride down the hall. "Us sitting here on our thumbs for the last hour and she waltzes in there and comes out holding Jesse's hand."

"She's a reporter," Elizabeth said, again feeling a wave of bone-deep weariness. Fear for Gina and worry about Jesse were taking a toll. "She's supposed to get results."

Louie rose to take a look down the hall for himself. "Uh-oh, brace yourself. Austin's back."

"Is he alone?" Elizabeth shook off fatigue and stood up.

"His lawyer's still with him, which I take as a good sign."

Maybe. Maybe not. In spite of the force of Ryan's personality, she wasn't counting on anybody being able to reason with Austin tonight. She stuffed the tissue deep into the pocket of her jeans, then smoothed a hand over her hair and tried to compose herself. Austin would seize upon any trace of tears or exhaustion as a sign of weakness.

It was Ryan who spoke. "Any word on Gina or Jesse yet?"

"No."

Ryan gave her a sharp look. "You look about ready to collapse, Liz. There's a vending machine with coffee down the hall. You want some?"

"I'm okay." So much for trying to look calm and collected.

"I insist."

Something in his tone made her bite off another irritable refusal. "Why, am I going to need it?" she asked, glancing at Austin, who merely shrugged with indifference.

"You've been cooped up in here for hours," Ryan said,

catching her firmly by the elbow. "C'mon, if you don't want coffee, you can at least stretch your legs."

His hand was warm and bracing. Oddly, she no longer felt skittish at being touched by him. "What if Jesse comes back?"

"The vending machines are near the elevators. We'll watch for Jesse."

"I promise not to kidnap her," Austin said with sarcasm.

Louie, thumbing through an ancient magazine, looked up. "Go, Liz. I wouldn't mind something wet and cold myself, but none of that diet stuff. I'll holler if Jesse comes back." He ignored Austin's remark.

After another moment, she nodded and went with Ryan. Actually, it felt good to be walking around a bit. Her head felt stuffed with cotton and her eyes burned as if they'd been washed with acid. She kneaded the small of her back as they passed the bank of elevators, still in sight of everyone in the waiting area. Beyond that was a small snack room with several vending machines. Ryan nudged her toward the first one, waited while she studied the choices, and then slipped a dollar bill into the slot.

"What'll it be?"

"Diet cola, please," she said. "And root beer for Louie. He loves it."

"But not diet." Ryan's mouth tilted in a half smile as he pulled the cans from the machine.

"He's almost a sugar junkie," Elizabeth said, still kneading the stiffness from the small of her back. "We nag him about it all the time, Gina especially. She's always—" She stopped as her throat went tight.

"Here, let me do that." Ryan put the cans of soda on top of the vending machine, then gently turned Elizabeth around. Before she could object, his hands were on her shoulders and both thumbs were pressing the knotted muscles along her spine. She made a tiny sound as he began a mesmerizing massage. "I—"

"Don't talk," he ordered in a low tone. "And don't think for a minute. Just relax...."

God, it felt so good. As for relaxing, she wasn't about to— Oh, now his fingers were seeking other places made tight and sore by stress. And she was allowing it. His huge hands, warm and strong, easily spanned her waist, found the small of her back and with his thumbs smoothed the soreness out of the muscles there. Then he moved skillfully up her spine and settled at her neck again where his fingers eased up, up, up into her nape. Nerves stimulated by his touch released such a rush of sensation that it stole the strength from her knees. If there had been a couch handy, she would have collapsed on it. Her head fell forward of its own volition.

"Feel good?" His voice, very close to her ear, held a smile.

That broke the spell. It was a spell, wasn't it? How else to explain that she'd lost sense of time and place for a minute? Maybe more. She straightened up, took in a breath, tried again for the second time in a short while to compose her face, then reached blindly for the can of diet cola still resting on the vending machine.

"You must have some professional training as a masseuse," she said, busying herself with the ring top on the can so she wouldn't have to look at him. "That was extremely...ah, pleasant."

"It's even more pleasant if you're naked."

That brought her eyes up to his in shock. "What?"

"To give a proper massage, one should be naked." Holding her gaze, he took a long swallow of his drink.

For a long second or two, she watched his throat as he drank. Strong, tan, so…male.

"We need to get back." She grabbed Louie's root beer and turned to go.

"Wait." Still smiling, he stepped in front of her, halting her. "I'm sorry, I shouldn't tease you, especially tonight when you've got so many serious things on your mind. I wanted to get you away from Austin to tell you what he agreed to."

His words banished everything else from her mind. "Tell me." She held the cans tight against her chest.

"He's agreed to let Louie take Jesse home tonight."

She released a disgusted sigh. "I'm underwhelmed, to say the least. Where else would she go tonight? He's forced, more or less, to stay here at least until Gina is out of surgery. There's no one at his house to leave her with."

"Granted." Ryan nodded. "But he probably could make a good argument to the court to get full custody while Gina recovers—"

"If she recovers."

"Yes, there's that possibility."

"And if she doesn't, possession is nine-tenths of the law."

"Not necessarily, Liz. Listen." He put a hand on her waist and guided her out of the tiny room. "I have a better idea of who Austin is now than when I took on the case. But you may have to face reality. He's Jesse's father and with Gina incapacitated, he wants her."

"He doesn't want her! Can't you get that through your head? It's a way of avoiding the financial burden the court has decreed. If, God forbid, something happens to Gina, I want Jesse…just because she's Jesse and I love her. I don't care about the cost."

"You don't think Austin loves his own child?"

She looked at him. "You want an honest answer? No."

He was shaking his head. "I don't know him well enough to argue that, but I have another suggestion if you'll just hear me out." They stopped, allowing a nurse wheeling a cart with medications to pass. "You remember my daughter, Jennifer, don't you? And you know the details about her accident. Her victim had an expensive bike that was totaled in the wreck. I thought the most effective way to force her to face the consequences of her behavior was to work off the cost of replacing it."

Her eyes followed the med cart as it entered the restricted entrance to the ICU. "What does this have to do with anything, Ryan?"

"Just this. You're going to be tied up here for some time once Gina is admitted to ICU. Luckily, you have Louie to baby-sit Jesse, but he's an old man. A kid that age has a lot of energy. How about Jennifer pitching in to help? She's out of school for the weekend and I think she'll agree to donate some time after school during the week."

The offer was almost too good to be true. In Jesse's eyes, Jennifer helping out as a baby-sitter, even on a spotty basis, would be second only to Britney Spears. "What makes you think Jennifer would be willing to do it?"

"She'll have no choice. She owes Rick for the bike, but I'm the one who's going to cough up the money. I get to dictate the terms."

"If that's the attitude you're going to use, I'm glad I'm not going to be around when you pitch it to Jennifer," Elizabeth said dryly.

"I'll be tactful."

Not his strong suit, but she wasn't going to quibble. Louie probably wasn't up to looking after Jesse 24/7, not that he wouldn't be willing. She'd have to look for someone to come in on a regular basis, depending on Gina's recovery period. The alternative—turning Jesse over to Austin—was not an option. Just now, as they approached the waiting room, Austin stood in the doorway looking restless and impatient.

"How about Austin?" she asked. "He won't be as easily manipulated as Jennifer."

"Let's take it a day at a time with Austin," Ryan said. "He's given in for the next day or so. He'll need a nanny, too. They don't grow on trees, which gives us some time."

Us?

"And I don't plan to offer Jennifer's services at his place," Ryan added.

"I'm glad to hear it."

Louie stood aside to let them enter the small room just as the elevator pinged. "Good timing," he said to Elizabeth, looking beyond her to the corridor. "Here's Jesse now."

Elizabeth turned around and saw Jesse leaving the elevator between Lindsay and a hospital aide in green scrubs. She walked hesitantly, her pink sneakers squeaking on the tile floor. Her small face was streaked with tears and so pale that her tiny freckles stood out like red pepper sprinkled on her nose. Her eyes darted nervously from one adult to another. There was a mark on her cheek and a white bandage circled one knee. Elizabeth's heart stumbled. She had only one thought and that was to get to Jesse. But Austin was faster.

"Jesse!" he called, striding toward her. "Come to Daddy, Jesse!"

One look at him and Jesse screamed, a high piercing sound that was like a shot straight to Elizabeth's heart. Panicked, Jesse dashed away before the nurse or Lindsay could react. Ryan swore and lunged after Austin, grabbing him in midstride and pulling him up short before he reached Jesse, who then scooted past two people waiting for the elevator and darted inside. Clearly terrified, she cowered inside the elevator with her eyes squeezed shut. A technician inside the elevator had the presence of mind to hold the doors open so that Elizabeth could approach slowly. She took a cautious step into the elevator, then dropped to one knee and held out her arms.

"Jesse, Jesse, don't be afraid," she said in a soft tone. "Open your eyes, darling. It's me, Aunt Lizzie."

It took a moment before Jesse's panic cleared enough so that she risked opening her eyes. Then, with another high, terrified wail, she hurled herself into Elizabeth's arms. For a long, long moment, Elizabeth simply crouched in the elevator and held the trembling child tight.

Fourteen

Another hour dragged by. Elizabeth rested her head on the back of the small settee. Austin had agreed to let Jesse go with Louie. Any other plan was impossible after everyone witnessed Jesse's reaction when she saw him. So, at least she was safe for the time being. She'd clung to Elizabeth, trembling and silent, but Ryan had taken Austin aside firmly and in a few minutes both men were gone, Austin still in a snit and Ryan with reluctance, as his daughter was home alone. Jesse's anxiety had visibly eased once Austin left, although she was still abnormally silent. To Elizabeth, her panic was more revealing than if she'd been able to tell them what happened in words.

Lindsay, impatient with hospital protocol, paced. She'd already made two trips down to the surgical floor to try to connect with Megan. She paused now to glance at her watch, then moved again to check activity in the corridor. It had been over three hours since they'd had any word about Gina.

"I don't know how you can sit so still," she said, studying Elizabeth as if she were a specimen from outer space. "You haven't moved in ten minutes. Megan's like that, too. It's weird." When she failed to get any response from Elizabeth, she said, "I wonder if our mother was quiet or vivacious. Was she outgoing or self-contained?

Am I the odd one out or was our dad the talkative one and I got that gene?''

A long moment passed before Elizabeth said, ''She looked like Megan.''

Lindsay's eyes lit up, encouraged by the first real information ever offered by Elizabeth. ''Really? Megan's quiet…to the extent that I sometimes feel as if I want to reach over and simply jerk a remark out of her, you know?''

Elizabeth rolled her head on the settee to look at Lindsay. ''She'd probably like to do the same to you now and then…in reverse.''

Lindsay laughed. ''Hey, a sense of humor lurks behind that cool mask. Megan's like that. She lets me rant and rave, then look out. She can really zing me one.'' She leaned against the doorjamb, her hands linked behind her. ''I wonder about our mother a lot, do you?''

''Not a lot, but sometimes…sure,'' Elizabeth said, after a moment. ''But I was only four years old when you were born. I just had the thought when meeting Megan for the first time that she looked like pictures I've seen.''

''Pictures of our parents? Would you consider sharing them sometimes? I'd love to just…you know…check 'em out. See if I feel some connection, you know?''

''I haven't looked at that stuff in a long time.'' The pictures were in a correspondence box that had been her mother's, along with the stationery she'd used to write all those letters to her father. She thought about the letters more often than she wanted to. None were ever returned. What had the post office done with them? They wouldn't have been delivered to a dead man, but she'd been encouraged by Iris Graham to keep writing. She'd been around ten years old when she'd finally realized the futility of it, so she'd closed the lid on the box and its contents, including the few mementoes of her parents. It was the right thing to do to share them with Lindsay and Megan.

"It must have been horrible for you when the judge died."

Elizabeth straightened, reached for the tall drink that Ryan had brought her before hustling Austin out of the room, and took a sip through a straw. "This is too morbid a subject to discuss tonight, Lindsay."

Lindsay's face was suddenly the picture of dismay. "Oh, I'm sorry. It is, it is. I'm just so—so damned clumsy sometimes. I'm all caught up in my own interests. I'm consumed with curiosity about my biological parents...and you, to be honest. You must think I'm just using you when I'm really just—" she spread her hands and gave a wry laugh "—just full of curiosity. It's the interviewer in me."

Elizabeth lifted a hand to shush her. "It's all right. Really."

Lindsay stood up. "I'll make it up to you by getting some word on Gina," she said with the light of battle in her eye, "even if I have to barge into the OR and grab my sister by her stethoscope!"

"You can't rush people when they're performing surgery." Elizabeth patted the settee. "Sit down."

Lindsay sat, but with reluctance. "Then let's talk about Jesse."

In spite of herself, Elizabeth managed a smile at that. "Okay."

"You really love that little girl, don't you?"

"How could I not? I was Gina's partner during child-care classes, I was her birthing coach during labor and I was in the delivery room when she was born. I've seen her at least three times a week since and most of the time, more than that."

"Tell me about her."

Elizabeth's face softened. "She's just a darling. She's smart and sassy and she has so much energy she makes me tired just watching her. She talks a blue streak and asks a million questions. Her mind is quirky and curious and bright as a star."

"She talks a blue streak," Lindsay repeated thoughtfully. "Then what does it mean that she wouldn't talk tonight, Liz?"

Exactly what Elizabeth had been worrying about. She got up and went to the door, restlessly surveying the emptiness. How much longer? "I don't know. You heard the nurse. Shock. Fear. Trauma. God knows, she's had so much turmoil in her life lately. Now tonight she's in an accident where her mother is critically injured and she's right there to see it. An adult might have the capacity to understand what's going on and still be bowled over by all that's happened. For a child...who knows?"

"It's probably temporary, don't you think?"

"Hopefully. I'll know more when I can get away from the hospital and be with her, but I can't leave Gina, not tonight. She might—" Her voice broke. It dawned on her that she was revealing far more to Lindsay than she ever intended. She took a deep breath. "You're a very good listener."

Lindsay smiled. "Not especially, although as I mentioned, I'm a good interviewer."

Elizabeth looked at her with quick suspicion. "You're not—"

"This is not an interview," Lindsay said, then rose to pace some more. "Talking helps to pass the hours. You're my sister." She put up a hand and stopped Elizabeth's automatic protest at that. "The reason you're breaking all your own rules tonight is that you're traumatized yourself.

Except for Jesse, Gina's the most precious person in your life and her life is in the balance.''

"I wish we'd hear something!'' Elizabeth cried suddenly. "What could be taking so long?'' She tossed the empty container in the trash. If she didn't hear something soon, she didn't know how she would be able to keep up a pretense of calm.

"Tell me about Gina,'' Lindsay said. "I was at the hearing, remember? I heard you testify to Austin's abusiveness. What I don't get is why he's making a big play to keep Jesse. Seems to me a guy like that wouldn't want the hassle of a little kid.''

"He doesn't want her. He just wants out from under the specifics of any financial burden the court has decreed.''

"Another thing puzzled me.'' Lindsay glanced toward the door to be sure no one was listening. "Why are there no records of the abuse she suffered? Did she never need medical treatment? From the point of view of the average person, that would indicate she didn't really get hurt all that much.'' She put up a hand to stop Elizabeth's instant protest. "I know, I know, I believe everything she said, but don't you see why it's difficult to convince other people?''

"Yes, I do. But she was very good at hiding the true situation in their private life.'' Elizabeth sank slowly onto the settee. "She was ashamed, I think.''

"Yeah, abused women are really good at assuming the burden of the abuse and the shame, almost embracing it personally.''

Elizabeth gave her a quick glance. "You know something about the subject?''

"I did a series of programs last year. I was stunned at the response. Women poured out their hearts in letters to the show—unsigned for the most part—while at the same time they were going to incredible lengths not to tell their best friends or proper authorities about the hell they lived daily.''

"I don't think Austin was violent every day, but when he was—"

Lindsay heard footsteps and got up to check. "But when he was bad, he was horrid, right?"

Elizabeth nodded. "Something like that."

"Here's Megan. At last."

"Sorry you've had to wait so long," she said to Elizabeth as she pulled off the surgical cap and ran a hand through her dark hair. She looked exhausted. A mask dangled from its strings at her neck and she still wore booties from the OR. She glanced at Lindsay. "Glad you could make it, Lin."

"How is she?" Lindsay asked while Elizabeth stood up slowly, her eyes huge and full of worry.

"We've just moved her from recovery to ICU. She survived the surgery, thanks mostly to Dave Hamilton's skill. He's the best. But she's critical. She's on life support and the swelling I mentioned before will likely do more damage. She's extremely unresponsive, in a deep coma. I want to warn you, Elizabeth, she's going to look nothing like herself. Her head is almost completely swathed in bandages, she has an airway and her face has cuts and bruises. Her eyes are taped over to keep them moist. People in a coma don't blink, therefore, their eyes get very dry. I wish I could tell you something more positive, but it's a very bleak situation. Dr. Hamilton will be out shortly to give you details and answer any other questions you might have."

"She can't die!" Elizabeth said in a fierce, low tone.

Megan's eyes went soft with sympathy. She hesitated,

then took Elizabeth's arm and drew her over to the settee, urging her down so that their knees touched. "She won't die because we've got the best equipment known to medical science keeping her alive, but if that were removed, she wouldn't breathe on her own, Elizabeth."

"No." She couldn't accept that. Not Gina, not her quick, funny, loving Gina.

"We've done all we can," Megan said. "The injury was just…too much."

Lindsay sat on the arm of the settee, rubbing Elizabeth's shoulders. Now she slipped an arm around her sister. "Elizabeth needs to see her, Megan. Is that possible?"

"Of course. As I said, she's in ICU. Two visitors are allowed, but for only ten minutes."

Elizabeth was already on her feet, but her legs, as she walked to the door, felt ready to buckle. She didn't notice that Megan was on one side of her and Lindsay on the other. A few weeks ago, she wouldn't have allowed it, had she realized. "I need to—"

Megan motioned to Lindsay to touch the button that allowed access into the restricted world of the ICU. "Yes. And we'll go with you."

She entered the ICU, braced to see Gina as Megan described her. Instead, she came face-to-face with Austin in conversation with a doctor who was explaining Gina's condition and warning him what to expect for the next few hours. Austin listened attentively, his face a mask of sincerity. He had a few questions, which the doctor conscientiously answered. Everything about him spoke of the concerned and caring lover.

"Dr. Hamilton." Megan interrupted, urging Elizabeth forward. "This is Gina's good friend. I've given her a general account of the surgery, but she probably has some questions."

Austin glanced up then, met Elizabeth's eyes, and for just a moment, the smooth mask slipped and she saw open hostility. But almost instantly, it was back in place. "Liz. I didn't know you were still around."

If he had the power, she knew, he would have barred her from the room. "I couldn't leave Gina."

"But you could leave Jesse?" There was insolence in his expression.

She ignored him and turned to the area of the unit where Gina lay. Her questions to the doctor could wait. A curtain was partially pulled around the bed, but Gina was visible. Someone—a nurse—was adjusting small round electrodes stuck to her chest. A plastic bag hung from an IV pole, dripping medication into her arm. Other equipment bleeped electronic data fed to it from unknown sources, displaying it on a TV-like monitor. Taking it all in, Elizabeth felt as if a dense weight had settled on her chest. She moved forward in mute anguish. The nurse glanced up and moved aside. Only then did Elizabeth see the full extent of Gina's condition. She shouldn't have been shocked, as she looked essentially just as Megan had warned her she would. But had she not been told, Elizabeth simply wouldn't have recognized her. She felt such a crushing sense of loss that it was hard to breathe.

"Oh, Gina…"

She was vaguely aware of Megan at her side. "She is in no pain, Elizabeth."

There was no comfort in knowing Gina felt nothing. The near-dead do not feel. With a heavy heart, Elizabeth groped beneath the sheet for her friend's hand. Oh, but Gina was so much more than a friend.

"What can I do?" she whispered, cradling the cold, limp, lifeless hand.

"You might try talking to her," Megan said softly.

"Some people believe that sensory stimuli, such as a familiar voice, has some benefit when a patient is…like this."

Elizabeth's gaze was fixed on Gina's hand, more familiar to her than the broken and bandaged form that lay like a mummy and still as death. "Do you believe it?"

"I don't know, Elizabeth. I've seen so much since my training began. I know miracles do happen."

"Are you saying only a miracle can save Gina?"

"She's very sick."

"Meaning it'll take a miracle?"

Megan's smile was fleeting, but genuine. "I make it a practice never to second-guess the Miracle-maker."

Elizabeth brought Gina's hand to her cheek. "Gina's a survivor. She won't give up."

Just then, Dr. Hamilton spoke Megan's name and with a parting touch to Elizabeth's arm, she moved away. Elizabeth kissed the lifeless fingers of Gina's hand and was tucking it back into place when she suddenly noticed some discoloration on the wrist. Turning it gently, she studied the odd markings with a frown.

"I guess we've got ourselves a helluva situation here, haven't we?"

She looked up to see Austin standing on the opposite side of the bed.

"What?"

"Haven't you got the word yet? She's brain-dead, Liz."

"What are you talking about? No one's said anything to me about that."

"Maybe they think you can't handle the truth. I could tell them a thing or two about how tough you are." He indicated the monitor with its array of electronic data. "A respirator's breathing for her, some kind of device is keeping her heart going, a tube poked into her intestines is feeding her. Face it, she's in a vegetative state, Liz. That's gentle talk for as good as dead.''

Elizabeth took in a deep breath and fought the rage almost choking her. Where was the tiniest spark of decency in this excuse for a man? But she couldn't argue the facts. Gina was being kept alive by machines, but she was alive. Her heart was beating. She knew what Austin was getting at and she wasn't going to allow it. ''The accident happened less than six hours ago, Austin. It's too early to make those judgments.''

''It's not a question of time,'' he said, dismissing her argument. ''They want a decision to pull the plug and I'm giving it.''

She stared at him in shock. ''You're crazy. That's— that's horrible. You haven't given her a chance, Austin. I'm not letting you do anything like that.''

''I don't have to have your approval,'' he said dismissing her as irrelevant. ''What's the point in keeping her alive knowing she'll never wake up? Get real, for God's sake.''

Still holding Gina's hand, she stared at the swathed head, a grotesque bruise on one cheek, the eyes slick with an oily cream and taped shut. The damage was temporary, she told herself, stroking the hand. Her gaze fell again to the telltale marks on Gina's wrist.

''What happened here, Austin?''

He frowned. ''What happened where?''

''Here. Gina's wrist is bruised.''

''Well, hell, stop the presses.'' He rolled his eyes. ''She's been in a car wreck, Liz. She's got cuts and bruises. Her arm's broken.''

''Her other arm, not this one. This arm hasn't a mark on it except for these which look suspiciously like the prints of someone's fingers.''

"Come again?"

"This arm is not injured, so how did she get these odd bruises on her wrist?" Watching his face, she lifted Gina's arm gently. "They look like the marks I've seen on Gina before...when you've manhandled her. I think these bruises were made by your fingers, Austin."

Austin quickly looked around, then leaned toward her over Gina. "You crazy, spiteful bitch! You better watch what you're saying or you'll find yourself in a helluva lot of trouble."

"Not as much as you if you manage to convince this hospital to take Gina off life support," Elizabeth promised in the same soft, but fierce tone. "You're not in charge here, Austin. You were not married to Gina and you have no legal standing."

His lip curled in a sneer. "And you do? As what? Her sister? Her mentor? Her other lover?" Satisfied he'd made a direct hit, he stepped back. "Right. So it's a standoff we've got here. But I think the court will find my argument more compelling. She's been living with me for the past eight years and she's the mother of my kid."

"Careful, Austin," she said. "If you make that claim, the hospital could very well stick you with the bill. The ICU doesn't come cheap, you know."

The look he sent her might have terrified someone else, but Elizabeth wouldn't be cowed. Instead, she stared him down in disgust. "And one more thing you should consider. Your belated concern might look odd to somebody reading the transcript of the hearing. It hardly agrees with what you said about her then."

"Yeah, well...we'll see." But his bluster was fading.

"Exactly. So I don't think you'll be considered the most logical party to dictate life and death for Gina, Austin."

"You are a first-class bitch, Liz."

"Insults and profanity are the last recourse of someone with no argument," she quoted, determined not to show him her rage and frustration. She was convinced something had happened between them tonight that set the stage for Gina's accident. If he had anything to do with it—and she could prove it—he wasn't going to slither out from under the consequences, as he was accustomed to doing. She'd expose him, even if she had to put everything else in her life aside temporarily. But to make that threat now would only put him on alert. Better to wait until she could prove her suspicions.

A nurse touched her arm. "Sorry, but time's up here."

Unaware of the tension in Gina's visitors, the nurse went about adjusting the IV, checking the airway, reading the monitor bleeping other vitals. With one last glare at Elizabeth, Austin turned and left.

"Wow, what was that all about?" Lindsay asked, watching Austin's angry strides out of the ICU. "He looks like he's gonna go kill somebody."

"Yes, but it's not going to be Gina," Elizabeth muttered. Her pace as she left the ICU forced Lindsay to skip keeping up.

"What'd you say?"

"Nothing."

"You two were having a pretty intense conversation in there."

"To put it mildly." Elizabeth made a disgusted sound in the back of her throat. "He's such a bastard, such a sorry excuse for a human being! The thought that Jesse might be raised by him is too vile to contemplate."

"Does this have anything to do with those bruises on Gina's wrist that looked a lot like the print of somebody's fingers?"

"Yes." Elizabeth didn't bother trying to spin it otherwise. Lindsay was too smart.

"You don't think those marks could have come from the accident?"

"No."

"Me, neither." Instead of going back to the waiting room, they stood outside the ICU. "That's very interesting."

"Not interesting, Lindsay. It's cruel, it's vile, but it's characteristic of Austin."

"What are you going to do about it?"

"I'm going to see that he doesn't get away with it."

"Even if Gina doesn't make it?" Lindsay spoke gently, with sympathy.

Elizabeth looked at her. "Do you know something that I don't?"

"I think you should talk to Megan," Lindsay said. "And Dr. Hamilton."

Elizabeth had intended doing just that, only after she'd cooled down. "So Austin's right. She's not going to survive."

"Nothing's certain in ICU."

"Which doesn't change anything I'm thinking right now. If Austin is somehow responsible for this accident, he's not going to get away with it, Lindsay. He's played fast and loose and viciously with Gina for eight years and I've had to stand by and watch, biting my tongue, comforting her, trying to shield Jesse from the reality of the situation she was born into. If it's the last thing I do in this lifetime, I'm going to make him pay."

Fifteen

It was raining when Elizabeth woke up. She lay without moving for a few disorienting moments, trying to figure out what was wrong. A strong wind whistled, and a lashing rain and small pebbles of hail fell against the huge window. She felt chilled and realized she was partially covered with a blanket. She pulled it more snugly around her shoulders. The movement triggered pain in her neck. And then she remembered. The hospital. Gina.

She blinked herself awake and sat up, glancing at her watch. She'd fallen asleep around 6:00 a.m. and consequently had missed a couple of visiting periods in ICU. She remembered someone lowering the lights in the waiting room to accommodate others with loved ones in the ICU. Before Lindsay left—reluctantly—at three o'clock, she'd made Elizabeth promise to get some sleep. Not to worry, she'd be back early. Nothing Elizabeth said had persuaded her otherwise.

"Tomorrow's Saturday. Actually, it's already Saturday and I don't have to go to work. I'm coming back. Consider it moral support." Lindsay held up a hand. "I know, I know, you don't need moral support. You don't need anything. You're perfectly capable of handling all the stress on your own. But, hey, I'm coming back anyway."

How do you reject somebody like that?

Elizabeth got up and went to the window. Had it been

raining when Gina had the accident? Could that explain why she'd lost control of her car? Austin hadn't mentioned it. But why would he volunteer information? The less information he gave, the better for him.

Elizabeth moved to the door, debating whether to try to get into ICU even though the official visiting time was still half an hour away. She wondered about Jesse, too, but it was still early. She'd call Louie a little later and check. Rubbing at the stiffness in her neck, she thought how ungrateful she must have sounded when Ryan offered his daughter to baby-sit. Now that she was thinking straight, she realized how helpful Jennifer would be while Gina was here. But other arrangements would have to be made. And soon.

"Hey, any news?"

She looked up to see Lindsay in wet rain gear bearing coffee and a paper sack with a familiar bagels shop logo. "If that's coffee, I'm putting your name in my will."

Lindsay grinned. "Starbucks wasn't open yet, so we'll have to settle for less high-octane stuff." She handed over a capped cup and dumped her shoulder bag, her raincoat and the sack of bagels on the settee where Elizabeth had slept. "I didn't know whether you take cream and sugar, but it's there if you do."

"Hmm, nothing, thanks." Removing the lid, Elizabeth took a sip.

"Where's Megan?"

"I haven't seen her since the 2:00 a.m. visit. I assume she went home."

"She's on an ER rotation. She can't go home. She might be catching a nap, but she's in the hospital. I bet she looked in here and saw you sleeping. I'll go check."

"Wait! I'll go with you."

Megan spotted them from across the unit. Giving a signal, she made a notation on Gina's chart and then with a final word to the nurse, headed toward them.

"Any change?" Lindsay asked, looking beyond Megan to Gina's bed.

"Not really." Megan took Elizabeth's arm and guided her to a spot out of earshot of others in the unit. "There's something I want to ask you, Liz. We've had a chance to do some tests. They're all routine. We do them on every patient admitted in Gina's condition." Looking her squarely in the eye, Megan asked, "Did you know she was pregnant?"

Elizabeth stared in shock and disbelief. "No."

"I'm afraid so. Just four weeks, but she's definitely pregnant."

Elizabeth put a hand to her mouth. "Oh, my God."

Seeing Elizabeth's distress, Megan touched her hand gently. "I thought you said she wasn't involved with Austin anymore. So, is there someone else that we should notify about this?"

Elizabeth was shaking her head, wanting to scream a denial. After all this time, then one foolish, impetuous moment— *Oh, Gina.*

"Elizabeth?"

She blinked and brought Megan back into focus, brought herself back into focus. "Oh. Ah, someone else? No. No one else." Her tone was flat and bitter. "Just Austin. She went out with him after the hearing. They didn't get home until late. There were bruises on her arms where he..." She drew a shaky breath. "She told me they had...sex. She felt awful about it. Disgusted with herself because she knew it was his way of manipulating her. Or trying to. He wanted her to drop the suit. He—"

She stopped, stemming the flow of words and looked at Megan. "I'm sorry. I know what you're thinking, but it's not true. She wasn't…easy. You have to understand her relationship with Austin. You have to understand how trapped she was in her need for him. It was neurotic…sick."

"You don't have to apologize for Gina," Megan said, giving her hand a squeeze. "I understand the syndrome. I see it in the ER too often."

"I'm not apologizing. I just don't want you to think she was promiscuous. She wasn't," Elizabeth said, adding bitterly, "She hasn't been with another man since meeting Austin eight years ago. She never looked at another man." She turned around and gazed sadly at Gina lying still and lifeless in the bed. A machine beeped with her every heartbeat. The respirator moved rhythmically, up and down, up and down. The monitor situated at eye level showed a maze of green lines, blips and numbers. "Have you told Austin?"

"No."

Elizabeth let out a breath. "There's no need," she said, her mouth turned down. "You can bet that's the reason Gina went out with him last night. I couldn't understand it until now. She had to tell him that she was pregnant."

Ryan had just stepped out of the shower when he heard the doorbell. What, besides an overnight parcel delivery would explain a caller at eight o'clock on Saturday morning? Peering through the peephole, he recognized the face of his troublesome client. With a grimace, he beckoned him inside.

"Ryan, we gotta talk." Austin looked around nervously, then managed a short laugh. "Sorry about this, but it's important." He cleared his throat. "I guess you wouldn't have a cup of coffee, by any chance?"

Gesturing him to follow, Ryan headed down the hall to

the kitchen. The pot was just brewed. He hadn't even had a chance to fortify himself, but he poured his client a cup and shoved it across the counter. "I hope you take it straight."

Austin pushed it back. "I could use a shot of something stronger."

Ryan looked at him hard. "The sun's barely up, Austin. What's with you?" But he reached into his store of liquor and took down a bottle of Jim Beam, poured a stiff shot into Austin's coffee and pushed it back. "You look like hell."

"Yeah. And I feel like hell." Austin drank half of it down in one gulp, then flexed his neck and released a sound, half sigh, half groan. "Thanks."

"Is this about Gina?" Ryan suddenly held his breath, thinking of Liz. It would hit her hard.

"No, no. Well, in a way." Austin wiped his mouth. He'd been sitting, but he got up abruptly and went to the window above the sink and looked out. "It's about Jesse. I need you to arrange it so I can ship her off to my mother in Arizona. She'll be better off there once Gina…" He took another gulp of coffee. "She shouldn't stay around here and be subjected to something like that."

"Didn't you say she hasn't seen your mother in a while? If Gina does pass away and Jesse is shipped off to be with people she doesn't know very well, aren't you concerned about how that'll affect her? Just think a minute, Austin. She was with her mom when the accident happened. She saw Gina's terrible injuries. Next, she's at the hospital where she senses that all is not well. She's smart, Austin. You're fooling yourself if you think she doesn't have a fairly good idea what's happening here. I'd be grateful, if I were you, that she can stay with Liz and Louie through the whole ordeal. From what I've seen, you can depend on Liz to help her understand her mom's death—if that happens. Liz knows what it's like to lose a parent when you're five years old. It happened to her.''

"Liz!" Speaking the name with disgust, he flung out a hand. "Everybody thinks the best of Liz. But what she's really doing is trying to set the stage to keep Jesse permanently. Don't you get it? Goddamn it! Has everybody lost it around here?" He hit the counter with his fist.

"She is concerned about Jesse, Austin," Ryan said patiently. "All of us are. Jesse's going to suffer the worst thing that can happen to a child. She's going to lose her mother. It's up to us—to you, especially, as her father—to see that she's not damaged more than is bound to happen anyway."

"Enough." Austin turned away. "I'm not here to convince you to agree with me on this, Ryan. I'm just telling you that I'm sending Jesse to my mother in Arizona. As my lawyer, I want you to do what's necessary to make it legal."

When it snows in Brownsville, buddy. Privately, Ryan longed to tell Austin to find himself another lawyer. This insensitive prick could take what was necessary legally and stick it where the sun didn't shine. But to do that would take Ryan out of the loop and leave Liz and Jesse vulnerable to Austin's self-centered plans. What kind of a father was he to even consider removing a child who was suffering from unspeakable grief and pain from everything that was familiar and sending her a thousand miles away? He flexed his jaw, took his time sipping his coffee while he thought how to handle this jerk.

"Tell you what, Austin," he said, "let's wait and see what happens with Gina today. And think about this. Judge Hetherington will probably think separating that child from Liz right now is not in her best interest. I don't know this for a fact, but I'm guessing that at the first hint Liz gets of you wanting to take Jesse away from Houston, she'll file for a restraining order. The facts are strong enough that she'll get it, too. Another point in her favor is that Hetherington's already familiar with the case.''

Ryan stood in his open door and watched Austin blast off down the street in the Porsche. His client was one very unhappy man, but hopefully Ryan had succeeded in stalling his plan to send Jesse away, for the moment. But in the back of his mind was a niggling unease about the whole thing. Why the urgency to remove Jesse? And what if he ignored his lawyer's advice and sent her off anyway? Finishing his coffee, Ryan decided he couldn't let that happen.

Upstairs, he heard Jennifer slamming drawers and banging doors. Then her boom box blasted at max level, Dixie Chicks chirping their latest. Somehow, he was more aware of his own neglect of Jennifer and he was working to change that. If it was within his power to do something to rescue Jesse, he was going to do that, too. Looking back on the last few years of his life, he couldn't see a lot to be proud of.

His cell phone lay on the hall table at the base of the stairs. He picked it up and punched in the digits for information. When he got an answer, he asked for Lindsay Blackstone's number. There was more than one way to skin a cat.

Sixteen

"What do you mean, I've got to baby-sit?"

"I think you heard me, hon. The ox is in the ditch."

Jennifer pulled her earphones off and looked at Ryan in complete bewilderment. "What does that mean?"

"It's in the Bible." His teenager lay on her stomach, her feet waving in the air. Her toenails, he noted, were painted a hideous bruise-purple. Why would a young girl think that color was attractive? He walked over to her bed and shoved aside half a dozen loose CDs to clear off a place to sit down. "An ox was as vital in biblical times as an automobile or a computer today, and there were very strict rules about what you could or couldn't do on Sundays, or the Sabbath as that day was called. Well, some guy's ox accidentally fell into a ditch and there was some criticism over pulling him out, seeing as it was forbidden to do any labor on Sunday. The alternative was just to leave the poor animal to suffer in the ditch, possibly die. The decision was made to pull him out. Compassion and logic triumphed over dogma."

Jennifer's expression had changed little while Ryan talked. She sighed deeply and pushed the button to silence her CD player before propping on an elbow to look at him. "And your point is, Daddy?"

It was Ryan's turn to sigh. What, had he expected instantaneous enthusiasm from his daughter? Keeping his tone even and patient, he gave it another shot. "Gina is lying in ICU close to death this morning. Liz is keeping vigil there. Jesse, who is probably very scared and bewildered, is being minded by her surrogate grandpa." He paused. "You met Louie, didn't you?"

She shrugged. "I guess."

"He's old, if you recall. Caring for a little kid takes a lot of energy, more sometimes than an elderly person has. Not that Louie's unwilling to watch Jesse right now, because as I said, the—"

She was already nodding. "...ox is in the ditch."

"Now, you've got it, baby."

Ryan smiled. "So I suggested to Liz that you might be able to step in and take up some of the slack this weekend. And maybe for a couple of afternoons next week depending on Gina's condition. The accident happened just last night and the first twelve hours after such a trauma are crucial. The prognosis isn't good, so Liz will probably want to stay."

"Well, I can't."

"You can't." His eyebrows went up a notch.

Jennifer shifted so that she was now sitting, legs crossed. "I have a life, Daddy. You can't just go around arranging stuff for me. It's a real pain to spend my entire weekend baby-sitting some little kid. What do you expect me to do there, read *Harry Potter*? Besides, how would I work it in with my prison sentence? I'm supposed to be the maid and general slave around here to pay for that stupid bike, remember?"

"I'm prepared to cut you some slack on the prison sentence," Ryan said, setting his teeth to keep from giving her a good shaking. "Instead of vacuuming and doing the dishes, you become a nanny for a few days. It'll go toward the cost of the bike."

"Sorry, but I'd rather do the toilets." She put the head-phones back on and reached for the CD player.

Dismissing him. Ryan sat for a moment just looking at her. Didn't she have a heart? Was there no sympathy for a little kid whose mother was probably dying? Music from the CD plugged into her ears came to him faintly, a solid, hard, rhythmic beat. Even if she told him the artist, he wouldn't recognize the name. He was so out of sync with Jennifer and her world that they might almost live on two different planets. So, why had he ever thought he could do a better job with her than Diane?

He reached for the CD player, ignoring her startled, angry reaction and punched the button that shut off the music. "Okay, back to square one, hon," he said, tossing the high-tech equipment on a chair nearby. "I want you to listen carefully. You don't get to agree or disagree. Get up, get dressed. We'll stop at McDonald's and get some breakfast and then I'll drop you at Liz's house where you will put on a happy face and be nice to that little girl who may be motherless soon. If she wants to hear *Harry Potter,* you'll be happy to read it. If she wants you to bake cookies, you become Martha Stewart, Jr. You will keep her entertained and tell her nothing about her mom that might upset her. Now, do I make myself clear?"

She was standing now, glaring at him. "This isn't about Jesse, is it, Dad? It's about that woman, Liz. Sending me over to baby-sit is just a backdoor way of you sucking up to her, isn't it?"

"Yeah, she's going to really like me a lot when she gets to know you better."

For a nanosecond, hurt flashed in her eyes. "I'm calling Mom to come and get me."

Ryan reached over and picked up her cell phone from the bedside table and without a word, held it out to her.

Keeping her gaze locked on his, she stood toe to toe with him. He could see the passion in her. Frustration radiated from her like heat on a summer beach. Half a minute passed, then with a muttered word that he wasn't meant to hear, she turned on her heel and headed for the bathroom, slamming the door with enough force to rock the room.

He crossed the room and stood listening. She was again banging things around and slamming drawers, but now in rebellion. Next, he heard the yank of the shower curtain. He winced, hoping it wouldn't be pulled off the rod. Then, the hiss of water. He spoke through the door before she had time to get in the shower. "You've got twenty minutes, princess."

Lindsay didn't know how he had done it, but Ryan Paxton had managed to reach her via cell phone at the hospital. At first, she'd assumed he meant the call to go to Liz, but no, what he had to say was meant for Lindsay. The lawyer was walking a fine line, she thought, as she scribbled notes in her journalist's shorthand while he talked. But she made a mental note to try to find a way to thank him once this was all over. She wasn't quite sure that Liz was ready to trust anybody who was in any way linked to Austin Leggett, but what Ryan was doing removed any doubt from Lindsay's mind.

She clicked her cell phone back onto its holder at her waist and made a big to-do of stretching the kinks out of her back and neck. "Boyoboy, Liz, sitting around and waiting like this is murder. I'm feeling almost claustrophobic and you've been cooped up for hours. How about us taking a walk to the atrium?" She moved to one of the windows. "It's stopped raining and we have another half hour before they'll let us back in to see Gina. What do you say?''

"I don't know...."

It was plain to see that Elizabeth was still in shock over Gina's pregnancy. Her suspicion, and it made sense, that Gina's reason for agreeing to go out with Austin was to tell him about it. What wasn't clear—and maybe never would be—was Austin's reaction when he was told. Nothing about the last few hours Gina spent with him that night would ever be clear unless Jesse knew something...and Jesse wasn't telling.

"There's something I want to talk to you about, Liz,'' Lindsay said, "and the ICU waiting area is a little too public."

Elizabeth sighed. "All right, but let's tell Gina's nurse. Just in case something happens."

"Sure, I'd already thought of that."

Ten minutes later, they were at the atrium, a lushly landscaped area on the ground floor of the hospital. The plants were heavy with colorful blooms at this time of year and small trees reached thirty and forty feet into the air. "The sun always seems so bright after a rainstorm, doesn't it?" Lindsay said as she slipped her sunglasses onto her face.

"That, too, but I'm always struck by how clean and sharp the world looks after it rains," Elizabeth said, bending over to pick up a deep-pink camellia bloom that had fallen. She gazed a long moment at its perfect composition. "Maybe *renewed* is a better word. Considering the reason I'm here, it seems someone has made an impossible, incredible error."

Lindsay touched her hand. "I'm so sorry, Liz."

Elizabeth could only nod.

"Since we do know that Gina's condition seems irreversible—or even if we don't yet know that for sure—there's still something that I wanted to suggest to you, something you might not have considered in all this. It has to do with Jesse.''

"I've done nothing but think of Jesse in all this," Elizabeth said dryly.

"But this is a legal matter."

Elizabeth drew a sharp breath. "Oh?"

"Let's sit down."

Water trickled from a rustic waterfall in a corner of the atrium. They headed to it and sat down on a stone bench. "Do you have Maude Kennedy's number?" Lindsay asked.

"Yes. Actually, I called her already. She promised to come, but after a nine o'clock appointment. I want to be sure we can block Austin on the life support."

Lindsay glanced at her watch. "If the appointment lasts an hour, she should be wrapping it up any minute. I hope you won't think I'm overstepping myself here, but I promise you, I'm thinking of Jesse's welfare. If we wait until we're blessed with hindsight, it'll be too late."

"What is it, Lindsay?"

"I think you should call Maude right now and ask that she file an injunction blocking Austin from being alone with Jesse and, failing that, certainly do whatever it takes to block him from shipping her off to his parents in Arizona."

Elizabeth frowned. "How did you know his parents were in Arizona?"

"I think I must have heard it when I sat in court that first day." She had not recalled that fact. Ryan had mentioned it. But Liz wasn't to know that. She didn't want Liz to know that this had been Ryan's suggestion. It amounted to a breach of legal ethics that he was advising

Liz when Austin clearly considered her his chief adversary.

"Do you think he would do that?" Liz asked with an expression of dismay on her face. Then before giving Lindsay a chance to reply, she added, "Well, of course, he would. He'd whisk her off to people she's seen only two or three times in her entire life without a blink."

"And why would you think he'd do that? I know why I think so, but just so we're on the same page, why?"

"Because he's a—" She stopped, looked sharply at Lindsay. "Because he doesn't want her to talk about what happened the night of the accident, right?"

"You'll have to admit, it's a possibility. And to be on the safe side—"

"Thanks, Lindsay. I should have thought of it myself." Elizabeth put out her hand. "May I borrow your cell phone?"

The phone was already in Lindsay's hand.

Jennifer's attitude hadn't improved a whole lot on the drive to Elizabeth's house, but at least she wasn't openly rebelling. Ryan hoped he was doing the right thing in forcing her to help out with Jesse. He hadn't exaggerated by telling her that Louie wasn't up to minding a five-year-old 24/7. It was bound to be a difficult day. Less than twelve hours since the accident and already it seemed like a week.

After Austin's surprise visit, Ryan had made two calls to the hospital, one to Lindsay and one to Megan Blackstone. Lindsay was one shrewd cookie. He hadn't had to dot any i's or cross any t's. She got it immediately. If anyone could make an end run around Austin, Lindsay was the gal to set it up. Liz wouldn't hesitate, given the stakes. Of course, as Austin's lawyer, Ryan might suffer an ethics charge as a result of that call, but he'd deal with that when it happened. He had a clean conscience, something he'd been neglecting lately.

What he wasn't quite sure about in his mind was why he was risking so much for Elizabeth Walker.

His call to Megan had left him feeling more somber and less noble. Gina's condition was grim. She wasn't going to recover, although Megan said she hadn't yet spoken so frankly to Elizabeth.

"There's just something about Liz's devotion to Gina—and her deep distress—that makes it difficult to destroy hope," Megan said. "Sometimes we decide to let a patient's loved one come around to the inevitable in their own way before actually telling them that all is lost. It's that way with Liz. She'll face it soon." He'd sensed a sad smile in her tone then. "I must admit to a personal interest in Gina's case. I keep trying to think of a way to make it less devastating to Liz, if that's possible."

"But it is hopeless?"

"We're doing all the tests, but she appears brain-dead."

Now, as he pulled into the driveway at Liz's house, he wondered if Louie knew. Beside him, Jennifer released her seat belt. "I'm not baking cookies, no matter what you say."

Obviously, his daughter wasn't feeling the same angst over the situation as he was. Ryan reached over and stopped her before she could get out of the car. "This little girl's mother is dying, Jennifer. If I find out you haven't done everything in your power today to ease the tragedy of that, then you'd better have a pretty good excuse."

Jennifer freed her wrist. "Oh, relax, Dad." She rolled her eyes and held up a trendy shopping bag. "I brought some old Barbie stuff that I used to play with. She might get a kick out of acting out stuff, you know. I read that somewhere...about traumatized kids.'' She pushed her door open and got out.

Ryan sat stunned into silence and watched her stroll nonchalantly up the walk to the front door. So much for thinking she had no heart. Did the female of the species start confounding men right out of the cradle, he wondered. Then, shaking his head with a mixture of fatherly pride and affection—and, to be honest, relief—he managed to get out and reach the door just as it was opened by Louie. Little Jesse stood almost hidden behind him, her blue eyes big and wary. The old man had a firm hand on the collar of the dog, who strained against his hold and barked with excitement. Ryan tried without success to recall the dog's name.

"Hi, Archie," Jennifer said, putting out her hand.

"That's enough, Archie," Louie said sternly, but the dog was already licking Jennifer's fingers. Then he smiled down at the wary-eyed child hugging his leg. "Look at this, Jesse-girl, here's Jennifer and her daddy come to visit you."

"Hi, Jesse," Ryan said gently and felt his heart twist at what she would soon face.

"Hey, kid." Jennifer didn't seem to notice that Jesse remained mute. Nor did she seem put off at being subjected to Jesse's unblinking stare. "I had some time this weekend and thought maybe we could hang out together. How'd you like that?"

Jesse didn't move or speak. She simply stared at Jennifer.

"I knew you'd like it." Jennifer held up the trendy bag. "You're not going to believe what I've got in this sack. Uh-uh, it's not Britney Spears zapped from life-size to

Barbie-size. It's…ta-dah!'' She plucked Barbie out of the sack. "Your basic Barbie."

There was a tiny flicker of the little girl's lashes.

"I've got a few more surprises in this sack, but I need a place to spread 'em all out…like your room, okay?"

"What do you say to that, Jesse-girl?" Louie bent with a crackle of his aging joints to look into the child's face. "You want to take Jennifer to your room?"

Jesse looked at Jennifer and the sack and gave an almost imperceptible nod.

"Okay!" Jennifer reached for her hand and without another look at the two men, they left the foyer together. Archie trotted beside them.

Louie and Ryan were silent, watching as they turned into the room that Liz had fixed up for Jesse. "Nice little girl you've got there," Louie said.

"Yeah, I was just thinking the same thing."

"They surprise you sometimes."

"I was thinking that, too."

Ryan still had not been invited inside. "You heard from the hospital today?" Louie asked, searching his face.

"Yeah, just before we left to come here. You?"

"Liz called to check on Jesse, but she didn't have much to say in the way of progress for Gina. It doesn't look good, does it?"

Ryan hesitated, wondering how frank to be with the old man. He didn't know whether telling Louie exactly how bad Gina was might cause a heart attack or something. Sensing his hesitation, Louie said, "Got time for a cup of coffee?"

"I wouldn't say no if it's already made."

Louie turned, gesturing with a jerk of his thumb for Ryan to follow. Once in the kitchen, he took a mug from a hook beneath one of the cabinets and poured coffee from

a carafe into it. His own was in the sink. He rinsed it out
and refilled it. Clearly, he was at home in Liz's house.
Ryan wondered how much time he actually spent here.

"You want cream or sugar?"

Ryan shook his head. "Black's fine." He took a sip
and made a pained face.

"I like it strong," Louie said with a twinkle in his eye.

"Uh-huh." Ryan gestured toward the French doors
leading to the patio. "Mind if we sit outside? I don't want
the kids to hear this."

He followed Louie outside, taking the lawn chair the
old man indicated. It was a great backyard. Tall trees cast
cooling shade. At the corner of the patio, water trickled
over a tasteful formation of stones, then pooled to form
an oasis with a variety of water-loving plants. He leaned
forward and caught a flash of color. She had it stocked
with goldfish. Very nice.

"What about Gina?" Louie asked after easing himself
down on the edge of a comfortable-looking chaise.

"It's bad. According to Megan, she's brain-dead.
They're doing tests, but I got the idea they were simply a
formality."

Louie gazed at a bird feeder that hung suspended from
the limb of the nearest tree. He looked sad and suddenly
older. "I'm thinking of that baby girl. She's already showing signs of trauma. Hasn't spoken a word since it happened. This is going to be bad."

"Yeah. And Liz is going to be crushed, too."

Louie got up with some effort and went to the edge of
the patio where he tipped his mug and poured out the rest
of his coffee. "Get ready for problems," he said, facing
Ryan again.

"What?"

"If Gina's brain-dead, that means there's a decision to

be made. Liz is stubborn. She isn't going to want to with-draw life support. On the other hand, Austin will.''

"It's not appropriate for me to discuss what Austin will or won't do," Ryan said. "I'm still his lawyer." And wishing every day that he wasn't.

"He never married Gina. He's got no power here."

"I could make a good case that he does, based on the number of years they were together and the fact that they have a child."

Louie looked at him. "He just wants to be rid of her."

Ryan believed the same thing, but he couldn't admit it to the old man. "Are you a lawyer?" He'd been curious about Louie Christian from day one. Now seemed as good a time as any to find out about him.

"It doesn't take a lawyer to know that Austin's position as Gina's next of kin is arguable."

Ryan smiled. "You talk like a lawyer."

"Maybe I was once." Louie dropped back onto the chaise.

"Was your practice in Texas?"

"Yes and no."

Stonewalling. "Speaking of Liz…" If he couldn't find out anything about Louie, maybe the old man would fill in some blanks about Judge Walker. "Do you know any-thing about her father?"

Louie stared at him hard. "Why do you ask?"

"I didn't make the connection until I read the article about her in the *Chronicle*. My father was a Superior Court judge, too. Coincidentally, he died at about the same time as Matthew Walker. They both served when Arthur Ramsey was mayor."

"A corrupt bastard."

"There was plenty of corruption to go around then, and

not only in the political arena. The judicial branch had its own share of bad apples.''

"But your father wasn't one of them?"

Ryan's gaze sharpened at that. "Did you know him?"

"That wasn't a statement. It was a question."

He wasn't going to trip up this wily old ex-lawyer. "No, my father wasn't one of them. In fact, I wish I had shown more interest in his work, especially the cases he was scheduled to preside over in those last few months. Maybe I would have had some warning that he was on the edge of an abyss. But I was a fifteen-year-old kid and full of myself. I didn't really understand or appreciate Dad's career. I've had a lot of time to regret that.''

"We all have regrets, son."

"Yeah."

"Actually, I did know John Paxton," Louie said, gazing again at the bird feeder where a cardinal was now perched, eating sunflower seeds. "He was a man of impeccable character. Defense attorneys with a guilty client literally quaked at the thought of appearing before Judge Paxton. His death was a great loss to the judicial system and the public.''

Ryan felt his heartbeat quicken. Louie didn't seem inclined to talk about himself, but he might be willing to fill in some of the blanks in those months leading up to John Paxton's death. He hunched forward in his chair, cupping the mug of coffee between both hands. "About that scandal in the judicial system during Mayor Ramsey's tenure, did you know about it?"

"Oh, yeah, I knew about it. Everybody knew about it. That's what makes a scandal—corruption, exposure, media blitz. Judges were on the take from lawyers who wanted verdicts in their favor. Some of the personal injury claims reached into the millions. Out of that came tax fraud, tax evasion, funny numbers from CPAs. You name it, several judges were ready to roll over if you could afford to pay. I don't mean a few, but twentysomething or more.''

''The way I understand it,'' Ryan said, watching Louie closely, ''the IRS stumbled on a large interest-bearing account in the Caymans with sizable withdrawals that seemed to go nowhere.''

''It was going to judges. Payoffs.'' Louie got to his feet, but it seemed to take some effort. Still, his gaze at Ryan was keen. ''Been a long time since I talked to anybody who remembered that scandal. It was ugly. Ruined a lot of lives.''

''Yeah. I've spent hundreds of hours researching Dad's cases at the time. He was not linked in any way to that scandal.''

Louie was frowning. ''I don't recall anybody ever suggesting that about John Paxton.''

''He killed himself, I guess you know that.''

Louie's face suddenly seemed older. ''I'm sorry you had that sadness to cope with.''

''He was driven to it.''

Again a dark frown. ''Driven to it? What—''

''It was Liz's father. Judge Matthew Walker. He was the last person to talk to my father in his chambers the night it happened. They were together, working late. The place was deserted when Walker left. Actually, nobody saw him leave at the time he claimed, so who's to know what really happened?'' Ryan looked down at the bitter near-black coffee and stood up abruptly, walked to the edge of the patio and tossed it out into the grass. Without turning, he said, ''I think Walker was in the scandal up to his sorry ass and that he tried to pressure my father into doing something, maybe ruling in a particular way and

Dad wouldn't budge. I think Walker had something in his back pocket to hold over my dad, some mistake on my dad's part...maybe something personally incriminating. I've scoured his records, everything in the house, a safe deposit box, his diaries, correspondence, but I've never found anything. Not a hint of something that would have disgraced him or embarrassed him or disbarred him. But whatever it was, it was a threat to his family or his reputation or his career. He killed himself rather than be outed on it."

"And you blame Matthew Walker for your dad taking that way out. Is that what you're saying, son?"

Ryan turned and looked at him. "Yeah, that's what I'm saying."

Seventeen

Thirty minutes later, he was drinking coffee again. This time it was from a machine in the hospital, but it was just as rancid as Louie's rank brew. Looking down at it, Ryan thought it suited his mood. He felt pretty rank and rancid himself. Which is what always happened when he allowed himself to think about his father. Only rarely did he admit his bitter resentment that John Paxton had taken a way out that seemed cowardly, no matter what the circumstances. He'd left a sick wife. And a son. What the hell was he thinking to just cash it in that way and leave them both hanging out to dry? Ryan believed there wasn't any situation bad enough to make him kill himself, not because he had more guts than his old man, but because it would hurt Jennifer. He couldn't do that to Jen. So, what the hell kind of threat had Matthew Walker hung over John Paxton's head that would make an honorable man turn his back on honor? The most frustrating part was that he couldn't get to either of them to ask. Not that he'd ask, if he had that opportunity. He'd demand.

He looked up now as Liz and Lindsay were returning from the brief visit to Gina allowed in the ICU. He'd arrived just as they were admitted. There was no sign of Austin. That puzzled and concerned Ryan. Austin had a lot at stake and from his attitude earlier, he'd seemed obsessed with controlling the events set in motion by Gina's

accident. When Ryan had left Louie, he'd warned him that
Austin might show up wanting to take Jesse and that he
was to refuse him, no matter what.

"Do what you have to to stall him," Ryan had advised
Louie, leaving his own cell phone and pager numbers.
He'd almost suggested they leave Liz's house and go to
his own condo, but Jesse didn't need to be in unfamiliar
territory right now.

He stood up as Liz and Lindsay entered the waiting
area. Liz looked exhausted. "How is she?" he asked, but
in fact, he was more concerned about Liz than Gina, who
was beyond help.

"No change." Liz pushed her hair back out of her eyes,
anchoring it behind one ear. She looked around blankly.
"Where's my coffee? I thought I left it here."

"I dumped it," Ryan said. Reaching out, he tipped up
her chin and studied her face. It was an indication of her
utter exhaustion that she allowed such an intimacy. "How
about taking a walk with me to the cafeteria? I know
you've got to be hungry."

"Great idea," Lindsay said, settling back on one of the
settees. "I've eaten, so I'll stay in case anything happens.
Take your cell phone, Liz. I'll call you."

"I had planned just to get something from one of the
vending machines," Elizabeth said, with a move that took
her just out of Ryan's reach. But there was a faint rise of
color on her face. She wasn't totally unaware of him, Ryan
noticed, and felt a surge of satisfaction.

"Go, Liz," Lindsay urged. She hadn't missed the small
byplay between the two. As Elizabeth turned to go, Lindsay met Ryan's eyes and gave him a thumbs-up signal and
a bright smile.

"I just left your house," Ryan told Liz as they waited
for the elevator. "Jesse was quiet, but she seemed agree-

able to having Jennifer around." With a hand at her waist, he guided her into the elevator. Most of the space was taken up with an elderly woman in a wheelchair accompanied by two family members. He waited until they reached their destination and got out before adding, "Louie's holding up."

"I talked to him earlier. I don't know what I would do without him." She stood uncertainly, looking over the crowd in the cafeteria. "I'm really not very hungry."

The place was packed with staff and visitors having lunch, too noisy to talk. And definitely the wrong choice to give Liz a break, Ryan thought, tucking a hand under her elbow. "There's a restaurant just a short walk from here. Getting outside will probably clear the cobwebs and I bet you'll be hungry once food is set in front of you. Remember, Lindsay will let you know if you're needed."

To his surprise, she didn't object, but simply fell into step as if to argue was too much trouble. He didn't jump to any conclusions about her unusual agreeableness. Fatigue, grief and fear were temporarily taking a toll, but the steel in her spine was still there.

"Where's your client?" she asked.

"Which one? I've got a few."

"You know which one. Austin hasn't been back since we argued over pulling life support from Gina." Her lips twisted with bitterness. "He has no love for her and he isn't going to be responsible for the expense of keeping her in ICU, so I've been wondering what's so urgent that he wants to end her life."

He touched her arm to stop her as they approached a cross street. "I don't pretend to understand what motivates Austin in anything he does. You may not believe this, but I don't know him very well. I agreed to represent him when asked by his father, who's one of the senior partners in the firm.'' The light changed and they started walking again. ''I haven't dumped him because of Jesse. I hope you believe that. Maybe I can do some good for her.''

A hint of a smile softened her face. ''I know the feeling. It's for Jesse's sake that I do a lot of things that I probably wouldn't otherwise do. Or make choices I wouldn't otherwise choose.''

''Such as—''

''Since you're still Austin's lawyer, I think I've said enough.''

They were approaching the restaurant now, which had half a dozen umbrella-covered tables set outside. She stopped and looked about, caught in full sunshine. Her hair was an incredible color, he thought, not red, but a dark auburn and shot through with rich fiery highlights. Thick and lustrous, it fell to her shoulders, wanting to curl in Houston's humid air. He guessed that ordinarily she spent a lot of time trying to tame it, but after nearly eighteen hours without benefit of vanity products and mirror, it was going its own untamed way. He preferred her looking natural and feminine, as she did in the jeans and soft T-shirt. And those green eyes... A man could learn to love the look of a woman like Liz.

''Liz—'' He stopped her as she started inside. She turned, giving him a questioning look. ''After this is over, would you have dinner with me? Could we get to know each other better without all the complications of Austin and...everything else?''

''I...don't know.'' She frowned.

''Are you seeing somebody?''

''No. It's just—'' Shaking her head, she looked sort of frantically at the traffic. ''I'm really not interested in...that.''

He smiled, a half tilt of his mouth, knowing the risk he

took teasing her. "Don't tell me Austin's tacky accusations were right after all?"

"Austin's—" She looked confused a second or two before she understood. "Oh, that Gina and I—" She stopped, giving a soft laugh. "No, his accusations were probably a fantasy in his own mind. He's just that sick."

"And tacky."

"Your words, not mine." She glanced at the door. "Are we having lunch or not?"

She hadn't promised to go out with him, but he hadn't been completely shot down either, he thought. He felt hopeful. "Want to sit outside?"

"I think so." She allowed him to seat her and thanked the waiter with a smile as water in a tall glass was placed in front of her. Again, he caught himself staring. Her smile was enough to make him forget the history they shared.

"You should do that more often," he said, waving the waiter off after they'd ordered.

"Do what?"

"Smile."

Instantly, her smile faded. "I don't have much to smile about today. I know it must seem as if I'm refusing to face reality about Gina, but I just can't accept that the life of someone so vibrant and loving could end this way. I just can't give up hope." She toyed with the raffia string tied around her napkin. "There's still Jesse to consider."

"There's always hope, Liz." He wanted to take her hand and bring her fingers to his lips to kiss, but he'd have to save that and other kisses for later. But it was going to happen. He was going to get to know Elizabeth Walker much better.

She frowned as she opened the napkin, the motion unhurried as if her thoughts were focused back in time. "I never understood her obsession with Austin. I think now, looking back, that I wasn't a very good friend." She looked into Ryan's eyes. "Gina knew Austin's faults without being constantly reminded by me. If she'd been able, she would have ended their relationship earlier. She simply wasn't able to put him out of her life and I never could accept that. I should have. I should have tried harder to understand."

Their food arrived, giving Ryan a chance to consider his reply. "You've been there for her during the times when she needed help. That's a true friend. And you've been a steady and loving presence to Jesse. Beyond that, I don't see what more you could do." It was all Ryan could think of to say, but her pain made him recall a long-forgotten memory. "My mother had a friend," he said, looking at the way she was shredding a roll into bird-size crumbs. "They knew each other in high school and all the way through college, but after they both married, they settled in different areas of Houston. In spite of the distance, they met for lunch occasionally and as friends they shared bits and pieces of their lives. Then one night my mother had a call and was told that the woman had been taken to a hospital. Seems she'd fallen down the stairs and was in a coma from which she never recovered. I must have been eight or ten, but I remember my mother's shock and anger. I thought it was odd to see my mother enraged over an accident. Her friend couldn't help falling down the stairs, could she? We went to the funeral and I remember hearing whispers and scraps of conversation that hinted at something other than an accidental fall down those stairs. Her husband was a well-respected business-man, and very successful. What were they hinting at? A man like that wouldn't do something so unspeakable as pushing his wife down a flight of stairs, would he? It just couldn't happen...could it? That kind of abuse happened in social circles different from ours. Didn't it?''

Ryan's smile wasn't quite straight. He picked up his fork and speared a shrimp, but held it untasted. Instead, he looked into Elizabeth's green eyes. "Afterward, my mother was filled with remorse. She felt guilty, even somewhat responsible, if you can believe that. I remember her telling my father that she should have done something. Intervened somehow. And I remember my father dismissing her feelings as the usual female tendency to overreact. Like many, he was blind to the truth. He didn't see anything but the man's public persona.''

Elizabeth sipped water and toyed with her salad. "It happens.''

"Yeah, it does. I'm wondering if I'm more like my old man than my mother. If Austin is as abusive as you believe him to be, then I might have been more helpful in keeping him away from her if I hadn't been assuming a man with Austin's background wouldn't behave like a common criminal.'' That was part of it. He hoped Liz would never know the other—how his objectivity had disappeared once he learned who her father was. Had he helped put Gina in jeopardy because he was blinded by Elizabeth's connection to his father? "So, if you're going to beat yourself up over the tragedy of Gina and her dysfunctional relationship with Austin, I'd have to get in line way ahead of you, Liz.''

Elizabeth was shaking her head, now pushing lettuce around on her plate. "Nobody could have prevented them seeing each other one more time," she said. "I don't know this for sure—I mean, Gina didn't confide in me— but I think she called Austin and set up the date. She was surely horrified to find herself pregnant. I think she knew he'd be unhappy to say the least and that's why she took

Jesse. He wouldn't attack her in front of Jesse." She pushed her plate away. "At least I don't think he would. Since Jesse hasn't said a word since, we haven't heard her account of the accident."

"Wait, wait. Go back a minute. Who's pregnant? Gina?"

She frowned. "Didn't you know?"

He put his fork down carefully. "No, I didn't. My client hasn't shared that particular bit of information."

She rested her hands on the edge of the table. "Should we be having this conversation, Ryan?"

He swore softly and signaled to the waiter. "Probably not." When the waiter appeared, he told him to remove their plates, then looked at Elizabeth. "Would you like dessert? Coffee?"

"No, thanks," she replied with a faint smile. "I didn't do justice to my salad and I've had enough caffeine in the last twenty-four hours to keep me wired for a week."

Ryan waited until the waiter moved away. "About Gina's pregnancy. She couldn't have been very far along, right?"

"It happened the day they left together after the hearing."

He stared at her. "You're kidding."

"Don't I wish."

"How do you know?"

"That she was pregnant? Megan gave me the good news."

"No, how do you know when it happened."

Another near-smile. "I know." She paused while the check was placed in front of him. "I think that's the reason she made the date. She had to tell him and I think the last thing he wanted from Gina was another child. I have no proof of any of this, of course."

No, but he could see how she'd worked it out in her mind. It sounded very likely to him, too. He pulled his wallet out and removed his credit card. How would Austin react to learning he was going to have to deal with yet another kid? The mental picture that produced was not pretty. But would he do more than just pitch a fit like a spoiled kid?

"Ryan…"

He looked up into her eyes, green as glass, clear and compelling. "What?"

"He mustn't be allowed to get his hands on Jesse."

They were entering the hospital foyer half an hour later when Elizabeth's cell phone rang. Her hands shook as she fumbled for it in her purse. One look at the read-out told her that it was Lindsay calling. With her heart pounding, she put the phone to her ear. "What is it, Lindsay?"

"Where are you?"

"In the lobby…at the elevators." She turned her back on a uniformed guard heading her way, no doubt to remind her that cell phones were not to be used in the hospital. "What's wrong? What's happened?"

"It's Gina. I don't know for sure, but everyone is crowded around her bed in the ICU. I've paged Megan." Lindsay's voice broke. "Hurry, Liz. They've called a Code Blue."

"I'm on my way."

Gina's heart stopped during a convulsion brought on by excessive swelling in her brain. It was Megan who told Elizabeth that she was pronounced dead after seventeen minutes of desperate effort by the ER team. Elizabeth listened numbly to the details, white-faced and frozen. This time, when Ryan slipped an arm around her, she didn't resist. She turned her face into his chest and gave way to unspeakable grief.

Eighteen

Elizabeth stood with her arms wrapped around herself, staring out the window in a private room off the ICU. She was dry-eyed and filled with a dark pain. She'd been given a few moments to say a final goodbye to Gina, but she still felt as if some terrible mistake had been made. It was like one of those moments in her teenage years when she was told that she was going to yet another foster home, except that this was so much worse. With her eyes fixed on the trees in the park across from the hospital, she recalled wondering then whether she would be able to survive. And, of course, she had survived and she would survive now.

There had been no sign of Austin, but she knew better than to assume he was no longer a threat. Since Jesse did not know yet, Louie had been told to take the girls, Jesse and Jennifer, to his house just to be on the safe side. Now, down the corridor, Ryan paced, his frown as dark as a Texas sky before a storm as he spoke out of earshot into his cell phone. Hospital rules go to hell. She suspected he was trying to locate Austin.

Hovering just outside, but within sight of Elizabeth, Lindsay waited. Clearly she was anxious. That, too, felt unreal. Inside, Elizabeth's heart literally ached. She'd heard that phrase all her life, but had never known what it really meant. Now she knew. It was a physical pain, as real as if something was actually piercing her chest. She heard a sound at the door and then someone coughed quietly, but she didn't look around. Whatever it was, it could wait. Whoever could wait.

"Ms. Walker. Elizabeth Walker?"

She closed her eyes, dropping her head. Closing him out.

"I'm sorry for your loss, ma'am. I'm with the Houston Police Department. Homicide division."

She turned at that and saw that he had a badge in a leather holder, opened to show a picture ID. Just like in a movie, she thought, utterly unable to read it.

"Detective Shepherd Steele, ma'am. I hate intruding on your grief this way, but it's my job."

She looked at his face then. Thirtysomething, tall and regulation-neat. Black hair. Brown eyes. On closer look, shrewd, but kind eyes. "Is that really your name?" It was a name she might have made up in one of her books.

"Since birth," he said with a smile that was slow, unthreatening. She thought it probably charmed the panty hose off any female under seventy and fooled murderers. "I need to ask you a few questions, ma'am. I'll be brief, I promise. But it's necessary."

"Why? Questions about what?"

"About your friend, Ms. D'Angelo."

"Gina?" She felt tears rising and with a hand to her throat, swallowed, hard. "What kind of questions?"

"What's going on here?" With a fierce look at the detective, Lindsay went to stand beside Liz.

"Police business, ma'am," he said, flashing his badge. The move was much quicker and without as much politeness as he'd shown Elizabeth. "If you'll just step outside—"

"I don't think so," Lindsay said, now joined at the hip

with Elizabeth. "This woman has just experienced a tragedy. She's been at her friend's bedside since midnight last night. That's—" she glanced at her watch "—nearly fourteen hours of hell. Now, if you have police business, it can wait. Her lawyer will make an appointment to meet with you downtown." She frowned. "What's this all about anyway?"

"Lindsay—" Elizabeth put out a hand to say it was all right.

"I didn't get your name," Detective Steele said, his handsome jaw set as stubbornly as Lindsay's.

"That's because I didn't give it," she said, her blue eyes flashing.

"Look," Steele said, slipping his badge back in his pocket, "I appreciate your concern for Ms. Walker and I understand this is awkward, but I'm also not going to ask you again to step outside until I've finished in here. This is, I repeat, police business and—"

Lindsay took two steps to the door. "Ryan, come in here!" She turned back, missing Ryan's quick frown. "Lucky for us, our lawyer is on the premises. Any questions you have can be directed to him."

"Lindsay, it's okay," Elizabeth said, almost seeing humor in the situation. The two of them were squared off like boxers waiting for the bell.

"What's going on?" Ryan joined the group in the now crowded room. He gave Detective Steele a hard look, then his face relaxed. "Hey, Steele, what's up?"

"You know him?" Lindsay asked as Steele and Ryan shook hands. Both ignored Lindsay.

"How's it goin', Ryan?" the detective asked.

"It's been better." Ryan glanced at Liz's pale face and took a step toward her. "Is there a problem?"

Steele tapped his notebook against his leg. "I've asked

Ms. Walker if she'd mind answering a few questions. She's consented and we—''

''Homicide's got an interest here?'' Ryan's frown was back. ''You want to explain that?''

The detective grimaced. ''Not to you, Ryan, unless you represent this lady. But I can tell you she doesn't need a lawyer for what I'm asking. It's routine.''

''Routine or not, it's not gonna happen today,'' Lindsay said. ''I've told him Elizabeth has just suffered a tragic loss, Ryan. I've also told him you're our lawyer. If he wants to talk to her, you can accompany her to the police station whenever.''

Shaking her head, Elizabeth rubbed a spot between her eyes. ''He can't be my lawyer, Lindsay. He's Austin's lawyer.''

Steele's gaze narrowed on Ryan. ''You represent Austin Leggett?''

''Yeah. Why is that relevant?''

''Wait outside,'' Steele said to Ryan in a tone that was suddenly devoid of the good-ol'-boy connection. ''I have a few questions for you, too.''

Lindsay made a choked sound. ''Don't you get it, Detective? We've had a family tragedy here. It borders on cruelty for you to intrude on this moment. I've said Elizabeth will be happy to talk with you downtown, but after she's had a chance to take all this in. Come on, be reasonable.''

''Ms. Walker consented,'' Steele said, then turned to Elizabeth. ''That's right, isn't it, ma'am?''

''Yes, I consented. Although I'm thinking that after all this time, we could probably have been finished,'' she remarked dryly.

''Yes, ma'am.'' He turned to Ryan and Lindsay. ''If you'll excuse us…''

Ryan looked at Elizabeth. "Liz?"

"If I think I need help, I'll call Maude Kennedy," she said. Then with a questioning look at the detective, she asked, "Don't I have that right?"

"Yes, ma'am."

She nodded. "Then let's get started." She moved toward Ryan and Lindsay, shooing them toward the door. "If Austin shows up, will one of you please let me know?" With that, she turned back to Detective Steele, who was smiling. Almost.

"You've got some good friends there looking out for you." He closed the door while she took a seat, but kept his eyes on her. "I wonder why they think you need protecting."

She considered that. She hadn't even known Lindsay's and Ryan's names a month ago and yes, they did seem…protective. No other word described their attitude. It was a new experience. Today it gave her a warm feeling, adding some small comfort to the hole in her heart left by Gina's passing. She wasn't sure how she'd tolerate that kind of attention under other circumstances. She'd been on her own too long and prized her independence. Not that it would become a problem. She didn't expect Lindsay or Ryan to continue to spend so much time with her after the crisis was past. If they went the way of most people in her life—with the exception of Gina and Louie—they would have forgotten she existed in a few weeks.

The detective's next words brought her thoughts back to the moment. "Ms. Walker, do you have reason to believe Gina D'Angelo was murdered?"

"Murdered? Why would you think that?"

"Why would you say that?"

"I didn't say Gina was murdered!"

He flipped a page back in his notebook. "We had a call from someone in the ICU here at Hermann. You were overheard saying you didn't believe Austin Leggett's version of the accident that injured Ms. D'Angelo and her daughter."

"Oh. That."

"Yes, ma'am."

"I didn't say he murdered her, Detective Steele. You'd have to know Austin and his relationship with Gina to understand, I guess. I simply question anything Austin says. He's good at equivocating. If the facts in a situation don't please him, he's perfectly capable of rearranging them to suit him."

"That's a pretty harsh assessment of a man's character."

"Nevertheless, it's the truth."

"And you don't equivocate?"

"No."

He jotted a note on a fresh page, then looked up again. "What made you suspicious about this particular accident?"

Elizabeth thought about the consequences of telling the truth or simply pretending that her reaction and what she'd said was the result of her shock. Or grief. But then she'd be doing the same thing Austin did, rearranging facts rather than letting the facts speak for themselves. Equivocating.

"Was that a hard question?" Steele asked.

"No. I saw some marks on Gina's wrist that looked suspiciously like bruises from the grip of a man's hand. They were not there when she left with Austin because I was in her bedroom as she was dressing for their date. I actually watched her buckle a tiny jeweled watch on her wrist that evening. I noticed the marks after she returned from surgery. There were some abrasions, too, which I guessed were made by the diamonds on the watch band. If he manhandled her by grabbing her wrist while she still wore the watch, his grip would make the bruises and the watch band would scrape her skin." She looked at him. "Does that sound like I'm paranoid?"

"I'm a cop, not a psychologist, ma'am."

"I probably wouldn't have noticed…or if I had noticed the marks, I might never have jumped to such a conclusion, but Austin had a habit of getting rough with Gina, especially when she took a stand that irritated him."

Steele was making notes. "And she took a stand that irritated him that night," he said. "About what?" He looked up at her.

"I'm only guessing, you understand."

"Noted."

"Gina was pregnant. She didn't tell me, but it was discovered when she was examined here after the…accident. I think that was the reason she made that last date with him. She would be convinced that having another baby would tick him off like nothing else. He was doing all in his power to get her out of his life. Another child meant even more in the way of a financial obligation. Judge Hetherington had already named a sum that shocked him."

"You think that was reason enough for him to kill her?"

"I didn't say that, Detective Steele. I said that hearing it was sure to make him mad."

"Mad enough to drive him to violence?"

"That, you'll have to ask him," Elizabeth said.

"Why did you file the restraining order?"

"Oh." She almost smiled. "Maude managed to get it done, did she?"

"She did." Steele rubbed the tip of his ballpoint pen up and down near his ear. "Your complaint alleges that he poses a threat to his little girl."

"He wants to take her to Arizona where his mother lives."

"And you believe that's wrong for a father whose wife—"

"Gina was not married to Austin, even though she longed to be his wife. He was a master at delaying what she wanted."

"Does that mean he shouldn't see his daughter now? That she shouldn't be with her grandmother now that her mother's gone?"

"He shouldn't see Jesse because he would not hesitate to ship her off to his mother. And that would be awful, first because Jesse doesn't know the woman. Since moving to Arizona two years ago, she's expressed no interest in Jesse. And second, Jesse will need to be in familiar surroundings, she'll need familiar people around her, because as soon as I get back to my house, she will have to be told that her mommy's gone forever. The most familiar people in her life are me and Louie, who's been her grandfather in every sense of the word since she was born. Also, there's kindergarten. Changing schools would mean further trauma. There should be as little major upheaval in her life as possible. Losing her mother is trauma enough for any child. She needs to be in a place where she feels safe, both physically and emotionally."

"You think you're better qualified to offer all that to Jesse than her father and her grandmother?"

Elizabeth's eyes suddenly narrowed with suspicion. "Why are you asking these questions about Jesse? I thought you were following up someone's statement that

Austin may have had something to do with Gina's death. I don't see how Jesse's circumstances relate to that.''

"Under the circumstances, I consider any and all information about the deceased to be relevant." He studied something in his notebook. "I'm simply following up on your remarks about Mr. Leggett's involvement in the accident. Are you suggesting he inflicted more injury after the crash? And if so, how, exactly, could that be possible? They were in separate cars. Gina lost control of her car and hit a tree. The accident report states Mr. Leggett was first on the scene. Do you think he attacked her rather than trying to get help, as he claims?''

Hearing it stated flat-out was enough to chill Elizabeth's blood. Was Austin capable of that? Did he use the accident as a convenient way to put an end to his problems with Gina? She knew him to have an ungovernable temper, but what Steele suggested was so diabolically evil. She looked thoughtfully into space before speaking. "I don't know the answer to that, of course. But Jesse was there. She didn't have any head trauma, so she never lost consciousness. He couldn't have hurt Gina in front of her. At least, I don't think…'' Her words trailed off as her imagination took over.

"The little girl is five years old?''

"Yes.''

Detective Steele closed his notebook and slipped it into his back pocket. "Would you mind if I spoke with her? I'd be very careful.''

Even before he finished, Elizabeth was shaking her head. "No, absolutely not. I haven't even told her about Gina yet. I don't know what to expect when I do. Louie told me this morning that Jesse hasn't spoken a word since they left the hospital together. And there's still the funeral to get through.''

He nodded, seeming to accept what she said. "We'll leave it for now. Remember, there's no evidence that Leggett had anything to do with the accident. But to learn exactly what happened, the little girl is our best source of information."

"No." Elizabeth got to her feet and looked directly at the detective. Jesse was not going to be the victim in all this, at least, not more than she already was. "You'll have to find another source of information, as you put it. It's your job to find out exactly what happened without further traumatizing a child. Jesse's already lost the person she loves best in the world. She's not losing her innocence, too."

Elizabeth began collecting her things to leave the hospital with her thoughts in turmoil. The endless paperwork that had been shoved at her was now completed. There might have been some dispute between herself and Austin over who assumed what responsibilities regarding Gina's body and preparation for burial, but as Austin had not made an appearance at the hospital since that one brief moment with the doctor in ICU, Elizabeth had assumed the role of next of kin. She'd called Maude Kennedy, and learned with no surprise that Gina had no will, nor had she left instructions in the event of her death for other practical matters or for Jesse's future. If she had life insurance, nobody knew about it or where the policy might be. It was so like Gina to neglect anything unpleasant, Elizabeth thought, even if such an event put Jesse in jeopardy. It was Gina's way to simply close her mind to life's difficulties.

"She should have learned by now," Elizabeth muttered, pulling a gym bag from beneath a chair in the ICU waiting room and stuffing inside it the papers she'd just signed. Lord, how she wished she could stuff her own grief and guilt and, yes, she admitted it, her anger. Both she and Gina had spent childhood dodging life's curve balls. Both knew from experience how quickly and unexpectedly a reversal of fortune happened. With a grunt, she stretched to reach a hairbrush that had fallen out of the bag. "I'll be damned if history repeats itself in Jesse," she vowed softly.

"What history is that?"

She settled back on her heels with the brush in her hand and looked up blankly at Ryan. "Just thinking out loud."

He reached to take the gym bag after she zipped it up. "I've spoken to Megan. There's nothing else you can do here. Lindsay's staying for a while to take care of any details that might crop up regarding Gina. She told me she would drop by your house later today to give you a progress report, if necessary."

Elizabeth handed the bag over and took his hand, letting him pull her to her feet. She swayed with fatigue and his arm went around her. For a brief moment, she actually leaned into him, unable to summon up any good reason not to. He was solid and reassuring and the rest of her world was tilted on its axis. She had a hazy thought that trying to hold both Ryan and Lindsay at arm's length required more effort than she had right now.

"C'mon, let's get you out of here." His voice so close to her ear was enough to stiffen her backbone.

"I don't think I have a car," she said as they walked out of the hospital into the dazzling brightness of midday. "Louie drove Jesse home in it last night."

"Not a problem," Ryan said, steering her to the sidewalk. "Mine's parked in a spot reserved for patient pickup."

At the car, he tossed her bag in the back seat, then

opened the door for her. "Kick back and relax if you can.
There will probably be a lot going on at your house once
it's known that Gina is gone. Your friends will be dropping by with food, neighbors will be knocking. Hopefully
you won't be bothered with reporters unless it gets around
that Shepherd Steele was asking questions." He went
around to the driver's side, got in and buckled up. "Unfortunately, you still have to break the news to Jesse.
That'll be rough."

"Yes." Lord, yes. It filled her with anxiety just thinking
about it. Jesse had been through so much. "As for the
other, there won't be any of that."

He slowed, giving her a quick glance as he signaled to
merge into the traffic on Fannin. "Any of what?"

"Neighbors. Food. Curiosity seekers." She rubbed her
temples with a thumb and one finger. "I don't know any
of my neighbors. Gina and Louie are the only friends..."
She stopped, almost choking up. "Louie. Louie's pretty
much it in the way of friends."

"Gina was well liked at LJ and B," he said, gently
contradicting her. "Her friends there will want to do
something to help."

"Oh. I guess so." She looked away. "I...this is
so...such a...shock."

"Yeah."

"Do you know if Austin—"

He was shaking his head. "I saw him this morning before I left my house, but not since. I've been trying to
reach him, but it beats me where he could be. I called
Curtiss and a couple of guys he hangs with sometimes,
but drew a blank. You'd think he would keep in touch,
considering Gina's critical status. To my knowledge, he
doesn't yet know about her."

"Why am I not surprised," she said bitterly, gazing out

the window on her side. She knew better than to think Austin wouldn't show up soon making demands that she would fight to the end, but for now, it was good not to have to see him. Not to hear him pretend he cared that Gina was dead. If she had to talk to him right now, she didn't know that she could be civil. It was probably nasty of her, but she couldn't help feeling a sneaky satisfaction that Shepherd Steele was nosing around. If he questioned Austin, it might at least give him a few uneasy moments. That would be of some comfort to her.

As good as his word, Ryan concentrated on driving, giving her a chance to clear her mind to try to prepare for the ordeal of telling Jesse about Gina. She closed her eyes, wishing for oblivion, but instead she simply opened the gate on guilt and remorse, two demons she'd managed to dodge since first hearing of Gina's accident. The thoughts she'd had about Gina's shortcomings as a mother now haunted her. Her resentment that Gina didn't seem to appreciate the precious gift that Jesse was now seemed petty and mean-spirited. Her carping about Gina's parenting skills now felt like sour grapes. Was it envy? Covetousness? She winced inwardly. Each were listed as one of the seven deadly sins. Hadn't she thought many times that if Jesse belonged to her, she'd be a better mother? How arrogant. What conceit. Jesse adored Gina, was blind to her faults. She saw only her mother's sunshine smile, her spontaneity, her generous spirit. Ashamed and grieving, Elizabeth covered her face with her hands.

Dear God, how am I going to tell her that Gina is gone forever?

Nineteen

"The house seems deserted," Ryan said as they pulled into her driveway. "Looks like Louie did as suggested and took the kids to his place. I didn't think Austin would follow through on his plan to ship Jesse off to Arizona, especially now, but just in case he decided to try something, I felt they'd be safer at Louie's." He got out of the car and walked around to her side.

"Thank you," she said, as he helped her out. "Detective Steele wanted to talk to her and I refused. Has it occurred to you that, other than Austin, Jesse is the only person who knows the truth about the accident?"

"Yeah."

"I'm not giving him access to her."

"I would advise strongly against it if you told me you would." While she struggled to figure out what he meant by that, he looked beyond her shoulder to the street. "Speaking of the devil, here he is."

A squeal of brakes sounded behind her. She turned and, together with Ryan, watched Austin get out of his Porsche. Clearly, he was in a temper. He slammed the door hard and headed toward them in trendy sunglasses and a Texans baseball cap pulled low on his face. "If I didn't know better," Ryan murmured, "I'd think that was a disguise."

"Why would he need a disguise?"

"Good question." Ryan moved so that Elizabeth stood

just slightly to the side of him, protected by his shoulder and watched his client stalk across the grass. Although the golf shirt was expensive and the khakis top of the line, both seemed a bit wilted and wrinkled. "Looks like he slept in those clothes," Ryan said.

As he reached them, Austin ripped the sunglasses from his face and shoved the bill of the cap up. "I need to talk to you, Ryan."

"So talk."

"Privately," Austin snapped, giving Elizabeth a hostile look. "But first, where's my daughter? This is the third time I've driven over here in the last hour and nobody answers."

Elizabeth moved from Ryan's shadow. "You're on my property, Austin, which means you're breaking the law. I know you were served, so don't pretend otherwise. I'm asking you to leave. If you don't, I'm calling the police."

Ignoring her, he glared at Ryan. "Did you know about this? They served a goddamn restraining order on me. Why didn't you do something to stop it?"

Ryan checked Elizabeth with a hand on her arm. "As you say, Austin, this is something we should discuss privately. But don't even think of disregarding that order to get to Jesse. You'll be in even more trouble than now."

"They have no right keeping my kid from me! You should have blocked them. You should at least have given me a heads-up."

"And give you time to ship her off to Arizona?"

"Whose side are you on anyway?"

"Jesse's side, Austin," Ryan said. "And I might have been able to keep you informed if I'd been able to reach you. I've left several messages today. Why didn't you respond?"

"I've been busy." His eyes cut away.

"So you got my messages and just ignored them?"

He gave a restless shrug of his shoulders. "I told you, I had business that kept me tied up. What was so important? Was it my old man? God, he can't let me have a minute to myself even on a weekend!"

"I was calling to tell you that Gina passed away."

Austin blinked with shock. "Jesus," he murmured, his rage suddenly spent. His jaw flexed and he swallowed hard. Then, feeling their scrutiny, he turned away. Some emotion was at work inside him, Elizabeth thought. At least he wasn't totally unaffected. Down the street a power crew worked with chain saws trimming trees. He seemed fixed on what they were doing. "What happened?" he asked finally, keeping his gaze on the workmen.

"Are you asking if we withdrew life support?" Elizabeth asked, unable to hide her bitterness.

He gave her a startled look. "Did you?"

Elizabeth met his gaze with disgust and simply turned away.

"Gina died from a convulsion brought on by the brain injury," Ryan told him. "It happened a few hours ago. It was quick. We were told she probably never knew anything from the moment of impact at the accident."

"What about the...ah...arrangements?"

"Liz took care of everything. I was just dropping her off as she had no wheels at the hospital. Jesse doesn't know yet. I think you'll agree that it's best for her to hear it from Liz."

"I want to be there when she tells her."

Ryan cocked his head, studying Austin as if he were some kind of alien being. "Why is that, Austin? You saw Jesse's reaction when you approached her last night at the hospital. She became hysterical. Are you willing to put her through that again to satisfy some kind of power thing with Liz? Don't you understand what's at stake here concerning your daughter? Don't you realize what damage can be done? Jesse's going to be told that her mother's dead. C'mon, Austin. You need to think of what's in her best interest.''

Austin was again gazing at the work crew, his face set. ''I want you to fix it so I can see her.''

''It'll have to be with supervision. You read the order.''

''So, when?''

Ryan sighed, looking as if he'd like to knock some sense in his client, but knowing it would probably be a waste of energy even trying. ''I don't know the answer to that. When Liz has talked to her, we'll know more about her state of mind. I'll talk to the judge if and when Jesse appears ready to see you. I think you're going to have to be satisfied with that, Austin.''

Austin turned and faced Ryan directly. ''And I think I'm going to have to get another lawyer. You're fired, Paxton.''

Ryan nodded. ''Suit yourself.''

Color flooded Austin's face, turning it a bright red. ''This time I'm not changing my mind.''

''I hear you. To be honest, I don't think we're on the same page here, Austin.''

Austin looked as if he were choking on frustration and rage. Unable to provoke anything more than bland detachment from Ryan, he turned to Elizabeth. ''I know what's going on, Liz, and you're not getting away with it. If I have to—''

''Enough,'' Ryan snapped, stepping again in front of Elizabeth. ''I think you've made your point. It's time to move on. But before you leave, consider this a friendly warning.'' Ryan paused and the gleam in his eye was diamond-hard. ''If you say anything else directly to Elizabeth, if you make any threats, veiled or otherwise, to her, or if you attempt to circumvent the restraining order and frighten your little girl, be prepared to answer to me. Not even Curtiss Leggett will be strong enough to save your ass.''

Austin stood with his eyes smoldering and his hands working impotently at his sides. Whatever he wanted to say, he swallowed with difficulty. Then, with a muttered curse, he turned on his heel and stalked to his car.

"Don't let him fool you," Elizabeth murmured, watching as he revved up the Porsche's powerful engine. "He won't give up that easily."

"Not a problem," Ryan said, with a knowing look in his eyes. "I can be one stubborn SOB myself."

"May I have a word, Detective Steele?"

Shepherd Steele glanced away from his conversation with Dr. Megan Blackstone to look at her sister. He'd recognized Lindsay earlier today when she'd leaped to the defense of Elizabeth Walker. It had been tough hiding his reaction when he found himself looking into those fantastic eyes, since for the past year or two she'd played the starring role in most of his fantasies. He'd been among the disappointed when her show was canceled. He still couldn't understand why the station had made such a stupid decision.

He tucked his notebook into his back pocket, smiled a polite thank-you at Megan, then turned to face Lindsay. "Over a beer?"

"What?" Her pretty face expressed confusion.

"I'm wrapping it up here, but if you have more information, I'll be happy to listen. You can tell me over a beer. How about the Black Labrador?"

"That's in Montrose! Besides, I don't have any information,'' she said. Irritation made her sound as chilly as an ice cube. ''And what I wanted to ask won't take long. You won't have time to drink a beer.''

''But my answer might.'' He took her by the arm and steered her toward the elevator. Her arm felt fragile in his grip, but her sleekness belied the feel of her bones. He'd bet she was as toned as a dancer. ''You work out a lot?'' he asked.

''Work out?'' She reclaimed her arm, and after hesitating only a second or two, stepped into the elevator with him anyway.

He indicated her shape with a hitch of his chin. ''Nice muscle tone in that arm.''

''Yoga and Pilates three times a week. And I eat right.''

He looked down at his feet with a wry half smile. ''My downfall. If they banned fast food in Texas, I'd starve to death.''

''You should learn to cook.''

''Never had the inclination.''

''Look, Detective Steele—''

''Just Steele. Of course, you could call me Shepherd, but only my mother and my five sisters are allowed to do that, so far.''

''You have five sisters.'' She seemed struck by the thought.

''And every one of them mean as Texas rattlers.'' The elevator opened and he nudged her gently into the busy lobby. ''So, what's your job at WBYH now?''

''Associate producer of—'' She stopped with a flash of gold fire in her eyes. ''What does it matter what my job is? I want to talk about your job. And what your plan of action is to gather evidence linking Austin Leggett to Gina's death.''

''Whoa. Big leap from what Leggett says happened to

proving him guilty of a crime." They stepped out into late-afternoon sunshine. Steele's hand again closed on Lindsay's elbow to steer her along the sidewalk. "My car's just a quick walk this way."

A glance at her face told him she wanted to argue, but she fell reluctantly into step beside him with an expression of impatient resignation. He smiled to himself. There was too much of the journalist in her to walk away from a source of information. He wasn't fooled that it was him personally that she found interesting. She wouldn't be giving him the time of day if there wasn't a story in it.

"I read Ms. Walker's write-up in the *Chronicle* a couple of months ago, but I never made the connection between you and Dr. Blackstone as the sisters she hadn't seen in twenty-five years. Interesting how people can have blood relations living within a few miles of one another for a lifetime and never even know it." They stepped off the curb to cross the intersection.

"It happens," Lindsay said, then turned at the sound of her name called by a guy in a Mercedes convertible who'd stopped for the traffic light. She waved and gave him a smile. "Hi, Barclay."

"Friend of yours?" Steele asked, treating the guy to his best hard look.

"An acquaintance." She halted as he approached his car, illegally parked. "Do you do this often?"

"Only when I need to stop."

The Black Labrador catered to a thirtysomething crowd in Houston. As it was still early in the day, happy hour hadn't yet commenced. Something bluesy and soft was playing as Steele guided Lindsay to a table in the rear where they'd be able to hear themselves talk. She was primed to shoot a dozen questions at him about Austin's role in Gina's accident, but in exchange, he'd get a half hour of her company. Maybe longer, if he was lucky.

To his surprise, Lindsay waited until their beer was set in front of them to start. "I think there's much more to Austin's account of the accident that killed Gina than he's admitting," she said, getting straight to the point.

He picked up the long neck, tilted it her way as a toast and then took a first satisfying taste. "That makes two of you."

"Two? You mean someone else thinks he's guilty, too?"

"Ms. Walker mentioned having some suspicions."

"Oh, Liz. Yes, I know. Does that mean you're unimpressed? Do you need a majority consensus among the general public before you seriously follow up on something like this?"

"There is no majority consensus and I am following up. Seriously."

"Such as?"

He leaned back in his chair, enjoying her. "I have talked to Ms. Walker, I questioned the medical staff in ICU and I'm here waiting with bated breath to hear what you have to tell me. Who knows where it might go from there?"

He was teasing her. He watched the play of emotion on her face as she fought an impulse to fire back at him, but again her journalist instincts won.

"In that case," she said, "hear this." Giving a little hitch to her chair, she moved her beer aside and leaned toward him. "I've been asking questions about Austin Leggett. Gina isn't the only woman he's been involved with. I don't know if you're familiar with the habits of men who abuse women, but their relationships more often than not follow a similar pattern. Austin's abuse didn't begin and end with Gina, you can bank on that.''

"How were you going about getting the goods on this guy?"

She frowned. "What do you mean?"

"You said you were asking questions. Of whom? Where? When?"

"Oh. People at his law firm," she said, waving a hand, "Leggett, Jones and Brunson. When word got out that Gina was hurt, friends of hers called the ICU expressing concern for her. I took the calls and made notes. These are people who would know about Austin. I'm betting they know other women he's been involved with.''

He was nodding. "I'm impressed." He picked up his beer. "Got any names for me?"

"No. I don't want to scare them off."

"Pardon me?"

"You're a cop. If what I suspect is true, these women in Austin's past have also been victimized by him. I bet Gina isn't his only victim. If they follow the usual trend of abused women, they'll be reluctant to talk about it. They're ashamed. Or they're afraid. Many of them are in denial, if you can believe that.''

"And you base all this on…what? Your degree in psychology, what you've read on the Internet or…personal experience?" He couldn't imagine Lindsay allowing any man to rough her up, but as a cop he'd seen stranger things.

"Personal experience?" She looked dumfounded. "Do I seem the kind of woman who'd let a man beat up on me?"

"No. But I sense a lot of passion in you on the subject and you do have more than a casual understanding of the syndrome.''

"I'm passionate on Gina's behalf. And what I know of the subject I learned when I did a series on 'Lindsay's Hour.'" Again, she gave a dismissive gesture of her hand. "But this isn't about me. It's about Austin and his past. I hope to persuade one or more of his women to talk about her relationship with Austin. And even if we never prove he had anything to do with Gina's accident, he'll at least be exposed. There'll be some satisfaction in that."

"And you think if these women know I'm a cop, they'll clam up?"

"That's what I think."

He looked at her beer. "How about another?"

She opened her mouth to refuse, then didn't. Instead, she took a moment to think. Appearing to come to some conclusion, she said, "I can flush these women out, Steele, but I won't be able to do as much with the information I get from them as someone in a more official capacity could." She settled back into her chair, idly twirling the long neck in front of her. "Also, if there are records, such as police reports or visits to the ER where he's named, I'd have difficulty getting access without a court order. You, however, in your official capacity could probably overcome that obstacle."

He liked hearing her say his name. "Getting access without proper documentation could get sticky, no matter what your official capacity is."

She gave him her best media-person smile. "You've probably overcome obstacles a lot worse than that."

His smile tilted. "Well, I once got the goods on a bag lady stealing coins from parking meters."

"My source at HPD says you got the goods on a criminal a lot worse than a bag lady. My source says you were almost exclusively responsible for gathering the evidence and building the case that convicted John Stephens last year.''

Stephens was a particularly violent sexual predator whose victims were young college women. Steele had spent countless after-duty hours and most of the first two years as a fresh new detective building the case against Stephens, who'd killed six students before he was apprehended. At the press conference, his lieutenant had taken the credit on the day of the man's arrest. How in hell did Lindsay find out that he'd done the work?

"If you help me build a case against Austin Leggett, I'll personally see to it that you get the credit,'' Lindsay said, still pushing.

He picked up his beer, not believing a word of it. He bet his badge she was looking to find something that would give her leverage at the TV station to negotiate a deal for a new show. But what the hell, he'd get to enjoy her as long as it took to nail Leggett. There was some compensation in that. With a grin, he tilted the bottle toward her. "It's a deal.''

She clinked her long neck to his. "I think I will have another.''

Twenty

Jesse was sleeping. Finally. Elizabeth eased herself up from the bed and tucked the blanket snug around the little girl. For a moment or two, her hand hovered over Jesse's head. The dark curls, still damp with tears, stuck to her temple and cheeks. Elizabeth gently caressed her silky mop and, bending low, kissed her softly. Telling her that Gina was gone forever had been unspeakably painful. Jesse had listened with wide, fearful eyes. Then she'd thrown herself into Elizabeth's arms, her small body trembling, sobbing as if her world had ended—as in some ways it had. Elizabeth had tried to find words to comfort her, but what was there to say to a five-year-old whose mother would never return?

Elizabeth had encouraged her to talk, to ask questions, but oddly, Jesse still seemed locked in a silent world. What was more worrisome was the look in her eyes. There had been grief, yes, but more than that had been the stark terror as she'd peered fearfully at windows and doors, jumping at sounds. The ring of the doorbell terrified her. Cars pulling up outside sent her flying to Elizabeth, clinging and pale. Trying to guess the source of her fear, Elizabeth had assured her that she was safe, that her new home was here. That her mother was in heaven and was now an angel who would watch over her forever. She still had not let Elizabeth out of her sight.

Straightening now, Elizabeth watched for a long moment to be sure Jesse was fully asleep, then she tiptoed from the room, leaving the door open and a night-light burning. Just getting Jesse into bed had been a challenge. Even without saying so in words, she'd made it plain she wanted Elizabeth to stay with her. Finally, she'd fallen asleep, but in Elizabeth's bed and only when Elizabeth had read her a favorite story over and over and had agreed to sit quietly beside her.

Now, almost swaying with fatigue herself, Elizabeth went down the hall to check that the house was secured for the night, all the locks thrown and the windows shut. In spite of the security system and the restraining order, she was still leery about Austin. If he reacted true to form, he wouldn't let a judge or a piece of paper deter him if he really wanted to get to Jesse. Elizabeth would need to be as determined as he. And she was, she told herself fiercely as she checked the dead bolt on the back door. Jesse's whole life was at stake and she vowed that the court system that had failed her at the same tender age wouldn't fail Jesse, too.

The door was a half-glass design and Elizabeth stood for a moment looking out at the night. In that moment of quiet, she finally let the reality of the tragedy sink in. Gina was dead. And in dying, Jesse was now hers. For the past two days since the call from Megan that Gina was near death, that selfish thought had been lurking in the back of her mind. Gina had been her sister, without a doubt closer to her than her biological sisters, and she'd loved her. Still, she'd seen her shortcomings as a parent and had longed to rescue Jesse, but not at such a price. Never like this. What was wrong that such a tragedy produced so joyful an outcome? Guilt, crushing and ugly, made her moan.

"Are you okay?"

Startled by the unexpected sound of Ryan's voice, she drew in a quick breath and wiped at her cheeks with both hands. "I was checking the lock." She didn't turn, afraid of what he'd see on her face.

"I've checked it and every other door and window in the house." He was behind her now, almost close enough to touch her. "The place is secure."

"I didn't know you were still here," she said, turning finally with a hand pressed over her runaway heart. Louie was often in the kitchen without exuding much male presence, but Ryan loomed tall and confident, almost filling up the space. Something about him made her feel crowded and breathless. "I thought everybody had gone."

"Leaving you alone?" His eyes, watchful and quiet, were intent on her face. "I don't think so."

"Did Louie go home?"

"He's in the den watching the late news. It'll be difficult to persuade him to leave. He seems to think you need all the support you can get tonight."

"That's really not necessary," she said, making a vague gesture. Only then did she notice the bounty in her kitchen. Every available inch of counter space held covered dishes and casseroles, containers of fruit, a cake on a pedestal plate, brownies in a cut-glass bowl, napkins, utensils and paper plates. Bottled drinks. Brewed tea in a tall jug. "Where did all this come from?" she asked, astonished.

"Your neighbors. Gina's co-workers. Friends. Your agent, your editor."

"How did they know?" She couldn't believe so many people had been so thoughtful.

He smiled. "I'm not sure, but if I had to guess, I'd say Lindsay and Louie thought it appropriate to tell the people in your life what happened." His gaze left her for a moment to look it over. "There will probably be a lot more tomorrow."

"Oh, my."

He was still smiling. "As for the brownies, I understand that Jennifer and Jesse made them." Shaking his head, he looked wryly puzzled. "I didn't know Jennifer could boil water, let along make brownies. She said she thought it would help to keep Jesse occupied."

Elizabeth nodded mutely. Who would have dreamed that Ryan Paxton's daughter would prove so sweet? Or that Lindsay would prove so thoughtful? Or that Megan so kind? Louie, yes, maybe, but expressions of concern from others were totally unexpected. "Is Jennifer here? It's so late."

"She got a phone call from Rick Sanchez a couple of hours ago and when he heard what was going on, he offered to pick her up and take her home."

"Isn't he the boy she struck on the bike?"

"Yeah. You'd think he'd run a mile to avoid her, but it seems the accident bonded them, so to speak." Ryan rested against the counter, crossing his feet at the ankles. He appeared relaxed, but his eyes looking into hers were dark and intent. Did he sense the turmoil she was feeling, she wondered. Did her face reveal the confusion she felt?

"Rick has befriended Jen at school," Ryan said, "and it's made her transition from Dallas to Houston a lot easier. I owe him more than a spiffy new bike."

"Are they alone at your house?"

Now his expression was almost funny. "They are and I'm praying my impression of Rick's character is reasonably accurate."

Elizabeth found herself smiling in sympathy. "Good luck."

"I laid down the law, but I'm not fooling myself that

they'll resist temptation forever. Rick's been raised right and he's aware of the circumstances here. I think they'll be okay until I get home." Leaving the subject of his daughter, he regarded her with a look of concern. "I didn't want to leave until Lindsay got here, Liz. She plans to stay the night. And even though Louie's dead on his feet, he's determined to stick like a burr, too."

Elizabeth didn't know what to object to first. That Lindsay was coming over? That she planned to stay? That Louie refused to go home? And Ryan. She couldn't even find words to describe the role he had assumed. She blinked as he straightened, watched the overhead light strike his hawk-handsome features and turn him into someone she should have backed away from. Instead she had to stuff her hands into her pockets to keep from reaching for him. It was a bizarre reaction. It was because Gina was dead and overnight her world was changed. She'd never adjusted easily to change. "Lindsay's coming here tonight? She's staying?"

"She thinks you need sisterly support. And she's right. And you know what else?" He straightened, then reached out and cupped her face in his hands. "You look like you need a hug."

With a flash of intuition, she knew he wasn't thinking about giving her a hug. He was going to kiss her. "Ryan—" She couldn't seem to tear her eyes from his or make a move that would tell him no.

"Yeah, I know. You never need anything. You're used to handling whatever comes your way—good or bad— alone. Besides, you've got a million things that you think you have to do for Gina." He was still smiling, his thumbs stroking her cheeks. "No doubt about it, Liz, you look like you could use a hug." His voice was low, almost a caress. Her heart was fluttering. "But would you settle for a kiss?"

She tried again to say something, to keep him from doing what he planned. For some reason, she knew that to be kissed by Ryan would change everything. Oh, God, more change. She felt dizzy at the prospect. Or was Ryan himself the source of her dizziness?

It was barely a whisper of a kiss...at first. His lips settled on hers, a nonthreatening touch of his mouth to hers. He was not touching her anywhere else. There was just that sweet, gentle blending of their lips and his big hands framing her face, and yet holding her in place. And then she was aware that he moved in a little, crowding her oh, so gently against the edge of the counter. Still nonthreatening, but firm enough so that she felt him, warm and solid, from her breasts all the way to her knees. It had been a long, long time since she'd been in a situation like this. On her rare dates, she never allowed a man to get so close. She was so caught up in the wonder of it that she was hardly aware of his hands leaving her face, skimming down over her arms, then slipping around her, closing about her until she was fully embraced. There was something elemental and so right in finding herself held fast by this man.

And then the kiss was suddenly much more than a sweet melding of his lips with hers. The whole tenor of it changed. It became deep and searching. Wondrously thrilling. He explored her mouth the way he might have the taste of something he'd wanted a long time, and would take his time, not rush and have it all over too soon. Or was that her reaction? Whatever, Elizabeth allowed herself to sink into the magic, to simply feel the heat of it spread deliciously through her. She'd once known something like this kind of pleasure, she thought dimly, but it had never come so close to overwhelming her.

And then a sound intruded. It was several seconds before, out of the delirium of the kiss, she identified it as the front door. Voices.

She stopped. Or was it Ryan who stopped? She honestly didn't know. Her hand went to her mouth and pressed hard as if to deny what had happened. She stared at him, dazed and shaken and appalled.

Seeing her face, Ryan reached to touch her. She must have looked shocked and unsteady on her feet. She certainly felt that way. "This isn't happening," she said shakily, catching his wrist and pushing it aside. "Gina—"

"Wouldn't deny you the comfort of a kiss," Ryan said, a rough edge in his voice. Had he been as caught off guard as she was? But he stepped back and allowed her to slip past him and out into the hall. If it felt like escape, she refused to admit it.

Their walk to the front of the house seemed a mile long. When they finally got there, Lindsay was in the foyer in conversation with Louie and the homicide detective who'd questioned Elizabeth at the hospital. "Hi, Liz. Ryan. You remember Shepherd Steele, don't you? From Homicide?"

"Of course." Resisting an impulse to put her hands to her burning cheeks, Elizabeth nodded politely, hoping her agitation didn't show on her face. It didn't help that Ryan remained close, his size and sheer presence a solid reminder of her insanity.

Ryan reached around Elizabeth to shake hands with the detective. "You're putting in some long hours, aren't you, detective?"

"He's not on duty now," Lindsay said. "We stopped at the pub to discuss the case and he insisted on driving me home."

"Her car's still at the hospital," Steele said. "I'll drive it over tomorrow morning and catch a ride back."

"I told him I was perfectly capable of driving," Lindsay complained with exasperation. "How many beers did we have?" she asked him.

"I had a couple," Steele said with only a hint of a smile. "You, on the other hand—"

She laughed suddenly and gave him a light punch on the arm. "He was probably trying to drive up my blood alcohol so he'd have an excuse to find out where I live." She shook a finger in his face. "I never, but never, reveal my address or my phone number."

"Area code 281-555-7628."

"Where did you get that?" Lindsay hit him again, still laughing. "Oh, I know. Probably from the same illegal source we're gonna use to flush out Austin's past relationships, huh?"

Grinning, Steele winked at Ryan. "She'll be a great investigative journalist just as soon as she learns to put a lid on it or drink less."

"What are you talking about, Lindsay?" Elizabeth asked.

"Nailing Austin," Lindsay said, without missing a beat. Then she looked at Ryan. "No offense, Ryan, but I'd rather you didn't hear the plan. I know he fired you, but you're still in a delicate position, legally speaking. Not to be forgotten also is his father, Curtiss Leggett. He's powerful in your law firm and if he suspects you have a hand in bringing Austin down, he could do you some real damage."

"Thanks," Ryan said dryly, "but I think I can survive whatever Curtiss and Austin may throw at me at LB and J."

"If we're successful, Austin won't be at LB and J to throw anything, isn't that right, Steele?"

"It depends." Steele had a hand on the door, ready to leave. He hesitated, looking now at Elizabeth. "It's damn difficult to get evidence in domestic violence cases, Ms. Walker. Women clam up, families retreat in denial, the courts won't act, even some cops turn a blind eye. Sometimes it takes a tragedy to wake us up."

"I'm aware of that," Elizabeth said, "but it's time that Austin was held accountable for his behavior."

Lindsay was staring at Steele with an open mouth. "Wait a minute. Something about what you said sounds very personal."

His brown eyes, teasing and friendly until now, were suddenly dark and unreadable. "I don't think we got around to the personal stuff tonight, did we?" She was shaking her head mutely as he pulled the door open. "My sister was married to an abusive bastard. The signs were all there, but we were blind. Until fourteen months ago when he killed her."

Gina's funeral was held two days later. Ryan spotted Austin the moment he appeared in the door of the chapel, mostly because he'd been on the lookout. Liz had mentioned using the restraining order to keep him away, but Ryan had promised to keep an eye on him to see that he didn't approach Jesse. Better to let him appear to pay his respects, ignore him and hope he'd leave quietly. Common decency demanded that he attend the funeral of the woman he'd lived with for more than eight years and Ryan was convinced that Curtiss Leggett would have laid down the law, too, forcing Austin to show if for nothing more than to keep up appearances. There would be employees of LJ and B paying their respects to Gina and the law firm

must appear to honor her memory. A huge spray of roses
from the firm was placed near the registry book, not to be
missed. Ryan felt disgust now watching Austin assume a
somber expression as he stood looking over the crowd.
Ryan noticed that he avoided glancing toward the flower-
shrouded casket.

Searching for Liz, he found her across the room talking
with one of Gina's co-workers. Heading her way, he saw
her eyes go wide with alarm as she spotted Austin. Her
gaze flew to the other side of the room where Jesse sat
with Jennifer. She ended her conversation and scanned the
crowd, found Ryan and sent him a look of wordless appeal. He reached her in another dozen strides.

"Don't worry," he said, touching her arm. "I'm keeping an eye on him."

She gave him a quick, concerned look. "Do you think
he'll try to get to Jesse?"

"He might try, but it won't happen," Ryan promised,
his grim gaze following Austin as he worked the room.
Liz was right to be concerned. In spite of his reassurances,
he was worried that Austin would try to approach Jesse.
He was a desperate man and as such Ryan considered him
a danger to the little girl. If he'd had any doubt, it had
been erased on the night Gina died.

He had driven home that night after leaving Liz in the
care of Lindsay and Louie to find Jennifer in her pj's ready
for bed, talking on the phone to her mother in Dallas. He
had stood outside her room listening as she told Diane
about her role as Jesse's nanny and described the household, including in her dialogue Louie, Archie, the dog,
and even Liz. He was relieved to hear none of the usual
bickering between them. He had smiled then, thinking his
little girl was growing up....

Jennifer heard him at her door and told her mother to

hold on. "Dad, can we drive to Dallas after all this is over and get Mocha? We could take Jesse. I don't think Liz would mind." She hesitated, then added craftily, "You could ask Liz to go, too."

He went in and sat on the side of the bed, no longer surprised at Jen's uncanny insight into his libido. As for her dog, he'd expected her to ask for Mocha before now. But the aging pet probably wouldn't transplant to the rather confined quarters of the condominium. "Are you willing to take on the responsibility of exercising her and seeing that she's taken outdoors to do her business?" He gave a tug on her hair. "She's old, baby. She might not adjust as well as you."

"We could ask Louie if she could stay with him. She'd be good company for Archie."

"We'll see."

She sighed and said into the phone, "That means no, Mom. But I'm not giving up. Talk to you later." She made a kissing sound and disconnected.

"That was Mom."

He smiled. "I guessed that." He pulled the comforter back and motioned for her to climb in. "How's she doing?"

Jennifer made a face, plumping up her pillow. "She's still dating that bald guy. His name is Gerald, can you believe that? It sounds so nerdy, doesn't it? Actually, he is nerdy, but I guess she likes that. It's light-years different from you."

"You don't see me as nerdy?" he asked, still smiling.

"You're hot, Dad. Every woman who sees you goes nuts."

"Hmm."

"Mom was really dumb to let you get away."

"Jen—"

*"I know, I know. We don't talk about how she got into
an affair with Sam, who turned out to be a turd."*

He forced himself not to chuckle. *"As opposed to a
nerd?"*

"Yeah."

"Hmm."

*"But about Gerald, he's really old, Dad. She just told
me, he's forty-five!"*

"Whoa, that ancient, huh?"

*"Well, it's a lot older than you. What does she see in
him, I wonder?"*

Ryan knew exactly the appeal of Gerald Winthrop from
Diane's point of view. He was wealthy, besotted with her,
semiretired so that he had time to lavish on her and did
not want her to have his child. Ryan had been forced to
listen as she'd gushed about Gerald a couple of days ago
when she'd called for an update on Jennifer. But telling
Jennifer exactly what Diane saw in her next husband
wasn't an option. *"He seems a nice man and I'm sure
they have a lot in common."*

Again, she made a face. *"I just hope they don't want
me to come live with them if they get married."*

He hoped the same thing. He'd found he liked having
Jennifer around. It was just a few short years until she'd
be in college and then she'd be gone forever. He planned
to make the most of the time he had with her while she
still thought he was cool. Or un-nerdy. *"So, how are you
and Jesse hitting it off?"*

*"She's a real sweet little girl, but she's got some ma-
jorly big problems, Dad."* Jennifer sat up, punched at her
pillow and shoved it against the headboard. *"She does
not talk at all since the accident. Isn't that weird? Because
that first afternoon when we met and had cookies and all,
she was a little chatterbox. She talked my ear off. Now—"*

Jennifer shook her head, looking troubled "—not a sound."

"Liz is concerned, too. Hopefully, it's a temporary thing."

"Like I said, it's weird." Jennifer wrapped her arms around her knees. "You know what I think, Dad? I think she's scared."

"Do you have any real basis for thinking that?"

"Well, all it takes to make her eyes go big and round and scary is to mention her scummy dad."

Ryan winced. "Jen. Describing someone as scummy is about as low as you can get." It was one thing for him to see Austin as he was, but to hear Jen express the raw truth was uncomfortable. It seemed that her perception of other people didn't end with her own dad. He didn't know whether to be impressed or alarmed.

"Get over it, Dad. Scummy's the right word. I think it describes him perfectly. You remember I told you Jesse used to talk about her dad scaring her mom and she'd hide under the bed listening to the yelling and screaming and who knows what all else. Then her mom would cry. Well, in all the time I've spent with Jesse, she's never mentioned her dad wanting to be with her. Now, ever since the accident, this guy's nagging everybody to see his little girl. Well, get real, for heaven sake." She rolled her eyes. "It's a lie, Dad. I mean, he wants to see her, all right, but it's not for love of Jesse. It's because she knows something about that accident and he doesn't want her telling."

"How do you know this, Jen? Or is it just something you're theorizing?"

"Oh, Dad, quit sounding like a lawyer again!" Jennifer ticked off points on her fingers. "One, Austin is hell-bent to talk to Jesse when he's always ignored her. Weird!

*Two, Jesse acts scared. She gets paranoid over stuff like
telephone calls. Or when the doorbell rings. Like, she'll
run to the bathroom and lock herself in. Me and Louie
have to talk her out of there and it's not easy, trust me.
And third, she drew a picture and wow, it was something
else!''*

"What kind of picture?'' Ryan asked.

*"Well, it was pretty crude, like she's not much of an
artist at five years old, but you could tell she was drawing
two cars on a road and you could tell it was night, too.
When I asked her who they were, she said her mom and
dad.''*

"I thought you said she doesn't talk anymore.''

*"She doesn't. I ask questions like, 'Who's in this car,
your mom? Your dad? Is this the night of the accident?'
and she'll nod her head. Or shake it if the answer's no.
But what made the picture scary was that she scribbled
all over it with black crayon. You could tell the whole
thing was...well, scary. Whatever she was drawing in that
picture, it was not a sunshiny message, Dad. It was mean
stuff. I'm even thinking, like dangerous stuff.''*

*Ryan rubbed his face with both hands. He hadn't antic-
ipated that having Jennifer baby-sit Jesse might expose
her to the chilling prospect of a father who posed a threat
to his child. "Did you keep the picture?'' he asked.*

*"Uh-huh.'' Jennifer scrambled out of bed and took her
backpack out of the closet. Rummaging around in it, she
finally produced a wrinkled sheet of Jesse's art. Ryan was
no child psychologist, but one look told him his daughter
had not overreacted. He could see terror in Jesse's childish rendition of that last ride with Austin and Gina. It was
unsettling that Jennifer came to the same conclusion as
Liz and Lindsay. Jesse was the only eye-witness to the
accident. What if she did, indeed, know something that*

*was damaging to Austin? And if Austin somehow managed
to gain access to Jesse, what would he do? And was there
any danger to Jennifer while she was taking care of Jesse?
Would he harm Liz if she put up a struggle, which she
was bound to do?*

"What is it? What's wrong, Ryan?" Liz's hand was on
his arm and she was looking up at him with concern.

He covered her hand with his own and managed a
smile. "I hate funerals."

"Don't we all," she said. Then he felt her fingers
clench on his arm. "Look, Ryan, he's moving toward the
girls."

Austin was moving amiably across the room, but was
steadily closing the distance between himself and Jesse
and Jennifer. At the moment, both were oblivious to the
mourners and guests paying their respects to Gina. Jennifer had given Jesse a new Barbie doll and both were
intent on dressing it. Austin, without making his true intent obvious, paused here and there to receive words of
sympathy from people who knew of his relationship with
Gina and assumed he was saddened by her death. Liz
guessed his purpose and headed quickly toward the children while Ryan moved in an oblique line to intercept
him. But just before Liz reached Jesse, she looked up and
saw Austin.

The sound of her scream, high-pitched with terror, startled everyone. The somber atmosphere in the room splin-
tered like glass shattering on stone. The shocked crowd
stared as Jesse scrambled off the couch, strewing tiny Barbie accessories everywhere, searching frantically for Elizabeth.

"Here, Jesse!" Elizabeth opened her arms and Jesse
flew into her embrace. She was swept up and held tight
as Elizabeth hurried through the door toward the private

office of the funeral director. Ryan silently congratulated
her for arranging the escape plan beforehand. He wished
she'd been able to whisk Jesse away before the child saw
her father.

Ryan stepped directly in front of Austin. "Nice of you
to drop by," he said with a tight smile, taking a firm grip
on his ex-client's elbow and steering him out of the room.
The maneuver was accomplished so smoothly that Austin
couldn't shake Ryan off without drawing attention to himself. Behind them, the funeral director began the business
of soothing the crowd, urging people back to their chairs.
After an awkward moment or two, they were indeed picking up the threads of their conversations. Hysterical out-
bursts were probably not uncommon at a funeral, Ryan
thought with grim humor as he frog-marched Austin, sullen and scowling, to the front door.

Once outside, he let go of the sleeve and brushed his
hands together as if ridding himself of something distasteful. "Don't bother signing the register," he told Austin
with disgust. "I'll take care of it. And I'll be sure to tell
Curtiss you paid your respects."

"What do you think you're doing, Paxton?" Austin
jerked the sleeves of his jacket into place and straightened
his tie.

"I'm attending the wake and funeral of a woman who,
until a few weeks ago was a damn good employee to LB
and J. As a partner, it seemed the decent thing to do."

Austin's mouth thinned in a sneer. "You don't give a
shit about Gina. You're here to play bodyguard to that
bitch Liz."

"Liz doesn't need a bodyguard, but it looks like Jesse
might."

Austin hesitated a beat, then his gaze slid away from
Ryan's. "I don't know what that was all about. I'm think-

ing somebody's working on her, trying to poison her mind against me. I'm not going to stand for it and you can tell the bitch that.''

''Such an idiotic accusation doesn't deserve an answer, Austin, but do you honestly think Liz would stoop to do something like that? She's never done anything except what's best for your daughter. You should be grateful.''

''Yeah, well, how's it best that a kid is kept from seeing her father? Especially after her mother's been killed in a car accident.''

''And under normal circumstances, I'd agree with you. But you saw Jesse's reaction just now. And it's the second time it's happened. Actually, the only two times she's seen you since the accident, she becomes hysterical. You want to tell me what that's all about, Austin?''

''How the hell do I know? She's traumatized from the accident, I guess. If I got a chance to talk to her, I could probably calm her down. The problem is, nobody will let me get near her,'' he added bitterly.

''Maybe she would calm down and maybe not. But it's out of your hands for the present. Look, I'm not your lawyer, but I'm giving you good advice, Austin. Stay away from your daughter right now. Abide by the terms of the restraining order and let things settle down.''

Austin's smile was hard. ''Yeah, you'd like that, wouldn't you? Stepping aside would leave the door open and make it even easier for Liz to grab my kid. Do you think I don't see what's happening here? You're suddenly tight with her, your kid's practically living over there and you want me to believe **you**'ve got my best interests at heart advising me to just step aside, be a gentleman and sign over my kid's life like she was a pet cat that I don't want anymore. What's with you, Ryan? That's nuts, man.''

"It would be nuts if I thought you were sincere in what you're saying," Ryan said quietly. "But there're too many unanswered questions about the accident and too much bad history is bubbling up, Austin. I'd get a lawyer if I were you and play it very quiet right now."

Austin looked at him suspiciously. "Was it you who sicced that homicide cop on me?"

"If you mean Steele, the way I heard it is he's following up on something he heard in the ICU. And if there's nothing there, you have nothing to be concerned about."

"Then I don't need a lawyer, do I?"

Shaking his head, Ryan turned to go back inside. "Suit yourself."

Twenty-One

Elizabeth walked into her kitchen and found Jennifer pouring brewed tea into a tall pitcher and Jesse standing beside her holding a sleeve of plastic cups. "What's up, you two?"

"We're making iced tea to take outside to the patio." Jennifer dropped a few slices of lemon into the pitcher, set it on a tray and picked it up. "Did you know Megan was here? Get that thing with the pink sugar in it, would you, punkin-pie?" she told Jesse, who did as asked and put the artificial sweetener on the tray. "Detective Steele already carried out the ice bucket."

"Detective Steele is here?"

"Uh-huh. He came with Lindsay and Megan."

Lindsay and Megan? Elizabeth had been struck by an idea for a book this morning and had gone directly to her office after breakfast. Besides herself and Jesse, only Louie had been in the house at the time. Louie, to her eternal gratitude, was almost a fixture since Gina's death a week ago. He'd practically appointed himself housekeeper, nanny and best friend and since Jesse needed all the support they could muster, Elizabeth had welcomed his presence.

Jennifer looked over the tray with a critical eye. "Okay, do we have everything?"

Jesse reached for sprigs of mint which lay on the table

and put them on the tray. Jennifer gave her a smile. "Whoa, can't have iced tea without mint, huh?"

Jesse agreed, solemnly moving her head from side to side.

Elizabeth went to the window. Outside on her patio, seated around a metal table in lawn chairs, were Lindsay, Megan and Shepherd Steele. Then her gaze lifted beyond the patio to the gazebo. She felt a little jolt of pleasure. Ryan sat on the glider with Louie. They seemed to be having a deep conversation. "Are we having a party?" she asked, bemused.

Jennifer grinned. "No, but we will if you say the word. Louie and I were going to keep Jesse occupied while you worked, but then Lindsay called and said she and Detective Steele had something to tell you and then when they got here, Megan was with them. Naturally, Jesse wouldn't let them disturb you. She's like a little tiger guarding your door while you're holed up in your office. I guess you've told her when you're working you don't want to be disturbed…or something. And boy, she can say a whole lot without making a sound. Right, punkin-pie? Then next, my dad came to pick me up, but when I told him who all was here, he just sort of stuck around."

Elizabeth felt a tug on her shirt and looked down into Jesse's face. "What is it, sweetheart?"

Jesse looked longingly at the group on the patio, then back to Elizabeth. Seven days since Gina's funeral and still Jesse refused to talk.

"She wants you to come outside with us and not go back to work," Jennifer said as if Jesse had spoken. Jesse nodded, her eyes pleading.

Jennifer was as skillful at interpreting Jesse's speechless communication as Jesse was in doing it. Elizabeth had spoken to a pediatric psychologist who'd advised her to wait awhile before seeking professional help. "Give her some time. Be patient and loving," had been her advice. "She'll probably come around. She hasn't just lost her mother, but she was actually in the accident. Added to that is the fact that the parents were separated and the family unit newly broken. Jesse might have survived all that, but you've told me the situation was somewhat chaotic. Frankly, I'd be surprised if the child didn't exhibit some unusual behavior."

"Can you break for a while, Liz?" Jennifer was at the French doors leading to the patio with Jesse, who was torn between wanting to go with her mentor and idol or staying with Elizabeth.

"I'll do better than that." Elizabeth went to the door and opened it for Jennifer. "I'll take the rest of the day off. Besides, it's Saturday. Is that okay, sweetheart?" She looked down at Jesse, who, with a pleased smile, tucked her hand in Elizabeth's and went with her out onto the patio.

The entire group looked up as one when she appeared. "Hey, it's Liz. And refreshments!" Lindsay jumped up and cleared a scattering of papers from the tabletop so that Jennifer could set the tray down. Steele rose quickly to offer her his seat. Megan did the same. There was a definite sense of flustered welcome in the lot. Had her appearance been so unexpected, Elizabeth wondered with a little spurt of irritation. It was her house, after all. Now that she'd discovered a gaggle of guests, wasn't it reasonable she'd join them?

"Jen and Jesse fixed iced tea," she said dryly.

Lindsay rubbed her hands together. "Iced tea, great. With lemon and mint, yet. Lovely. You can hang out at my place anytime, Jen." She looked down at Jesse, who was tugging on her shirt. "Oh, what's that you say, Jesse? You helped, too?"

Jesse took one of the mint leaves and went to a pot on the edge of the patio where the herb grew, lush, green and fragrant.

"You grew the mint?" Lindsay grinned. "Cool."

Jesse went pink with pleasure. Archie ambled up, tail wagging, and bumped against her knees. Then suddenly, he gave a joyful bark as Cody appeared, slipping shyly through the backyard gate. Jesse's face brightened and followed Archie to greet her little friend.

"Will she talk to Cody?" Lindsay asked, watching them.

Jennifer picked up the pitcher, ready to pour. "Nope, but they still have a lot of fun." With her eyes on the two little kids, she worried her bottom lip. "I think Jesse wants to talk, but she's afraid to. All we need to do is figure out why."

Steele smiled. "You think you can do that?"

Jennifer began pouring iced tea. "I don't know, but I'm working on it."

"You must think we're a thoughtless bunch," Megan said to Elizabeth in her quiet voice a few minutes later. "Here we are descending like a swarm of locusts and on a Saturday, too. Did we do much harm, interrupting your work?"

"Not at all," Elizabeth said politely. "But your days off are far more precious, I would think."

"What could be better than this?" Megan waved a hand indicating Elizabeth's yard with its tasteful landscaping. "The water garden with the goldfish is especially nice. I love the sound of water trickling over those stones. So restful. You have a beautiful place here."

Elizabeth smiled. "Thank you. I like it."

"Perfect for Jesse to grow up happy and untroubled."

Elizabeth's smile faded a little. "If Austin can be reasoned with."

"Or removed from the picture altogether. That's definitely Lindsay's plan and I understand from her that you're just as determined."

"We can't turn Jesse over to Austin," Elizabeth said fiercely. "It would be a travesty."

"And that's why we've all descended on you this morning. Lindsay's found some interesting stuff and she's roped me into the project, as usual."

Elizabeth looked at Lindsay. "About Austin?"

"About Austin." Lindsay reached for her cell phone. "Wait'll you hear."

Elizabeth sat in the chair that Steele vacated for her and waited while Lindsay punched a few buttons, looking intently at the read-out. Apparently the cell phone was a state-of-the-art product that functioned as a telephone and a small computer. As Megan said, Lindsay had vowed to dig into Austin's past to see what might turn up. After being around her for only a couple of weeks, Elizabeth had soon realized that, once on a mission, Lindsay was like a dog with a bone. And nailing Austin Leggett was her mission.

As she waited, Elizabeth couldn't resist looking across to the gazebo. Ryan and Louie made no effort to join the group on the patio, but as if he sensed her watching, Ryan turned his head and saw her. His smile was slow and seductive, rich with an intimacy that took her breath away. She quickly reached for the glass Jennifer handed over.

Not missing the moment, Lindsay said, "Ryan's banned from our discussion. He's agreed that he can't have access to our research. Although he's champing at the bit to get involved, he was Austin's lawyer and he's bound by ethical considerations whether he likes it or not.'' She flashed a smile. ''His loyalties have changed, but I don't think that would cut much ice with his ex-client.''

''Hardly.'' She took a taste of tea, barely hearing Lindsay. She'd avoided being alone with Ryan since the night of the kiss, but she hadn't been able to avoid seeing him altogether. Nor had she been able to blank out thoughts of him that popped up, sometimes when she was at her computer, sometimes while going about household routine. Sometimes in the middle of the night. He'd been very thoughtful in driving Jennifer over often after school, but he didn't come inside. The only reason he was here today, she suspected, was that Louie had waylaid him.

''Okay, I've got a few names of women who figure in Austin's past.'' Lindsay scrolled through the material she'd put in the data base. ''First one, Kristin Jordan. I got her name from a paralegal who worked closely with Gina.'' She looked up at Elizabeth. ''Did you ever hear Gina mention Kristin?''

Elizabeth thought back. ''I think so, but only vaguely as nothing comes to mind. Was she someone in his past?''

''Not in the distant past as in before Gina, if that's what you're asking. According to my source, he was fooling around with Kristin while living with Gina. Anyway, Kristin didn't want to talk other than to tell me that Austin was a real piece of work. She had nothing nice to say about him, but denied he'd ever been violent. So—'' she pushed a button to scroll to the next name ''—dead end there. Olivia Barton.''

Elizabeth frowned. ''Olivia is…was Gina's hairdresser, wasn't she?''

''Uh-huh. And she was Austin's, too. I noticed his spiffy hairstyle at the hospital and thought at the time that it was every bit as good as anything our makeup staff at the station did. She was also very talented in the sack.''

"He was involved with Olivia?'' Elizabeth asked with a look of astonishment.

"Yes, ma'am. And she, unlike Kristin, was much more forthcoming. She seemed genuinely sorry for the affair after I told her about Gina's accident and death. Said she always felt real guilty as Gina was a nice person.'' Lindsay paused with a better-late-than-never look, then added, "But not guilty enough to end the affair...until Austin coldcocked her one night. It happened at the San Luis Hotel in Galveston, she told me. The rendezvous was an idea Austin cooked up.'' She stopped and veered off her report. "He did this often. He'd get his eye on a woman, then begin a seduction campaign that had to be pretty expensive. He'd arrange dinner at an upscale restaurant, or he'd spring for a trip. For instance, he took Olivia on a junket to Las Vegas. Anyway—'' she was shaking her head "—on this particular night, they called room service and ate in. According to her, they had a little too much vino and got into an argument over Gina, of all people, if you can believe that. Next thing Olivia knew, she was on the floor and seeing stars, he slapped her that hard. She thinks she was actually out for a moment or two. Unfortunately, she didn't report it to the cops. She left, called a friend of hers who is an EMT, he checked her out, said she didn't have a concussion, and Olivia vowed to steer clear of Austin Leggett. Which she has done ever since.''

"We might get a statement from the EMT,'' Steele said, making notes in his notebook with a pen.

"You need one of these, Steele,'' Lindsay said, leaning over to show him the tricks her cell phone computer was performing.

"Yeah, and I'll get one when the Homicide budget gets

as cushy as yours at WBYH,'' he said dryly. Then, without looking up, ''What else do you have?''

''You're welcome,'' Lindsay muttered, making a face. But she did as he asked and scrolled to the next name. ''Patricia Ellis.'' She looked up at Liz, who shook her head with a blank look. ''Patricia is our best bet, boys and girls. Along with Erica, that is.''

Steele looked up. ''Who's Erica?''

''I haven't gotten to her yet,'' Lindsay said.

''Then why did you mention her?''

''Because she—oh, never mind. Where was I?''

''Patricia Ellis,'' Steele said evenly, showing her his notebook.

''Anytime you two get ready,'' Megan said, smiling, ''Elizabeth and I are listening.''

Lindsay shot Steele a wicked look, then went back to the subject at hand. ''Okay. Austin knew Patricia before Gina ever came into the picture. He was actually engaged to her right after law school. They were deep into plans for the wedding and suddenly she broke it off. She went into seclusion—'' Lindsay made quotation marks with her fingers ''—or something for a month. Word put out by her family was that she was recovering from the emotional trauma of it all. But her maid of honor said she was hospitalized with a broken jaw that had to be wired until it healed.''

Elizabeth was leaning forward, her drink clasped between both hands. ''Please tell me she pressed charges.''

''Indeed, she did.''

''About time,'' Megan muttered.

''But it'll be a miracle if we can get our hands on it. Maude Kennedy would have found it for the custody hearing if it still existed.''

"Could Austin's father have pulled some strings to have it destroyed?" Elizabeth asked.

"Nothing's ever destroyed," Steele said. "He could have influenced a judge to seal the file."

"Or..." Lindsay sent a thoughtful look at Ryan, still talking with Louie. "Maybe this is where Ryan could be useful. If Curtiss Leggett thought we'd gotten hold of those records, I wonder what his reaction would be?"

"I could mention it to Ryan," Steele said, "in the course of my investigation. And if he feels compelled to mention to Austin's old man that some of the kid's past transgressions are cropping up, I wonder what the fallout would be?"

"Ooo, Detective Steele, that's so devious." Lindsay grabbed his pen and scribbled something on a napkin. "I like it. I like it. I'll enter it into my data base."

"Using my pen? My outdated pen?" Steele made a sound, something between a laugh and a snort and reclaimed it. "What else do you have?"

"This is amazing," Elizabeth said with an admiring look at Lindsay. "How did you do it?"

Lindsay grinned. "Wait, I'm not through."

"The out-of-order Erica," Megan guessed.

"Yep. Erica Johns was the homecoming queen the year that Austin graduated from high school. She was his date for the prom and instead of enjoying a late-night breakfast at some spiffy hotel in Houston, she spent the night in the emergency room at a hospital after he roughed her up. My source said gossip has it that he raped her and she's almost certain the hospital was Hermann."

"Another sealed document?" Elizabeth said in disgust.

"Probably. But the hospital's records might not be so secure." Lindsay looked at Megan. "What you could do in your spare time, Meggie—" she grinned at Megan's expression ''—is to dig through the records at Hermann. If Austin's thirty-four now, it would have been sixteen or seventeen years ago that he graduated from high school. Would those records be accessible?''

''I'm not sure.'' Megan took the scrap of paper that Steele handed her with Erica Johns's name and the date of the incident written on it. ''I'll give it a shot.'' She glanced up, her face unusually animated. ''So to speak.''

They were all getting a little punch-drunk at the thought of bringing Austin down, Elizabeth thought. She glanced around the table, looking at the faces of her sisters and felt kinship, not resentment. The defenses that for years she'd been so careful to keep intact were slowly but surely being undermined. How had it happened? The changes that she'd resisted so long were upon her whether she was ready or not.

''She begins to get next to you after a while, doesn't she?''

Ryan turned from a deep study of Liz and met the smile in Louie's eyes. What had he given away by the look on his face? ''Which one?'' he asked.

Louie chuckled softly. ''Oh, I think we both know which one. She has a very **complex** personality, Liz. She won't be easy to win—'' he paused and looked deliberately at Ryan ''—even without the complicated history that exists between the two of you.''

''What history? I had never met her until Gina's court hearing.''

''The history linking your father and hers, son. You told me yourself you blame Matthew Walker for the death of your dad. That's a serious charge and an even more dangerous secret to keep from Liz if you plan to act on what you're feeling for her.''

"I don't have a clue as to what I feel for her, Louie."

Louie chuckled again. "I think you do have a clue and that's what's bugging you. You're not sure you can walk away from Liz once you've got her where you want her. Isn't that the way you've handled all your women since you divorced Jenny's mother?"

"Diane had an affair," Ryan said, sounding defensive in spite of the rightness of his behavior then. "Divorce was inevitable. Hell, she was married again within six weeks of the date it was final."

"I guess you showed her."

"Yeah." There was silence as the two men mulled over private thoughts. Then their eyes met and both laughed. "You're right. Wounded male pride played a big part in making me push for the divorce, although I didn't admit it then."

"Understandable."

"I think Diane regretted the affair and probably wanted to stay married." Ryan's gaze strayed to Jen, half child, half woman, now passing around napkins to the group on the patio. "It's only recently that I've come to see the damage done when a couple splits. A kid's loyalties are divided, discipline goes by the board, there's chaos all around. It's Jennifer more than Diane or me who became the victim."

"Live and learn, I reckon." There was no malice, but just what seemed shared sympathy from Louie.

"It's too late to change things back to the way they were," Ryan said, adding, "Even if I wanted to. Diane's second marriage broke up after a couple of years and now she's ready to take the plunge with a new guy." He leaned forward, resting his elbows on his knees. "Jen says he's bald and old and she doesn't know what her mom sees in him. He's forty-five, Louie."

"And you're what, thirty-five, six?"

"Close. I'm thirty-seven."

"Huh. Eight years to go before you get old, eh?" He was still smiling. Both men watched as Jennifer left the patio and headed toward Jesse and Cody carrying two small boxes of juice. "Jen's been a godsend for Jesse," Louie said. "Instead of making a fuss over the fact that the little one won't talk, Jen acts like it's the most normal state of affairs. She's one sweet little girl, your Jennifer."

"Yeah, but I sure can't take the credit. I haven't always been a good father. You'd think that being deprived of a dad myself, I would have made a better effort to see that Jen had everything I missed." He had been uncomfortably aware of his shortcomings as he'd watched Liz fret over Jesse since Gina died. He should have blocked Diane from moving to Dallas after the divorce. He should have insisted on being a real father, sharing in Jen's life far more than he had. Those years and that opportunity were lost to him now, but he planned to make the most of the time they had left before his daughter went off to college. And he was going to do his dead-level best to see that the outcome for Jesse was safe, secure and happy.

"You wouldn't be the first father in the world who didn't measure up," Louie said with a look toward the group on the patio that Ryan couldn't read. "Take my advice and make the most of the time you've got with your daughter."

"Am I hearing the voice of experience?"

"Experience?" Louie looked at him. "You're asking if I've ever been a father? The answer is no…not in the real sense of the word."

Depends what the meaning of no is. Louie's reply was no more enlightening than the famous line by a former president. The old guy might be retired, but once a lawyer, always a lawyer. "Sorry," Ryan said. "I didn't mean to get personal."

Louie gave a crack of a laugh. "Hell, son, this is about as personal a conversation as two men ever get. You've just told me some pretty strong stuff about yourself. I guess I can do the same."

Ryan had been waiting for the right moment to satisfy his curiosity about Louie Christian ever since that first day when they'd talked here in Liz's backyard. The man had a past that would be helpful to Ryan in trying to straighten out the mystery of his dad's death. He just hadn't figured out how to go about enlisting Louie's help. Except for the brief facts he'd offered then, the older man seemed to shy away from any questions about that time. Was this the right time? Rather than say the wrong thing and have Louie clam up again, he kept his mouth shut and waited.

There was no humor left in Louie's voice when he spoke. "I once was a father, but a damned piss-poor one. Oh, I didn't get a divorce and I didn't do the stuff we're thinking Austin Leggett has done, but I failed in other ways and the failure was just as catastrophic."

Ryan noted the older man's unsteady hands as he braced himself to get to his feet. Concerned, Ryan started to rise, but Louie made a grunt of a sound and gestured to keep him in his seat. Walking to the edge of the gazebo, he leaned both arms on the railing and looked out across the lawn where the three women and Steele sat discussing Austin's downfall. His voice had a rough edge when he spoke. "I've been thinking about what to tell you, Ryan. And I'm not talking about myself now and my shortcomings as a father. First of all, I owe you. You've been generous about letting Jennifer help out here and I know you're going to help Liz." His gaze had moved to the children where Jennifer supervised Jesse and Cody throwing the Frisbee to an ecstatic Archie.

"You don't owe me, Louie. I'm righting a wrong in seeing that Liz gets custody of Jesse. I let my own personal prejudice get in the way of my objectivity. I have an obligation to fix it."

"We'll talk about that, too," Louie said, rubbing at his beard. "But first—"

"Is this about Matthew Walker?"

Louie turned, giving him a surprised look. "What makes you ask that?"

Ryan raised a shoulder. "It just makes sense. You've admitted you knew my dad and we know he was a colleague of Judge Walker's. I've been thinking you probably knew Walker, too."

Louie went back to the glider and, with a creak of arthritic knees, sat back down. "Yeah, I knew him, son. And it's been worrying me that you believe he had something to do with your father's suicide. I hope you won't insist on worming the details out of me, but I can put your mind at rest about a couple of things. Of course, you'll have to take me at my word. No way to confirm what I'm about to say."

"I don't believe you'd lie to me about something like this, Louie."

"Yeah, well, I've lied before and I'll probably burn in hell for it, but what I'm about to say is the God's truth. Matthew Walker didn't have anything to do with John Paxton's death. And your dad didn't commit suicide, son. He was murdered."

Ryan focused on his hands clasped between his knees. Here it was. Confirmation of a suspicion that had been in the back of his mind a long time. He turned the idea over and over as a multitude of chaotic emotions tumbled around inside him. Relief. Confusion. Disbelief. Rage. And a thousand questions.

He turned his head to look at Louie. "Don't tell me, let me guess. You're not going to tell me how you know this for a fact."

"What you should do is concentrate on your life now, son. It should give you some peace of mind to know your dad didn't abandon you and your mother. I knew Elaine Paxton, too. She was a brave, beautiful woman, a wife any man would be proud to have. Her illness was tragic. John never would have taken the coward's way out and left her, not to mention abandon his son."

"You're positive about this?"

"That he was murdered? I swear it on my own wife's grave."

Ryan believed him. He knew he wouldn't get anything more out of Louie at the moment, but he didn't have any intention of giving up. Still, there had been something else Louie had mentioned. "What else was it you wanted to tell me?"

"Well, I guess it's advice. Not that I've got any right giving advice, but I've never stopped buttin' in when I've got an opinion. It's about Liz."

Ryan grunted but said nothing.

"You're not denying you have special feelings for Liz, are you?"

Ryan's mouth hiked up at one corner. "What you should do is concentrate on your own business, old man."

Louie rubbed at the smile on his face. "Guess I asked for that. But I'm serious when I tell you that Liz isn't going to like being surprised. You better tell her about your dad and hers before you get much more involved."

"Yes, Father." Grinning, Ryan stood up. Louie hit the nail on the head in guessing his attraction to Liz. His obligation to right the wrong done to Jesse wasn't the reason he found himself at Liz's house so often lately. It was Liz herself.

"One more thing," Louie said as Ryan stepped down out of the gazebo. Ryan turned, looking back over his shoulder. "I have some old files that might interest you about the cases on John Paxton's docket when he was killed. You can drop by to look at them later tonight." He gave a gentle shove with his foot and set the glider in motion. "That is, if you were planning to ignore my advice about getting on with your life."

"I'll be there." Ryan walked off, shaking his head and regretting he'd never get a chance to see Louie Christian in action in the courtroom. He would have been a worthy adversary.

Twenty-Two

The hours Elizabeth spent writing stories for children had always been her greatest source of pleasure and escape. Survival during her childhood had fueled her rich imagination. Long nights of fear were the fertile ground to grow characters who overcame great odds. The pain of being shunted off to yet another foster family produced plots where rejection grew into strength.

After she'd escaped the prison of state bureaucracy, she'd learned to her delight that it was possible to live in the adult world without giving up the fantasies of her childhood. Publishers paid for her stories. And the value they paid her in dollars didn't begin to match what the writing of them gave Elizabeth. From time to time, Gina and her turbulent life were a distraction, but not even that robbed Elizabeth of the magical escape to be found in weaving tales for children.

Unfortunately, it wasn't working lately.

She'd been at her computer for a couple of hours since her guests had departed and nothing had been produced that Jesse couldn't have done. With a sigh, she closed down her computer and went to check on Jesse.

Jesse. Was she the problem? For the past hour or so, she'd been in the den playing with Cody. The quiet was disconcerting to Elizabeth. The little boy had never been a chatterbox and Jesse's muteness was not the magic that turned him into one. Consequently, they played in an eerie silence. Watching them, she thought they didn't seem hampered by not talking, but communication among children wasn't always done with words. Something adults might note, Elizabeth thought dryly.

No, it wasn't Jesse. Having the gift of Jesse bestowed on her so unexpectedly was the source of much conflict and guilt, but she was dealing with that. She could work around it. She would work around it. For one thing, Gina would literally turn over in her grave if she knew that Elizabeth had a single moment of guilt over circumstances that were truly beyond her control. And for another, the alternative—handing Jesse over to Austin—was simply not to be considered.

The other possibility—her resistance to knowing her sisters—was greatly diminished. There was no mistaking their sincerity in wanting to reconnect after all these years. It wasn't their fault that their adoptive parents had rejected a third child. That had been a stroke of bad luck for Elizabeth, but it was unbecoming and petty to resent it now that they'd discovered her and wanted to build a relationship with her.

As she stood watching the children and thinking, the doorbell rang. Instantly Jesse dropped a handful of Lego and sprang up, scattering the pieces everywhere and looking around wildly for Elizabeth. She rushed over and grabbed the tail of her shirt while looking fearfully toward the front door. Elizabeth bent and cupped her little face with both hands, forcing their eyes to meet. "It's okay, sweetheart. You stay here with Cody and I'll see who it is. Nobody will come into our house and hurt you."

Jesse's head moved back and forth frantically.

"Nobody," Elizabeth repeated firmly. "See, I'm going

to close the den door and you and Cody will be safe. Don't worry."

Jesse reluctantly backed to the couch while Cody watched with apprehension. The little boy clearly didn't understand Jesse's fear, but as the days passed, he'd come to respect it. He took her hand and led her behind the couch where they both dropped out of sight, hiding. With a worried sigh, Elizabeth closed them up in the den and went to see who was at the door.

"Hi." Ryan stood on her porch with one hip cocked, jiggling his car keys. His grin was off center, just short of embarrassment. "I was in the neighborhood."

She nodded, feeling a now familiar flutter of nerves in her stomach. "Again?"

He spread his hands with boyish nonchalance. "It's probably my car. It keeps swerving toward your house."

Like a bolt of lightning, she finally pinpointed the reason for her distraction. It was an incredible case of denial that she hadn't faced before this moment. "Your car," she repeated, trying to keep a smile in check. "Is that the reason Jennifer keeps turning up?"

"That and her newly developed sense of self-esteem. It's pretty satisfying to do something worthwhile—and I'm talking about befriending Jesse—when there's nothing in it for yourself except the warm feeling you get."

"She is an angel. You're a lucky dad."

"Yeah." His smile waned as he moved closer and instead of looking at her, turned his gaze to Louie's house next door. "Louie's expecting me at his place soon, but I wanted to talk to you first." He glanced at her, then down at his feet. Whatever was on his mind seemed to rob him of some of his usual male confidence. "Can I come in?"

"Okay." She stepped back to let him inside. Lean and broad-shouldered, he took up a lot of space. As always when she found herself confined in a room with him, her composure suffered. He was the only man on the planet who could do that.

"Jesse and Cody are playing in the den. The doorbell frightened her, so I need to tell her who's here. She'll be fine when she knows it's you."

"Have you figured out what's going on with that?"

"Isn't it obvious? She's afraid Austin will come for her."

"Jen agrees with you." He dropped his gaze, studied his feet. "I wish I could tell you that's not gonna happen, but Austin's behavior has defied all logic lately. In his present state of mind, he's capable of ignoring the restraining order and trying to force his way in here to talk to her."

"I wish I could believe he only wants to talk to her." Elizabeth worried her lower lip. "What's more likely is that he wants to take her."

"There's a word for that. The penalty for kidnapping is serious. Even if it's your own kid."

"But as you say, Austin's behavior lately is not logical. He's desperate, Ryan."

"He hasn't made any attempt to see her recently, has he?"

"Not to my knowledge, and she's seldom out of my sight unless she's with Louie or Jennifer."

"Just be cautious, okay?"

He watched her walk to the den and open the door to reassure the kids. No sound from Jesse, but Cody's question to Liz was revealing. "That's not Jesse's bad daddy, is it?" the boy asked.

"No, it's Ryan and he's Jesse's good friend."

After settling them, she left the den and found him looking up at a series of her book covers, framed and hanging on the wall going up the stairs. "I'll be so glad when all this is resolved," she said.

He turned. "Yeah, me too." He gestured toward the book covers. "That's very impressive, but it's not everything you've published."

"No, those are my earlier works. I used to have more ego," she said, smiling.

He stood uncertainly for a moment, then drew in a breath. "I wouldn't say no if you offered me a beer."

"And I'd offer you one if there was any in the house. I'm not much of a beer drinker, but I do have some wine."

"I'm not particular."

She didn't believe that for a minute. The trappings of a very upscale lifestyle were evident in Ryan's career, his home, his wardrobe. Even in the casual clothes he seemed to prefer. She was glad that she could offer him good wine.

"Red or white?" she asked, her hand hovering over a wine rack.

"You choose."

She took down a bottle of Frog's Leap, then pulled a drawer open looking for the corkscrew. When she found it, he reached and took it gently from her. "Here, let me do that." In a few deft twists, he uncorked the wine. "We'll let it breathe for a minute," he told her.

"Okay." An awkward moment passed before she thought to get wineglasses. She moved to the opposite side of the bar and removed two from a hanging rack. To Ryan, she seemed a little breathless. Flustered.

"I had a talk with Louie this afternoon while you were tied up with your sisters and Steele," Ryan said, picking up the bottle. "He's had an interesting life."

"I agree. That is, what I know of his life. He's not very forthcoming with details of his past." She gave a soft laugh. "It's the writer in me, I suppose, but sometimes my imagination leaps to some pretty wild what-ifs."

"I would think that's normal, for a writer."

"Normal or not, it's what I do. There's probably nothing very mysterious in his past, but what a disappointment if he tells me one day he was a mailman."

"I think you can strike that one. He admits he was a lawyer."

"Really?"

She looked interested, he thought, pouring some of the wine in the two pretty stems she'd chosen. But not particularly surprised. If she knew more about Louie, she was good at concealing it. They each took a glass. "Hmm, nice," he said as he tasted it.

"I like it," she said, inhaling the heady fragrance. "Usually you can only find Frog's Leap in restaurants, but there's a place on West Gray that stocks hard-to-find labels. Actually, Gina told me about it. She was the wine connoisseur." She stopped, as if mentioning Gina had been unintentional. And painful.

"She had good taste," he said quietly. "And not only in wine."

In another second, she would be crying. Seeing it, Ryan made a motion toward the French doors leading to the patio. "Can we talk outside? I'd rather Jesse and Cody didn't overhear our conversation."

The April night was mild. The sweet scent of night-blooming jasmine wafted on just a whisper of a breeze. There was a chaise longue on the patio. Ryan watched her go to it and curl up on it. Something about her body language suggested she was folding into herself. He suspected it was self-protective behavior learned during her tumultuous childhood and that thinking of Gina was the reason. He hoped it was Gina and not him.

"I've said it before," he began, wanting to put her at ease. "You've got a great house here, but what you've done with the grounds is even better."

"I like puttering around in the yard, but I can't take all the credit. The overall plan came from a professional."

They sat for a moment listening to night sounds. There was a full moon and it cast pale shadows on the delicate bones of her face. He wished he had nothing else to do tonight except to spend it with Liz. They hadn't had enough time together and he worried that after tonight when she learned what he had to tell her, that she might cut him out of her life altogether.

He drank some of the wine and then set the glass aside carefully. "Louie knew my father. Did you know that?"

"What?" She seemed to take a moment to change mental gears. "No, I didn't. Is that what you wanted to talk about?"

"Yes and no. I mentioned my father to him a while ago. I suspected it from some of the things he said that he'd had more than just a casual acquaintance with him. I think they worked together, although he didn't tell me that in so many words." Ryan hesitated, then took a seat on the end of the chaise. "I take it you didn't know any of this."

"No, but I'm not really surprised. Louie's never admitted that Houston was a part of his work history, but he's often revealed a knowledge of Houston politics as it relates to the legal community. Of course, a news junkie would be in the know, too. I suppose I assumed that was the basis of his interest. But to be honest, it was not something that mattered much to me." She took a sip of her wine. "Of course, I can understand why it would interest you. At one time I was hungry for information about my parents. My father especially."

Did that mean she no longer was? He wondered why. He could tell her that a good source of information on Judge Walker was in and out of her life daily, but she clearly didn't know Louie was acquainted with Walker. It wasn't up to Ryan to tell her, especially not tonight. Besides, he was getting more and more curious about Louie Christian as an individual himself.

"I've never been able to get much information about my dad's career on the bench," he told her. "Now today, I find out from Louie that he's sitting on a pile of papers that may answer questions that have tortured me since the day he died. Do you have an idea what that's all about?"

"You're asking me?" She spread the fingers of one hand on her chest.

"I figure you know Louie Christian better than anyone else."

She gave a brief laugh. "Then you know more than I do. As I said a minute ago, Louie's very private. We don't talk about his past."

"And you've never been curious?"

"No."

He studied her face, now turned in profile from him. Studying her, he was aware of something, a scrap of a thought that he couldn't quite pin down. It was not the first time, and it always slipped away. "I guess I find it interesting that someone as private as you would open yourself to a friendship with anyone whose past is a mystery."

She stirred restlessly. "Why are you asking me all these questions when you conclude that I'm even more in the dark than you are?"

"Because there's something I need to tell you that's related to all this. In a way." He saw the wariness that came over her and thought she was going to get up, possibly ask him to leave. But she didn't.

She brought her wineglass to her lips. "Now I'm really confused."

"My dad knew Judge Matthew Walker."

"You learned that from Louie today, too?"

"No, I've always known they knew each other."

"My father and yours—" She looked bewildered. "Were they friends?"

"Maybe, I don't know. Maybe not. I've thought for years that they weren't."

"Based on what?"

He gave a short laugh. "My own imagination, or so it seems now."

"Why have you never mentioned this before?"

This was turning out to be more dicey than he'd thought. He got up from the chaise. "I'm wondering the same thing myself and kicking myself because I didn't." He watched her set her wineglass down carefully on the patio and draw her knees up close to her chest. More defensive posture. "I had what I thought was a good reason for not telling you. I thought Judge Walker was responsible for my father's suicide."

She was silent for a couple of heartbeats, looking at him. "You thought. Past tense."

"Yeah, past tense. I guess you could call this a confession," he told her. "I left my objectivity in a hole somewhere when I went into the courtroom to argue Austin's case against Gina that day. I'd learned our connection—yours and mine—only a couple of days before the hearing. I'd spent all the years since I was sixteen hating Matthew Walker, so I was out for blood."

She was turned from him now, looking at the windows visible in the rear of Louie's house, but she said nothing.

"Afterward, I felt like...well, I didn't feel good. I'm not usually that vicious in the courtroom. I've been trying to think of a way to tell you."

He moved around the chaise, needing to see her face. A feeling of dread was building inside him over what was at stake. Somehow, Liz had become more than just an interesting woman who appealed to him sexually. He'd sensed that she was as aware of the attraction between them as he was, but she had far more reason to be wary even without knowing the connection between their fathers. And Louie had been right. She was a complex person. She didn't like surprises. Her whole childhood had been a series of ugly surprises. Now, with his heavy-handed confession, something precious and vital and rich with possibilities was in danger of slipping away from him.

"Why tell me now?" She was still not looking at him.

"Promise you won't laugh?" Maybe playing it lightly would work.

"I'm not finding anything you said funny."

"Then how about this? I think I'm falling in love with you."

That brought her up and off the chaise. He watched her wrap her arms around herself and pace to the edge of the patio. Something about her looked so vulnerable that he ached to take her in his arms and reassure her. "Is that so bad?" he asked, coming up close behind her.

"It's impossible. You never met me until a few weeks ago. You don't know me."

"I do, even if that knowledge has been crammed into a very brief time. Think about it. I've been with you in some of your darkest hours. In fact, I've probably contributed to them, but I swear I'll make it up to you. And I've learned more about you from Jennifer singing your praises when she gets home. I've seen you with Jesse, watched you open up to your sisters. You're generous and kind and smart and creative.''

"Oh, please—"

"And beautiful." Setting his wine aside, he reached from behind her and took her chin in his hand, turning her face gently toward him. "And I swear that wasn't the first thing I noticed."

She did look up then into his eyes. "Have you been drinking?''

He laughed. "Yeah, some very good red wine, but less than four ounces." His smiled stilled. "It's not alcohol talking, Liz. I want us to be together. I want to spend time with you, get to know you better. I want you to know me. I've been with a lot of women since my divorce, but I haven't met anyone I'd miss if they went out of my life."

Her gaze roamed over his features, searching. "I don't know what to say."

"Just say that you're willing to give us a chance."

Her lips curved and he felt some of his tension fade. "I'm willing to think about it."

With a smile, he caught both her hands in his and unwound the tight lock she had on herself. "Will you think about this, too?''

Catching her face, he brought her mouth to his. The kiss was slow and deliberate, telling her without words that he meant what he said. He savored the sweet taste of her for a long moment, then reluctantly broke the kiss and tucked her head beneath his chin. "I'm going to do my dead-level best to be patient, but I've gotta tell you, patience was never one of my star qualities."

She let out a short laugh. "Don't you have somewhere to go tonight?''

Louie. "Yeah." He heaved a sigh and stepped back

reluctantly. "I'll walk over from here." Still holding her hand, he looked into her eyes. "Will you have dinner with me tomorrow night? Or we can go to a movie. Your choice. Or both. Jennifer can baby-sit."

"We'll see."

He'd have to be satisfied with that. "Lock up," he said.

Elizabeth stood watching Ryan's long strides take him deep into the shadows of her lawn, using the path the children had made through the thick oleander border separating Louie's place from hers. She put a hand to her mouth where the taste of him lingered. Everything that was considered and deliberate and wise in her cautioned against letting herself get involved in an affair just now when her entire life was in turmoil. Her primary concern should be Jesse and winning the custody battle. She was struggling to adjust to Lindsay and Megan coming into her life. She was struggling to adjust to Gina leaving her life. No, too much was happening. Adding Ryan to the mix was a complication that she didn't need.

I think I'm falling in love with you. She shivered and turned to go back into the house. What woman wouldn't be tempted upon hearing those words from a man like Ryan?

As she opened the French doors to go inside, she heard the phone in the den ringing and rushed to pick it up. Telephone calls were another source of anxiety for Jesse, who now sidled up to Elizabeth and hovered anxiously as she talked.

"That was your mom, Cody," Elizabeth said, keeping a hand on Jesse's shoulder. "Time to go home. Your dad's walking over now. How about I help you both pick up these toys?"

Jesse stayed close, but pitched in with Cody to put away

the things they'd played with from the toy box. A moment later, the doorbell rang. And again Jesse's face filled with fear. "It's okay, sweetheart. I'm sure that's Cody's daddy." Jesse hung back as Elizabeth went with the little boy to the front door, checking the peephole before opening it. She chatted a moment with Ben Knight, said goodnight to Cody, then closed up, threw the dead bolt and activated the alarm.

"There, we're all set, sweetheart."

Jesse emerged from the den, tucked her hand into Elizabeth's. "Are you ready for your bath?"

Jesse nodded, but her big eyes swam with tears, her still-babyish lips quivered. "What's wrong, sweetheart?"

Jesse cast a fearful glance to the door.

"That was Cody's dad." Elizabeth put an upbeat note in her voice. "He came to take Cody home. I locked the door tight. We're safe. We can go to bed now."

Jesse still stood motionless and Elizabeth tried to guess what she wanted to say. So much about her was unchanged since Gina's death. Her small T-shirt was grimy from a day hard at play with Cody, as always. Her tiny jeans had a new tear in one knee. One of her sneakers was untied, the strings soiled and trailing. But so much was utterly different.

Damn you, Austin.

Sleep was elusive when Elizabeth turned out the light an hour later and tried to blank everything from her mind. Beside her, Jesse's warm little body was relaxed. Whatever demons plagued her when awake blessedly seemed to depart once she slept. Elizabeth longed for the same respite, but it was a long time in coming.

She must have finally dropped off, because she was suddenly brought out of a deep sleep sometime later. In the distance, a dog was barking wildly. She lay for a moment without moving. Archie, she thought vaguely, pinpointing the direction. Louie should check to see what was wrong with Archie. He wasn't easily agitated and this was clearly an urgent, insistent, something's wrong kind of bark. Then, checking to see that Jesse wasn't disturbed by the sound, she carefully sat up, pushed the comforter aside and got out of bed. With the vague idea in mind of checking the grounds around Louie's house, she padded across the carpeted floor in her bedroom.

And then she went cold all over. A moving shadow caught her eye. Living alone, she didn't close her bedroom door. And since Jesse's trauma, there were night-lights here and there, both upstairs and down. Someone was in the house near the stairs.

Fear, instantaneous and wild, hit her in the stomach like a fist. Her brain racing, she stood for a heartbeat wondering frantically what to do. She didn't own a gun. She couldn't pick Jesse up without waking her and he'd surely hear that. She turned silently and went to her bedside table. Hands shaking, she quietly lifted the cordless phone and took it deep into her walk-in closet. Whoever it was had headed upstairs. The master suite in her house was downstairs. Did he not know that? Or did he have some other purpose?

She pressed the first number for 911 before changing her mind. No, Louie was closer. He could be here faster. Holding a folded sweater to muffle the sound, she punched in his number. Waited. One ring. Two. Outside, Archie had stopped barking. "Damn," she whispered, thinking Louie was dealing with the dog. She was ready to hang up and call 911 when a voice said, "Hello."

Ryan? *Ryan!* She went weak in the knees. "Someone

is inside my house, Ryan,'' she told him in a whisper. "Please call the police and tell them to hurry."

"Where are you?" he asked in a hard tone.

"In my bedroom closet. Downstairs. With Jesse. He went upstairs."

"Is your bedroom door locked?"

"No, I—"

"Goddamn it! Lock it now. And don't hang up. I'll be there in thirty seconds."

"Why—" She heard the clatter when his phone hit a hard surface and stood for a second getting herself together. Holding on to the cordless, she crept out of the closet, crossed to the door of her bedroom and closed it as quietly as possible. The sound of the lock shattered the silence. He was sure to have heard it.

Leaning against the door, she heard his footsteps coming down the stairs at a fast clip. Trembling, she held her breath, bracing herself for the moment when he'd try her door. Footsteps now, heavier and closer, actually running. But it wasn't the intruder who spoke. It was Ryan.

"Liz!" She almost jumped out of her skin, then she whirled about and with fumbling fingers managed to turn the lock. He pushed it open and reached for her, pulling her over the threshold and into his arms.

She simply clung to him for a few seconds while her heart thundered in her chest and her legs threatened to fold beneath her. "Don't wake Jesse," she whispered in his ear.

"What?" He muttered the word against her temple. She could feel the heavy beat of his heart as out of control as her own. His breath heaved in his chest. She realized he must have run all the way over.

"I don't want to wake Jesse if possible. This is all she

needs to convince her there's no safe place on the planet for her.''

"Oh. Right. That's good.'' He sounded as if he had to concentrate to manage a calm tone. ''Here, I'll close the door.''

''Wait, let me get my robe.'' Still shaken to the core, she went into her room and scooped up the silk kimono that lay at the foot of her bed. Jesse, thankfully, was still sound asleep. Moving silently, she slipped on the kimono, but her hands seemed all thumbs when she tried to tie the sash. Seeing it, Ryan gently moved her hands aside and finished the job for her. His own hands, she noticed, weren't completely steady either. They'd all had a good scare.

He then pulled the door to very quietly, put an arm around her and guided her toward the den. ''Thank God you got here so fast,'' she said, her voice shaky. ''I don't know what I would have done if he'd come into my bedroom.''

''Yeah.'' At the den door, he flipped on a light and she saw his face. He looked furious. Now, in the light, she saw that the French doors stood wide-open. ''Oh! Did you do that?''

''I came in that way, but so did your trespasser,'' he said in an even tone.

''But how? I thought everything was locked up. And I set the alarm, too. Why didn't it go off?''

''Damn good question.''

Archie materialized out of the night and dashed inside the open door, quivering with excitement. Behind him, Louie appeared holding a piece of an electronic device. ''Looks like your alarm system was deactivated at the source,'' he said.

Ryan was already examining the door frame. He was

scowling when he turned to look at Elizabeth. "There's no evidence that he jimmied the lock here. Did you lock these doors after I left?"

Chagrined, she realized she couldn't remember. She'd been rattled by his kiss and all that he'd said. She thought back. Then Cody's mother had called and she'd hurried to answer the telephone because phone calls upset Jesse. She might not have locked those doors. "I'm not sure," she said and she could see in his eyes that Ryan guessed the reason why. Or part of it. Wisely, he said nothing.

Louie came inside and closed the doors behind him. "Is Jesse okay?"

Elizabeth could at least be confident of that. "She's asleep in my bed. She didn't hear a thing."

"Did you get a look at him, Lizzie?"

"No, I only saw shadowy movement as he crept up the stairs." She rubbed her arms briskly, recalling the terror of that moment. "I was out of bed because something about Archie's bark was unusual. I was going to take a look at your house from my window." She reached down and gave the dog a pat. Archie, his job done, flopped down at their feet and rested his head on his paws. "Did either of you see him?"

Louie gave a rueful shake of his head. "Not me. The minute I released Archie, he was off like a shot, but my days of running at that speed are long gone." He jerked his head toward Ryan. "And Ryan was hell-bent to get to you. So, looks like whoever it was got away."

"It wasn't necessary to get a look at him," Elizabeth said, sinking onto an ottoman. Suddenly her legs didn't feel strong enough to keep her upright. "I know who it was. He headed upstairs because he assumed Jesse would be in the bedroom she shared with Gina. Thanks to Austin, she's so traumatized that she's afraid to sleep alone now," she ended on a bitter note.

"Austin." Louie shook his head in disgust. "You see any flaw in her logic, Ryan?"

Ryan's gaze as he stared beyond them into the night was dark and intense. "It probably was Austin. He's just stupid enough to try something as reckless as kidnapping his own daughter."

"I told you a restraining order wouldn't be enough to stop him," Elizabeth said bitterly. "He's desperate and for good reason. The consequences for violating a legal document aren't as serious as being implicated in Gina's death." She shot a look at Ryan. "He knows that Jesse can do that once she feels safe enough to talk again. It's the only thing to explain why he'd do something as risky as this."

Neither of the men contradicted her. At that moment, a clock on the mantel began striking the midnight hour. She looked at it as if it couldn't possibly be right. It seemed as if the night should be far more advanced. She stood up. "It's late. Thank you both for responding the way you did. Louie, you should have been in bed two hours ago." She watched him get creakily to his feet, then glanced at Ryan, who still looked as if he wanted to smash something. "He must have roped you into a game of chess," she said.

"Chess," Ryan repeated with a look at Louie that was impossible to read. "No, we didn't actually play that game tonight, but I bet you're good at it, Louie."

"Lizzie's pretty good, too," Louie said. "C'mon, Archie, we're heading home, boy."

"I'll pick up those files in a few minutes," Ryan told him. "I'm going to make a check of the house to be sure

Austin didn't leave himself a way to enter another time. I don't think he'll try again tonight.''

"Do you think that's necessary?" Elizabeth asked a few minutes later as Ryan came down the stairs. He'd already canvassed the entire lower floor of the house, running his fingers over the tops of the windows, checking the locks. He'd even gone into the garage. "I really don't think he had time to go anywhere except that one bedroom."

"Humor me." Ryan still had a brooding look about him. "I feel responsible. I'd stay the night if possible, but I can't leave Jen alone." His smile, when it came, was unexpected. He seemed briefly amused as he fiddled with the controls on the defunct security system. "She's already reading something into the fact that I can find no end of excuses to be here."

Elizabeth put her fingers over her mouth, hiding a smile. "Oh, no."

He turned, cutting a sharp look at her. "You think it's funny?"

She gave a tiny shrug, but her eyes were bright with humor. The terror that had prompted the panicked call to Louie's house was gone. She wasn't the only one shaken by the incident. He wouldn't soon forget how he'd felt when her call came.

"What did you mean," she asked, "by saying you feel responsible tonight?"

He snapped the cover shut on the electronic gadget. "I should have waited to see that you locked the French doors tonight when I left."

"That's ridiculous. It was totally my own fault. I've lived alone since the age of eighteen. The thing is, I was—"

She stopped, but before she could move away, he

caught her chin in his hand and turned her face up and looked into her eyes. "You were what?" he asked huskily. "Upset? Dizzy from a kiss? All shook up?" He chuckled softly. "Well, honey, that's my excuse, too. It was all I could do to leave without finishing what we started." His gaze strayed down to her mouth.

"Ryan—"

"Umm, I love it when you say my name." His mouth came down on hers then, not with the care he'd taken on the patio, but with a deliberate demand that plunged them both instantly into a vortex of sensation. Her arms went up and around his neck. Her mouth was soft and sweet, opening to his with a hunger that matched his own. Embracing her more fully, he wedged a leg between hers and took the kiss deeper. Heat pooled heavily in his groin. He wanted to see more of her, needed to touch her in more intimate places. He slipped the knot of the kimono and pushed it away from her shoulders onto the floor so that all she now had on was the skimpy little gown.

He'd been on an adrenaline high when he'd crashed into her bedroom tonight, but he hadn't been too far gone to miss the look of her in that little gown. He hooked a thumb around a spaghetti strap and bared her breasts. And when he bent and took a nipple in his mouth, she moaned, a low and throaty sound. The taste of her was almost as good as the scent of her, intoxicating, arousing him on some purely elemental level. The bed, he thought. He needed to carry her to the bed and put an end to the craving in both of them.

Oh, God, not possible. Jesse was in the bedroom and if they went upstairs—on the off chance Liz would go—Jesse might wake up and come looking for her. God damn. With a groan, he sought her mouth again like a hungry man whose chance at a banquet had been seized. Then, unwilling to stop altogether, he let his mouth trail down her throat. He pushed her little scrap of a gown even lower and gave himself the pleasure of roaming a hand over the flat of her stomach. She was like satin, warm, enticing, tantalizing. Then, unable to resist, he went lower and found the sweet, glorious heat of her.

She made an urgent, keening sound and he smiled to himself. *Oh, yes. Open for me, sweetheart. Let me.* He chanted it soundlessly, urging her beyond her conscious mind, knowing if he broke the spell with a word, she would come to herself and it would end. But if he couldn't have all of her tonight, he wanted to give her something to remember. And something to hold him until he could have all of her.

Elizabeth clung to him weakly, feeling his fingers like torture—wild, irresistible torture at the heart of her—moving mercilessly, giving no respite. There was too much happening to stop it now. "Let go, Liz," he murmured. "Let me give you this. Just let go."

And then the pleasure erupted in a flood of sensation, rushing over her, through her, stealing her mind, her breath, her everything. He shuddered with her, pressing her head with one hand hard against his throat as she reached her peak and then holding her as she slid weightlessly, bonelessly back into reality.

"Oh, my God," she said long, long moments later. She couldn't—or wouldn't—look at him.

It took some effort, but he smiled against her hair. "Was it that good?"

"I've never—"

"Yeah, well, you could have fooled me." He could barely speak. It had been an awesome moment when she came. He chuckled soundlessly. She owed him now. Oh yeah, she owed him. He felt her shoulders shaking and realized she was laughing, too. "What?"

"Do you always bring your women to their knees with sex?"

His smile broadened. "That part comes later."

She pushed back then and looked up into his face, going all serious on him. "This doesn't mean anything, Ryan. We were both under a lot of strain tonight. Add that to...everything else and...something like this happens. We shouldn't rush into anything." She took the kimono he held out to her wordlessly and clutched it to her body. She smoothed her hair. She held one slightly unsteady hand to her cheek. "Shouldn't you be heading over to Louie's?"

He studied her, knowing she'd have some trouble coming to grips with what she'd allowed. But he could live with that. "Okay. But this time, I'm waiting until I hear the sound of the dead bolt on those doors."

And for the second time that night, he crossed her patio and the shadowy lawn, heading for Louie Christian's house, one very frustrated man.

Twenty-Three

Lindsay had the phone in one ear, taking notes on a laptop computer about a smashup on the I-610 loop when Elizabeth walked into her office at WBYH-TV the next morning. She flashed a smile at Elizabeth, held up one finger and indicated a chair, all this while typing the particulars of the accident. She spoke a few words to someone on the other end and hung up.

"Give me a minute, Liz." She rose, sailed down the hall calling someone by the name of Harry. No more than a minute later, she was back, closing the door and flopping down in the chair next to Elizabeth. "Now, what's up? I've been on pins and needles since you called."

"It's about the list of names you told us about yesterday."

"Okay…"

"I know this is an imposition," Elizabeth began, "but if you could just give me what you've got on the woman Austin was engaged to, I'll take it from there."

"Imposition? Are you kidding? Every spare minute of my life has been spent digging into that scumbag's life. Helping to nail him isn't an imposition, it's a pleasure." Lindsay reached for a file on her desk and opened it. "Let's see…you're talking about Patricia Ellis, only her name isn't Patricia Ellis anymore. It's Mrs. James Bartlett Parks. J. B., as he's known, is an architect and they live somewhere in the Woodlands. It's a long drive, but the rush hour is over." She got up and grabbed her handbag and laptop. "We can be there in about forty-five minutes provided we avoid the accident on the loop."

"Wait, is it okay for you to leave in the middle of the day?" Elizabeth stood up, glancing at the desk piled high with files and a mix of other stuff that looked as if it would take a month to sift through. "You don't have to do this. I just needed her name and address. I can take it from there. Really."

Lindsay gave her a look of disbelief. "You're serious, aren't you? No way do you get to do the good part on your own, honey. Besides, it may take the two of us to persuade her to—" She stopped. "Now that I think about it, what do we want? We could ask for a copy of the police report she filed, if she has it. But I vote for trying to persuade her to visit the judge." Urging Elizabeth along, she headed for the elevators. "Hetherington's an old fart, pardon my French, but he was pretty fair-minded in deciding the merits in Gina's petition. I bet if he heard Patricia Ellis Parks swear that Austin broke her jaw two weeks before they were to be *married*, he would put an end to any hope that weasel has to ever even see Jesse."

"That would be helpful if it happened."

"Helpful? Hey, I see persuading her to testify as the whole enchilada."

Elizabeth smiled and followed her into the elevator. "It's half the enchilada. I'll probably get legal custody if that happens and I used to think that would be the happy ending. But Jesse still isn't talking and the reason is that she's afraid that Austin will somehow appear and take her away. If Patricia will agree to testify, that will be a major first step, but what we need ultimately is to get Austin out of the picture altogether. And the only way to do that is to prove that he contributed to the accident.''

"Not a problem,'' Lindsay said breezily. Steering Elizabeth out into the foyer, she urged her toward the door. "Steele's working that end.''

"But how?'' Out of the building now, they began weaving through a sea of parked cars. Apparently, Lindsay planned to drive. "Even if Jesse spoke, I'm not sure the word of a five-year-old would be enough.''

"Steele has some leads and I think Ryan is doing some stuff behind the scenes.''

Ryan? Elizabeth put a hand on her tummy, remembering the cataclysmic encounter with Ryan last night after Louie left.

"Meanwhile, tell me all about what happened last night.''

Elizabeth gave her a startled look. "Last night?''

"The break-in.'' Lindsay clicked the remote in her hand and a chirp sounded from an SUV twenty feet away. "Austin's stupid attempt to end life as he knows it.''

"Oh. That.''

Behind the wheel now, Lindsay turned and looked at her. "Was there anything else last night I should be asking about?''

"No!'' But Elizabeth felt a flush warming her face. She waved a hand blindly. "Just drive. And you're right, for Austin to break into my house was beyond stupid. Fortunately, Archie barked like crazy and woke me up. I called Louie instead of 911, which proved to be a good thing. In two minutes, Ryan was at my door.''

"Ryan was at Louie's house last night at midnight? You didn't mention that when you called this morning.'' Lindsay took a left turn onto an up-ramp and merged at a hair-raising pace—to Elizabeth—into a maze of vehicles on the interstate.

"Ryan has just learned that Louie knew his father," Elizabeth explained. "He thinks Louie worked with Judge Paxton. Ryan's obsessed with the court docket at that time as it relates to Paxton's cases. He thinks Louie may be able to shed some light on whatever was happening then."

"Whoa, this is really interesting." Lindsay whizzed past an eighteen-wheeler. "Now, when did you say this happened?"

"At about the same time our father died. In fact, Judge Paxton and Judge Walker were in the same judicial jurisdiction, according to Ryan. They knew each other."

"Well, what d'you know about that?" Lindsay murmured. Deep in thought, her speed actually slowed to the legal limit. "This is very interesting as I've been doing some research into the circumstances of Judge Matthew Walker's death myself. You'd be surprised how difficult it's been getting access to what should be public files. Were you aware of the Caymen Islands caper that resulted in the disbarment of several crooked judges and lawyers at about that time?"

"Somewhat." Elizabeth did know about it. As an undergraduate when she'd still aspired to be a lawyer, she'd read extensively about it. But the affair with Evan Reynolds and her pregnancy had killed not only her interest in her father's profession, but she'd let go her obsession with all things relating to her father.

Lindsay went on, "Someone, some *entity* doesn't want us poking around in that old scandal or Matthew Walker's role in it. Every time I'd get onto something, the trail would just fizzle out."

"You're that curious about Matthew Walker?"

"Well, he is my biological father. And he was a charismatic political figure at the time. How could I not be? And remember, I didn't know my connection to the judge until your write-up in the paper.''

"I keep forgetting that.''

"Uh-huh. And in case you're thinking I'm just too nice, I have to confess something else. If there was something fishy about the judge's demise and it does have to do with that Cayman Islands scandal, it would make a delicious feature for a local news special.''

"Your ticket to your own show again,'' Elizabeth guessed.

"Very possibly.'' Lindsay took her eyes off the road and grinned at her. "I'm shameless, right?''

"You're ambitious, which is nothing to be ashamed of. Only when you hurt other people with your ambition does it become a vice.'' She returned Lindsay's smile. "I don't think you're the back-stabbing sort.''

Lindsay waved at senior citizens in a van who'd recognized her in passing. "Thanks.'' She signaled suddenly and zoomed off the interstate at the exit for the Woodlands. "Now let me see if I've got this straight.''

"You don't know the address?''

"What? Oh, for Patricia, you're mean? I think I can get us there. But I was still mulling over the connection between Ryan's father and Judge Walker. And now you tell me that Louie knew them both, possibly worked with them. How come he's never mentioned that to you?''

"Maybe he sensed that I shied away from any mention of my parents and out of consideration he didn't go there.'' What was more surprising to Elizabeth was that she was no longer shying away from that time. The defenses she'd spent years building were crumbling at a pace that made her almost dizzy. This discussion with Lindsay

was an example. They were delving into places she
wouldn't have allowed just a few weeks ago.

So many changes.

"Well, I think it's odd," Lindsay said, "very odd. And
I'm gonna put it to him the next time I see him. I want
to know what he knows about Judge Matthew Walker.
Heck, I've encountered nothing but obstruction and frustration using more conventional methods. What reason
could Louie have to stonewall? The guy was my father,
after all. If necessary, I'll weigh in strongly on my personal right to know."

"Speaking of odd," Elizabeth said, now thinking back
to that time when she'd been obsessed with learning about
Judge Matthew Walker, "you mentioned the Cayman Islands scandal. And we know Louie, John Paxton and Matthew Walker were all judges at the time. What I don't
recall is ever seeing Louie mentioned. Nowhere in all the
hundreds of pages of transcript that I reviewed did the
name Louis Christian ever appear."

"Yes, very odd," Lindsay said, turning onto Woodlands Parkway. "We'll ask him about that, too."

Patricia Ellis Parks could have been Gina's twin. The
resemblance was so striking that both Elizabeth and Lindsay were caught off guard when she opened the door. Dark
hair, crystal-blue eyes, petite to the point of delicacy, the
look of her sent a swift, piercing pain straight to Elizabeth's heart. So like Gina.

"Mrs. Parks?" Lindsay flashed her best smile and stuck
out her hand. "Lindsay Blackstone. I called you a couple
of days ago, if you recall. This is Liz Walker, ah, you may
know her as Elizabeth Walker, author of children's
books?"

Patricia Parks's manners demanded polite acceptance of

Lindsay's hand and a cordial acknowledgment of Elizabeth. "How did you know where I live?" she asked. Although still courteous, she didn't invite them in.

Lindsay gave one of her charmingly wry shrug-and-a-smile movements. "Well, it wasn't too difficult after we talked on the phone. I hope we haven't shocked you by just showing up, but we'd *love*—no, we *need* to talk to you."

"Is it about Austin?"

"Yes," Lindsay said and rushed to add, "and we understand you probably hoped you'd never hear his name again as long as you lived, but men like Austin don't just fade away, they keep on wreaking havoc in the lives of other women. We hoped you'd agree just to talk to us, hear us out...for Jesse's sake."

Patricia frowned. "Jesse?"

Elizabeth spoke up. "Jesse's my goddaughter, Mrs. Parks. She's five years old. My foster sister, Gina D'Angelo, is...was her mother. Gina died last week in an accident after spending the evening with Austin and there is some question about his culpability there. Austin is Jesse's father."

Patricia stood for a moment, still uncertain about welcoming them into her home. Elizabeth could almost imagine the conflict going on inside her. She, unlike Gina, had been clever enough to put Austin out of her life after only one brutal incident. What if she'd had a child before she learned his true colors and then something happened? Elizabeth saw on her face that she could imagine the fate a child—worse, a girl child—would have growing up in Austin's care.

Suddenly arriving at a decision, she stepped back and invited them in.

* * *

Ryan was in his office the next day even before his paralegal arrived. Jean Johnson was an early bird, often at work an hour before others in the firm. She was fifty-five, single, and efficient almost to the point of obsessive-compulsive behavior where her job was concerned. This morning, when she did appear, she gave him a curious look and asked if he needed her assistance. She'd returned to her work space after he'd told her to let him know when Austin made it into the office. She'd be shocked if she knew the chaos in his thinking this day. Good thing he didn't have to appear in court, he thought. Rage was not conducive to straight thinking.

Turning in his chair, he studied the Houston skyline through the tall windows without really seeing anything. He needed to get his ducks in a row before confronting Austin. No chance of the boss's son arriving before anybody else, so he had plenty of time to lay out a plan before Austin showed. He'd spent most of the night thinking up and discarding ideas. Clearly, the restraining order wouldn't keep Austin from grabbing Jesse, first chance he got. The file now on his desk might do the job. He owed Shepherd Steele for helping him load his guns. Austin had to get the message in a way that gave him no option but to back off, to get out of Jesse's life. And Liz's.

He still went cold thinking about the son of a bitch invading Liz's home and giving her the fright of her life. He'd already admitted to himself that Liz was special to him. He'd meant it when he said he'd fallen in love with her. But he hadn't realized how much until last night. The turmoil inside him was almost as strong as if the threat were to Jennifer. It had been a defining moment for him.

"Ryan."

He swiveled back to find Jean in the doorway. It was

an indication of his state of mind that he hadn't heard her. He stood up. "Is he here?"

"Yes. Ryan, what's going on?" She watched him scoop up a single file folder on his desk, snag his jacket from the coatrack and shove his arms into it.

"Just a little problem with Austin," he told her. "I'll call if I need you, Jean."

A walk thirty feet down the hall and around a corner brought him to Austin's office. Like Ryan's, it was a spiffy corner location with a stunning view of the Galleria. Austin sat in a luxurious executive chair and, like Ryan earlier, seemed preoccupied with his thoughts, not the view. Ryan gave a perfunctory rap on the open door and without waiting for an invitation, closed it behind him and didn't stop until he stood directly in front of his ex-client's desk.

Austin pushed his chair back a fraction, but didn't rise. The last time they'd talked, Ryan had threatened him and had been fired before he could quit. There was nothing in Austin's demeanor now that spoke of hard feelings. "Hey, big guy." Going for humor.

"Austin." A grizzly bear would seem friendlier than Ryan.

Now, as he got a closer look at Ryan's face, Austin's expression was suddenly wary. "Man, you're looking real serious. What's up?"

"Where were you at midnight last night, Austin?"

"Midnight? Last— What the hell are you talking about?"

"I'm talking about breaking and entering. I'm talking about attempted kidnapping. I'm talking about your ass being in deep shit if you don't persuade me that you were at home in bed at midnight last night."

Now Austin was on his feet. "Now look, you son of a bitch, you can't come in here accusing me of—"

"You sneaky little worm!" Ryan was around the desk and gripping a handful of shirt and tie before Austin could scramble out of the way. "You went to Liz's house, dismantled her alarm system and entered in violation of a restraining order so you could take that innocent child and ship her off to Arizona." Ryan had him up on his tiptoes now, both of them nose to nose. Then, with a disgusted sound and a hard shake, he let him go, watching Austin drop in his chair, almost missing it when it scooted sideways.

"I've always had my doubts about you, Austin," he said, now prowling the space near the desk. "But to kidnap your own little girl is too low for even you. What about when she woke up and saw you? She freaks out at the mention of your name, man. How did you plan to cope with that?"

"I'm calling security." Austin reached for the telephone.

"And you'll tell them what?" Ryan stared him down. "Right. Yeah, that's what I thought." Grabbing the folder he'd tossed on Austin's desk when he came at him, he shoved it toward him. "Read that and then instead of calling security, let's call your old man. No, I've got a better idea, let's you and me go together to his office. See what his reaction is when I fill him in on what you've been doing at night lately."

Austin hardly seemed to hear him. He'd opened the folder and was staring at the single sheet of paper it contained. "Where did you get this?"

"Read the letterhead at the top, buddy. Fourteen hundred and forty dollars for paint and repair of your Porsche, the way I read it. Dated the day that Gina died. The day

I tried to call you about six times trying all your numbers and getting nothing but voice mail. Hell, no, you were in Beaumont getting the nicks smoothed out and traces of the paint from Gina's car buffed away.''

Austin shoved the folder aside. ''That's a damn lie! The damage to my car had nothing to do with Gina. There was street repair going on right outside the hospital the night of the accident. I bumped into a blockade put up by the city crews. I was upset and didn't see it until I was on top of it. Hell, Gina was half dead and Jesse'd come close to a serious injury that night. I was rattled.'' He straightened his tie and sat back down. ''Anybody would be. That's what happened.''

Less enraged now that he'd worked off some of his frustration, Ryan stood at the front of the desk again. ''You tell a touching story, Austin, but if it's true, why the urgency to get to Jesse now? Are you afraid she'll be able to blow your story to hell and back?''

Austin still wore a sullen look. ''My concern for my daughter is normal. And I deny ever trying to get to Jesse, as you put it. As for threatening to haul me up in front of my old man like a kid who's been caught smoking dope, go ahead and try.''

''You think you can blow this off, Austin, but I'm warning you, you're treading on some very dangerous ground. Curtiss may cover for you as long as there's no hard evidence, but if you keep on trying to get to Jesse, you won't be able to rely on his connections. Kidnapping is a serious felony.''

''Yadda, yadda, yadda.''

Ryan stood looking at him for a beat or two, then shaking his head, walked out. Back in his office, he picked up the phone. There were two things on his agenda that day and the second one wouldn't give him as much pleasure as confronting Austin. He dialed a number, setting the stage for what had to be done. Turning in his chair, he again fixed his gaze on the view from the tall windows and waited through several rings. On the fourth, Louie Christian finally picked up.

Twenty-Four

Elizabeth had not dressed for a date with a man for many months. And if dating brought on a case of nerves as intense as what she was experiencing tonight, she'd have been careful to avoid dates forever. She should have refused him, but he kept coming up with arguments to counter her objections. Remembering Ryan's methods in court, she shouldn't have expected less than steamroller tactics. She'd worried that it was risky leaving Jesse, but he'd reminded her that she couldn't be safer than in Shepherd Steele's care, after arranging for Lindsay and Steele to take Jesse and Jennifer to the movies.

Standing before her mirror, she studied the effect of the outfit she'd finally chosen. Black-and-white silk capri pants with a lime-green top, black sandals. Silver jewelry. Did lime green make her hair look too red? Were the pants too trendy? "Casual dress," Ryan had advised. "Where we're going, you'll want to be comfortable."

They went to a restaurant in Kemah, a town on Galveston Bay catering to the yachting crowd. The main attraction was a number of waterfront restaurants lining the ship channel. Within sight of the Bay was a string of touristy shops, but Ryan avoided them and headed to the waterfront area. The sun was setting and the western sky was a stunning display of color, burnished orange radiating from the center before darkening at the horizon to near-purple.

He parked the SUV in sight of the channel and the fiery sky and went around to help Elizabeth climb down. It was almost a two-foot drop from the car to the street below. Instead of allowing her to step down, he lifted her and swung her about before setting her on her feet. "I'd kiss you, but you'd probably grumble and stop to put on more war paint."

"I certainly would," she said, one hand trying to save her hairdo. There was a stiff breeze blowing in off the Bay and her hair wanted to fly everywhere. "And why didn't you tell me we were going to Kemah? I would have put a clip in my hair." She pushed a strand from her face, but it was a useless effort. "It'll be a mess by the time we get inside the restaurant."

"That's exactly why I didn't tell you." His hands still lingered at her waist and before she knew it, he'd slipped his arms around her. Leaning forward, he buried his face in her hair, inhaling the scent of it. "It's gorgeous. Like that sunset, all color and light."

"My hair's orange and purple?" she said, laughing. It struck her that she laughed a lot when she was with Ryan.

"Your hair's perfect. I fell in love with it at first sight." He held her for a moment longer, swaying a little, enjoying the intimacy as if they weren't standing in view of dozens of people. Then he caught her hand and they began walking toward the restaurant.

Like lovers. She shivered with the thought.

"I saw Austin today," he said, minutes later as they waited outside for a table. He played idly with the fingers of her hand. "He denied ever being near your house last night."

"What a surprise," she said dryly.

"However, when I showed him the receipt from the body shop, he couldn't deny the fact that his Porsche needed repair and that he had it done within hours of the accident."

Elizabeth watched a flock of seagulls overhead, enjoying their flashy antics. "I'm amazed that Steele managed to dig that up. Did Austin question how you happened to have such a damaging piece of evidence? Incidentally, how did he get it?"

"He didn't acknowledge that it was damaging. And Steele got it as a result of good police work. He canvassed the neighborhood within a mile of the accident hoping somebody would have seen something. Fortunately, somebody did. As he was walking his dog, a man had noticed two speeding cars, the Porsche tailgating the Toyota. He was irritated and tried to get license numbers, but they flew by so fast it was impossible. He told Steele the Porsche bumped the Toyota from behind and it looked deliberate to him."

"Which would explain why Gina lost control and went off the road."

"Yeah. But it happened about a mile farther down from where the eyewitness saw them."

"So he didn't actually see the accident."

"No, but from that eyewitness, Steele guessed the Porsche was probably damaged and that led him to look for a shop where Austin had it repaired. His search took him all the way to Beaumont." Ryan was shaking his head. "I can't figure why he'd be so stupid."

"To leave a trail when he got his car fixed?" Elizabeth asked.

"No, to give chase and actually ram Gina's car from behind like a maniac. His own child was in that car."

Elizabeth imagined the terror Gina must have experi-

enced in the minutes before the crash. Austin had been in
a rage, probably after she told him about her pregnancy.
Seeing his reaction, she knew to get away from him to
avoid a scene or before he hurt her or Jesse, but she probably hadn't expected him to go so far as to chase her on
a public street. That he had was an indication of just how
furious he was with her. "I suspect it was a culmination
of several things," Elizabeth said, watching the gulls
swoop down on an incoming tugboat. "Gina had challenged him in court, embarrassed him publicly and was
going to put the squeeze on him financially. But in spite
of all that, he may have thought he could still talk her
around. Then she throws a pregnancy in his face."

"Like I said, only a maniac would react the way he
did."

"I really don't think he intended to kill her," Elizabeth
said, thinking about it. "He just lost it, as he has done so
many other times."

"Maybe. But this time his temper tantrum had dire consequences. If the circumstances are as we suspect, he's
definitely responsible for the accident and her death."

"Would that be manslaughter?"

"If it could be proven."

"That's a big if."

"Sir." The hostess approached them. "Your table's
ready."

Ryan got to his feet, put out a hand to help her up and
they followed the woman inside.

"Sounds like you and Lindsay had some success with
Austin's former fiancée," Ryan said after they were
seated.

"Patricia Parks is her name." Elizabeth accepted a
menu from the waiter. "And she was very nice, too nice

to slam the door in our faces, as I'm sure she wanted to do when Lindsay first launched into her sales pitch.''

"Lindsay wouldn't be where she is today in her profession if she didn't have guts.'' He sampled the wine proffered by the waiter and nodded approval.

Elizabeth's lips curved in a smile. "Some might call it gall.''

"But it worked.''

"Actually, I think it was Jesse that turned the trick. When I mentioned that Austin was fighting for custody of a five-year-old girl, she suddenly overcame her reluctance and invited us in.''

"Was it true that Austin broke her jaw two weeks before their wedding?''

"Yes. And for Jesse's sake, she's willing to testify to that before Judge Hetherington.'' She took a sip of wine, recalling the visit. "It was déjà vu, Ryan. Their relationship as she described it was like a rerun of Gina's with Austin. In fact, both Lindsay and I were struck by how much she looked like Gina. Apparently, Austin's taste runs to petite women with dark hair and pretty blue eyes.''

Ryan's face was grim as he studied the menu. "The hairdresser and the homecoming queen were similar types?''

"Yes.''

"Did she tell you how it happened?''

Elizabeth closed the menu and put it aside. "They were at a house party Austin had insisted they attend, but it was inconvenient, so close to the wedding date. Patricia was unenthusiastic about going. You can imagine the thousand and one details waiting for her at home regarding the wedding. But he pushed it and she caved, or at least, compromised. She'd go, but only for half the weekend. They'd be there Friday and Saturday, but were to leave Sunday morning. It was after they were in the car that she realized how furious he was. They had a terrific argument and she wound up with a broken jaw."

"He's lucky she didn't hang his ass."

"Charges were filed, as Lindsay learned when she first talked with Patricia's friend and maid of honor, but the records are sealed. Which points to Curtiss Leggett's friends in high places. But it doesn't matter. Patricia's willing to testify now, thank God."

Ryan watched her sip from the wineglass. "Now that I know how he treated Gina, I guess I shouldn't be surprised at anything, but to break the jaw of the woman you're planning to marry? And two weeks before the wedding? The guy's a mental case."

"It's rage, not insanity, the same emotion that drove him to chase Gina in a car going sixty miles an hour when she made him mad. Abusive men are, by and large, angry men. Why they're angry and with whom are intriguing questions, but I'm uninterested in poking and prying into Austin's psyche," Elizabeth said, feeling a surge of frustration. "I just want him brought to justice for what he did to Gina and put out of the picture as far as Jesse's future is concerned."

Ryan lifted his own glass of wine. "I'll drink to that."

An hour and a half later, they were both pleasantly sated and mellow after an entrée of fresh sea bass and a little wine. Ryan suggested a stroll along the boardwalk after dinner before tackling the drive home, telling her that they needed to change the subject. "Enough about Austin's dark side," he said. Then, he spent the next ten minutes educating her on the particulars of this or that boat passing on the inlet of Galveston Bay. He seemed especially partial to the sportfishers.

"I bet you have a boat," she said as he admired a huge and very expensive Bertram cabin cruiser with a Miami registration.

"I do," he told her, guiding her to a wrought iron bench facing the water. "See that one behind the Bertram? Mine's similar."

"Nice," she said, thinking that although it wasn't a cruising yacht, a boat of that style and quality meant boating was more than just a casual hobby. It also explained his deep tan. "Where is it docked?"

"Galveston. We'll drive down soon and I'll take you out." He sat with one ankle propped on a knee and threw his arm over the back of the bench. "There's nothing like it, Liz. You get about thirty miles offshore and the water's so blue it looks like it can't be real. And clear. Sea creatures you'd only see in an aquarium are swimming all around you. And the fishing! You haven't lived until you've landed a billfish. It's great."

"What's a billfish?"

"Could be a blue marlin, a striped marlin, nothing small. We're talking big babies."

She smiled. "I can guess what you do in your spare time."

He grinned. "And with my spare money. You know what they say. Owning a boat's like opening a hole in the ocean and pouring money into it. But, God, I love it. I can't wait to take you out."

She was frowning over a scrap of memory. "Do I recall that Austin has a boat? I think Gina once spent a weekend cruising off the coast of Mexico with him."

"Not Austin, it belongs to Curtiss. It's a yacht, not a boat. A Bertram. He's an avid yachtsman. Beside his, my sportfisher is chopped liver."

"Does Jennifer like going out with you?"

"She does. In the past, it's been our best time together. But Diane hated it. She suffers from seasickness. Nothing seemed to help." He turned his head to look at her. "Have you ever been on a pleasure cruiser? Did you ever sail? It's all the same. If you were good to go then, you'll be fine on the *Jennifer Jay*."

"Named after you-know-who," Elizabeth guessed, still smiling. A couple with two sons strolled past, a toddler and his brother, who looked about eight years old. She saw, with a pang, that the older boy had dark hair and eyes and wondered if she'd ever be able to overcome the pain of never seeing the child she'd given away. She wondered, if this thing with Ryan turned into something serious, what he'd say if he knew what she'd done.

"What's wrong?" Ryan asked, looking at her with concern.

"What?" She realized he'd seen something on her face. "Oh, it's nothing." She glanced at her watch. "Do you think we should be getting back? I worry about Jesse. I can't help it."

"In a minute." He took her hand, idly stroking her knuckles with his thumb. "Jesse's okay. She's safe. But before we go back, there's something else I wanted to discuss with you. And I hope you won't go home tonight thinking that Austin's always going to dominate the conversation when we're together. He's dead meat once we get the trouble with Jesse straightened out."

She felt a little flutter in her tummy. "Is it something about Jesse you want to discuss?" He'd volunteered to check the paperwork she'd signed at the hospital when Gina died. And, as Austin's former attorney, he was familiar with the particulars of Jesse's situation.

He was shaking his head. "No, it's about Louie." She gave a confused nod, waiting. "You know I went to his house last night…at his invitation. He promised to let me look at a bunch of files dating back to the time when my father died. He was as good as his word. He pulled them out of a trunk that looked as if it had been in the Ark and when I realized what they were, I asked if I could take them home with me. He didn't object and suggested several which I might want to read carefully. Those, I realized when I got home, were cases where my father was the judge, as well as a ton of case files where Matthew Walker was the judge. But what I found most interesting was the number of files he had regarding the Cayman Islands scandal. Have you ever heard of it?''

''Yes.'' She turned her gaze to the channel where a boat was slowly passing followed by a swarm of seagulls. A fishing boat, she thought vaguely, not a pleasure craft. ''Lindsay and I were talking about it today,'' she told him, ''among other things. It's odd that we're getting little trickles of information from Louie after all these years. We wondered, why now? And in all this material that's surfaced lately, why is there no mention of Louie himself?''

''Good question.''

She brushed a speck of something from her pants. ''When I was a senior in college, I planned to enter law school. I did extensive research about that case. I never read anything about a player named Louie Christian.''

He brought her hand up, idly rubbing it along the side of his face, his thoughts elsewhere. ''I don't think there was anyone named Louie Christian back then. In fact, I don't think there ever was anybody with that name, period.''

''What are you saying?''

He shifted so that he was facing her directly, now catching both hands. ''I worried half the night about mentioning this to you. I know how close you are to Louie. I know what he means to Jesse. His role in her life and yours will only increase now that Gina is gone and hopefully Austin is out of the picture.''

"Just tell me straight out, Ryan. Stop dancing around what you want to say.''

"I think that for some reason Louie is living under a false identity.''

"What?'' She looked incredulous.

"Just hear me out, Liz. Maybe he was one of the lawyers involved in the scandal somehow. Or maybe he wasn't a lawyer at all, but one of the bean counters. The transcripts show that accountants were vital in pulling off a scam like that. He claims to be a lawyer, but how do we know it's the truth? With no credentials to show, he could be a CPA just as easily as he calls himself a lawyer. He could have been a court clerk.'' He gave a could-be shrug. "In that role, he'd have access to a helluva lot of information, damaging information. It would also explain where those files came from.''

"What?'' she asked with asperity. "You're saying he ripped off a bunch of files and disappeared for twenty-five years? And for some reason, he's suddenly decided to hand them over? For what purpose, Ryan?''

"Another good question.''

"No.'' She was shaking her head. "No, you're on the wrong trail here. Louie's past is a mystery, I grant you that, but he's not a criminal. He's just too—'' She didn't finish. Couldn't. But she couldn't deny that Ryan's suspicions provoked reasonable doubt. She'd had flashes of something—more déjà vu?—from time to time over the years, but had never let herself dwell on it. She didn't want to dwell on it now.

"Well, maybe he was a whistle-blower,'' Ryan persisted. "It's not clear how the Feds got involved, but somebody had to give them a heads-up."

"It was twenty-five years ago, Ryan!" She looked at him with distress and tried to pull her hands away.

"Some things aren't erased just because time has passed."

She made a skeptical sound. "Tell me some facts, Ryan. Not suspicions or what-ifs or maybes."

"That Cayman Islands scandal was a big deal, Liz. There were some really unsavory characters involved in it. If Louie has any connection to it, I want to know about it. He has carte blanche at your house. He walks in and out at will, no questions asked. I don't feel comfortable with that until I get some answers to the questions that popped up from those files he gave me."

"But why would he give you files that would cast doubt on him personally?" When she tugged at her hands this time, he let her go. "It doesn't make sense."

"And yet another good question," Ryan said.

"This is not happening," she said, her voice only a whisper. She fumbled for the tiny purse on the bench beside her and started to get up.

"Wait." He touched her knee to keep her on the bench. "There's one more thing. When Louie gave me those files, he told me he knew I'd have a lot of questions. He said he'd try to answer them, but that I was to tell you what I found out first."

"Why?" She searched his face, confused and upset. "Why would he tell you that?"

"Only Louie can answer that, Liz."

She looked away from him, unwilling to acknowledge the emotion in her chest. It was night now. Another luxurious yacht cruised slowly past, heading for the open sea, lights ablaze. "I would like to go home now," she told Ryan.

He stood up and offered a hand to her, but she got to her feet without his help and this time when they walked back to the car, they didn't touch.

She took Jesse to nursery school the next morning and after again warning the staff not to allow anyone but herself to pick her up, she drove straight back home and called Louie. Whatever had been Ryan's purpose in sharing his suspicions about Louie Christian, she couldn't ignore what he said. She'd spent the hours of a long, restless night trying to make sense of everything, but in the end nothing made sense. What wouldn't be ignored was that Ryan had forced her out of denial.

From the time she'd first met Louie, she'd been drawn to him by something more than neighborliness. It hadn't been his thoughtfulness in bringing her newspaper in out of the rain or his gifts of tomatoes and cucumbers from his garden. It had been something deeper, but she had preferred not to examine it. There was a little frisson of something that danced just out of reach, or bits and pieces of—not quite memory—that she couldn't pin down into a recognizable picture. But as she'd gradually spent more time with Louie, friendship had blotted out those notions. Had she simply refused to acknowledge something that her subconscious recognized?

But what?

She walked to his house, as always, across her lawn and through the oleander border. He and Archie were waiting for her beneath the shade of a wisteria that grew over the lanai covering his patio. Archie wagged his tail in welcome, but he seemed to sense tension. She put out a hand and he licked it.

"Can we talk in the gazebo?" Louie asked in a voice that lacked his usual gentle humor. Without a word, she turned and started toward the ornate structure that sat almost on the property line. Louie had approached her with the plans for the gazebo four years before, insisting that the location between two huge live oak trees was the best spot. That particular spot was definitely on Elizabeth's property. He'd already hired a contractor, he told her, and she could, of course, refuse permission. She hadn't. It was the first act of trust she'd made since the betrayal of Evan Reynolds. Now she had to ask herself why.

In the gazebo, Louie took a seat on the glider. Elizabeth watched him ease himself down and thought he looked as if the night he'd spent was no more restful than her own. He'd promised to get a full medical checkup and she wondered whether he'd done it yet. Last month, she'd threatened to make the appointment herself and push him into keeping it, but she'd been distracted by Gina and Jesse and their situation. Now, looking at him closely, she didn't like his color. He looked—

She brought her thoughts up sharply. If he'd been as deceptive as Ryan seemed to think, she needn't worry herself over his health anymore. She brushed a few leaves from the cushion of a matching chair and sat down.

"Actually," Louie said, studying her intently through his bifocals, "I thought you might call last night after Ryan brought you home, Lizzie."

Lizzie. She wasn't sure when he'd started calling her that pet name. He was one of the few people in the world she allowed to call her that. "I was too upset last night. I had a lot to think about after what he told me. I'm still trying to understand why you didn't tell me some of this stuff yourself. Why didn't you tell me you knew my father? Why, in all the time we've known each other, did you share the information you have about the judge with Ryan and not me?''

He smiled sadly. ''It seemed at the time that I had very good reasons, Lizzie.''

''But those reasons didn't extend to Ryan? You knew his father and you were quick enough to tell him.''

''Because he'd believed a lie since he was sixteen. He was angry and bitter and blaming Matthew Walker for something I knew to be wrong. I knew the truth about his dad and to tell him meant I'd have to admit I knew John Paxton.''

''So what was the problem with that?''

''Well, for starters, it would open a big can of worms.''

She stared at him, vexed that he refused to give her a straight answer. ''Louie, did you know my father?''

Archie had sidled up to Louie and now gave a plaintive whine. Louie put a hand on the dog's head and Elizabeth saw that it was unsteady. She frowned and perched on the edge of her seat, ready to go to him. ''Are you feeling okay?''

He managed a smile and waved away her concern. ''Too much coffee,'' he replied, adding with a wry lift of his bushy brows, ''and, to be honest, a guilty conscience.''

''You're supposed to be drinking decaf,'' she said, while the guilty conscience remark echoed in her mind. But her purpose in confronting him seemed less important when he appeared to be so fragile. And old. She never thought of Louie as old, in spite of his white hair and beard. ''Maybe we should have this discussion another time. Did you ever make that appointment with your doctor?''

''Forget me and my pesky health, Lizzie. We need to have this discussion.'' He seemed to shift to get more comfortable on the glider. ''And don't stop me until I've said it all. For months I've been trying to find a way to tell you. And I've been thinking about it for years."

Years?

He appeared to try to get to his feet, then changed his mind and sank back with a disgusted grunt. "I should never have gone along with it. It was wrong to deceive you and I knew it. Ignored that, to my shame. Hell, I thought I had good reason, but you know, looking back now and seeing the consequences, a man gets a different perspective." He gave a rueful shake of his head. "It took me a few years in exile, but I finally saw the light. Course that was after it was too late. Way too late. Back then, they said it was the only way and I was in up to my neck by that time, but I swear to you and to God that I thought I was doing what was best at the time."

"Louie, you're not making any sense. What are you talking about?"

"My past, Lizzie-girl." Archie whined and put his front paws up on the glider. Louie put a calming hand on the dog's head. "And my past is what wrote the script for your future, God help me."

For the first time, Elizabeth thought he might be suffering some dementia. They'd played a hundred chess games over the years and there had been no indication that he wasn't as sharp as ever. But still... "Ryan mentioned the Cayman Islands scandal that turned the Houston legal community upside down," she said. "Is that what you're talking about?"

"That and the people it ruined. That's what I'm talking about, Lizzie." He put a hand on his face and rubbed over his beard briskly as if to clear his thoughts.

"And my father? Did you know Matthew Walker? Is that what you've been trying to tell me?"

"I knew him, Lizzie." He was breathing shallowly

now, his head resting against the back of the glider. Whatever he was intent on telling, it was taking a toll. His face,
she saw, was pinched and pale. Almost gray. He looked
ready to pass out.

"Louie, what's wrong?" Going to him, she picked up
his wrist and was alarmed to find his skin was damp and
cold. "Please, tell me what's wrong. Are you having chest
pains?" He took a shaky breath and denied it. "Stay
here," she told him. "I'm going to call 911."

"Wait, darlin'. I need to tell you. There's something—"

She was at the steps. "It can wait, Louie. Just hang on.
Don't try to get up. Stay calm. I'll be right back, just as
soon as—"

"Stop, Lizzie. I need to say this." His tone was suddenly strong enough to halt her. "I'm trying to tell you
that I knew Matthew Walker, Lizzie."

"I heard that, but it doesn't matter now, Louie. I'm
sorry I upset you."

"My God, darlin', you didn't upset me. I'm the one—"

"Louie." Now she was the one using a firm tone. "I'm
going to call 911. Don't move."

"Lizzie." Something in his voice should have warned
her. "I *am* Matthew Walker."

The next hour was, forever after, a blur in Elizabeth's
mind. It hadn't taken more than ten minutes for the EMTs
to arrive, but Louie was unconscious when she returned
to the gazebo after calling for help and to her it seemed
as if time stood still. She'd never been so frightened. But
they'd stabilized him, thank God, then loaded him into the
ambulance. They'd refused Elizabeth permission to go
with them, ignoring her pleas, so she'd had to watch helplessly as Louie was taken away in a blaze of flashing lights

and screaming sirens. Then, cell phone in her hand, she ran to her car to follow.

It was Ryan she called first. And then Lindsay. And then Megan.

Later, she would think about how right it had seemed that in a time of deep turmoil and fear, she'd turned to Ryan and her sisters. In the span of a few weeks, the defenses she'd used to protect herself for most of her childhood and all of her adult life had been abandoned. However, the bombshell Louie had dropped before passing out, she kept to herself. She simply didn't believe him.

He didn't have a heart attack. According to Megan, the scary episode was a reaction to new medication for hypertension that had been prescribed for him. "This is not uncommon," she told Elizabeth in a reassuring tone. "The drug caused his blood pressure to drop to a dangerously low level. I suspect his hypertension is newly diagnosed and that his doctor has been trying to find the drug that's right for him."

"I didn't even know he'd scheduled a physical exam," Elizabeth said, still shaken to her core and feeling guilty for upsetting him. With her arms wrapped around herself, she gave Megan a bewildered look. "We—Gina and I— nagged him for months, but we thought he had ignored us. And then after Gina—" Her voice broke and she fought to bring it under control. "All along, he must have been receiving treatment. Why keep it a secret?"

"Men of his age often don't want the people they're closest to thinking they're beyond coping. He's not an old man, nor is he young anymore. It's a common reaction." Megan squeezed her arm. "Just be glad that he apparently took you at your word and had the exam. Hypertension's known as the silent killer. It's too late to take a pill after a stroke." Her lips curved in a smile. "Of course, we don't want the cure to be worse than the disease. Passing out is an extreme reaction. I'm betting his doctor will want to keep him here for a day or so until he can be stabilized with the correct meds.''

"Come on, let's find you a place to sit down," Ryan said, urging her toward a waiting area that looked eerily familiar. It wasn't on the same floor as the room where she'd waited all those hours after Gina's accident, but it was close enough. Too close.

"I can't," she said with real distress. "Jesse's at kindergarten. I have to pick her up. They're under strict instructions not to release her to anybody except Louie or me.''

"It's too early," Lindsay said, glancing at her watch. "But when it's time, I'll go. If you call and authorize it, they'll release her to me. It'll be a couple of hours yet, right?''

Elizabeth touched her forehead, having no idea of the time. It seemed forever since she dropped Jesse off at the school that morning. "Her class is dismissed at eleven-thirty. Thanks, Lindsay.''

Lindsay smiled. "What are sisters for?''

"Right." Megan leaned against the door, crossing her arms. "You know, I see a lot of elderly people taken into the ER in situations like this and sometimes they're totally alone. There's nobody to worry about them, nobody to go in and give them a word of encouragement. Louie's lucky to have someone who cares.''

Elizabeth closed her eyes. The moments before Louie's collapse returned in a vivid flashback. Beside her, Ryan was quiet, deep in his own thoughts, it seemed. She glanced at him and then away. How much did he know? Had he guessed why Louie wanted to talk to her after giving up the files? "Can we all sit down for a minute?

There's something I need to tell you." She lowered herself onto a sofa.

"What is it, Liz?" Lindsay perched on the arm of the chair that Megan took.

"You want me to stay or go?" Ryan asked.

"Stay. I think you've probably already guessed what I'm going to say."

"What's going on?" Lindsay demanded, looking from one to the other.

Elizabeth put a hand to her forehead, looking at her knees, but realized she would have to look her sisters in the face to tell them something like this. "I think I'm responsible for Louie's attack."

Megan looked confused. "It was the medication, Liz."

"Maybe. But if the two of us hadn't been...talking, he wouldn't have reacted as he did." Her hands twisted together in her lap. "He knew I was...upset with him and it bothered him. He probably would have realized he needed to call his doctor, but—"

"Liz." Ryan sat down beside her and covered both her hands with his. "You're making it more difficult this way."

She looked at him with tears in her eyes. "You know what he told me, don't you?"

"Maybe." He shrugged. "Probably."

"I don't believe it." She blinked her tears away, but her voice rose with her distress. "It can't be true."

"Tell us, for God's sake, so we can decide whether we believe it or not!" Lindsay said, then added with exasperation, "whatever it is."

Elizabeth put both her hands to her cheeks, looking at her sisters. "Louie claims he's Matthew Walker."

"Oh, my." Megan looked from Elizabeth to Ryan and back again.

Lindsay, for once, was silent.

"I don't believe it," Elizabeth said, calmer now that she'd told them. She looked at Ryan. "I mean, he moved into the house next door five years ago. If what he says is true, he could have told me a thousand times before today." She was shaking her head, but her lips were trembling. "I just don't believe it."

Ryan reached out a hand and cupped her cheek. "Yes, you do, Lizzie."

Her eyes suddenly flooded with fresh tears. She still shook her head mutely.

"What about the fire when he died?" Megan asked quietly.

"I didn't ask," Elizabeth said, wiping her cheeks. "I mean, I didn't have time. He took sick while trying to tell me. I rushed to call 911 and when I got back, he was unconscious. I was so scared."

"You must have been," Megan murmured softly.

"It was the longest ten minutes in history before they got there." Elizabeth realized Ryan now had slipped his arm around her, and she felt comforted by it.

"This is incredible," Lindsay said, finding her voice. She looked at Megan, her face alive with excitement. "Didn't I tell you something about that whole thing was fishy, Meg? Didn't I tell you that Duke always had his suspicions about that fire? That stuff was hushed up? But even he didn't guess the real zinger, that the fire was staged. My God!"

"Who is Duke?" Ryan asked.

Megan was shaking her head. "Some aging detective connection that Lindsay pumped for information about Matthew Walker's death."

"His name is Duke Collins. And it was before Gina's accident, Meg!" Lindsay turned to Elizabeth. "I was intrigued by the details of the judge's death from day one. Maybe because it was all new to me, but I thought it seemed a little too dramatic. To me, that is, not you as you probably accepted the story the way it was told to you from the time you were five. We all know how that is. You grow up hearing the way something happened and you just accept it. Well, I didn't find it that...acceptable. I mean, here's a judge, very well-connected politically, who's involved in a very scandalous case. Careers are over for half a dozen judges and more lawyers. So Judge Walker's house catches fire and he's the only casualty. His three children are miraculously unharmed, plus nearly all the valuables of his career and what he might have been involved in are destroyed, too.'' She gave a meaningful lift of her eyebrows. ''Including most photographs of him. It's the investigative reporter in me, I guess, but this story had all the makings of a really good exposé.''

''If there was anything to expose,'' Megan said dryly.

Elizabeth looked all around the room. ''Am I the only person who doesn't believe Louie is Matthew Walker?''

''It would explain a lot if it's true.'' Lindsay was up and pacing. ''I mean, he's totally devoted to you, Liz. And he's nuts about Jesse. He knows what she means to you. You said yourself he's informed beyond the norm about Houston's legal community. You name a judge, he knows him.''

''Now we know why,'' Ryan said dryly.

''Even the full beard and mustache are in keeping with a man whose face might be recognized,'' Lindsay said.

''Which explains the vague familiarity I felt when I saw the framed photo of a much younger Matthew Walker in your office, Liz,'' Ryan said. ''You look like him.''

''In other words,'' Elizabeth said, ''you all believe he's Matthew Walker.''

Lindsay shrugged again, rather apologetically.

Megan stared at her feet.

Ryan gave her shoulder a sympathetic squeeze.

"Okay." She watched a nurse pass by. "Fine." She held up a hand. "I'm not saying I believe my own father has been deceiving me for twenty-five years, but just for the sake of argument, say it's the truth. That he has." She shot Ryan a tentative sideways glance. "The question is, why? Why would he do that?"

"If I knew the answer to that," Ryan said, picking up her hand and kissing it, "I would have pushed Louie to tell you. But it's his story to tell. That's what opening the trunk was all about. That's why he handed those files about my dad over to me."

"What files? What trunk?" Lindsay demanded, in full investigative reporter mode.

Elizabeth looked at her watch. "It's almost time to pick Jesse up, Lindsay. Does your offer still hold? Can you go now?"

"Of course," Lindsay said, then added, "but as soon as I've left her safe in Jennifer's care, I'm coming back here to get some answers from Louie."

"Don't you mean Judge Matthew Walker?" Elizabeth asked with sarcasm.

"Yeah, that's what I mean," Lindsay said, grinning.

"Isn't Jennifer in school?" Megan asked, ever the practical one.

"It's a teacher's conference or some sort of thing," Ryan replied. "She's hanging out with a couple of new friends and they're cool with taking Jesse."

Thank God for Jennifer, Elizabeth thought. She released her cell phone from the clip on her handbag. "I'll call the school."

Twenty-Five

Jennifer sat in one of the soft club chairs near the coffee bar in the bookstore and watched Jesse solemnly studying the display of children's books. For a little kid who couldn't read yet, she definitely knew her way around a bookstore. She finally spotted the book she was looking for and picked it up. Big surprise, Jennifer thought, giving Jesse a high five from across the aisle. Her choice was Liz's Newbery prize book. "You've already got that one at home, Jess. Pick something else, my treat."

Jesse nodded and pulled out *Bob the Builder*.

"You have that, too, love bug."

Putting her hands on her hips, she gave Jennifer a fierce frown.

"Okay, convince me that we should buy a book when you've already got it at home. I'm listening."

For a beat or two, Jesse seemed on the verge of speaking. She opened her mouth. Jennifer held her breath. "Say it, Jess. Tell me why you want to take home a book you've already got."

But the moment passed and Jesse disappeared into the next aisle to find something else.

Jennifer looked at Rick. "Did you see that? She almost said something."

Rick nodded, taking a swig from his smoothy. "Almost, but not quite. She's gettin' there, Jen. But it beats me how you know what she's thinking. She doesn't even need to talk when she's with you. You interpret those big-eyed looks and her funny little face quirks like they're real words.''

Jennifer brushed the crumbs of a brownie into a napkin. ''It's easy when you know her, but she really needs to talk. It'll mean she's finally getting over the trauma.''

''You mean her mom and all.''

She folded the napkin over and then over again, studying it thoughtfully. ''It's not just Gina dying and all, you know? A lot of it's about her sleazy dad. She's really scared of him. You should see her whenever you just mention his name. She goes all quiet and it's like she gets, you know, kind of smaller. Like she goes into herself. Just a minute.'' She stood up suddenly and crossed the aisle to check the section where Jesse was browsing. In a moment, she was back, giving Rick a quick smile as she sat back down. ''I know it's silly, being so paranoid about keeping an eye on her 'cause this is a nice store and how could anything happen, but you can never be too careful, Liz says. And my dad.''

Rick smiled. ''And when she's with you, you're responsible.''

''A lot more than when we first met,'' she said dryly.

''Jeez, I hope so. You were hell on wheels then…so to speak.'' He laughed, dodging sideways, when she tried to land a punch on his arm.

Jennifer knew the grin on her face looked stupid, but Rick was so cool. And he was nice, too. Like going with her to the bookstore to give Jesse a treat when he found out she needed to baby-sit. He could be hanging out with his friends instead or doing more training for his marathon. She couldn't think of a single guy she knew in Dallas who would do that.

"Speaking of your dad," Rick said, "how're things going with you and him?"

"Great. I mean, really. This will sound crazy to someone like you with a regular family and all, but I didn't know my dad as well as you know yours because of the divorce and everything. But he's a good person, Rick. Just look at the way he's tried to make up for almost handing Jesse over to creepy ol' Austin."

"This isn't exactly a news flash to me, Jen. I knew your dad was cool five minutes after meeting him."

"Well, my mom probably influenced me, but I've got my head on straight now. And you know what?" She glanced over at the aisle where she'd last seen Jesse. "I think my dad is serious about Liz. I bet they're gonna have a serious relationship."

"You mean an affair?"

She frowned. "I don't think Liz is the type. I think if a man got serious about her and she felt the same way, she's the kind of woman a man marries."

Rick grinned and stood up. "I think you're right. Come on, let's check on the brat again." He reached for her hand and pulled her up from the chair.

The trip to the bookstore wasn't something she'd ordinarily do when she was in charge of Jesse. It was Lindsay who'd suggested it, saying it might keep Jesse from worrying about Louie being sick in the hospital. Having another person so close to her in the hospital was bound to be scary and Jesse had had enough scary stuff in her life to last any little kid always and forever.

They went to the section where she'd last seen Jesse sitting on the floor looking at a pop-up picture book. No sign of her in that aisle now, so Rick went back one aisle and she checked the next one. And the next.

The store was arranged so that parents could keep an

eye on their kids and drink cappuccino at the same time as the kids went through the torturous process of choosing a book. The entire section was in full view of the café. Almost.

"Rick, do you see her?"

"No." He stood with his hands on his hips, looking around. "She's got to be here. No way she could have disappeared without us seeing her."

"She wouldn't have gone anywhere without me," Jennifer said, beginning to feel panic. "Quick, you go upstairs. That's the music section and books on tape and stuff. I don't think she'd go up there without me, but check anyway, would you? I'm going to the rest rooms."

"Tell the checkers at the exit first," Rick advised. "I mean, just in case she's with someone and he tries to take her out of the store."

"She'd scream bloody murder if that happened," Jennifer said, beginning to get a stomachache. She took off in a run to the front of the store where she breathlessly explained there was a lost little girl. Then she dashed to the ladies' rest room. Empty. As she left there, she hesitated only a second before going into the men's room. Empty in there, too.

Rick met her coming down the stairs. "Nobody's seen her in the upper level. What'd they say at the checkout?"

"I could tell they thought I was in a panic over nothing. Nobody saw anything." Her mouth trembled. "I'm scared, Rick."

"Yeah, it's really weird for her to just disappear into thin air with us sitting right there." He ran a hand over his hair. "I'm gonna ask to see the manager. Meanwhile, you go check the stockroom. She might just be hiding to scare you."

"Well, it's sure working."

The stockroom was crowded with cartons and books stored on metal shelves arranged in aisles. Jennifer raced down the first few, turned a corner and came upon the rear exit of the store. She read the sign, Emergency Exit Only, and hesitated for two seconds before pushing it open.

Austin Leggett stood at the door of an SUV in the act of hefting Jesse up into the passenger seat. "Hey!" Jennifer shouted and dashed toward him.

She stopped in her tracks as he jerked Jesse back, covering her face with his hand. "Shut up, you little bitch, and get over here if you don't want to see her hurt." Jennifer's stomach dropped to her feet. Jesse was struggling, clawing at Austin's hand, trying to breathe.

"Don't hurt her," she said, struggling to sound reasonable, although her heart was beating so fast she was almost light-headed. She put her hands out and walked toward them. "You can do whatever you want, but just don't hurt her."

"If she makes a sound—"

"Jesse! Don't scream, okay? He's not going to hurt you."

"Why the hell didn't you stay in the goddamn store!" Austin bit off the words, infuriated by the necessity of altering his plan. "We've got to get out of here. They'll be all over us like flies on shit as soon as they realize she's gone." Still holding Jesse with a brutal grip, he chewed his lower lip. "Okay, get in with her. I'll decide what to do—" He broke off as if just realizing he was wasting time talking to two children.

Jennifer climbed in beside Jesse, who threw herself into Jennifer's arms and buried her face in her midriff. Cursing, Austin reached over and closed the passenger door, then started the SUV with a roar. They were almost out of the alley when, through the side mirror, Jennifer saw the emergency exit fly open. Rick! But it was too late.

Austin eased into traffic on Kirby, driving much more sedately than he wanted, to avoid drawing any attention to the car just in case the kid was missed a lot sooner than he expected and they started looking right away. The risks in a kidnapping were substantial and he'd taken as many precautions to reduce the chances of being caught before he'd accomplished what he set out to do. Still, you never knew.

He wasn't in the Porsche. Freakin' car had brought him enough grief. This time, he'd rented an SUV. Half the male population in Houston owned one. Nothing conspicuous about it. And to delay anybody missing him as long as possible, he'd called in sick at the office and told them he wouldn't be at his condo, but at his father's place instead. Curtiss still employed the housekeeper who'd raised him. She'd vouch for him—that he was there until they actually checked—which would kill a few hours if he was lucky. Consuelo was the closest thing to a mother he'd had during his rotten childhood. If he told her to say he had gone through a sex change, she would. For this job, he didn't need a sex change. He just needed three days.

But, goddamn it, the Paxton kid could screw up the whole plan. Another minute and he would have had Jesse in the car and been out of there. Then the girl had to come running out, hell-bent for leather to save her. He couldn't just leave her after she'd seen him and taking her would jeopardize his plan. He felt himself breaking out into a cold sweat. Ryan Paxton wasn't the kind to overlook a threat to his kid without retaliating. He had to come up with some way to get rid of her.

Beside him, Jesse now sat buckled securely in the seat

belt, sharing it with Jennifer as she sat on her lap. With her knees together and her feet in the cute little pink sneakers dangling, they looked almost like a normal family traveling. At least, that's what he hoped anyone looking would think. Face turned, she was intent on the scenery from the passenger window, as prim-looking and distant as…as…that stuffy Liz Walker. Give her another few months in that house and Liz would have cloned herself in Jesse.

"Not in my lifetime," he muttered darkly and gave in to a deep rage by accelerating up the ramp onto the Southwest Freeway.

"Where are we going?" Jennifer asked.

"Shut up."

He'd made it clear to Jesse when he'd grabbed her in the bookstore that he'd take his hand off her face only if she promised not to scream. Then, he'd told her with his mouth at her ear that if she did scream, he'd break her freakin' neck right then and there and he'd hurt the Paxton teenager as well. His threat worked. Pale and big-eyed, she'd walked as nice as you please out of the kids' section of the store into the stockroom in back and on out the emergency exit. He'd never have made it that far if Jennifer hadn't been more interested in her boyfriend than Jesse.

Rotten luck that she'd missed Jesse before he got her in the SUV and drove off.

"I don't know how you can treat your own little girl like this," Jennifer said.

"I'm telling you to shut up, kid."

Hell, he didn't hate Jesse, but having her around was now a definite risk. It was the damnedest stroke of good luck that she'd been struck dumb over the whole thing. When he told her after the wreck that she was to keep her little mouth shut or he'd see that she paid a price, he hadn't realized she would literally take him at his word. In fact, he didn't believe her version of the accident would have carried much weight in the beginning. It was only after she started freaking out whenever she saw him that people began to get suspicious.

The plan might still work out, but he needed both kids in a more cooperative frame of mind. "C'mon, Jesse, quit acting like a baby. You're not gonna be hurt now. You were a good girl back there in the bookstore. See, I'm keeping my word. I didn't hurt your friend. You're in the car and we're going on a nice trip."

Jesse picked at the laces on one sneaker, tying a knot and then untying it. Over and over. Jennifer had a hand on one small shoulder, gently stroking.

"You can talk now. You were a good girl about that, too, but now it's just you and me, so you don't have to stay quiet."

Jesse reached for the scrunch that held her hair in a ponytail and pulled it off. A curtain of dark, silky hair instantly fell forward shielding her face.

Austin reached out to touch her and she flinched, huddling against the door, still not looking at him. "Hey, I'm not gonna hurt you. Daddies don't hurt their little girls."

Now her skinny little legs were drawn up and she rested her face on her knees, her body turned away.

In spite of himself, Austin felt…something. The kid wouldn't look at him, hadn't actually looked in his face one time since he'd grabbed her. Maybe she thought if she didn't look at him, he wouldn't be there, he thought with a certain wry self-derision. And why would she want to look at him? He'd been a shitty daddy. No denying that to himself. But he didn't bear all the guilt for the unlucky hand the kid had drawn. Gina had been a pretty shitty mother, too. She might try to convince the judge and anybody else who'd listen that she'd always put the kid's best interests first, but he knew stuff about Gina that nobody else would believe. And if it ever came down to the nut-cutting, he'd tell that stuff.

But first he had to get her out of Houston and over to Arizona to his mother. Time enough afterward to figure out what to do with Jennifer.

Louie hated being confined to a bed in the hospital. He suffered through another check of his blood pressure by a male nurse who made bad jokes about the effect of hypertension on his sex life. He had rarely been in a hospital, but mostly, as he recalled, nurses had been women. Grumbling, he took the new pill in the silly little paper cup— what happened to just handing a man a pill?—and settled back to wait and wonder if they'd let his family in to see him.

Lizzie would have told them by now, of course. He turned to stare morosely out the window. Maybe they wouldn't show up to see him at all. Maybe they'd wash their hands of a father who'd seemed to wash his hands of them, as babies yet. He wouldn't blame them. In truth, he didn't deserve to have them acknowledge him as father at all.

It was Ryan who came into his room when they finally said he could have visitors. "I'm afraid Liz will need a little time to adjust to the news, Louie. After they told her there was nothing seriously wrong and that you would be released within twenty-four hours, she decided to go home." He stood with his back to the window. It was midday and bright, the glare throwing his face into shadow so that Louie couldn't tell what he was thinking.

"What about Lindsay and Megan?"

"I think they felt bound to honor Liz's feelings."

"I guess they were pretty shocked."

"Liz, definitely. Lindsay and Megan seemed startled, but you have to remember they've both had a very stable childhood and the emotional impact wasn't as significant as it was for Liz. At least, that was my reading of the situation. It meant dire consequences to her when you disappeared." He ran a palm around the back of his neck. "She'll come around, Louie. As I said, it may take some time."

Louie lifted his arm and rested it on his forehead. The few years he'd had living near Lizzie might very well be at an end. She'd be within her rights to cut him out of her life, now that she knew the depth of his deception. He wouldn't blame her if she did. "I should never have done it, but it was too late when I realized they hadn't honored their promise," he said quietly.

"You'll need to explain everything to her, Louie. To all three of your daughters. Nothing makes any sense."

Louie released an empty, hopeless laugh. "It's gonna sound pretty sick when I explain that I traded their lives to save my own worthless, criminal ass."

"I'm not following you, Louie."

He brought his arm down and looked Ryan in the eye. "I went into the Witness Protection Plan twenty-five years ago."

Ryan gave just one single nod of understanding. "Ah…"

"Yeah, it was the Cayman Islands thing." He studied the IV taped to his left arm. "I guess the reason I didn't tell Lizzie who I was when I first showed up after all those years was that I was too ashamed. I felt too much guilt.

But I swear to God, I didn't know it would turn into such a disaster.''

"The Feds staged your death in the fire," Ryan guessed.

"Yeah. In exchange for my testimony. It was that or prison. But they didn't have to apply much pressure. In fact, I didn't expect any leniency. I knew I was going to serve time, me and a whole slew of judges. But John Paxton, your dad, had stayed clean, resisted the lure of all that money. The night he died, I was in his office. He told me he was going to the Feds and tell them what he knew. A case that was on his docket had been pulled abruptly and reassigned to me. You have the file in that stack I gave you. He'd had his suspicions all along. He told me that night that he intended to blow the whistle on the whole lot of us.''

Ryan was on his feet now. "Did you kill him, Louie?"

"No, no, son." He moved restlessly, got up on one elbow and added earnestly, "I didn't try to talk him out of it, either. I was pretty sick of the whole thing. Like other judges at the time, I'd started out taking just a little here and a little there. I don't have an excuse that will hold water. My wife had died giving birth to our last baby girl, Lindsay, and I was depressed and sort of overwhelmed with the care of three small children, but I wasn't the only man in the world who'd been in that fix before. Look at your dad. John had a wife with an incurable disease. Medical bills were piling up, he said as much to me once. But he was steadfast in his devotion to her and in his duties as a judge." He reached for a cup of water on the bed stand and raised it with an unsteady hand to drink. "And even if I were overwhelmed, it didn't justify compromising the integrity of the bench or dishonoring the oath I took to uphold the law. No, anyway I looked at myself over the years, I was a pretty miserable human being.''

Ryan sat with his hands clasped loosely between his knees. "I won't lie to you, Louie. It'll be difficult for Lizzie to hear this.''

The old man nodded solemnly. "I'm prepared for the worst.''

"You said you were in the office with my father the night he died. Do you have any idea, then, who murdered him?''

"No, not at the time. I was as shocked as everyone else. But later I heard what I think is probably the truth from one of my contacts once I took up my new life. John was killed by the same assassin who would have done the same to me had I not been hustled off to a safe house after I agreed to testify. His name was Josef Reiner. He was later linked to a money-laundering scheme in Florida, tried and convicted. He died in prison of AIDS about five years ago.''

"Was that when you decided to come out of the program?''

"I'd been thinking about it long before that. I actually made the break when Lizzie was finishing college and getting ready to go into law school.''

He frowned. "Liz is a lawyer?''

"No, she dropped out." He pushed the button that brought the bed up to a near-sitting position. "You might ask her about that one of these days. She's had a lot of pain in her life and a lot of it's my fault. If she'll forgive me—and I include Lindsay and Megan in that, too—I'll spend the rest of my life being the best man I have it in me to be." He sat up and pushed the sheet down over his bony knees, then swung his legs over the side of the bed.

"What're you doing?" Ryan asked as Louie studied the

IV apparatus taped to the back of his hand. "You need to go to the john?"

"What do you know about taking this thing out?" Louie lifted his hand with the IV apparatus taped to it.

"Your IV?" Ryan stepped to the bed to take a closer look, then glanced up at the bag of fluids suspended from a metal pole. "Is it uncomfortable? Looks to me as if it's working all right, but I can call somebody if you think it needs to be reinserted."

"I don't want the damn thing reinserted," Louie growled. "I want it removed. And for God's sake, don't ring for the nurse. He's a dumb son of a bitch who thinks he's a comedian."

"You can't just remove it, Louie. It's dispensing medication. They're trying to stabilize your blood pressure. You want to pass out again?"

"I'm stabilized. No medication in that sack for that, just fluid 'cause they said I was a little dehydrated. I've been peeing every few minutes since I got here, dang it. The blood pressure pill is just that, a pill. It'll work fine. If it doesn't, I'll know next time not to wait 'til I pass out before I tell somebody and they can give me a new one."

"Liz will be upset," Ryan warned.

"Lizzie isn't even speaking to me, so that's a pretty weak argument. I gotta get home and try to find a way to fix what I screwed up twenty-five years ago. Besides, that baby girl, Jesse, needs me. Lizzie won't admit that now, but it's the truth." He gestured toward the wall cabinet with his white head. "Hand me my pants, son. No telling what they did with my shorts, but I'll make do without 'em if I have to."

Fighting a grin, Ryan did as ordered. Judge Matthew Walker was probably a force to be reckoned with in his heyday. And it was now clear where Liz got that streak of stubborn independence.

"You're in luck," he told the old man, handing over underwear, shirt and pants. His cell phone rang as Louie was dressing. He'd forgotten to turn it off, as requested by the hospital. Now, glancing at the number, he saw that it was Rick Sanchez.

"What's up, Rick?"

"It's Jen and Jesse, sir. They're gone."

"Gone? What d'you mean, they're gone?"

"We were at the bookstore on Kirby letting Jesse pick out a book and Jen went to check on her in the children's department and she never came back. Sir, I think they've been kidnapped."

Twenty-Six

One look at Ryan's face and the receptionist at LJ and B leaped to her feet. "Mr. Paxton, what's wrong?"

"Is Austin in his office?"

Patti Gardner hesitated, taken aback. It was unlike Ryan Paxton to be abrupt. He was known in the firm as an all-around nice guy, one who was invariably courteous to employees, no matter how far down the food chain they were. She glanced down at a notation in the sign-out book. "Uh, no, sir. He never came in at all today. He called in sick."

"Did you make a note of the time when he called?"

She traced the entry with a finger. "Ten-fifteen."

"How about Curtiss? Is he in?"

"Yes, sir. Shall I buzz Marta?" Nobody got in to see Curtiss Leggett without going through his longtime secretary and bodyguard.

"Yeah." He headed toward the executive suites, passing his own without a glance. "Thanks, Patti," he added, clearly an afterthought.

The receptionist watched him stalk down the hall—there was no other word for it—then quickly dialed the number for the old dragon who guarded Curtiss Leggett's inner sanctuary. She'd never seen Ryan Paxton looking so severe. He was different in the courtroom, of course. His tactics there were legendary. This must be the Ryan Paxton he morphed into before a judge and jury, she thought.

"Look out, Mr. Leggett," she murmured with a wicked smile, then reverted to professional receptionist mode in response to Marta's clipped, "May I help you?"

Curtiss Leggett was standing when Ryan strode through the door of his office. "I wasn't expecting you, Ryan." He took a closer look and frowned. "Is something wrong?"

"I'll get right to the point, Curtiss. Two nights ago, Austin violated the restraining order Liz filed to keep him away from Jesse. He actually got into the house, but bungled the attempt to kidnap his daughter as she was sleeping in the bedroom with Liz, and not where he thought she would be. An hour ago, he finally succeeded. He abducted Jesse and my daughter, Jennifer, from a bookstore on Kirby. Tell me that you know where the sneaky little creep may be headed."

"Now see here—"

Ryan cut him off with a slice of his hand. "Don't fuck with me, Curtiss. My daughter's more precious to me than anybody or anything on this planet. If he harms a hair on her head, I'll personally see him on death row."

"This is preposterous. Austin's judgment may be faulty at times, but he wouldn't stoop to kidnapping." Curtiss fiddled with a paperweight on his desk, anchoring a sheaf of papers he'd been reading. "How do you know he was involved? Was there an eyewitness?"

"He's involved, all right. And yeah, we've got an eyewitness, someone who got a glimpse of them as Austin left the alley behind the bookstore in an SUV. Rick got the license number."

Leggett lowered himself to his chair, looking shaken.

"You must be mistaken. You know Austin drives a Porsche."

"He probably considered it too risky to pull a caper like this in his car, knowing he'd be recognized. He's driving a rental. The license number is being released to all units. And just so you'll know this is serious, Shepherd Steele at Homicide is all over his case, Curtiss, and has been since Gina's accident. He's running scared."

Leggett was clearly startled. "Homicide? Surely you don't think—"

"That Jesse's life is in danger? That Austin's capable of violence? That he'd hurt my daughter if he felt she threatened his plan, whatever the hell it is? Yeah, I think all of the above." He moved forward, shoving aside a photo of Curtiss and his yacht, and put both hands flat on the lawyer's desk. "For once, Curtiss," he said, looking him in the eye, "think of something besides the goddamn firm and whatever embarrassment this might cause you personally. Think of that little girl. She's your granddaughter, for God's sake! Think of Jennifer."

Leggett's color was up. He fumbled for a handkerchief and used it to mop his brow. "You can believe this or not, but I have no idea where he is. I'm completely unaware of the details of Austin's personal life. I certainly didn't know about a restraining order." He stared at the handkerchief for a long moment, then looked up at Ryan. "All that said, I can't believe he would hurt either one of those children."

"He would, Curtiss. He's been abusive to every woman he's ever had a relationship with and he'll hurt Jesse or Jennifer or both if he's pushed to the wall. We just need to find him before he becomes that desperate."

"What would he hope to accomplish by kidnapping his own daughter?"

"If Jesse's version of Gina's accident didn't match his own, he might want her out of the way before she begins to talk again."

He frowned. "Begins to talk? What does that mean?"

"Didn't you know Jesse has been utterly mute since the accident?"

"I understood she was unhurt."

"Physically unhurt. Emotionally, it's another story."

Leggett turned to gaze at the view of Houston from his windows. "He used to run to his mother when he got in trouble," the lawyer said, and added with disgust, "she always bailed him out." He stuffed the handkerchief back into his pocket. "I don't know whether she'd welcome having a little kid dumped on her. She's been essentially out of his life—and mine, thank God—for years."

"If he's planning to send her off to his mother," Ryan said, feeling a sick dread building in his belly, "I'm concerned about how Jennifer fits in his plan. She's certain to be a complication he wasn't counting on." He backed away from the desk and prowled the luxurious office, thinking. First it was Jesse who could incriminate him and now Jennifer. Ryan felt cold knowing Austin's options.

"I'll put a call through to his mother," Curtiss promised. "That would be my best guess. Otherwise, I don't know what else to tell you, Ryan."

Ryan stopped at a table displaying several small framed photographs, most of them taken on Curtiss's yacht or in the Galveston area. None of the people were recognizable, he realized, and noted vaguely that Austin's face was missing. Curtiss's first love was his yacht and his yachting friends, not family.

Family. Jennifer. God, how terrified she must be right now. And Jesse, whose paranoia about her father had become a real nightmare. Where the hell could he have taken them? Where to start looking for them? And Liz. His heart literally ached for Liz. First losing Gina, then the shock of Louie's deception. Now Jesse. How much more could she take?

Elizabeth's house was overrun with people. From where she stood in her den, she counted eight familiar faces, as well as half a dozen strangers, some in uniform, some not. She pressed a palm to her stomach, still queasy with panic ever since Ryan's call. It was almost impossible to believe that Austin thought taking Jesse would solve his problems. There was no logic to what he'd done. Even if he returned both children unharmed, he would face dire legal consequences. That left him with no motivation to do the right thing and that was the scariest thought of all.

Ryan was across the room with Shepherd Steele discussing what to do next. Steele's expertise was not in kidnapping, but he'd refused to be excluded from the search for Austin on the grounds that his own homicide investigation took priority. He'd introduced two of the men and one woman as an elite team specializing in cases involving missing children. The woman, Sheila Wyckoff, had suggested that Jennifer was at the age to think it was cool to disappear and give her parents a fright. Elizabeth and Ryan both had instantly set her straight. "Not even a remote possibility," he'd told the woman. Both Lindsay and Megan had agreed.

"It's more likely that Jennifer would put herself in harm's way to try to protect Jesse," Lindsay had shot back. "What you want to do is find Austin. You locate him, you'll find both the girls."

If we're not too late.

What Elizabeth feared most was that Austin was in a mental meltdown. If she was right, the girls were in ex-

treme danger. She watched as Steele beckoned a pair of
uniformed police officers over, and gave them instructions. They then turned smartly to leave to carry them out,
she assumed. What instructions, she wondered. If anything
was known about where Jesse and Jennifer had been
taken, she and Ryan would have gone there hours ago. A
parent on the run with a child could disappear for years.
It happened all the time, according to the media. Also,
Jennifer was a complication that Austin couldn't have
counted on. He would be unhappy having to cope with a
teenage girl. He had no patience with his own five-year-
old.

Aware of a stinging pain in her palm, she relaxed her
hold on the picture frame in her hand. She'd removed the
photo of Jesse to be copied by the search team and was
clutching the empty frame to her chest. A picture of Jennifer had come from Ryan's wallet. By now, Steele had
informed her, hundreds of law enforcement people were
on the lookout for both children.

Moving to the French doors, she looked out and saw
Louie standing on his patio, his solemn gaze fixed on her
house and the activity in and out of it. He looked lonely
and isolated. Her throat tightened in a rush of emotion and
suddenly tears blurred her view of him. In spite of her
efforts to put Louie out of her mind, it was almost as
impossible as forgetting about the girls.

*Damn you, Louie. You're supposed to be in the hospital,
not fretting over Jesse and Jennifer. Go back inside and
lie down.*

Lindsay appeared beside her, handing over a cup of hot
tea. "He's fretting over you, too," she said, following
Elizabeth's gaze.

She cupped both hands around the warm mug. "Was I
talking to myself?"

"I guess so, since there's nobody else within earshot." Her face went sad. "He's suffering, Liz. He loves those girls and it must be unbearable to be shut out at such a terrible time."

"You can keep him informed," Elizabeth said bitterly.

"I can't acknowledge him until you do. Megan agrees with me."

Elizabeth's face took on an expression of misery and her voice rose in pained bewilderment. "How could he do this to us, Lin? Didn't he think of the consequences of abandoning his children? And don't say he wasn't aware. He appears on my doorstep after nearly twenty years with a new name and no past and we're supposed to just open our arms and say welcome home, Daddy? How could he expect welcome and forgiveness after perpetuating such a hoax?"

"It wasn't a hoax, Liz. You heard what Ryan said. It was a huge criminal investigation and what Louie agreed to do jeopardized his family as well as himself."

She sighed when Elizabeth made a disgusted sound. "I can see you're thinking he wouldn't be in that pickle if he hadn't corrupted his position on the bench. Don't you think one of the reasons he failed to tell you is that he doesn't come out looking very honorable in all this?" Her hand was moving very gently back and forth on Elizabeth's shoulders. "Would it hurt so much to give him a chance to explain?"

Oh, but it did hurt. She'd spent most of her childhood trapped in a bureaucratic nightmare as a result of her father's duplicity. It was no thanks to him that she'd finally been reunited with what was left of her family. And it was Lindsay who'd been the driving force there, not Louie. Pushing her hair from her face, she let her gaze wander

over the wide expanse of lawn to where he still
stood…waiting. Hardening her heart, she turned away.

Across the room, Ryan was still in conversation with
Steele, who was interrupted by one of the male members
of the search team. When they headed toward the front
door, Ryan must have sensed her watching, for he turned
and saw her, then came straight across the floor to her.
He put an arm around her shoulders in a wordless expression of shared anxiety.

"What are they planning to do?" she asked.

"There's an all-points bulletin out on the vehicle.
Thank God that Rick managed to get the license number.
The rental agency will be able to confirm that it was Austin. Wyckoff's team will watch for credit card charges and
any withdrawals from Austin's ATM. Curtiss promises to
notify us if he hears anything." He gave her shoulders a
squeeze. "We'll find them, Liz."

"Have you called Jennifer's mother?" she asked.

"She doesn't answer. I think I remember Jen saying
something about her leaving on a trip with Gerald, the
man she's been seeing lately." He turned so that his chin
rested against her temple. "California, maybe. L.A.? I
don't remember and if she doesn't answer her cell, there's
no way I can get in touch with her. I don't know anything
about Gerald except his name. Jennifer—" He cleared his
throat. "Jen knows all that stuff."

She knew his terror over the children went as deep as
hers. "I'm so sorry about this, Ryan. If Jennifer hadn't
been so generous in helping with Jesse, she at least would
have been spared this."

"Jen gained more from her experience with Jesse than
she gave. She would be the first to tell you that."

Elizabeth turned her face into his chest. "What can we

do, Ryan? I feel so useless just standing around occupying space.''

"Steele says try to stay calm. And pray. They're the experts—the team headed by Sheila Wyckoff, not Steele—although he has a stake in the outcome. He wants Austin for the accident.''

"What will the charge be?''

"Reckless endangerment, at the very least.''

"On top of kidnapping now.''

"Yeah, he's really messed up this time. But back to Steele. He says let them do their job.'' He pushed back a fraction, holding her with his hands on her forearms, forcing her to look into his eyes. "We don't have much choice but to go along with that. Where would we go to search? Curtiss will call if he hears from Austin. And his mother has promised the same. Both are aware of how thoroughly Austin has screwed up and if they attempt to stonewall, they'll become accessories to kidnapping. I don't think Curtiss wants to jeopardize his reputation or his cushy life by shielding Austin this time.''

"It's just so difficult to do nothing,'' Elizabeth murmured.

"There is something that I think would be helpful.'' His hands moved idly up and down on her arms in a warm, comforting caress.

"What? I'll do anything.''

"It won't help us find the girls, but it will make you feel better.'' Ryan tucked a wave of her auburn hair behind one ear. "I think we should respectfully ask these people to go. Megan's shift begins early tomorrow morning. Lindsay would stay until she dropped with exhaustion, but she has a job, too. I've already sent Rick home. He has school tomorrow. The cops and the search team are getting ready to fan out and do their jobs.''

"Are you leaving, too?" She felt a pang of dismay, realizing that if Ryan left, she'd be alone. The idea of facing this ordeal alone was terrifying.

He gave a low near-laugh and bent to kiss a spot at her ear. "No, Liz. You're stuck with me until we get our children back."

She felt color warming her cheeks, but he wouldn't let her look away. "I haven't told you the part that's going to make you feel better," he said, now stroking her hair. "I think we should go over to Louie's house and clear the air." She pushed against him in protest and tried to turn away, but he held her in place. "You need to try to get some rest tonight, but do you really think you can with the thought of Louie all alone, pacing and hurting? He loves Jesse, too."

The image he'd painted was difficult to dismiss. She wasn't a cruel person and the thought of Louie in pain made her feel terrible. Actually, she was feeling a range of conflicting emotion. Everything was out of control. If it weren't for Ryan, so rocklike in spite of his fear for his own daughter, she might have given in to terror by now. And clearing her house was a welcome idea—even though she knew people were there for the most thoughtful reasons. He was also right, of course, that she should make peace with Louie. Harboring anger would drain precious energy, energy she needed to deal with what might come if Austin wasn't apprehended soon.

She stood studying Ryan, admitting to herself the enormous effect he was having on her life. Oddly, she wasn't fighting the changes anymore. The more she thought about it, the more natural and right it felt to open herself to Ryan and what they might have together. He made her feel cared for…cherished.

"I wasn't going to rest tonight," she told him. "I couldn't."

He smiled. "Then it won't cost you anything to have a conversation with Louie."

Less than an hour later, Elizabeth walked beside Ryan on the well-worn path between her house and Louie's. "I should warn you that I'm far from accepting everything he's done no matter what he comes up with by way of an explanation," she said, brushing past a planting of bright-yellow lantana. "I'm mostly doing as you suggest because being at odds with Louie is something I don't need right now. Unlike everyone else, I'm not entirely convinced he's who he says he is."

"Your father."

"And," she added, ignoring that, "I'm also concerned that he left the hospital against doctor's orders. What was he thinking? What were you thinking to help him?"

Ryan took her elbow and guided her around a water garden stocked with goldfish, a project—like the gazebo—that Louie had installed for Elizabeth and Jesse's pleasure. "It was a choice of him catching a taxi or driving him myself," he said. "He was leaving come hell or high water. What would you have done?"

"He's a sick man," she said, adding with exasperation, "He'd collapsed just four hours before that. You could have been more forceful."

"Maybe I sympathized with him too much. I know how much I'd hate to be stuck in a hospital."

She didn't have a chance to continue the debate because Archie was suddenly bounding toward them, barking joyously. Beyond him on the patio, Louie began to rise slowly from his chair, holding a small box that had been on his lap. She felt a ridiculous urge to rush over and help him to his feet, to give him a hug. Instead, she stepped onto the patio sedately, unconsciously holding on to Ryan.

Louie placed the small box on a table beside him. "Lizzie," he said, searching her face anxiously. "Are you all right? Do you have any word on the children?"

"No, nothing." Lighting on the patio was poor. As long as they were outside, she wasn't able to judge how well— or sick—he looked. She took a breath. "Ryan thought we should talk." Emphasis on Ryan.

"Then once again I owe him my thanks." He gave Ryan a wry smile. "I may never live long enough to pay all my debts to Ryan. He's surely his father's son." He bent and picked up the box. "Shall we go inside?"

Holding out an arm, he ushered them to the door. Elizabeth had participated substantially in decorating Louie's place. When he first moved in, he'd accepted everything just as it existed, but after they became friends, he'd asked for her suggestions. The result had been an attractive, comfortable look that a bachelor could easily maintain. At the time, she'd assumed Louie to be a bachelor, she thought with some bitterness now. More dishonesty if what he claimed was true.

"I thought we could talk in the den," he said, leading the way.

"You should be in bed, Louie. You look awful."

"I was waiting for you."

"How did you know I would come?"

"I would have waited until you did, no matter how long it took." He put the box down on the coffee table and waited until they were both seated on the sofa before lowering himself into a worn recliner. During the redecorating phase, Elizabeth had not been able to persuade him to replace it with something as comfortable, but more stylish.

"Are you taking the medication the doctor prescribed?"

He fumbled in his shirt pocket and pulled out a card with pills enclosed in foil. "These are physician's samples. Megan got 'em for me and Ryan brought 'em over."

"You're taking them according to the doctor's instructions?"

"Yes, ma'am. And I'm feeling fine." He tucked the medicine back in his pocket and said almost humbly, "I'm a hundred percent better now that you're here, Lizzie."

She felt her throat tighten. "Why did you do it, Louie?"

He sat for half a beat with his hands on both knees, then he leaned over to pick up the box on the coffee table. "Before we talk about that, there's something in this box I want you to see." Without opening it, he held it out for her to take.

Elizabeth hesitated, then took the box. It was cherry wood and beautifully made. Something about it seemed familiar, but she couldn't place where she had seen it— or one like it—before. Then, there was a brief flash of memory. More déjà vu? Her heart began to beat with a feeling that she couldn't quite define. Her father had had a box very similar. Matthew Walker had been a great golfer and he'd kept a few golf balls in the box on his desk. She remembered watching him practice putting on the carpet. He would let her collect the balls and put them back in the box. The recollection was so clear that it might have happened yesterday.

She rubbed a hand over the satiny finish of the cherry wood, pausing when she felt a slight imperfection. Examining it, she saw that it was a burn scar. It had been polished over, but the damage was still visible. Polished brass hardware secured a small catch. Her fingers were unsteady as she worked at the catch. Then, holding her breath, she slowly lifted the lid of the box. She sent a quick, startled glance at Louie. Inside was a collection of letters. She recognized them instantly.

They were letters from the child Elizabeth to her father, Matthew Walker.

"Mr. Leggett, I wish you'd stop and think about what you're doing." Jennifer stood with Jesse on the deck of the boat watching Austin readying it to cast off. She'd had a dozen chances to get away herself, but she'd been forced to go along with everything he thought up because he threatened to hurt Jesse. Jennifer wasn't sure she believed he would do it, but he had a crazy look in his eyes. And with every passing minute, he got crazier. He mumbled a lot to himself and he seemed ready to jump out of his skin at the least little thing. "If you take us out in this big boat, how is that going to help you? Sooner or later you're going to have to put in at a dock somewhere to gas up and the whole world is going to be waiting for you."

"Shut up and make yourself useful." Austin tossed the line to her and Jennifer caught it smartly. Going out with her dad on his boat had always been her favorite thing, so she was accustomed to playing deckhand. She made it fast on a cleat and watched him jump awkwardly onto the deck. He was no yachtsman, she thought in disgust. And she was willing to bet this Bertram didn't belong to him.

"Whose boat is this?" she asked, looking around to locate life jackets.

"My father's."

"My dad's got a boat, too." She removed the cushion on a hatch cover, one logical location for life jackets. No way she would let Jesse go out on this boat without one. Worse yet, it was getting dark. Did this clown know anything about navigating at night? "His isn't in the class with this one, though. I bet you had some good times when you were a kid growing up with a yacht like this in the family.''

''I hate boats,'' Austin muttered, beginning to fiddle with switches and check gauges at the helm. He definitely wasn't as confident as her dad when he was at the controls of his boat. It would be really risky going out to sea with a man who hated boats. At night. This baby probably had power to spare, she thought, and they could be miles from shore within no time flat. What could she do to delay casting off? ''Where are the life jackets? All of us need one. I bet you don't have anything small enough for Jesse, do you?''

''Do you ever shut the hell up, kid?'' Grumbling, he left the pit and began searching for life jackets. Which turned out to be a bust as far as safeguarding Jesse. Nothing small enough, just as Jennifer guessed.

''Now what?'' she asked, keeping Jesse close. ''We can't even think of taking Jesse out to sea until we get her a life jacket.''

''We'll all go without life jackets if I say so,'' he snarled. Slamming a door inside the cabin, he came out looking harassed. Jennifer watched him shove his fingers through his hair, muttering to himself. He stood looking around as if the life jackets would just magically appear out of thin air. What a dork! But they could be hurt by a dork the same as a maniac and she had to do something.

''I've got an idea,'' she said brightly. ''It's not exactly honest, but we're desperate, isn't that right? I could just pop over to one of the other boats around here and sort of borrow some life jackets.'' She waved a hand at the boats moored in the surrounding slips. ''I mean, the ox is in the ditch, as my dad would say, so we gotta do what we gotta do. It wouldn't be too criminal since our lives would be at stake if we go out in the Gulf without 'em.''

"Will you shut up, for Christ sake!" He turned from the console to look at her, cursing furiously. "Did anybody ever tell you kids are a major hassle in a man's life? It's no wonder Paxton dumped you on his ex. Drive a man insane flapping your gums.''

That hurt a little, but she didn't show it. Her daddy loved her, she knew it. She felt it. When Mom married bald-headed Gerald, she was going to stay with Ryan and he wanted her. It was gonna happen. Really.

"You didn't answer my question, Mr. Leggett." She wondered if pushing his buttons was smart, but she just couldn't let him leave this dock. "Aren't you afraid you'll be spotted and get in trouble when we have to dock?"

"I don't think you need to worry about docking," he said viciously. "What you need to worry about is whether or not I throw you overboard.''

Jesse made a sound, a soft little whimper. Jennifer instantly threw her arm around her small shoulders and hugged her close. "He was just kidding, love bug. He's your daddy. He's already promised he wouldn't hurt us." She looked up, glaring at him over Jesse's head. "Isn't that right, Mr. Leggett?"

"Yeah, yeah." Austin was preoccupied now with the mechanics of starting up the boat. "Just keep the chatter to a minimum and we'll all be okay.''

Jennifer bent to whisper words of comfort in Jesse's ear. But as Austin fired up the Bertram's powerful engines, she was filled with fresh fear. Austin, the creep, had confiscated her cell phone right away, so she had no way of calling anybody unless she could somehow get hold of his before they got too far out. Once you were a certain distance out in the Gulf, you couldn't use a regular cell phone. And he was probably too stupid to even know that.

She closed both arms around Jesse, her mind racing. What to do? What to do? There was still a slim chance that somebody was aware of the vehicle Austin had rented...if Rick had recognized them as they'd left the alley. And, if he did, was he able to get the license number? Once they'd arrived at Galveston and were pulled up at dockside, she'd noticed that Austin had obscured the numbers with mud or something. So, if somebody was looking for an SUV of that make and model, would they stop and clean off the tag?

"You never said where we're going, Mr. Leggett," Jennifer said, raising her voice over the sound of the engines. Meanwhile, she noticed anxiously, it was getting dark, big time.

Austin was busy studying a map.

"Mr. Leggett? Mr. Leggett!"

He turned around furiously. "This is the last time I'm warning you, you little shit! Put a lid on it!"

"But I think Jesse's getting seasick." She wasn't, but anything to delay them leaving the dock.

If she thought his use of cuss words was bad a few minutes ago, now she'd never heard some of the things he'd said. Not even on MTV. "Maybe we better wait a few minutes," she suggested. "And we really need to get life jackets. What if we run into bad weather?"

"You—" He pointed a finger at Jennifer. "One more word and you're overboard, you hear me?"

We'll probably all be overboard whether I talk or not, you creep. You're about as capable of operating this boat as your five-year-old daughter.

Jesse squirmed around and looked up at Jennifer, big eyes seeking reassurance.

"We'll be okay, love bug." She put her lips close to the little girl's ear. "Jen's gonna think of a way to get us out of this mess, don't worry."

Jesse seemed to relax somewhat, but there was still an anxious look in her eyes. For herself, Jennifer had never been so scared. That they were stuck on this boat with a lunatic was bad enough, but it was night. His inexperience was an even bigger threat. If it was true that panic was a spur to creative thinking as she'd once heard some psychologist say on The Learning Channel, then she'd come up with something brilliant. She just hoped her brilliant idea would come soon.

Twenty-Seven

After leaving Louie, Elizabeth and Ryan were both silent all the way back to her house. Instead of relieving tension and making her feel better, Louie's confession had drained her of what small reservoir of energy she had left. She had imagined herself being able to listen to his explanation of the incredible circumstances of his life and then simply deciding whether to believe it or not. But, in any event, it would mean nothing to her except that Louie was now not the man she'd come to know.

But it had been nothing like that.

At the door, she fumbled in her pocket for the key to her house, then after a couple of attempts to fit it into the lock, Ryan finally took it from her gently. "I don't know the code for the security system," he said, pausing before opening the French doors. "Can you manage that?"

"Yes." She stepped inside and punched in the code. He closed and locked the doors. They'd had no calls from Steele or from Jennifer's cell phone. There was nothing to do now but wait. And think.

The mental turmoil of the past few weeks was taking a toll. It was devastating to hear Louie tell of his criminal past, of his fear for the safety of his children, of his decision to testify and disappear from their lives. Coming so close on the heels of Gina's death and Jesse's disappearance, it was just too much. How could she have thought otherwise?

She stood in the middle of the room, willing her mind to shut down. If she could manage that, she might be able to make it through another long night. Not to sleep; sleep was utterly out of the question. Bursting into tears, however, just might happen. It was probably the aftershock of all she'd been through, she thought, making her way quickly to the leather sofa. Shedding her sweater, she kicked off her shoes and settled into the corner. With her legs tucked beneath her, she hugged a big cushion and concentrated on heading off an embarrassing display of guilt and self-pity.

She had almost forgotten Ryan when he appeared carrying two snifters of brandy. Taking one, she sipped it, closing her eyes and savoring the fiery taste flowing over her tongue. Hopefully, it would soon dull her senses. "Where did this come from? I don't have any brandy in the house."

"I thought you might need something stronger than that expensive wine you stock." He went to the wall and switched off the overhead light, leaving only a small lamp burning on a table across the room. The effect was one of quiet intimacy, enhancing the feeling that the two of them were suddenly alone with their fears and regrets. "I made a list and one of the cops went to Spec's to pick it up for me."

"Thank you." Tears were threatening again.

Taking a seat within touching distance, he leaned forward to set his glass on the low table in front of the sofa, then leaned back, resting his arm behind her. "Want to talk about it?"

"What is there to say? Louie is my father. He was a corrupt judge. He took bribes in return for handing down favorable rulings to well-heeled clients. He abandoned me and my sisters and left us at the mercy of the state of Texas knowing it had been only one year since we'd lost our mother.''

Ryan reached for his drink. ''That pretty much summarizes what he said.''

Hugging her cushion, she studied his profile in the faint light. ''And your own father might not have died if Matthew Walker hadn't chosen that night to talk to him. Don't you feel any resentment for that?''

''Have you forgotten that I spent my life hating him from the day Dad committed suicide?''

''You were a boy hating a faceless person, someone you'd conjured up in your imagination. I'm talking about Louie.''

''My dad's fate was set when he made it known he was going to the Feds, Liz. It was a reckless decision to advertise his intentions before actually doing it. And it killed him. Matthew Walker had nothing to do with my dad's murder.''

She cupped the brandy snifter with both hands. ''I'm sorry, but it feels a lot more personal than that to me.''

''It was personal for both of us, Lizzie.''

''Yes, but you have the comfort of knowing your father was honorable.'' She looked at him with anguish. ''My father was not.''

''He did the right thing in the end. And I think he's spent years trying to atone. He's been a doting father to you for the last five years, even if you didn't realize it was biological as well as emotional. Can't you give him some credit for that?''

''I don't know, Ryan. I have such painful memories.''

He finished the brandy and leaned back, resting his head

against the leather, looking at her. "Tell me about the letters."

"You heard him. A little kid's fantasy." She released a weary sigh. She felt tired, and so incredibly sad. "They were the desperate attempts of a child to convince herself that she still had a father. A family."

If Ryan noticed that she spoke of herself in third person, he gave no sign. "It sounds to me as if that was Louie's motivation, too. He must have been as hungry for a connection to you as you were to him."

"I poured out my heart in those letters, Ryan. It would have meant so much to me if he had acknowledged one. Just one."

"It might have taken only one to blow his cover, did you think of that? It was risky for anybody out of the protection program to know anything." He waited for her to consider that, then asked, "When did you stop writing?"

"When realization dawned." She lifted the glass to her lips and sipped more brandy, but it had taken on a bitter flavor now. "It finally hit me that only crazy people write to someone who's dead."

"Your caseworker, Iris—isn't that her name?—must have guessed he was alive. Louie's contact would have had to go through her to get your letters. Did she never give you a hint?"

"No, never." She rubbed idly at a spot between her eyes.

"You're exhausted." He took the glass from her and set it on the coffee table. "You've had two nasty shocks today. Do you think you could sleep if I ran a warm tub for you? You could take your drink with you and—"

She leaned forward and touched his lips with her fingertips to silence him. "Enough about Louie and about me and my miserable fate as an orphan. There are other things so much more important tonight and we've both been doing everything we can not to think about them." She put a hand on his chest, looking him in the eye. "Tell me something, Ryan. In your heart of hearts, do you think Jesse and Jennifer will be returned to us unharmed?"

"Liz—"

"Be honest with me, Ryan."

He caught her hands, both of them, and held them fast. "We can't allow ourselves to go down that road. Austin's unstable, we both know that, but he's still capable of weighing the consequences of doing anything vile to the girls. I think he's selfish enough not to throw his life away, which is what'll happen if he hurts them."

She held his gaze, fighting the tears welling in her eyes. "I feel like this is my fault, that I'm being punished."

He was shaking his head, genuinely puzzled. "How could that be? You've been a stable presence in Jesse's life since she was born. The only stable presence, if you ask me."

"That's just it. I was incredibly arrogant in the way I thought. I was always so critical of the way Gina behaved as a mother. I would have been different, I told myself, had Jesse belonged to me. I told myself I would have done a much better job as a mother."

"What's wrong with that? It's probably true. Gina definitely made some questionable choices. She really wasn't a model mom."

"No. No-ooo!" She pulled free of his hold and covered her face with her hands. "Gina was kind and funny and loving. I really loved her, I did. It was wrong of me to covet her child behind her back. I feel so guilty about that. And now this awful thing has happened and she's dead." Her words were muffled behind her hands. "It's as if Jesse was handed over to me and then snatched away to punish me for being so…so…presumptuous, thinking I could do better."

"Listen to yourself, Liz. If that were true, then Jesse's paying a price for something she didn't do." His voice was close to her ear, deep and quiet and reasoning, his hand stroking her hair. "Come on, it doesn't make any sense."

She felt his arms go around her, pulling her close. "And if we're going to start looking for reasons that this is personal punishment, then I'm far more guilty than you." His voice caught, but he cleared his throat and plowed on. "I have been a lousy father to Jen. Even before the divorce, I wasn't a hands-on dad. I had so many other priorities before my little girl. I spent more time on my boat than I did with Jen. And she knew it. Kids do desperate things when they're neglected. That's what the hit and run was about."

"The hit and run was an accident," she said. It was much easier to defend Ryan's shortcomings than her own.

"An accident, yeah, but the way Jennifer reacted in a crisis was disappointing to me. I'd stake my life on this though—if it happened today, Jen would do the right thing."

She raised her head to meet his eyes, uncaring now that he saw her tears. "It's just so hard to think we might…lose them."

"We won't. He'll turn up. The car will be spotted. He can only go so far." He nestled her head beneath his chin. "Steele and that Wyckoff woman are a formidable pair."

"Don't forget Lindsay." Safe against his chest now, she sniffed and wiped her eyes with her fingertips.

He urged her face up with a finger beneath her chin. "Will you take that bath now? You need some rest."

"I'd rather wait here with you." If there was to be bad news, she wanted Ryan nearby when she was told. She didn't have the kind of discipline to keep her thoughts at bay that he apparently had.

"It might be a long night."

"I never thought otherwise."

"Then let's get comfortable." Reaching behind him, he put a cushion against the arm of the sofa and leaned back, bringing her with him. Fortunately, the sofa was oversize and there was plenty of room for him to stretch out his long legs. Too tired to think anymore, Elizabeth relaxed against him and was asleep almost instantly.

There had not been many moments in Ryan's life when he felt helpless. With Liz curled next to him, he should have been rejoicing. She was right where he'd wanted her since that first day in the courtroom, although then he'd been in a state of denial. It hadn't lasted long. She was his, even if she wasn't ready to admit it to herself. Especially not now while she was frozen with fear for the girls and aching with the painful truth about Louie. He'd never thought of himself as a patient man, but Liz would be worth the wait.

He'd felt the gradual relaxing of her limbs as she surrendered to exhaustion and wished his own system would also shut down. She wouldn't sleep long, he suspected. No one with an imagination as vivid as hers would be able to keep the demons at bay. She was terrified for Jesse's life.

Just as he was terrified for Jennifer.

His brain ached from the intensity of his fury and frustration. Where was his daughter? There was no way Austin would choose to be saddled with two kids. If he wasn't headed for Arizona and his mother, where would he go? What kind of insane plan did he have?

Ryan stared at the ceiling, watching the play of moonlight reflected off the light fixture. From the moment this happened, he'd felt as if there was something right in front of him, something he knew but couldn't quite pin down. Whether it was the key to what Austin might be up to, he didn't know. But he couldn't shake the feeling he was missing something. He just needed to bring it into focus.

Liz stirred, made a small, anguished sound. Even in sleep, she wasn't able to let go of her fear. In that, she was like all the mothers in the world whether she'd given birth to Jesse or not. Her child had been stolen and she was living a parent's worst nightmare. He turned his head and pressed his lips to her temple, filled with a protectiveness he'd never felt before for anyone except Jennifer. Austin had a lot to answer for.

"Mr. Leggett?"

Austin dropped his head for a second, going very still. He spoke through clenched teeth. "What now?"

"I think I saw some streaks of lightning on the horizon. Did you check the weather?" Jennifer knew he didn't, because he'd never turned the TV on in the salon, which is where he'd have gotten a fix on the weather. And she'd seen no sign of a weather radio. Her dad always kept an eye out for weather, but this guy had already admitted he hated boats, so she'd bet he wasn't up on the stuff you had to do when you planned a trip. Furthermore, she'd bet his father didn't even know he was taking the boat out. Which made her wonder how he'd gotten the keys. Did Mr. Leggett senior just leave them lying around so anybody could rip off a million-dollar Bertram?

She watched him trying to maneuver the boat out of

the slip. He'd had a couple of failed attempts and been forced to put it in forward gear and start all over. She cast a worried look at the dock, hoping to see something or somebody who might help before they were off and running, but it was deserted at this hour. And there might be some storm warnings keeping other craft from starting out. The Gulf looked pretty choppy.

"Did you check the weather?" she repeated.

Suddenly, he turned from the console, stumbled over something he'd left on the deck and lunged at her. Grabbing her shirt, he lifted her off her feet. Jennifer's heart was in her throat when he stuck his face in hers and yelled, "What does it take to shut you up!" giving her a vicious jerk that tore her shirt. Drawing back, he slapped her hard, putting the force of his anger behind the blow. Stunned, she saw stars for a moment or two, then she felt herself slung around and slammed against the bulkhead. Sharp pain pierced her side and she lay for a few dazed seconds, unable to move.

Still dizzy, she heard Jesse scream. But Austin was caught in a red rage and didn't spare a glance at his daughter. He came at Jennifer again, grabbed her arm and yanked her painfully to her feet. With his arm cocked back to land another blow, he failed to notice Jesse scrambling away from the skirmish to the other side of the boat. Climbing out of the cockpit, she balanced for a heartbeat, then jumped.

"Jesse!" Jennifer screamed. Wrenching free, she lunged to the side of the boat and leaned over, searching frantically for a trace of the little girl. There was nothing but black water. Black, filthy water. And she knew it was deep. Oh, Lord, Jennifer thought, almost paralyzed with terror, could Jesse swim? Had it been fear of Austin that sent her over the side? Whatever the answer, there was no time to think about it. Taking a breath, she said a quick prayer and jumped overboard, too.

Elizabeth came awake slowly, realizing the clock on the mantel was striking the hour. A few seconds ticked by before she recalled where she was. With a wave of despair, she remembered Jesse and Jennifer.

Her pillow, warm and firm, turned out to be Ryan's arm. He lay wedged in the bend of the sofa and she was snuggled against him, her hand on his chest, as if in her troubled sleep she'd given in to the need for intimacy. She could feel the even movement of his chest and thought he must have been able to sleep, too. She lay for a moment thinking she should move. This was so terribly inappropriate. She should slip away and sit in the big club chair across the room and wait for news of the children. She shouldn't disturb what rest he was able to get. He had as much at stake as she. But that would mean waiting out the rest of the night alone in cold panic. Instead, she lay in the warm cocoon that almost shut out the harsh reality they shared. His chest was broad and warm, she discovered, cautiously moving her hand over the crinkly feel of hair through the fabric of his shirt. She wished his chest was bare so that her palm, opened wide now, could touch skin and muscle. She drifted a while in her fantasy and was startled when he suddenly gripped her wrist.

"You're going to have to stop that, darlin'," he said, his voice a deep, low rumble near her ear, "or be ready to take the consequences."

She lay very still, not mistaking his intent. To stop now would be to risk nothing. There was safety in staying free of involvement, which is what she'd been doing for more years than she wanted to count. Evan's betrayal had made her feel less of a woman. Ryan, she knew, would take pleasure in erasing that insecurity. And yet he wouldn't go where she didn't wish. Still, she felt the impatience in him now. He was a man who pushed an advantage, as she'd experienced in the short number of weeks she'd known him.

Her nod was barely a whisper of movement, but he felt it. With one hand, he began working at the buttons on his shirt. When he had it open, he took her palm and placed it flat on his skin. "Try it that way," he said in a thick tone.

The skin was firm and warm to her touch, the muscle as solid as the thud of his heart. She sifted through the hair on his chest with delight, moving her hand leisurely, savoring the smooth, male texture of him, tweaking the tiny pebble of a nipple. Then she cautiously touched her tongue to it, drawing from him a muffled sound, a cross between a groan and a painful wince. Now her own body was heating up, going weak and urgent at the same time. She moved restlessly, pressing her thigh against the erection he could not conceal and she felt a thrill that she could arouse a man like Ryan. Then, with a shock, she realized that her own need was as fierce as his. She slipped her arms around him and lifted her face to his.

His eyes, locked with hers, were ablaze in the dark. "Are you sure?" he managed to say.

She nodded, burying her face in his chest. "Make me forget, Ryan."

He hesitated as if her reply fell short of what he wanted to hear. When he didn't move, she looked up again, both her hands on his chest. "I need this. I need you," she said.

And for an instant, she thought he was going to stop. She felt panic, a tiny spurt of fear that she'd taken the risky step she'd carefully avoided for years only to have it thrown back in her face. She could feel his heart running away. He wanted her. And yet he wanted something more from her than she was ready to give. He might be tempted to reject whatever she was offering, but she knew it would cost him.

"I'm not going to hurt you, Liz."

"I know." It would not be intentional. He didn't have a wife tucked away somewhere. She was free. He was free. Still, she was one heartbeat away from pushing back and running to hide in her bedroom. But then he seized her face in his hands. "And I'm not going away, lady. If it's not tonight, it'll be soon."

"I would survive even if you did." But would she? That was the source of her panic, she admitted, the certainty that Ryan had come to mean more to her than any man she'd ever met in her life. That she wouldn't be able to throw herself into something—anything—and pick up the pieces and go on as she had once before.

"Are we having an argument?" he asked, his smile a little off center. "I have to tell you, it's not a good time."

"I think you started it."

He lowered his lips to hers, barely touching her. "Then I'm ending it."

The easy caress of his hands had her muscles turning to water and her doubts slipping out of reach. With his mouth at her ear, he had her blouse open before she came to her senses. Heat radiated all through her as he curled a hand around a breast then bent to kiss a tingling nipple. "I could do this a lot better in a bed," he told her, all the while he was slowly undressing the rest of her, laying kisses on her skin as it was bared.

In a daze, she stood up and let him take her by the hand to her bedroom. By the time he lowered her to the bed, her shirt and pants lay on the floor in a tangle with Ryan's.

But she had no time to admire the look of him wearing nothing, because he was touching her everywhere. He was so good at this, she thought with distraction, dizzy with the pleasure of his hands and mouth and tongue streaking over her. She had a fleeting worry that she might disappoint him. She had loved Evan passionately, but their actual lovemaking hadn't been particularly satisfying.

But this. This! Ryan made her feel feminine and desirable. He made her feel that she was everything he needed, that his need for her wouldn't be satisfied with a single night in her bed. Then the ability to think was gone. She came once with his hand between her legs, then again when he entered her. She rose to meet him and they moved together, their pleasure heightened by the sheer joy of discovering how well they fit. And when she was ready to erupt again, he buried his face in her auburn hair and took them both over the edge.

Twenty-Eight

"Louie told me that you once wanted to be a lawyer," Ryan said in a quiet voice. There had been other hints dropped by Louie about Liz's past and he hadn't followed up on anything. Now he found he wanted to know everything. "Why did you give it up?"

She lay facing him, propped on one elbow. "Circumstances. When it was time to enter law school, fate intervened. Besides, writing for children gives me far more satisfaction than arguing the rights of defendants in a courtroom."

"Fate intervened. What does that mean?"

Taking her time, she traced the shape of his biceps with one finger. "A few weeks before I was to enter law school, I discovered that I was pregnant." She raised her eyes to his.

"Pregnant."

"Yes."

She'd pulled up the sheet and covered her beautiful breasts after they'd made love. He'd thought her endearingly modest. They hadn't turned on a lamp in their haste to get to her bed. Now, he wondered if there were signs, not that he'd care. As a lover, she was warm and responsive and giving. And oddly innocent. "Was it a love affair gone wrong?"

"It was never love, although I thought it was the real thing at the time."

"Did the baby not survive?"

"Or did I have an abortion, you ask? No, neither."

"Am I asking too many questions?"

She touched his mouth with the tips of her fingers, smiling softly. "You're a lawyer. That's what lawyers do."

"I don't want to ask anything you don't want to tell me, Liz."

She shifted, settling back on two pillows propped against the headboard. "When I was a senior in college, I got involved with a married man. Here's a joke. He was a judge."

Ryan now lay propped on one elbow, facing her. "I bet he was older than you, too."

"A lot," she said dryly. "I know what you're thinking and it's probably true. I was looking for a father figure. But what *I* was thinking was that he was handsome and sophisticated and wise, and why in the world had he chosen me?" She touched her chest with her fingers.

"Because you were special? And intelligent, beautiful and young? Just a guess," he said with a shrug.

"I discovered he was married when I told him I was pregnant." She turned her face to the window. "I will never forget that evening. We never went anywhere that he might be recognized—which shows how genuinely dumb I really was. I'd prepared a special meal in my apartment. He'd said he loved me, many times, so I assumed that he'd be pleased about our baby." Her laugh was short and humorless. "Not only was he displeased, but he was furious. He accused me of deliberately trying to trap him into marriage. He said I was a scheming little—well, he used a word that I hate—and that he already had a wife. She was in academia as well and spending a year in Europe. He said that he wasn't about to be stuck with child support for the next eighteen years and I was to get an abortion immediately.''

Ryan forced himself to breathe evenly, wishing to have just five minutes with the bastard. "But that wasn't an option, right?"

She looked at him. "I seriously considered it. I even made the appointment and showed up at the clinic. Gina went with me."

"Were you going to get rid of the baby thinking to continue the affair?"

"I was going to get rid of both the baby and the judge."

He didn't know if she was aware that her hands were cradling the place where her child had once been. He placed a hand over hers. "What happened?"

"When it came right down to it, I couldn't do it. But I was lucky," she said. "Many young women who screw up and find themselves pregnant don't have options. My father left a trust fund. I had enough income to live on, so I went to work in a bookstore, mostly to keep myself from thinking and brooding over what a fool I'd been, and it gave me something to do to pass the time."

"Did you intend to keep the baby?"

"No, although I wanted to with all my heart. I knew what a childhood without both parents was like. I couldn't subject my child to that." She pulled one hand from beneath his and turned his palm up, linking her fingers with his. Her eyes, when she looked at him, were too bright. "Giving him up was the hardest thing I ever did in my life. It was sheer hell."

"But very unselfish."

"It didn't feel unselfish. It just felt painful."

He could imagine her anguish. And now that he knew, he understood why she was so protective of Jesse. Why she fretted when Gina neglected the little girl. Why guilt would kill her if anything happened to Jesse now. And why it was so difficult for her to trust a man. Any man.

"He had black hair," she said in a dreamy voice. "And probably dark eyes, but you don't know so early. Seven pounds, six ounces, twenty-one inches long. He's ten years old and lives in Denver today."

"Wow."

She turned so that their faces were almost touching. "I had a chance to be a mother and I gave it away, Ryan. If something happens to Jesse or Jennifer, I just don't think I can survive it."

"We'll find them, Liz."

She lifted a shoulder in a helpless little gesture. "I keep worrying about Austin's mental state. He has to find a way to get Jesse away from here. That has to be the purpose of this crazy stunt. If he uses the car he rented, he'll have to be on public roads. He can't fly. So what would he do? I keep asking my—"

"The boat." Ryan sat up abruptly. "Curtiss Leggett's boat." He threw off the sheet and hit his forehead with the heel of his hand. "That's it! Son of a gun, why didn't I think of it before? I *knew* there was something—"

"You think Austin has them on a boat?"

"Yeah, I do."

"I can't see Curtiss Leggett being a party to a kidnapping."

Ryan was up now and reaching for his pants. "I don't think Austin would ask permission, but Curtiss has a Bertram that could easily cruise for days, long enough to get Austin to his destination. And there's a way to find out fast." He rammed his arm through a shirtsleeve. "I can put in a call to Steele and have him check the Galveston marina where Curtiss docks his boat."

"Is he as skilled operating a boat as his father?"

"No. And that's why we have to hurry."

Steele picked up his cell phone on the first ring. "Ryan, I was just about to call you. We've spotted the SUV and you'll never guess where."

"Galveston?"

"Uh, yeah," Steele said after a surprised moment. "It's parked at the yacht club and we're in the process of checking the people who're registered for rooms there tonight."

"Send somebody else to do that," Ryan said, sweeping up his car keys. "Go down to the marina and find Curtiss Leggett's Bertram. If it's put out to sea, notify the Coast Guard to try and intercept it. If not, see that it doesn't leave the dock. Meanwhile, Liz and I are on our way."

The water was cold. Jennifer fought her way up to the surface, gasping from the shock as much as the need for air. She'd dived near the place where Jesse had jumped, or so she hoped. And prayed. The water was filthy, slick with the oily stuff that boats gave off. And now that she was in the water, she realized how slim the chances were of finding Jesse. Little kids who couldn't swim could drown in a heartbeat.

Can you swim, Jesse?

Above her on the boat, Austin was cursing and pacing, but he wasn't jumping in to save his daughter, Jennifer noted with disgust, although he was looking real crazylike over the side of the big Bertram. It was all going to be up to her. She took a frantic look around and then drew in a deep breath, prepared to dive.

"Jennifer, here I am."

Jennifer thought her heart would jump right out of her chest. The words came in a hissing kind of whisper, but it was Jesse, no doubt about it. And she had enough sense not to say it loud enough for her nutty dad to hear. Jennifer squinted across the black water, trying to locate her. Beneath the dock were countless pilings which made it difficult to spot anything, especially a little kid.

"Where are you, Jesse?" She kept her voice as low as possible. Not that there was much chance of the nutcase hearing anything. He was still ranting and raving and he hadn't even had the brains to turn off the engines. Actually, he was calling Jesse's name over and over. Maybe he got some credit for that, she thought.

"I'm over here. I'm holding a big thing that's sticking out of this pole."

A hook or cable thingy of some kind. Good. "Okay, hold on. I'm swimming over there. Say something else so I'll go in the right direction."

"Like what?"

"Just keep talking. Say a poem."

"One fish, two fish, red fish, blue fish."

Good choice. Jennifer almost chuckled, except she was too cold. "Way to go, love bug. Did anybody ever tell you you're the bravest little girl in the whole world?"

"I'm really cold, Jennifer."

Jennifer guessed that from the unsteady way she was talking, but she was talking. Hallelujah. And from the sound, she knew she was getting closer. She gasped when something brushed her leg underwater and realized she'd bumped right into Jesse.

She was so glad that she threw her arms around her, almost sinking herself. Jesse was hanging on to a large steel hook driven into the side of a barnacle-covered piling. She'd be all scratched up when they were finally out and dried off, but she couldn't afford to think about that now. And she wasn't going to sink as long as she didn't get too cold to hang on to the hook while Jennifer tried to figure out how to get them out of the water and find a safe place without Austin spotting them. How she wished she'd been able to find those life jackets. They'd sure come in handy right about now.

"He made my mommy have that accident," Jesse whispered in her ear. "He ran right into the back of our car."

"Oh, baby..."

"He told me not to say a word, but he was going to hurt you, too. So I jumped."

Jennifer held up a finger. "Shhh, I'm glad you're talking again, but you need to save it for when we get home safe. Now, listen." She put her lips next to Jesse's ear. "We're gonna have to get out of this cold water, love bug. Here's the deal. Your daddy might see us if we try to climb up on the pier right here, so we need to move among the boats that're docked until we're sort of away from him. I guess you can swim, huh?"

"Uh-huh. I had lessons. Aunt Lizzie made me."

Thank you, God, and thank you, Aunt Lizzie. "Okay. I'm going to help you as much as I can, but I need you to swim the best you ever have. Think you can do that?"

"Yes."

"Good girl." This kid deserved a medal if and when they managed to get out of this mess. Between Gina and that stupid Austin, they'd created an awesome little girl. Why he would put her at risk was a mystery. But no time now for figuring out mysteries or idiot fathers.

They were still within earshot of Austin, but as they were under the pier, he couldn't see them. She was getting ready to push off, to head away from the Bertram when she realized that he'd stopped yelling. What now? She strained, waiting to see, trying not to think what might be in the water getting ready to take a taste of them. Then, she heard a splash and saw a big cushion from the hatch floating a few yards from them.

Oooh, she wanted that makeshift life raft. But not enough to show herself and somehow wind up a kidnap victim again. "Stay here, Jess." She took a deep breath—it was going to be awful—and dived toward the cushion, planning to grab it from underneath and drag it back to where Jesse waited. Okay, she had it in her grip. She began to tug on it and realized he'd tied a rope to it. It was like the creep was fishing for them!

Damn! Sorry, Dad. Just let me and Jesse get out of this alive and I'll never cuss again.

Abandoning the idea of the float, she swam back to Jesse. In a minute, she had her breath back. "No choice, love bug. We've gotta swim for it. Try not to swallow this nasty water. Ready?"

"Uh-huh."

"Okay, you know the plan. Let's roll!"

The risky part was getting away, unseen, from the Bertram. Once they cleared that slip, it would be relatively easy to keep out of sight. She eased away from the piling and glanced back to see Jesse following in a respectable doggie paddle. Good girl. She had dark hair, which would be a little more difficult to spot if Austin had an eagle eye, but as for herself...

"Blondes have more fun," she muttered and took in a mouthful of water.

But they were clear now, and in another minute or two, were hanging on to the line of another cabin cruiser, a big one. The trouble was, it was really cold. April was not the month to swim, not even on the subtropical Texas coast.

"I'm really c-cold, J-Jen." Jesse's teeth were chattering.

"Three more boats and I think we can get out, Jesse.

Ready?'' And when they did, she'd need something to dry this little girl off.

Please let there be something.

By the time they reached an area of the marina that Jennifer considered safe, she was using a life-saving technique to pull Jesse along. Say a thank-you for her own swimming lessons, she thought. When she had kids of her own, she'd have to remember. Swimming lessons. As soon as possible.

She chose a boat that had a ladder left out. Her dad would never allow that, as it was an open invitation for someone to climb aboard. Okay, two uninvited guests, but she sure wasn't looking a gift horse in the mouth. ''Can you climb up, punkin-pie?''

Jesse couldn't. Jennifer cast an anxious look over the keel of the boat trying to spot Austin. From where they were, it didn't seem as if they were visible to him, but movement of any kind once they cleared the keel and made it into the pit of this boat might change that. It was a chance she had to take. Jesse couldn't stay in the water another minute.

She pushed at the little girl's tiny rump, literally shoving her up the steps. She was helpless to keep her from tumbling to the deck like a rag doll. Jennifer cleared the ladder herself in seconds. With Jesse lying still and spent on the deck, she searched the boat frantically for any-thing—anything!—to cover the little girl. The careless owner had left his hatch cover unlocked. Inside she found only life jackets. Not much warmth there, but better than nothing. Grabbing a couple, she draped them over Jesse until she could find something better. She'd lost her shoes; they both had, but she still wore her jeans and a skimpy little T-shirt. Jennifer wasn't sure whether you should leave wet clothes on or take them off in a rescue situation.

But without adequate covering, it seemed dumb to take them off.

"Are you okay, Jesse?" she asked, gathering her up into her arms. Holding her close, she squeezed water from the dark curls, then took both small hands in hers, rubbing briskly and tucking them into her own armpits. She'd read somewhere that a person's armpits were very warm. "Talk to me, Jess."

"C-cold."

"I know, baby. Jen's gonna fix that." But oh, Lord, how? She tucked the little girl back among the life jackets and sat back on her heels, shivering. They had to have something to cover themselves.

Her own body was chilled to the bone. Rubbing her arms briskly, she tried to ward off the strength-sapping effect of the cold. Here on the Gulf, there was always a breeze. She'd known it to be worse, but any wind was too much when you were wet.

Looking around, she searched for a blanket. But there was nothing. Only a pile of something that looked like a net. A fish net. She kicked it in her frustration and realized it was soft. Shaking it out, she found it holey and smelly, too, but it was better than nothing. She lay down beside Jesse, keeping the life jackets in place around and on top of her, donning one herself, then she draped the netting over them, folded over and over again. Fortunately, the thing was huge, and by the time she'd used it up, she realized they would soon be relatively warm. Not totally dry, but not cold enough to endanger Jesse, either. They were hidden, too, in case Austin started looking for them. Then she settled down with her arms around the love bug—body heat was good, she'd read that, too—and waited for daylight when there was bound to be somebody showing up. People who liked boats were early risers.

Twenty-Nine

Ryan made the trip to Galveston in record time. He was stopped for speeding by a highway patrolman and sat drumming his fingers with impatience on the steering wheel counting the minutes while his story was verified in a call to Shepherd Steele.

"I'm not surprised," Elizabeth said, keeping a smile in check. "You can't drive so much above the speed limit, no matter what excuse you have. Even in Texas." Once, she'd glanced at the speedometer hovering at ninety-five miles an hour and had chosen not to look again. Galveston was less than fifty miles from Houston and traffic on I-45 was at a minimum at this hour. She couldn't argue with his motive for wanting to reach the marina as soon as possible. But, according to Steele, Austin had already been prevented from taking the girls out on the Gulf in his father's boat. So much speed was overkill. But, she wasn't in the mood to argue with Ryan about anything, not after tonight.

She had been right in thinking that Ryan would erase her doubts about herself as a desirable, sexual being. Everything about the hour they'd spent together was meant to tell her that he thought her feminine and exciting and appealing as a lover. Evan's rejection had made her feel less of a woman, but she viewed that experience now with new insight. She wasn't the one who'd failed to measure up; Evan was. And that was his problem, not hers. Carrying that burden for years had been crippling. She felt liberated now that it had been removed.

Her thoughts were interrupted when the highway patrolman approached the SUV once again. He'd made the call and told Ryan that he would escort them. It was a safer ride from that point and, although they exceeded the speed limit, it was less than Ryan would have done if he hadn't been stopped. He was anxious to get to the girls. They both were, but he was quiet to the point of testiness and he had a stern look about him. She would not want to be in Austin's shoes when Ryan got hold of him.

The sky was turning pink with the promise of a new day when they approached the marina in Galveston. They drove past the yacht club where Austin's rental SUV was parked. Ryan had learned from Steele that there were lights and activity aboard Curtiss Leggett's cruiser and that he had given no one permission to take it out. At the marina, no less than six patrol cars blocked the parking area, blue lights flashing. Boat owners, arriving early for a day's fishing or for a simple pleasure run out in the Gulf were forced to jockey for space. Their escort patrol car pulled into the pack, adding to the congestion.

Ryan's door was open almost before he stopped. With her hands shaking and her heart in her throat, Elizabeth climbed out, too. "This time, Austin has gone too far," he said, looking narrow-eyed toward the end of the marina dock where he knew Curtiss's slip was located. Every light on the cruiser was lit. From this distance, they could see several people on the deck and in the pit. No doubt others were in the Bertram's luxurious salon.

"Do you see him?" she asked.

"No, but Steele says he's here."

They'd reached the pier now and Elizabeth picked up

her pace, almost running in her eagerness to get to the
end. She was still a few yards away when Ryan caught
her arm and stopped her. "Wait, Liz."

She pulled to get away. "No, I want to see her. I
need—"

He took both her arms and forced her to look at him.
"I didn't tell you before, but Steele says the girls aren't
on the boat with Austin."

"Where are they?" Confused, she strained to catch a
glimpse of them somewhere on the dock. Naturally, they
wouldn't want to stay on the boat a moment longer than
they had to. With the police swarming onboard, they
would gladly have seized the chance to get away from
Austin.

"According to Austin, they jumped overboard," Ryan
said.

"What?"

"He claims Jesse jumped and then Jennifer followed."

"But it's too cold...." She waved a hand weakly.
"That's impossible. No, Ryan. No."

"They're looking, sweetheart. They're trying to find
them."

"When?" She pressed her mouth with shaky fingers.
"When did they—"

"Two hours ago, according to Austin."

She was moving her head from side to side, denying it.
Now she noticed diving equipment on the dock. A diver
in full gear was hoisting himself up from the water. He
made a negative gesture with his head. A black, painful
despair rose in her chest, almost crushing her ability to
breathe.

"I want to talk to Austin," she said, refusing to panic.
"I want to hear him tell me to my face that he let Gina's
baby and your...and Jennifer jump into this filthy, black,

bottomless hole." They were nearing the Leggett yacht now. She slowed, spotting Austin sitting dockside on a chair, handcuffed, head hung low.

Steele went to meet them a few feet short of Austin, but she had no thought for the detective. Her gaze was locked on Austin, who must have sensed her scrutiny. His head came up. "Liz, I—"

"Where is that little girl?" she asked coldly. Her teeth clenched against the urge to fly at him and scratch his eyes out, to hurl at him all the rage and pain eating at her.

He looked away, his gaze going to the black, oil-slick surface of the water. "I threw them a cushion. I couldn't find the life jackets. She just jumped when I—" The handcuffs prevented the instinctive movement he made to bring his hands up.

"She jumped when you what, Austin?" she asked, her voice rising.

His gaze slid away from all eyes. "It was Jennifer. She wouldn't shut up. She had a million questions. I was rattled. You know how it is when kids won't shut up. Your head rings and you—"

"You shut them up the way that comes naturally to you, right?"

"You hit her?" Ryan made a lunge, but was blocked by Steele. "You son of a bitch! You hit Jennifer and then what? Did you shove those kids overboard, Austin?"

"No, no! I—"

"I swear, if they're hurt I'll kill you!" Ryan stood with his fists curling and uncurling at his side. "I thought I knew how low you could sink, but by God, this time—"

"I didn't push them overboard!" Austin surged to his feet. "Jesse jumped and then Jennifer went in after her. I swear it. I told you, I threw them a cushion from the hatch cover. I put a rope on it so they could grab it. I yelled for them, over and over.'' His face crumpled into shapeless misery. ''I kept calling and looking, but the water was so black....''

''Too black and too deep and too cold for you to jump in and try to save them. Is that the way it was, Austin?'' Ryan's chest heaved with rage and disgust.

''I didn't mean it,'' Austin said, shoulders now shaking with sobs.

Ryan strained against Steele's grip. ''You never mean it when you attack a female smaller than you.'' He shook free and reached for Elizabeth who stood with her hands on her face, tears running down her cheeks. ''Get him out of my sight, Steele.''

''Hey! Hey, over there!''

Steele frowned and motioned for one of his men. ''You know my orders! Keep those people back!''

The policeman started toward a man who was now moving toward them at a fast trot. ''I've got a couple of kids on my boat!'' he yelled.

''Oh, my God.'' Elizabeth released a shaky sob, then broke away from Ryan. Her sneakers squeaked on the boards of the pier as she took off, heading for the fisherman. ''Where? Where are they?''

They were exactly where the man said they were—tangled in a nest of shrimp netting in the pit of his boat, bedraggled and damp and sleepy-eyed. ''Wait, ma'am, it's a little tricky, that step from the dock to the cockpit.'' He put out a hand and she took it, literally leaping the distance. Arms wide, she swept both Jesse and Jennifer up in a desperate embrace and held them close.

His daughter was fine. Safe. And thanks to Austin's own idiocy, Jesse was freed forever from his screwed-up presence in her life. Ryan shoved his hands deep in the pockets of his windbreaker and scowled at the horizon. A few feet away—Ryan couldn't bear Jennifer out of his sight just yet—Steele was taking her statement. A brief one, he'd promised, knowing Ryan was anxious to remove his daughter from the scene. There was so much he wanted to tell her, so many promises he planned to make to her. God, his cup ran over this morning, he thought, thinking of Liz's face when she knew the kids were safe. They'd both come close to an experience they might never have survived and both knew it.

"Okay, Ryan, she's done here." Steele handed over his clipboard to a uniformed cop standing by. "I'll want a more complete statement, but it can wait a day or so." He flashed a smile at Jennifer. "This little lady is the hero of this event, no doubt about it."

"I know." Ryan pulled her close, tucking her in the V of his shoulder. He was still weak in the knees from terror. "On the drive home, she can think up a suitable reward."

Jennifer grinned up at him. "A car would be a good start, Dad."

Steele laughed. "Way to go, Jen!" He walked off, shaking his head.

"In your dreams, brat," Ryan said and couldn't resist another quick, fierce hug.

Jennifer looked beyond him toward the Leggett yacht. "Where is he?"

"Austin?" Ryan moved a strand of blond hair away from her eye. "He's already on his way back to Houston in a patrol car. He won't get another chance to cruise on his daddy's yacht for a long time." Frowning, he turned her face to get a better look. A dark bruise had blossomed on her cheekbone and there was a tiny cut near her eye. Rage simmered in his chest, but it could wait. He vowed to settle with Austin later, one way or another. "He admitted to hitting you. He won't be doing any more of that, either.'' He made an effort to ease his tight jaw.

''I think he's a mental case, Dad. He's kinda pitiful, you know?''

He looked at her, amazed that instead of exhibiting trauma, she expressed a sort of nonjudgmental understanding of Austin. Pride and a wave of pure fatherly love edged out some of the rage. ''And you're a psychiatrist, now, huh?''

''No...'' She gave him a playful punch on the arm, grinning.

His face sobered. ''Are you hurt anywhere else, Jennifer?''

''I bumped my backside when he tossed me across the deck, but since I'm standing and walking I guess there's no permanent damage.''

''And that's all? Nothing else?''

She frowned. ''What else could—'' Her face cleared and her mouth shaped a round O. ''Oh, you mean *that?* Like rape or something.''

He winced. Was there anything that daunted a teenage girl? ''Yeah, that.''

''No, Dad. I'm still a virgin.''

God, give me strength. He took her arm. ''C'mon, let's go to the car.''

''Where's Jesse?'' she asked, realizing the little girl was nowhere in sight.

''While you were talking to Detective Steele, Liz took her to the yacht club. I got us a couple of rooms there so you can get cleaned up before the drive back to Houston. After you shower, you can put something on that doesn't smell like fish.''

She looked down at herself. ''Dad, I didn't exactly get

to pack a suitcase for this trip. I don't have anything else to wear.''

"Not a problem. Lindsay's on her way with clothes for you and Jesse.''

"Wow, okay! She's like a model, you know?''

"I know." With his arm still around her, they started up the long pier to the car. "You really are the hero of the day, Jen," he said, giving her another quick squeeze. "It was pretty ingenious using a shrimp net to keep warm. And we're all impressed with your resourcefulness. You're one smart cookie, sugar.''

"A girl's gotta do what a girl's gotta do.''

"Like I said, a real smarty-pants.'' He tweaked her ear. "But it took pure, raw courage to jump in that cold water. I don't know many men who would have had the courage to do that, Jen.''

"It was that or let Jesse drown, Dad. I really didn't have any choice.''

"We always have choices. You were presented with a hard one. Austin failed and you didn't. I'm so proud of you, Jen. I don't know if I could have measured up in a crisis any better than you did today.''

"Better than I did the day I drove off and left Rick bruised and hurting on the street, huh?'' She was still smiling, but there was an anxious look in her eyes.

"I'm thinking this cancels that debt, honey. You risked your life today.''

"It was a second chance to do the right thing,'' she said quietly.

Ryan stopped. There was a piling that made a good place to sit. He urged her over and crouched down in front of her. "That's an interesting way to look at it. We don't always get second chances in life. You learned it early.'' He paused, looking beyond her to the Gulf, hoping to find the right words. "I've had some time to think about second chances myself these past weeks, Jen. It's been great having you in my house, seeing you every day. I'd like for you to think about staying."

"You mean like...forever?"

He smiled. "As long as forever, yeah, if you're willing." His smile faded again. "I haven't measured up as a father, Jen, and I'd like a second chance. You know the reasons for the divorce. At the time, I wanted to blame your mother. But I've been thinking lately about the reasons she was unhappy enough to seek something she didn't find in our marriage. Maybe if I'd spent as much time being a good husband and father as I spent on furthering my career, there wouldn't have been a divorce."

"Are you thinking you and Mom might get together again?"

He studied her face, hoping an honest answer wouldn't dash a secret fantasy. He knew many kids of divorced parents dreamed of the time the family would be whole again. "That's not going to happen, Jen. I hope you're not wishing for it."

"I might have once, Dad," his daughter said with insight beyond her years, "but to tell the truth, I don't see you and Mom making a go of it now. Mom's not exactly the constant type, you know? I mean, I love her and all that, but she did have an affair while still married and that's wrong. Then she got married again but that didn't last, either. Then she found somebody else. I guess I should be glad she didn't decide to marry him, too. It would have been hubby number three. I could get confused with all those stepfathers. And now it's Gerald, baldheaded and rich, sure to be number three. When'll she stop?" She was shaking her head. "No, I think you stand a better chance of a good solid marriage with Liz."

"Liz."

"You're in love with her, Dad. I've known it for weeks."

"Weeks, huh?"

"You're not gonna deny it, are you?"

He stood up, pulled her to her feet, wrapped an arm around her and started once more toward the car. "You're something else, Miss Jennifer Paxton. Did I ever tell you that?"

"You're something else, too, Dad." She looked up at him with a devil in her blue eyes. "And the next time we talk, you can tell me the facts of life."

He laughed, grabbed her head with one hand and ruffled up her hair. "You wish, brat."

"If I live with you, it's your responsibility!" she shrieked, laughing.

God, he felt great! He glanced up and saw that it was going to be a beautiful day, bright and sunny and warm. Yeah, he had a lot to be grateful for. "I love you, Jen."

"I love you, too, Daddy."

Jesse lay quiet and still as Elizabeth read the last words in the story. *Miss Spider's Wedding* was still Jesse's favorite. Smiling, Elizabeth closed it. She liked it herself. If the book had been written for adults, it would have been a romance novel. A lady spider looking for Mr. Right. "Okay, that's it, sweetie. Time to say good-night."

"Is the door locked, Aunt Lizzie?"

Elizabeth sighed, caught the little girl's hand and held it to her cheek. "Yes, love, the door is locked. You and I are safe in our house."

"Because my daddy is locked up, right? He did something bad, so the good policeman took him away in his car with the blue lights."

Oh, Lord, what to say that wouldn't further damage this child? Jessie'd seen it all on the dock: Austin's meltdown, Elizabeth's near-hysteria, the divers searching the water. There hadn't been any way to prevent it in the confusion of those first minutes when Jen and Jesse emerged from the boat. "Yes, your daddy did something bad, Jesse. It's wrong to kidnap children. It's a serious crime. And when grown-ups commit a crime, they are punished by being locked away in a special place."

"For how long?"

Until hell freezes over was not an acceptable reply. "For a long, long time, Jess. You will not be seeing your daddy for several years."

"I'm not sad."

Elizabeth stroked a soft cheek. "That's okay, too."

"I'm sad about Mommy."

Elizabeth's throat went tight. She waited a moment, then spoke huskily. "I'm sad, too, darling. So here's what we'll do. We'll think of ways to always remember your mommy. We have pictures and we have things she's given us. Best of all, we have so many memories of your mommy."

Jesse looked up at the ceiling in deep thought. "I'll get some paper when I get up tomorrow and I'll color something and decorate it and I'll use some of that glue on a stick to put real flowers on it. Papa Louie will let me pick any of his flowers that I want."

"Papa Louie is very good to you and that's because he loves you." Elizabeth managed a smile. "I love you, too."

"You want me to count the people I love?" Jesse asked, preparing to sit up. Elizabeth touched her gently.

"You can tell me lying down."

Jesse held up both hands and counted off the people

she loved, one on each finger. "I love you and I love Jennifer and I love Papa Louie and I love Archie." She wrinkled her nose, thinking. "Is that all?"

Elizabeth laughed softly. "I don't know, is it?"

"I guess I love Ryan, too, because Jennifer says he's the best daddy in the world. She told me that and I asked if he could be my daddy, too, because I didn't have such a good one." She looked earnestly into Elizabeth's eyes. "Do you think Jennifer would share?"

"I think she just might, love."

Once Jesse was asleep, the house seemed too empty and still to Elizabeth. How soon she'd changed from a semi-recluse to a person who welcomed the presence of those she loved. She walked through the den, opened the patio doors and slipped outside. She could hear Jesse if she woke up, but Elizabeth didn't think that would happen. A miracle really, considering everything yet somehow—incredibly—the whole episode seemed to have brought about much needed closure to Jesse. Odd, that. Rather than trying to puzzle it out, Elizabeth was simply thankful tonight that both Jesse and Jennifer were safe and that Austin was in custody, hopefully no longer a threat to anybody else, ever.

Night sounds were everywhere around her. Comforting sounds. And the pleasing scent of her flowers, of Louie's roses. She breathed it all in. But still…

Across the way, she could see lights in Louie's house. He had been waiting today when she and Ryan arrived in the SUV with the girls. Both Jen and Jesse had run to him and been gathered in a grandfatherly hug. He was visibly shaken as he met her eyes over their heads. Then afterward, there had been a melancholy look about him and

Elizabeth knew that her own joy wouldn't be complete until she and Louie were reconciled.

As late as it was, he should be in bed, she thought now, falling naturally into the role of well-meaning friend. But she wasn't his friend any longer, she reminded herself, or an abandoned child. She was his daughter. And she knew Louie loved her. For the first time since learning his secrets, she let herself test the feeling. Standing there watching his house, she let herself explore the possibilities of that most natural of relationships. It felt right, she admitted with a deep sigh. Just as she'd taken the risk of loving Ryan with rich reward, she would have to let go of her bitterness by forgiving Louie.

Turning, she went back into the house and hesitated only a heartbeat before going to her office. She was articulate and even eloquent when writing her thoughts on her computer, but what she had to write now—tonight—was best done with a pen in her own hand. She opened a storage closet, reached high on a shelf and took down a stationery box. Clearly old, it had not been used since she'd closed her mind and heart on the memory of her father years ago.

Sitting at her desk, she clicked her pen and began writing.

Dear Daddy:

How familiar that sounds, even after all these years. Funny, but back then when I had something on my mind or in my heart, it felt so natural and right to pour it all out in a letter to you and I guess that's what I'm doing tonight. So, where to begin?

I wish that I had behaved more gracefully when I learned who you really were. I wish I had been able to throw my arms around you and tell you that keeping your secrets didn't matter. I wish you hadn't had to leave. I wish I had known you were reading my letters. I wish I had had one—just one—in reply. But if all those wishes had been granted, we wouldn't be where we are today, would we? And so, I'm glad that we now have a second chance and can try to build on the affectionate relationship that has been growing in the five years since we've been neighbors.

I don't know if I would have been able to get beyond all this at another time, but I have so much in my life to be thankful for now. After denying myself all the things I wanted most, fate literally pushed me into a situation I never anticipated. My life was safe and orderly until Gina and Jesse came. It's painful to me to know that Jesse is now mine, but at what price? I loved Gina as a sister and a friend and I always will. I will cherish her memory— and her daughter. Then, next thing I knew, there was Ryan and Jennifer, and then Lindsay and then Megan and then you. Suddenly my world wasn't so safe or so orderly. There was chaos and excitement and energy and ups and downs and…there was love. It was Ryan who urged me to forgive the past and start a real life, one with ups and downs and chaos, yes, but with all the goodness that comes with family, too. He snuck his way past my defenses before I could see it coming—and so did my sisters and you.

I will try to be the best mother to Gina's little girl that I can possibly be. And while I work on that, maybe you and I can get beyond the past to enjoy a loving future. I love you, Daddy.

Thirty

Standing at the door to her patio, Elizabeth watched Jesse and Jennifer regaling the group outside with the details of their adventure. If there was to be any lingering trauma from their harrowing escape, it wasn't yet evident. It was she and Ryan who were feeling the aftershocks of what could have been a double tragedy. Austin's desperation—and his deteriorating mental state—might well have brought about a far different outcome. She sensed Ryan moving up behind her and leaned against him when he slipped his arms around her waist.

"Counting your blessings?" he asked, following her gaze. Steele stood with Lindsay at the barbecue. Megan and Louie were sitting at the picnic table. Rick Sanchez, who'd rushed over when he heard the girls were rescued, sat beside Jennifer.

She looked up at him. "Yes, aren't you?"

The look on his face answered that. The terror of the long night was slowly receding, but neither would ever forget how it felt fearing the girls had drowned. "You must be so proud of Jennifer," she said.

"Yeah. And Jesse's pretty spunky, too." He watched his daughter help Jesse fill her plate from the food on the table, then both walked with Rick to the gazebo. "I want Diane to know how Jen behaved in this situation. Maybe it will help smooth over some of their problems."

She gave him a quick glance. "You're not sending her back to her mother?"

"Not a chance. We've talked. She's here with me as long as she wants to stay. I think she knows now both her mom and I love her, even though we don't love each other."

Elizabeth looked out at the gazebo. It was sweet of Jennifer to indulge Jesse when she must have wished to have Rick to herself. "I don't think you'll have any problem keeping Jennifer in Houston," she said dryly.

He saw where she was looking and grinned. "So, you think it's Rick and not me keeping her here."

She shrugged. "Two great guys. What female would complain?"

He shifted so he could look at her face. "You think I'm a great guy?"

Her lips curved. "Are you fishing for a compliment, Mr. Paxton?"

"No, I'm asking straight out for one."

She laughed openly at that. "Yes, you're a great guy."

"How great?"

She pretended to be exasperated. "Like on a scale of one to ten?"

"No, like am I great enough that you'd consider a proposition I've got in mind?"

Her heart made a little skip-beat. "What kind of proposition?"

"The most meaningful kind—marriage."

She felt genuine shock and pressed a hand to her cheek. "Wow, this is...I mean, I didn't think—"

"You didn't think I'd want to marry the woman I love?"

Of course, he would. And springing his proposal right now was so typical while no less than six pairs of eyes were on them. As she tried to gather her wits, Lindsay called her name. She motioned to them from the patio, waving her arms. "Come out here, you two. Steele's getting ready to put the chicken on the grill."

"In a minute!" Ryan said and caught her before she could open the door. "There's only one reason you went to bed with me last night, Liz. And it's not that you got carried away. Or that you needed escape. A woman like you makes love because you feel love. I just need to hear you say it. Isn't it time to put aside all your bad baggage? You've got Jesse now. That's a battle won, a done deal. But do you want to be just another single mom? You did the right thing with your baby boy, but you're facing the same thing again." He held her by her waist, her hands on his forearms. "Marry me and we'll be a real family, you, me, Jess and Jen."

When he slowed to take a breath, she was smiling gently. "If I could get a word in, please...or is this a filibuster?"

"I'm not joking, Liz. I'm—"

She lifted a hand to his cheek and smoothed away his tension. "I won't marry you just to create a traditional home for Jesse, Ryan. That—"

"It wouldn't be—"

Her hand on his face tightened in a little shake. "Will you let me finish just one sentence?" His response sounded very like a growl, but he subsided. "I'm not silly enough—even with my baggage as you call it—to get married for Jesse's sake. But yes, I'll marry you," she said, rushing on because his mouth was open to argue more. "I'll marry you for the best reason of all. Not that it'll surprise you," she said dryly, "since you practically put the words in my mouth. I do love you, Ryan. How could I not?"

He closed his eyes and rested his forehead against hers for a sweet, but brief moment. "Okay. Okay." After a quick, hot kiss, he reached around her and pushed the door open. As she stepped outside, he said in her ear, "And it's gonna be soon, 'cause it's too damn difficult to get you alone around here."

Elizabeth was worried she must appear painfully pink in the face to the group on the patio, but they were more interested in discussing Austin than her love life.

"What will happen to him?" Lindsay asked, setting a platter of grilled chicken and corn on the cob on the patio table.

"Austin?" Steele helped himself to a juicy drumstick. "His arrest warrant will have a long list of charges. Not only did he violate the restraining order, but he added kidnapping to the crime. Even if his lawyer tries to argue that Jesse is his natural child, Jennifer certainly isn't."

"Don't forget he caused Gina's accident," Elizabeth said, pouring a glass of iced tea. "Now that she's talking, Jesse is telling more and more details about that night. She says he bumped their car from behind. That's what made Gina lose control of her car."

Steele wiped barbecue sauce off his fingers with a paper napkin. "There may be some difficulty there. Jesse's only five years old. All of us believe her version of the accident, but it's hard to convict a man on the testimony of a five-year-old."

Lindsay halted in the act of spooning coleslaw on Steele's plate. "You mean he'll get away scot-free? No. Uh-uh."

"Maybe for the accident," Steele said, "but not for the kidnapping."

"On the other hand," Elizabeth said thoughtfully. "I'm

not sure I'd want to subject her to actually testifying. There could be psychological problems later when she realized she was the key to her father's conviction for murder.''

''It would probably be reckless endangerment, not murder,'' Louie said, speaking up for the first time. Elizabeth was well aware that she'd been avoiding him. She was still struggling to come to terms with the truth about his past. More than once today, she'd felt his eyes on her, anxious and hopeful. ''His lawyer will argue that it was not a premeditated act, but a crime of passion.''

Passion. To label it *passion* when rage and violence come together to end the life of a person was a shameful desecration of life's most perfect emotion, she thought. Passion was her fierce love for Jesse. Passion was what drove her to create fiction for children. Passion was what she and Ryan shared. Passion as an excuse for murder was an abomination.

Across the lawn, Archie began barking at a squirrel teasing him from the fence along the rear property line. When he didn't cease, Louie rose from the table and headed toward the dog. Jesse, seeing Louie, left the gazebo and the two teens and ran to ''help'' Louie. As Elizabeth watched, he took the little girl's hand. Jesse wasn't burdened with bothersome questions of integrity and honor. She simply knew Louie loved her and responded in kind. Elizabeth turned her attention back to the adults around the table.

Lindsay was talking. ''Could it be possible that Gina was not as critically injured in the accident as Austin claims? Do we think he's capable of seizing an opportunity when nobody would know to free himself of a ton of trouble?''

''By ton of trouble, do you include Gina's pregnancy?''

Elizabeth took a potato chip from a basket. "I'm convinced she told him about it that night. He would have been furious."

"So she left in her car to avoid a scene right there in the restaurant—"

Elizabeth interrupted. "And to protect Jesse from emotional, if not physical, damage."

"And he was crazy-mad enough to chase her, butting the rear end of her car hard enough and often enough to make her lose control?" Lindsay finished.

"I think that's exactly what happened," Elizabeth said.

"And then he approached the car after the crash and finished her off?" Megan asked with an expression of horror on her face.

Ryan sat straddling a chair nearby. "I don't know, ladies. That part of the scenario is pretty cold-blooded. It doesn't seem to fit with the way his violence was usually triggered. We know from Gina and from his other women that when his buttons were pushed, he exploded into quick violence. Walking up to her car after seeing it crash, he wouldn't know if she was badly hurt. But say he realizes she is. He'd have to find a weapon—a tool from his car or her car, cope with Jesse who was not unconscious, do the deed and then dispose of the tool. There was nothing found at the accident site. Most important, Jesse didn't say anything about that."

Steele reached for another drumstick. "The truth is, we'll never know exactly what happened. Once Austin is lawyered up, the case will probably focus on the kidnapping, which is a serious offense. Couple that with the fact that his career's ruined and you have a certain degree of justice. It won't bring complete closure for you, but he's one less brutal guy to prey on other women." He put the drumstick on his plate without tasting it. "My sister's killer was never charged. He left no evidence, no eyewitnesses, and no closure for my family.''

Everyone grew quiet, each with his own thoughts. The trauma of the past night was not forgotten, nor was Gina's untimely death. But there was a general feeling of gladness in everyone gathered at the table. For herself, Elizabeth could have named many things, not the least the quiet joy of knowing Ryan loved her and they would have a life together. Somehow the terrible event that took Gina had worked to enrich Elizabeth's life. It was something she'd have to come to terms with. She knew it wouldn't be easy.

She watched now as Louie and Jesse, with a subdued Archie, headed for the fountain. Jesse, chattering away, urged him down beside her on the low stone wall and began a spirited account of the kidnapping, complete with the moment when she clung to a ''big hook stuck in a pole in really, really cold water, Papa Louie,'' and felt a crab nibbling on her toes. He'd heard the story several times already, but he listened now as attentively as if hearing it for the first time.

Looking up, Louie caught Elizabeth watching them. His face sobered, searching hers for the forgiveness he believed she still withheld. She took in the slight stoop of his shoulders, his silver beard, his hand cradling Jesse's tiny one. It came to her that there had always been a kind of sadness in Louie's eyes and that she had it in her power to take away that sadness. She turned, found Ryan watching her, urging her. She felt a great rush of emotion, a fullness that was both affection and gladness. The letter was in her pocket. She slipped a hand inside and felt its crackle, ran her fingers over and around it. It was so emotional. Had she written it to give to Louie or was it a sort of catharsis for herself? As closure perhaps, much as

Jesse's abduction had put an end to her silence and eased her childish fears?

She saw Jesse jump up to catch Archie, off again chasing the squirrel. Then, hesitating for a heartbeat, she found herself moving toward her father. She had so much now, life's greatest gifts: love, family, friendship, justice. She stopped at his feet and pulled the letter out of her pocket. As she handed it over, a look of surprised joy lit his face. He studied the envelope, holding it with unsteady hands. His name, Judge Matthew Walker. The return, Elizabeth Walker. His eyes, when he looked up and met hers, shone with tears. "This time, I promise to answer," he said.

She smiled, and left him reading.

This deeply moving novel proves once again
that nobody tells women's stories
better than Debbie Macomber!

DEBBIE MACOMBER

BETWEEN FRIENDS

Debbie Macomber tells the story of a remarkable friendship—a story
in which every woman will recognize herself...and her best friend.

The friendship between Jillian and Lesley begins in the postwar
era of the 1950s and lasts to the present day. In this novel,
Debbie Macomber uses letters and diaries to reveal the lives of
two women, to show us the laughter and the tears *between friends*.

*Available the first week of April 2003
wherever paperbacks are sold!*

*Introducing an incredible new voice
in romantic suspense*

LAURIE BRETON

FINAL EXIT

Ten years ago tragedy tore them apart....

But when FBI Special Agent Carolyn Monahan walks back into
the life of Homicide Lieutenant Conor Rafferty, the sizzle
is undeniable. They are back together, albeit reluctantly,
to find the serial killer who is terrorizing Boston.

As the pressure builds to solve the murders, so does the attraction
between Caro and Rafferty. But the question remains:
Who will get to Caro first—the killer or the cop?

Available the first week of April 2003 wherever paperbacks are sold!

MIRA®

KAREN YOUNG

66471 FULL CIRCLE   ___ $5.99 U.S. ___ $6.99 CAN.
66306 GOOD GIRLS   ___ $5.99 U.S. ___ $6.99 CAN.
(limited quantities available)

TOTAL AMOUNT $_____
POSTAGE & HANDLING $_____
($1.00 for one book; 50¢ for each additional)
APPLICABLE TAXES* $_____
TOTAL PAYABLE $_____
(check or money order—please do not send cash)

To order, complete this form and send it, along with a check or money order for the total above, payable to MIRA Books®, to: **In the U.S.:** 3010 Walden Avenue, P.O. Box 9077, Buffalo, NY 14269-9077; **In Canada:** P.O. Box 636, Fort Erie, Ontario, L2A 5X3.

Name:_____
Address:_____ City:_____
State/Prov.:_____ Zip/Postal Code:_____
Account Number (if applicable):_____
075 CSAS

*New York residents remit applicable sales taxes.
  Canadian residents remit applicable
  GST and provincial taxes.

MIRA®